# Perfect

## ALISON CLAIRE

This book is a work of fiction. Names, characters, places, and incidents are either the product of the author's imagination or are used fictitiously, and any resemblance to actual persons, living or dead, business establishments, events, or locales is entirely coincidental.

All rights reserved.
No part of this book may be used or reproduced in any manner whatsoever without written permission except in the case of brief quotations embodied in critical articles and reviews.

Cover illustration and layout by Carrie Rose.

This book is available on Amazon.com, CreateSpace.com, and other retail outlets. For information — alisonclaireMI@gmail.com.

Copyright © 2014 Alison Claire

All rights reserved.

ISBN-10: 1500976326
ISBN-13: 978-1500976323

# DEDICATION

To my muse, the ladies and everyone
that said, "You should write!"

Take pains; be perfect.

-William Shakespeare, *A Midsummer Night's Dream*

# PERFECT

# 1

"So, can I have that?" he asked, his hand tugging at mine.

Unintelligently, I mumbled, "Um. Yeah. Sure." I knew that I was staring at him.

"Are you going to let me eat this sandwich or do I have to hold your hand at the same time?" he asked, a droll expression on his face.

Rattled, I realized that I had a death grip on his turkey club.

"It would be nice," I responded, dropping my hand. Eyeing me uncomfortably, he shifted his weight, pulling the sandwich to his chest.

"What's your name?" He took a step back, guarding that sandwich as if it were his last.

"Sarah," I stammered.

"You have a last name, Sarah?" he asked, taking out his phone and fiddling with it.

"Over drinks," I ventured. He glanced quizzically over his phone.

"Ha. That's a good one. Do you always wear that dog collar?" he asked, pointing at my studded leather choke.

"It's not a dog collar," I responded confidently.

"My apologies. It matches your dreads nicely." He shook his head. "But answer the question, if you will—is that standard attire?"

This is precisely why I wore a leather collar. Unless the guy was a creeper, I liked the extra attention. If you want people to think more about you, to wonder about you, collars work.

"Most women just tell me what I want to know but I am going to go out on a limb and say you're probably not like most women." He marveled at my shoulder length dreads.

"That sounds like a line," I said, preparing to get back to work.

"Sarah with a sandwich," he said, relishing the sound. He stared unapologetically at my face.

"Sarah without a sandwich. You took it." I motioned to his club which was all but forgotten, hanging at his side.

"Well, I did pay for it, Sarah without a sandwich. Thanks again for this." He waved it in the air as he turned to walk away.

I exhaled loudly. Until that moment, I didn't know I'd stopped breathing. I just exchanged a nonsensical conversation with Captain J. Melchior Orion and my heart was about to explode. I watched him walk away, repeating to myself, 'Sarah with a sandwich.' That's cute, I thought. He's cute, I thought. Come back here now, I thought. And he did.

Walking back into the store, he said, "You know, Sandwich Sarah, I don't have your last name nor do I have your phone number. How can we do drinks? Or, did you mean that I should pay for a drink and sit here while you make sandwiches for the masses?"

"I feel like I am being punked," I said, wiping my hands on my apron.

"Sometimes the best things in life feel like bad jokes. Back to the question at hand," he said, holding his phone out to me.

"Call yourself, Sarah." He reached across the counter and deposited his phone in my hands. I typed in my phone number and was mortified when the *Enemies of Orion* theme song emanated from the recesses of my purse.

"Coincidence?" he asked.

"I have a fondness for the Captain. I have a fondness for ALL the *Enemies of Orion* cast, actually," I said, turning a polite shade of rose as my phone finally stopped ringing.

"Well, Sarah with a sandwich—good to meet you. I have to get back but I would love to get those drinks and your last name." He saluted me as he left.

One of my coworkers came out of the back at that moment. "Holy shit! Was that Captain Orion? Sarah, can you confirm that was Christopher

Sparks?" Hand on my shoulder, she spun me around and said, "Earth to Sarah! Was that or was that not Chris Sparks?"

I dumbly nodded as the door closed behind him. As he walked in front of the window, he turned and gave me one of the biggest grins any man on earth has ever given. I was blinded.

~~

Concentrating on sandwiches for the rest of the day was challenging in a way that deli meat never has been before. Thankfully, it was a slow afternoon and there were only a few customers here and there. It gave me the time to think about the Captain and daydream all sorts of scenarios that always ended blissfully.

These dreams continued to make my week as I picked up extra shift after shift, making myself available for his sandwich making needs. When the weekend rolled around, I was behind the counter texting when I received a text that made my fingers lock.

'Sandwich Sarah—How're you with ham? I am feeling like a ham n' cheese.' I flicked the screen and reread it several times knowing he was there on the other end, trying vainly to come up with something witty to say, something that would say, visit me. Call me. Save ME. And now, please.

Then, the next message came, 'Heads up.' Doing so, I saw him casually walking through the door once again, looking so damn good that I wanted a cigarette.

"Hi," I managed meekly.

"Hi, Sarah," he said engagingly. "What's new?"

"The ham," I said brightly. "The ham is new and a great choice if you're tired of turkey."

"Can anyone ever be tired of turkey?" he asked, raising a wonderfully sculpted eyebrow at me.

"I get tired of talking turkey, I can tell you that. People ask an awful lot of questions about the turkey and you know what, it's just cheap fast food turkey. It's not worthy of Thanksgiving. I doubt this bird ever walked around on grass but customers ask if they did. People ask all sorts of weird crap about food." I paused. "Are you really here for sandwich shop talk or can I get you something?"

"Wow. Is there a line? I didn't realize that we had to move things along. You are unusual," he said, cocking his head ever so slightly and putting his hands in his pockets. Awkwardly, I waited.

"Okay," he said sharply. "I know that you don't want to talk shop. Good to know. Can I get a cup, please?" He rifled through his wallet.

As I handed him the cup, he said, "Do you get to take breaks around here or is it all work and no play?"

"Depends on if I expect to get paid," I said a little too seriously. "That's $2.56 please."

"Well, there's no one else in here. How about I get my drink and—can I talk to you from a table or is that against the law?" As I tried to hand him the change, he waved me off, pointing to my tip cup. He turned and helped himself to lemonade and I desperately tried to come up with something to say.

"Chris," I said. Using his name made me feel like we were friends. "It is okay that I called you that, right?"

His laugh was beautiful, sinewy. "That's my name, Sarah. I'm rather relieved that you used it. I thought we weren't going to get anywhere quickly but now I know there's hope." He chose a table and was about to sit down when he said, "You know, I never did introduce myself. It's so hard sometimes to introduce myself when I know that you know who I am. It's like going to see Santa Claus as a kid. You sit in his lap because you know it's Santa. There's no formal introduction. It'd be really weird to introduce yourself to Santa and expect some kind of response."

I agreed. "Hey, you smiled." He grinned. "It suits you. Add to list of what I know about Sarah, 'Talk of Santa brings smiles.' Excellent." He closed the distance between that table and my counter in three easy strides. Extending his hand, he said, "Hi. My name is Chris. I love your sandwiches even if they're cheap fast food."

Shaking his strong hand, I softly laughed at the ridiculousness. "Hi, Chris. I am still Sarah. I am glad that The Sandwich Shoppe has your needs covered."

"I think I'd like that sandwich now. All this chatter and I'm working up an appetite. Throw some chips on that, please." I began pulling out the bread. Taking a sip, he said, "What do you think about getting those drinks tomorrow night? I could pick you up here, or if they actually let you out of this place, at home?"

I locked on to his dreamy eyes, the eyes that were politely asking to take me out for drinks. I didn't need a drink. I was drunk right now. I could feel that warm flush creeping into my face. I put down the mustard and obsessively wiped my hands on my apron, trying to formulate any words that didn't make me sound like I was on something.

"They do let me out. They've found they don't get their money's worth when I am sleeping. Tomorrow'd work. I would, I mean—it would be amazing!"

"Cool. If you're amazing, that's just as well. No need to correct yourself," he replied, handing me cash.

"Is this how you find your entertainment for Saturday nights? Do you hit a sandwich shop and hope for the best?"

With a grin on his beautifully chiseled face, he shook his head. "No, Sarah. I don't eat crap food with any regularity and I certainly don't go trolling for sandwich shop workers. Or any workers. You just—there's something about you that made me strike up a conversation. You from around here?" He plopped down at one of the empty tables.

"You and I both know that no one is from Los Angeles," I said, coming around the counter with my dish rag.

"True, but I was attempting to glean how close to the Sandwich Shoppe you live." His body turned, his eyes following me as I wiped down the soda fountain. "Where are you from originally, now that you've brought it up?"

"Connecticut with a layover in Rhode Island," I responded, walking over to his booth. "You?"

"You profess to be a lover of the Captain yet haven't IMDB'ed me? Inconceivable!" he said, leaning toward me.

"I said I have a thing for the *ENEMIES OF ORION*. You were just lucky enough to be *in* it." I rounded the booth and sat opposite him. "And I never said I was a stalker!" I said mercurially.

"Hey, OUCH. I do have an ego. How well do you know Massachusetts? I'm from Newburyport, outside of Boston."

"Sar—HOLY shi—Sarah? Are you—is that?" Amy rounded the corner of the counter at an astounding speed. Tugging down on her shirt and smoothing out her apron, she stepped right up to him. "You are Chris Sparks! Hi! I'm Amy. What brings you to our restaurant?"

She crossed her legs, dipping her right hip, and batted her eyelashes. This was my Amy—always ready to meet a star and unashamedly invite herself out to dinner, the movies, a premiere. It hadn't worked out for her yet but she was never bashful and for that, she amused me.

"Sarah. Sarah brings me to your restaurant, Amy. Good to meet you. What would you think if Sarah were to take off with me for a little bit? Could you hold down the fort?" he asked, putting his hand on hers.

I watched her melt. Her body stiffened when she addressed me.

"Well, Sarah. I thought it would be the two of us in here tonight but if you have to go— " Her eyes said it all. How on earth was this happening to *me* when she was the one who always put in the effort? I met her gaze and held it as I processed what he said to her. My mouth opened and closed repeatedly. I felt very unsure of myself.

Picking up on this, Chris leaped in. "I would really appreciate that. She can be back here—when does it get busy? I could have her back by then. If you need her." He turned on his charm, unleashing one of those movie star smiles that makes your heart skip a beat. Amy and I were frozen in time, enchanted by his lovely face.

I finally broke the trance, standing up and pushing Amy out of the way. "Great!" I said, "I can be back here by four or so as we're not going that far." Amy was riveted. Slowly, she smiled and silently gave me permission.

Chris got up, threw out his more or less uneaten sandwich and waited for me to get my purse. "Amy—thanks again. I really appreciate you spotting Sarah like this. You're really a good coworker for covering for her." He took my elbow and led me out the door.

~~

After strolling the better part of a block, I realized that I had my apron on. Charming, I thought. He mentioned the apron while we were waiting for the light to change but he did so in such a kind way that I was totally disarmed and had to keep it on.

"Where're we going?" I queried as I don't usually wander off with strange men.

"I thought I could walk off that sandwich. Do you need a destination?"

"You mean there really isn't one?"

"Nope."

"Huh."

"I didn't mean to make you uncomfortable. We can stop over here." He motioned me to a street side table, pulling out the chair for me. Never in my life had I even contemplated sitting at a place this tony. I couldn't wait to get home and tell my roommate. She was going to strangle me and cheer me on all at the same time.

As the waiter approached, Chris asked me, "Do you want anything? Get anything you like. It's on me."

The waiter's eyes flicked from Chris to me, giving me such a sugary sweet smile that I knew he wanted to vomit on me. Glaring at my apron, he handed me a menu. He turned to hand one to Chris but Chris just shook his head.

"Nothing for you, sir? Very well. And for the lady?" he asked, turning that syrupy smile on me again.

"It's going to be a minute. Thank you."

"Sure. Take your time." He strolled back into the restaurant.

"This menu is something else. Do you eat here regularly?" I asked.

"Never been here before but I needed a destination, STAT!"

"I don't know what half of this stuff *is*. It sure doesn't sound like food to me. Duck confit with roasted quinoa and apple demi-glace? This is what L.A. eats for lunch? Now I know why the Sandwich Shoppe does so well."

Chris smiled, a smile that melted my heart and made me think that I needed something hearty or I could pass out.

"I'm certain that we could get a soda? Maybe even something crazy like a strawberry lemonade? A Green Grass smoothie? What's it gonna be? Don't make me feel badly about choosing this place as our stop. I wanted to get you away from—was it Amy? There are too many people like Amy in my life so when I see someone more honest, I can't help myself." He shrugged and eased back into his chair.

"Amy's not too bad. It's actually entertaining to watch her work. She tries so hard when we get people like you in there. It doesn't happen often but when it does, she's like white on rice—all over herself, trying to be memorable even if the food isn't." I set the menu down. "I think I will take a lemonade but I don't like to drink alone. It makes me feel desperate. What are you getting?"

"Let's just make it two." He surveyed the restaurant, making eye contact with the waiter. "You'd be surprised by how often they try to get a picture of me or get me to sign something. It can get a little weird."

"What is the strangest thing someone's asked you to sign? In a place like this, I mean. I'm sure you could get wilder stuff in other locations but a place like this?"

The waiter approached, hands clasped at his waist.

"Did we come to any decisions?" he asked. After taking our order, he took about two steps away from the table before doubling back.

"I am sorry, but I just have to ask. Would you sign my apron? I have been a fan of yours since the *Enemies of Orion*. You're just—that suit. You look like you were born in that suit and it suits you. It would mean so much to me if you could. Here. Here's a pen. How about, could you write, 'Alan, love your buns!' That'd be so great!" He turned to the side, handing Chris a pen and smoothing out part of the apron on the table.

"Alan, huh? I didn't even know you had buns to love. Or maybe it's a menu recommendation?" he smirked, signing the apron, 'Alan, keep it up—Chris Sparks.'

The waiter bubbled on, full speed ahead about his desires for more and how thrilling his weekend would be as he would just have to tell his friends about this chance encounter. Chris never stopped smiling but there came a point when he lazily checked out the other diners. The waiter must have seen it, too, because he apologized and scurried away, untying his apron as he went.

"Do you want to stay? You look like you're ready to go," I said, putting my purse in my lap.

'Should I stay or should I go?' Song of my life!" he said, smiling genuinely at me. "I'm not sure but I am rethinking Saturday night." He was scanning the tables for our waiter. "I think we should have our drink and I will get you back to work as long as we have agreed that there *will* be a Saturday night?" He leaned into the table, arms crossed.

I acquiesced, blushing at the sound of his invitation. My mind was going places that were not even on the menu. Hell, they weren't appropriate for polite conversation.

~~

I went straight for my housemate's bedroom. There was no way I wasn't going to share this with her. Swinging the door open, she was not at home. This is the person that I tell everything to and she *should* be here at this hour on a Friday. Determined to tell her first, I sat down and started barraging her with texts.

'Where are you?' No response. 'DUDE. You should be here. I have something that I just can't text to you.' Nothing. I started to pace and think about what on earth Plan B should be when I decided to IMDB him and check out his official record. As I was reading, I received a text from him.

'Hey.' That's all it said.

'Have you seen my roommate?' I inquired. 'She should be here and she's not. I have stuff to tell her.'

'You have a roommate? Relieved to see it's a 'she.' What are you up to?' I could feel the need for Jessica lessening. I was downright annoyed when she finally walked in the door, talking to me like I wasn't busy.

"I saw your texts. What's up?" she said, chucking her stuff on the couch by my feet. Instead of answering, I handed her my phone. She scrolled through the texts. She lowered herself slowly on to the couch.

"Who *is* this? I didn't know that you were texting anybody. He's funny, though. I just might approve." She looked at me, waiting for an answer.

"Read the name."

"Chris Sparks. Is it supposed to mean something to me?" she asked forcefully.

"I know it's totally out of context and I realize that it seems highly unlikely—" I paused and took the phone back to let him know Jess was home. "But it's Captain James Melchior Orion! He came into the Shoppe earlier this week and today he came back. He said, he told Amy he came back for *me*." Her eyes betrayed her enthusiasm for the story that she knew was to come.

As we were catching up, she chortled. "Do you know that you're caressing your phone?" I didn't have to look down to know that she was right. Even though I was eager to tell her my story, part of me was very curious to know if he had gone on about his business for the evening.

"You're going out with him tomorrow, right? *Put the phone down. Let him wait. It'll be okay.*" When I casually set my phone on the table, she reached for it and took another look at the texts.

"I wonder how often he does this?" she said to herself, rereading them for the umpteenth time. I had no good answer but wasn't sure that there was a wrong one. I was going out with a cool guy tomorrow, a guy who came back for me, and that was something.

~~

# 2

After a beauty-less rest, I was up at the crack of dawn getting everything in order for his visit. I cleaned the living room, the kitchen, the bathroom and even my bedroom. With a critical eye, I surveyed everything on the walls, the furniture—what others would call 'décor.' My roommate and I had this little game of hiding pictures of hot men in strange places so that we were always pleased to change the toilet paper roll or put away the dishes. I knew it was silly and I loved it. Now I was wondering if there were any that I should be concerned about. We regularly put the Captain around the house. I calmed myself down by thinking that the likelihood of him seeing much more than the living room was unlikely. He certainly would not be changing the toilet paper roll.

Now it was time to prep myself and I didn't know where to start. Anything would have to be an improvement over the apron. I cocked my head, taking in all of my faults in the mirror. Before I knew it, I was baring my fangs and putting pony tails in places that made me look pretty darn special.

Stress relieved, I took my hair down and addressed the things that required care. I never hated clothing more than at times like this. Do I have to care what I wear under my clothes? If I do care, is there anything that is better than 'good enough' in my collection? How much effort should I look like I put in? This is a big deal but I don't want to look desperate. Worse, I don't want to look like I calculated everything. I want to be me, to be natural and honest but what *is* that?

I settled on a simple shirt and colorful skirt. I felt confident, comfortable and ready for anything. As we left it, he was picking me up at seven. We were going to go somewhere but he wouldn't tell me where. He apologized for withholding the destination but did tell me that it didn't require special clothing; that I could wear anything except an apron. I took that to mean no high end restaurant, no clubbing, and nothing out of the ordinary. This I could do. This would be fun.

For the last hour, Jessica was just as buzzed as I was. She didn't know if she should stay or go. I finally encouraged her to park it. This was possibly the most exciting thing that was going to happen to us this weekend or any weekend in the foreseeable future. She settled down on the couch and was as nonchalant as I wanted to be. I am awed by people who determine a course of action and then seem to be so at ease with it. Me? I was unable to sit.

I firmly grasped the edge of the kitchen sink, thinking about the moment he would arrive. As I was practicing my hello, I heard the doorbell and my heart dropped. My grip became a white knuckler.

I knew I had to turn around when I heard Jessica say, "Sarah, would you like *me* to get that?" I spun around and locked eyes with her. I purposefully strode to the door just as it rang a second time.

As I unlocked it, I glanced at Jessica. She was giving me a 'JUST OPEN IT ALREADY' glare which I returned just as vehemently.

He was casually lounging on my stoop, candy to my eyes. I was never overly conscious of clothing but his choices were spot on—distressed jeans, Fender t-shirt, well-loved black leather jacket. He smelled of soap and aftershave. Add to that his mega-watt smile and dark blue eyes, and I was captivated.

"Hi, Sarah. It's good to see you." He rocked slowly on his feet.

"Glad you could find it. Would you like to come in?" I said, swinging the door all the way open and motioning him inside.

"Hello, there." He confidently addressed Jessica on the couch. "I'm Chris." He offered Jess his hand. Rising, she shook it ever so formally as she introduced herself.

"Chris—are you full of bologna? I gather that Sarah knows something of your meat predilections, but as her caring roommate, it's my job to ask." I took it to be a good sign when they continued to smile at each other as I stood mortified, front door still open.

"Ha. That's one meat I never understood," he said, turning to see what had become of me. I closed the door and joined them. "I guess we will have to wait and see what you think." His eyes scanned the house as Jessica patted the couch, imploring him to sit.

"Nice place you have here. I particularly like that poster." He pointed at the *Enemies of Orion* right outside the bathroom. "What other secrets does your house hold?" he asked, flashing me another star powered grin.

I showed him around the house. He seemed so at ease in my house that it was almost infuriating. How can he walk into the house of two women he barely knows and be one hundred percent at ease? We looped back to the living room where Jessica was picking up her things.

"Sarah was telling me those are your photographs. Do you sell them?" he asked, eyes combing the nearest print. "You should. The nautical theme reminds me of home."

Holding her laptop to her chest, she said, "It's my understanding you're from the Boston area, so they should feel like home. I took most of them in Rhode Island. And thanks." She picked up her purse. "It was good to meet you, Chris. I hope to see you again."

I watched her close the front door. I turned expectantly to Chris as the front door burst open.

"Sarah, I am going to be out for a couple of hours but you know you can get me if you need me," she said, waggling her phone.

"Thanks." I waved. "That girl does look out for me. We've been together for a long time." I contemplated whether or not I should ask him to sit. Mercifully, he took the driver's seat.

"I know how important destinations are to you. I have a couple of options that I thought might work better than the more obvious ones." He put his hands behind his back, his eyes glinting. "Choose a hand. They're both good choices. And if you find them otherwise, we can always do something else. Feel free to explore both before deciding."

He popped to attention and remained rigid, like a soldier. Screwing up my face and trying very hard to decide how to make my choice, I finally leaned in and took his left bicep. It was rock hard. I felt awkward holding on to it but it was the first time I touched him. He was real. He was in my living room and my hand was on his finely chiseled body. As I continued to hold on for dear life, marveling at how inviting his arms were, he said, "Okay. So—I would rather not go *out* on a first date." He dropped his head, his gaze so intense that I felt my grip strengthening. I had no idea what he meant but I did hear him calling this a 'first date.'

"What would you think of coming to over to my place? I know it's not much of an offer but—maybe you should get ahold of your other option," he said, wiggling his other arm. Without releasing the first, I put my hand on his other bicep which he intentionally flexed, smiling.

"What are you thinking?" he asked intently.

"Ha! That's for me and me alone. What's the other option?"

He leaned into me. "We could stay right here." I felt his breath on my face and flushed. I was dumbstruck. "I don't want you to think I am lame but I am not That Guy either. I grew up with sisters. I will take you out if that is what you really want, if that will keep a smile on your face, but I'd really like to get to know you."

He put his hands on my shoulders, sliding them down my arms and causing me to let go of his. With his hands in mine, he said, "What do you think?"

"I don't particularly want to share my evening with your adoring public. I don't share well." I shrugged apologetically. "Hazard of being an only child. For that *same* reason, I don't much want to stay here. Jess will do her best to be gone but she does live here. She will be back at some point. We don't have the square footage. We will cross paths with her. So, I guess what I am thinking is that it would be—I'd be game for your place." His exquisitely sculpted mouth twitched.

"Now that you know where you're going, do you need a minute?" he asked, still holding my right hand.

My body swayed, mesmerized by the experience.

"Give me just a sec." If opportunity presented itself, I didn't want to come home tonight. I scratched Jess a note on the fridge. "I don't want Jess to come home to an empty house and freak out." Finishing that, I practically ran to my bedroom to get a bigger purse. I was startled to see him at my bedroom door, leaning on the frame.

"You sure that it's okay not to go out? I felt a little awkward asking. Maybe if I lived somewhere else, where people don't expect me to be on all the time. I don't know. I love my life, don't get me wrong. It's *great* but time off from it is also satisfying."

I choked back a chuckle. "I'd think I'd love your life, too."

~~

The ride to his place was everything that a girl deserves. His red Mustang smelled like new car. I sank easily into the cool leather seat. The sun was setting and a warm breeze flowed through the open windows as we drove. Keeping up the conversation, the half hour passed like nothing at all. When we finally pulled into a parking lot, I was surprised. I assumed that he must have one of those big Hollywood houses but this was very ordinary.

Parking the car, he said, "The studio is putting me up." Hopping out and opening my door, he added, "It's nothing special but it's home for the next couple of months."

His apartment was the cleanest, most antiseptic and white one I had ever seen. There were no hints of who he was except for a stack of books on an end table and a brightly colored grannie square afghan on the couch. Beyond that, it looked like it hadn't been lived in.

"Not what you expected, huh?" He closed the door and took a couple of steps into the foyer.

"Would you like the grand tour?" His hand closed on my elbow, sending waves of excitement through me. It's always a good sign if someone's willing to touch you, right?

He steered me down the hallway pointing out the kitchen, office and bathroom. Going upstairs, there were two bedrooms and a sitting area that overlooked the living room down below. The bedrooms infused me with both fight and flight. My guts were flip-flopping and I wanted a reason to touch him. Badly. I couldn't remember the last time I wandered into a man's arms so recklessly.

I don't know how long I scoped out the bedrooms but it must've been beyond reasonable. When he softly cleared his throat and offered to get me something to drink, I returned to my senses.

After scrounging around his empty kitchen, he smirked. "Maybe we should have gone out. I don't have much to offer you." We took our beers and chips to the couch. He flipped on the TV and threw me the remote. Catching it, I used it as an excuse not to make eye contact. I flipped and flipped, answering his questions about what I do, how I came to Los Angeles and then he put his hand on mine, stopping the incessant flipping. It was *The Walking Dead*, which was fine with me.

I felt his eyes boring into the side of my head. My mouth went dry. When I finally looked in his direction, he scooted down the couch until our thighs were brushing each other. "Can I tell you a secret?" he asked conspiratorially.

"Riley," I blurted.

"Riley?" The hint of a smile on his lips, his eyes darted around my face, connecting it with my name. "That's your last name."

"How about I tell *you* another secret?" I offered playfully. He closed the remaining inch, his thigh pressing delightfully on mine. He put his arm around me on the back of the couch.

"Please do, Sarah Riley."

"I don't want this to end," I barely whispered into his handsome face. "I've dreamt of wrestling Captain Orion." I was pleased with myself for being so forward. I smiled slyly at him, his arm curling snugly around me.

"Wrestling," he said appreciatively. "You do know I'll win."

"I'm counting on it," I purred, my breath catching. He athletically kicked off his shoes. Then, stood up, pulled off his jacket and flung it dramatically over his shoulder.

"Do you have any pregame prep to undertake, Ms. Riley?" he asked, rubbing his hands together and striking a professional wrestler's pose.

"I think I'm good." I strode purposefully toward him. Smiling broadly, I grabbed his head with both of my hands and planted a big kiss on him. I felt his posture changing as he instinctively put his arms around me.

Nuzzling into my neck, he said, "This doesn't feel much like wrestling." I savored the moment then did my best to trip him. He didn't move. He chuckled sexily. Why was his laugh such a turn on?

"Is that *all* you've got?" he asked throatily, backing me up to the couch. He tripped me slowly and elegantly. I felt like he was teaching me how it's done. I couldn't help myself and started laughing.

Seeing an opportunity, he launched himself on top of me, pinning me to the couch.

"Now—this. This has potential," he said, getting a dread out of my face. I was in my element, engaged in full body contact. I squirmed, feeling every inch of his body pressing into mine. I freed my arms and pushed up on his chest. He repositioned a knee between my legs and I liked it.

Not ready to give up the fight, I pulled the afghan over his head.

"HEY. That's cheating!" he howled, as I pinned his head and arms under the blanket. I freed my legs and fell on the floor while he wrestled with the blanket. I was back up and straddling him before he'd even locked on my new position.

His face glowed like a child. He was enjoying himself profoundly. When he tossed the balled up blanket at me, I knew this was the best game in town. I rolled the afghan into a tighter wad and pitched it on the floor.

"He who hesitates is lost!" he growled, grabbing my hips and pivoting me to the back of the couch. One more move and I would be under him again. I went with the obvious maneuver—another kiss. He foolishly relaxed and I felt myself doing the same. When his hands went under my skirt, I sat bolt upright and unintentionally said, "HELLO!"

His face was impossible to read. He was gauging my expression.

All too quickly he pounced and rolled me beneath him. Two could play the clothing game. I pulled his shirt over his head. His body was just as smooth and flawless as you'd imagine the Captain to be. I ran my hands up and down his back, exploring his body until I remembered this was a wrestling match.

Feeling the rigidity of his muscular arms was the biggest turn on. I wasn't going to win but I was certainly going to lose it all in the most delightful way. I was aware of him tugging at my undies. I helped him by pulling off my shirt. I was delirious. He was no longer playful but had ravenous bedroom eyes.

He stood up and gave a little boxer's jump in place, rolling his neck. I was a little confused. I picked up the blanket in some attempt at modesty. He leaned down, took my head firmly in his hands and gave me what I would expect a movie kiss to be. Muttering something, he scooped me into his arms and trucked me up the stairs as if my body were as weightless as my soul. He looped directly into bland bedroom number one and managed to pull back the sheets without dropping me. Lowering me to the bed, he shoved the rest of the bedding out of the way and slid in next to me.

"You're incredible," I said.

"You haven't seen anything yet," he responded, running his hand down the front of my neck, and my cleavage. I shivered with delight as his head disappeared under the blanket. As engaging as it was to have this man kissing my soon-to-be-clothes-less body, I wanted to see that tuft of blond hair. When he'd successfully tugged off my skirt, I pulled on his arms, bringing him back up to me.

With a questioning look on his face, I felt obligated to say something and told him the truth; that I wanted to see his face. I was treated to a childish grin as he again smoothed my hair and covered my neck with kisses. When I felt him disappearing again, I rolled him over and straddled him. He was not going to get lost in the blankets today even if what his lips promised would be incredible.

What followed was the best give and take one can hope to encounter between the sheets. He was both gracious and masculine. I was his queen. The afterglow was just as fantastic. His arm around me, we were both trying to decide if sleep was in the cards.

Eventually, I broke the trance with some simple, few-word questions. What I really wanted answered was—how long was he going to be around Los Angeles?

"I am going to be here for a while," he said, kissing my hair. "You will be, too?" His gaze was so intense, so warm that I turned to mush in his arms. "Everything about you is alluring. From your tattoos to your collar, and crazy skirts. I feel like you've got a secret hiding behind your brilliant blue eyes." He pulled me tightly against his body. "Hey, if I'm lucky, will you share it with me?"

My eyes danced. "You *were* lucky, dude," I said, stroking his chest.

"Then, about that secret?" He kissed my fingers.

"You've seen it all. I've got no secrets."

"Hmm. Somehow, I doubt that. We've all got secrets." He shook his head. "Are you here permanently?"

"How would I ever give up life at the Sandwich Shoppe? I never thought I would thank it for introducing me to anything other than a new proto-meat but here I am." I rolled over, draping myself across his chest. "I am not much of a planner but I do know what to expect on a daily basis.

Right now, I feel like my feet are nowhere near the ground and I don't know how to fly." His gaze met mine and he seemed to work on his response.

"You worry more than is healthy, don't you? Let it go. Let it go for this moment and any we spend together. I promise you that I will treat you as you should be treated. You will have no regrets." I pursed my lips and peered into his deep, searching eyes.

"Why is it that when *you* say it, it sounds completely plausible? You might be the one to talk me into jumping off a building. I might not even fear the splat."

"Good. That's not a negative so don't try to spin it as one," he said, tickling my back. "Life without fear is so much better. Live in the moment. *Enjoy* it." He touched my wrist. "Is that what your tattoo means?"

"Pretty much," I responded, watching him trace my 'now' tattoo. "Like I said, I don't really have any deep secrets. What you see is what you get."

He pulled the blankets up over my body. "Los Angeles evenings do get rather chilly. Do you need anything? Do you want to sleep?"

"Sleeping is for those who need to dream and refresh. I am both dreaming and refreshed! I am living in the now, baby!"

I smothered him in kisses, from his now-whiskery face to the backs of his knees. I had this boy humming and I loved it. Every time he tried to reposition, I kept control. It was killing him.

This second round of foreplay was gonna be a show stopper. And it was mine to design.

~~

"I think I need a cigarette," I joked, spent.

"Ah, just like the movies," he said mildly into my hair. "I was thinking more along the lines of breakfast. I am going to need breakfast." As if on cue, his belly growled. "Ah, reality approaches," he said forlornly.

He swung himself into to a seated position. Beaming over his shoulder at me, he tugged on his boxers. "How do you feel about going out for breakfast? It's either that or more beer and chips."

"That sounds like another dose of reality."

"I guess I should warn you, too, that if we're seen together, it won't be long before everyone will be lamenting our entanglement."

My brow furrowed. "Already? But I hardly know you!" I couldn't decide if he was serious. His comment was the weirdest thing anyone'd ever said to me after a first date.

"Have you seen that they even put information about my relationships on IMDB? True story."

"I'm amused that you read about yourself. Doesn't it make you uncomfortable?" I felt around under the bed for my shirt.

"It's just another adjustment I've made in the past ten years. Some of it is amusing. Other elements are uncomfortable." He had his hands on his hips, admiring me. "Your shirt's downstairs. Would you like a t-shirt?"

Accepting, I continued, "I did see your romantic moment with Svetlana Alvarez—something about a bath and candles. I thought it was sweet. Definitely a strange note on what was really your resume." He handed me a t-shirt. "Unless being a romantic falls under special interests?"

"I like that. There's no reason that I can see for showing anything less than appreciation for anyone who is important in your life." I slid into his shirt. "That looks better on you than it does on me." He moved quickly around the bed. "And if we don't get out of here quickly, I may need an appetizer!" He encircled me in his arms.

~~

Not too far from his condo, we strolled into his usual breakfast place. It was jam packed but everyone parted like the Red Sea for him. They quickly found us a table in the back, as far away from the crowd as they could.

The people here knew him and were quick to bring his coffee and a menu for me. Not knowing how long the experience would last, I appreciated every unusual gesture from getting a table without a wait to sharing a booth with one of the most beautiful men on the planet.

It was hard to read the menu. I could feel his gaze resting on me.

Putting the menu up between us, I asked, "Any recommendations? I could be here all day trying to make a decision."

"How do you feel about French Toast? Theirs is really good. It's got some kind a cereal-almond crust that I find myself dreaming about."

"That sounds pretty damn special. I'm in."

Breakfast was great. It was more low key that I would have thought possible. He chatted it up with his usual waitress. Because of his genuine attention, Gloria became animated. She glowed. It was a joy, watching this guy work women. He did it effortlessly and with so much warmth that it no longer amazed me that he was so successful.

When it was time to head out, he gave me another warning. "It's good to see you smiling. Hold on to that."

"Why?"

"Because some of these people are about to turn into piranhas." I made it into the center of the restaurant before they descended. A little boy who couldn't be more than six squeezed between us. Chris dropped down on one knee.

"Hello," he said. The little guy smiled nervously and glimpsed at his parents who were still sitting at their table.

"I like your *Ninja Turtle* shirt," Chris said. The boy yanked on the hem of his shirt and ran back to his parents. Holding his hand, the family approached, triggering a cascade of others. Chris waved at the little ninja fan, took my hand and strode purposefully out the door.

"Not too bad but I did commit one cardinal sin." He swung my arm. "I like to know where I'm going before I even get up. I seem to have an easier time getting out when I look like I have somewhere to be."

"Have you made a study of this? I'd love to test that theory." He put his arm around my shoulders.

"Please do." He pulled me closer. "That means I will see more of you." He kissed the top of my head.

"I think I'd like that." I heard my phone chirping. I yelped, digging around in my purse. I fished out my phone just as it went to voice mail. "It's Jess. She's probably pretty close to piranha, too."

"Never forget to feed the fish. They're much nicer when they're full," he said, unlocking the door.

"Who made you such a sage?" I queried, sending a quick text.

"I don't know about sage," he said holding the door open for me. "But the Church would probably like to take the credit."

"The church?"

"Yeah. Raised a Catholic with indoctrination every Sunday. I learned a lot growing up from my family, obviously, and the Church," he said openly.

He dropped the keys on the counter, taking a peek in the fridge.

"You can't seriously be hungry again," I said, peeking up from my phone.

"Just checking out what's next. Don't want a repeat of last night's beer and chip dinner."

"How about this—we go to *my* house? I know that I have food and it should probably get eaten. Jess will be heading out tonight for a writer's workshop."

"This just may be the beginning of a beautiful relationship." He shot me a quick smile and bounded up the stairs. I flipped on the TV before climbing onto the couch. I ran my hands over the cushion, reminiscing.

"You're on TV!" I squealed. "It's a little weird seeing you in that tight outfit now." It was hard to believe I was in his living room. "My fondness for the Captain has increased a good tenfold in twenty four hours."

Coming down the stairs with a duffle bag, he said, "It's in heavy rotation. The next one's coming out soon." He stared at himself. "And you should put that thing on and stand under the lights. It's not pleasant."

He set his bag by the couch. "I need a shower. You're welcome to join me, if you like, or hang out with the TV Captain."

My heart skipped a beat. "I think I will sit this one out. The best part is only minutes away."

He put his hands on his waist. "You're going to sit this one out? Like I *bore* you?"

My eyes widened. "Oh, no! That's not it."

He surveyed himself, arms outstretched. "Do I stink? Cuz I am headed to the shower."

I bit my lip.

"Okay." He shrugged and crossed between me and the TV. He leaned right in front of my face, putting his arms around my body, hands resting on the back of the couch.

His lips touched my ear. "Is there anything that I can do that would make you change your mind?" he asked huskily.

His voice was like no other. I shivered, bathing in his suggestion.

"You're something else. You know that? You have known me for, what, twenty four hours and you can't get enough of me?" I pulled my neck back so I could make eye contact.

"Something like that. Yup. Hey, I'm a guy and I can't help myself. Do you want me to beg?" He brushed his whiskery face on my neck.

"Dear god. Don't do that. Don't beg. But please—feel free to keep doing what you're doing." A little growl escaped. Feeling my toes curling, I caved. He was divine.

"Damn you!" I pushed him off. *"Fine. Fine. Fine!"* I stormed up the stairs with him hot on my heels.

~~

# 3

I was still sorting through the whirlwind when we landed on my couch. What a glorious weekend it had been and if it ended now, I'd relive it indefinitely.

Hand innocently resting on my thigh, he greeted Jessica like an old friend. She eyed the bag on the floor and rolled her eyes.

"You moving in, Chris?" She nudged the duffle with her foot.

"Not today," he said, turning on the charm. "And I promise that I will try not to overstay my welcome."

I sighed multiple times. They ignored me. My mind was on a crash course of what ifs. Maybe a nap would help to settle me down. I slouched down against his chest and closed my eyes while they embarked on a marathon conversation.

I opened my eyes when Chris shook me gently. "You're still here." That's a good sign, I thought.

I stretched. "How long was I out?"

He ran his fingers over my dreads. "A while. Jessica offered to make dinner. I like her."

"Jessica is making *us* dinner? Damn. What did you say to her?"

He raised his eyebrow quizzically. "I think it was more that you were sleeping and my stomach started growling." Patting his stomach, he added, "I am a growing boy."

"You're in your thirties. Haven't you *stopped* growing?" I asked, through closed eyes.

"Hey, don't go to sleep on me again! I'll tickle you," he threatened, poking my ribcage.

"My god, you're cute," I said, sitting up. "How do you stand yourself?"

"I'm rarely myself. That's key," he said flirtingly.

"Let me see if I can help Jessica. Do you want anything to drink?" I asked, entering the kitchen.

"Nope. Happy as a clam, thanks." He picked up his phone.

"Thanks for making dinner," I said to Jess as she handed me a beer.

"You were out cold." With a wicked smile, she added, "Must've been one *hell* of a night."

"It's been unreal. Just about as unreal as you would expect if you met some famous guy in a sandwich shop and then found yourself not only hanging out with him but sleeping with him. Pretty fuckin' incredible."

"Fuckin' incredible. Glad to hear it was incredible." She sampled her beer. "I'm just making pasta with chicken. It's easy and who doesn't like chicken?" I leaned up against the counter, spying on Chris who was texting away. Tipping her beer at him, Jessica asked, "Is he spending the night?"

"Sort of. He has to be on set at something like four in the morning. Probably a good thing, too, because I could really use some sleep."

"I can't even believe you're saying that! You can sleep when you're dead. *Enjoy* this, girlfriend. I know I would."

As she finished up the pasta, I hovered.

"He's pretty cool, Sarah."

"I think so, too."

"Why're you hiding in here with me, getting in my way?" She dug the Parmesan cheese out of the fridge.

"I'm *not* hiding. He's texting and I am helping you."

"Your version of reality is pretty funny. You've spent quite a bit of time with him so I think it's fair to say you're hiding. Do you want me to leave?"

"No. It's your place, too." I picked at the label on my beer. "I'm afraid I may be getting my hopes up. That's all. This weekend has been a dream. There's no other way to put it. I don't want it to end but I want to be ready for it if it does."

"The weekend *will* end. That's a given. Shake it off. He seems to be a really sweet, genuine person and he has really taken a shine to you. When he's gone, I can fill you in on what you missed." She arranged some pasta on a plate. "He's a good guy. I can feel it and I think you know it, too. Is it scaring you?" She studied me intently.

~~

I set the dishes in the sink, hoping that I was interesting enough. I knew he was leaving at four. It could be for good. I was startled to feel him behind me, reaching around to put the empty bottles on the counter.

"Let me do the dishes." He steered me away from the sink.

"You even do dishes?" I asked, handing him the sponge.

"Not often but then as you noticed, I didn't have much in the way of food in my place either." He did a three-sixty. "Where's your dishwasher?"

"We don't have a dishwashing machine." I flipped the cap open on the soap.

He squeezed it onto the sponge.

"Will you dry?" he asked, checking out our limited counter space. I turned on some tunes and started dancing as I waited for dishes to dry.

"We make a good team," he said, appreciating my smooth moves and adding a few butt bumps of his own. When he'd finished washing, he opened a cupboard to put the plates away. He backed away from it and looked at me. "Mike Rowe? Doesn't he belong with the toilet bowl cleaner?"

"Hey, be nice to Mike. He may not be a captain but dirty never looked so good. I miss his show."

"Who came up with the word bubble? Sounds like it could be either of you." Chris put the towel down, staring at the picture.

"Jess. Mike was for me." I looked at the little picture taped into the cupboard fondly. 'Hey, sexy. I'm still feelin' dirty.' Jess knew me well. I contemplated paper Mike and the real Chris. They couldn't be more different yet both were damn attractive to me.

"At least I can see the incentive you two use to get the dishes done. Genius," he added, approvingly. "You might consider an Etsy store for these. If you can make Mike Rowe work, you've got some talent."

"Leave Mike alone!" I pinched his rock hard obliques. "He's my paper towel guy and has been there when I've been lonely or had a spill." Grabbing my arm, he pulled me in to a snug embrace.

"*You* leave Mike alone! I've got your dirty jobs covered." He nuzzled my ear and slid his hands into the band of my skirt.

"I think I can part with him if you're willing to take care of my needs—and my spills." I slid my hands into his pants, eliciting a groan from him.

"Is Jessica likely to come home because I can think of a few dirty things we could do. Right here." He started kissing my neck, maneuvering us to the small kitchen island. He kicked a couple of stools out of the way.

"Yeah. No—probably not the best idea unless you're very voyeuristic. Look out that window. That's my neighbor, Ann. She's been watching for a few minutes. Probably recognizes you."

He waved at her before locating the pull cord on the blinds.

"Voyeurism isn't all bad," he said, lowering the blinds. "I wouldn't want to wear out my welcome with Jessica, however, so again—think she'll be back soon?" Letting go of my waist, he opted for a tug o' war with my bra.

"This is like a chastity belt!" He grunted, dramatically pulling at the clasp. "Usually I can get these with one hand."

"Listen to you, stud! Lots of practice, huh?"

"You phrase it like it's a bad thing." His eyes flashed. "Appreciate the skill. The talent. The desire!"

"What about it—love 'em and leave em? Is there a trail of tears behind you?" I asked coyly.

"Worried again? Don't be. I am right where I want to be."

"I can see that," I said, ducking out of his grasp. "But the question is—*Is* there a harem in your history?"

"Harem! I *work* with the guys who have harems. I don't think I am of that caliber. I don't have stalker-fans."

"That you're aware of. But I am asking about your pedigree."

His eyes narrowed. "Has to come up sooner or later, doesn't it?" He took my hand, guiding me toward my bedroom.

I dropped his hand and took a different approach.

"Are you a serial monogamist?" I queried from my bedroom door.

He threw his bag over his shoulder, his body moving so fluidly that I couldn't take my eyes off him.

"Odd question," he responded. Even his measured gate was such a tease. "But yeah, I guess so. If what you mean is—are you the only gal that I am currently involved with and do I intend to keep it that way?" He met me at my door and backed me up to the bed. He bag dropped with a muffled thud.

"I treat people as I hope to be treated. And you're worrying." He cupped my face in his hands. "Don't worry. Life is a lot more fun if you leave some things to fate." He kissed me and I swooned. A gorgeous man was saying all the right things.

"What is your weakness?" I put my arms around him and wrenched the stuffing out of him.

"You're not likely to find one by squeezing me!" He glided to the other side of the bed and pulled back the sheets. As I watched him undress, he continued, "Hopefully any shortcomings won't be catastrophic. I would like to think that I'm a pretty good guy. Dependable. Romantic. Employed. And a captain." His boyish grin was infectious.

I climbed in on the wrong side of the bed. While I arranged my pillows, he took off his watch and opened the nightstand drawer. As my head hit the pillow, he chuckled, deep in his throat. I closed my eyes and listened to that husky sound. His voice was even better in person.

"Hey! It's Mini-Me." He hadn't even finished his sentence when I knew what he'd found. The pictures of hot men were not the only secrets in my apartment. He had found my very special Captain J.M. Orion vibrator.

I cringed. I kept my eyes shut and went on the attack, "Mini-Me, huh? You think an awful lot of yourself, Captain. That's a good eight inches of pure power." I cracked one eye. He was rotating it in its clear case.

"Oh, I think I've got that covered."

"You haven't *measured* your junk, have you?" I sat up, fixated.

He continued to fondle The Captain and took his time in responding. "Not lately."

"Oh, but you *have*, haven't you? How does that happen?" I bounced the bed. "You're sitting there one day and decide it'd be cool to pull out a ruler? Or are you sitting around with a bunch of dudes and the inspiration is overwhelming?"

"Maybe a little bit of both. People do strange things. He tapped the case. "I can safely say I've never been asked to sign one of these before."

"Ooh, Chris! Will you sign it? That'd be pure awesome."

"If I sign it, you couldn't use it any more. It'd be a collectible." He propped himself up on an elbow, eyes dancing.

"Indelibly!" I jumped out of bed and ran to find a marker.

When I hopped back in, he was lounging in my bed like we'd been together for years. He was the epitome of comfortable. He took the marker. "Did you bring a ruler, too? Want to see if that's my shortcoming?" He shook the comforter, revealing his naked torso.

"How well do you know the *Enemies of Orion* movie?" he asked, uncapping it with his teeth. He chewed on the cap, staring at me. I could have watched him all day. His eyes lit up devilishly. He tore into the case, holding my vibrator valiantly.

I craned in to see what he was writing, 'Rocket, baby - Captain J.M. Orion.'

"Well, that's fitting," I said.

"I hope so! You paid good money for this." He winked, holding it rather fondly.

"No complaints." I put my hand on it and kissed him. "The original is *much* better." He tossed the marker over my shoulder.

"Originals are the inspiration." He took another good look at it. "Did they have to duplicate the texture of my costume? It's a little creepy."

"Can you put it away now, please?" I said sweetly, forcing his hand toward the open drawer.

"More proof that this job is mine!" he said proudly. He stashed it and closed the drawer. "I gotta say, I do like toys. This job's got its perks." His head disappeared under the quilt.

~~

When the alarm went off around three, I was not coherent. I never get up that early for any reason. He, however, bounced out of bed like it was the most natural thing in the world.

"You're like the Energizer Bunny. Don't you ever need rest?" I moaned, hugging his pillow to my chest.

"I am that merry wanderer of the night—" His eyes twinkled mischievously.

"Is that—are you quoting Shakespeare at three in the morning? Before coffee?"

He crossed his arms. "Sarah—is there a wrong time for the Bard? I think not."

"What's it from?"

"*A Midsummer Night's Dream.*"

"Do you have it memorized?" I asked, my head clearing.

"It *is* my favorite."

"And you have it all in there?" I queried, poking myself in the head.

"You can test me some time," he said, tousling my hair.

"As long as you don't expect me to keep up with you."

He pouted. "I'll make you a fan. You stick around long enough and I guarantee you will have an appreciation!"

"Hard to believe I'd appreciate anything from high school." I closed one eye.

"He transcends high school!"

I groaned. "That's great but there's a wrong time for consciousness. Save it for later. I need my beauty rest!" I pulled a pillow over my head.

"You're already tantalizing," he said, squeezing me through the bedding.

He peeled back the pillow. "I will be outta here in less than five minutes but I will leave you with another quotation." He brushed my ear with his lips. "'You spotted snakes with double tongue, thorny hedgehogs, be not seen; newts and blind-worms, do no wrong, come not near our fairy queen.'"

I smiled under my pillow. "What's that?"

"It's a lullaby to *Titania*, the fairy queen."

~~

Amy never beat me to work but she did today. She was literally bouncing up and down when she saw me opening the door.

"Sooooooooooo!" she squeaked, handing me an apron.

"Hi, Amy. So—what?" I knew that I would tell her but it was fun to make her work for it. Peeking into the store, there were no customers. We assumed our usual positions, prepping vegetables by the counter.

"Sarah Riley—you can't do this to me. I *know* you went out with him. How do I know? Because. You of all people walked into Sunrise Café yesterday morning, didn't notice me, and he followed YOU. So, you can't deny it! And if you were there for *BREAKFAST*, then you were there for the night and if you were there for the night, you damn well better give it up!"

"I don't think you left much to your imagination."

"Sarah—" she whined. "Pleeeeaaassseee!"

"Amy, Amy, Amy! Do you live around that Café? Have you had their French Toast? It's incredible." I met her heated gaze.

She stopped chopping. When her shoulders sagged, I figured she'd suffered enough. I told her about his condo and what he was working on, the stuff she really wanted to know. She didn't care what part I played in the weekend but rather used me like a fanzine to fill in the gaps. I didn't mind. Talking about him made me feel more at peace that I really was.

"Damn, girl." She sighed. "I think I need a cigarette." She took off her gloves, grabbed her bag and went out for a smoke.

Left to my own devices, I took a moment and checked my phone. No texts. No calls. That stunk. At least Jessica sent me a note, 'filthy whore.' That's my girl and she didn't even hear the vibrator story.

At closing time, Amy had another slew of questions, chief among them, "Did you get his autograph?" I sure did, I thought. She was quite relieved.

It promised to be a quiet and boring evening. This would be the weakness whether with him or myself I wasn't sure. I was having a hard time going from full throttle to empty. I idly watched TV, wishing he were there to rope me into another shower. I heard the muted tune from the *Enemies of Orion*.

By the time I found my phone, there was a missed call and a text, 'You ignored our song? How's Amy?'

~~

# 4

The monotony of life eased when he strode into the Shoppe. His hair was a different color and shorter but he still looked mighty fine.

"Hi," he said, approaching the counter.

"Hi," I replied shyly. Having the counter between us was awkward. He leaned over hesitantly and pecked my cheek.

"It's good to see you. Can you throw together a turkey club—make it two, to go?"

"Sure thing. You're not going to hang around? This is literally a drive by?" I asked petulantly.

"Actually, the *food* is to go. I'd rather spend what time I have with you. You better hurry. It's taking all of my super human strength not to join you on that side of the counter!"

We both laughed. As I was bagging the sandwiches, two customers walked in the door, talking to each other. While ordering, they cast sidelong glances at Chris. It was pretty obvious that they felt they should know him. He parked himself at a table, checking out the restaurant. As soon as they'd paid, I came around the counter to join him. My 'to go' customers sat one table over, ogling him.

"I thought the counter was awkward," I said, glowering at them. One of the young women mouthed the word, 'sorry' and averted her gaze.

I handed him the bag. "Have you ever thought about doing something else somewhere else?"

"Yeah. But I get stuck on the how. And then the what and the where."

"How 'bout the movies? You could take your mad skills and work for one of the craft services. You'd fit right in." He glanced at the ladies at the other table.

"Hi, ladies. How are you today? I hope you tipped Sarah for those."

The girls giggled. The older of the two smiled faintly and finally managed a sentence. "You're Christopher Sparks, right? Sorry to interrupt you but could you—" She handed me her phone. "Could you take a picture with us?" She motioned her girlfriend to stand up.

"What do you think, Sarah? Are you up to it?" He winked at the girls, "Or a selfie, perhaps?" Chris slid out of his seat.

Mischievously, I snapped off a picture of the much-shorter girls, cutting off his head. "Nope. Sorry. Can you guys get in a little closer? Chris, can you—" I trailed off as he put his arms around them causing them to squeal. "That's a keeper." I handed the phone back.

The girls thanked him profusely. Heads down, they energetically stumbled out of the restaurant. They were probably sending that photo to the far ends of the earth.

He took a gander at the empty store. Happily, he stood behind me. His arms around my waist, he rested his chin on my head. "Any chance you can come with me to the set? Your company would make the down time far more pleasurable."

I leaned into him. "I still need a paycheck and that means I have to work."

"But you don't have to work *here*. Come with me. I'll introduce you."

"How about you do reconnaissance and I will jump when I know there is something to jump to?"

"Fine. That's respectable." He pulled me into his lap as he sat down. "Feels like I haven't seen you in days. I actually had a harder time focusing. Usually, I can bang out a scene— but even the makeup gal, she told me I looked tired. I have never heard that before."

"I told you that we should sleep."

"Ha." He kissed my nose. "I'll work on it. Promise." He put his hand behind my head, pulling my face into his. Our foreheads bumped. "I have to go. I don't want to go." I put my arms around his neck, content. "I go! I go! Look how I go!"

When the door bell sounded, I jumped out of his lap, embarrassed. "Dude, where have you been? We didn't realize that you were taking off. You left without our order!" said a cute, young guy with a scruffy face.

"Sarah, this is Arthur. He's a grip on the set. He and I have spent a lot of time together talking sandwiches. I mentioned your Cowabunga Slider. Sorry, Arthur." He scratched absently at his neck. "At least you get to meet Sarah. I was trying to convince her to bring her recipes to craft services. What d'you think?"

Arthur pretended to examine me through a monocle. "You look like you'd be a lot of fun. Why don't you come with us? We could probably talk them into hiring you on the spot. Or we could play cards. I love cards and a sandwich!"

"I'd love to. Do they just let people wander in off the street? Somehow, I don't see me getting very far even with you two to vouch for me," I said over my shoulder, returning to the counter.

"Let me get my sandwich before you leave!" Arthur wailed as Chris wandered back to the counter.

"I've never been here before. Nice place," he said, appreciatively. "Have you ever been to a movie set? It's pretty cool. And a great job."

"I haven't but then I haven't been in Los Angeles for that long." I handed him a slider.

"Well, now that Chris has invited you, it's a done deal. You can pretty much come and go as you please," he said cheerfully. "It's amazing what *the talent* gets when *the talent* asks."

~~

The days passed. I had a text here or there but I began to feel like a woman scorned, like 'he went to work and all he got me was this crummy t-shirt.' Jessica did her best to cheer me up. She reassured me that I was now ensnared with a high commodity. He had a life before me with its prerequisite obligations. I wanted to be one of those obligations! I wanted more of his time and waiting for it was a bitch.

I took myself to the beach after work on Friday. It was glorious. Rhode Island had the same blue skies but it also had Nor'easters. The west coast was aces, smog aside.

There were people crawling over each other today because it was one of the nicer evenings that we'd had in recent weeks. I found an unoccupied spot and sat down, pulling my legs up to my chest. The ocean always made me feel grounded and rejuvenated. It's surprising how little time I spent here.

I had been really good for the past couple of days, only checking my phone around lunch, after work and before bed. I was usually treated to a brief note which kept me on the hook, squirming. He was something with words. As I scrolled through the day's news, I was excited by a text.

'Hey, I'm outta here in about an hour. I'm off tomorrow. Are you free or can you get free?'

My fingers flew, 'YES. Good timing! I am at Matador Beach right now.'

'Want me to meet you there?'

'Only if you're bringing dinner. I know you're going to need to eat and I don't have anything with me.'

'Will do. Requests?'

Yep. I like this guy.

'A blanket. Be quick about it.'

'One hour. Sparks' out!'

I relaxed into the sand and made a sand angel. The sand was warm on my skin. My mind drifted off into thoughts, prayers and wishes for the next forty eight hours. Not one of these included much of my reality. There was no job, no apartment. Just time with him somewhere secluded and beautiful. My dreams were becoming quite visceral when I sensed someone kneeling over me.

I shielded my eyes.

"You look peaceful. I didn't want to interrupt your thoughts," he said, landing next to me with the basket.

"I picked up a few things." He handed me a glass and poured me some red wine. I had never been much of a wine drinker but then I'd never been romanced at the beach either.

"It appears you picked up *everything*—even the basket?" I said, fingering with the still-hanging price tag.

"You saw my place. I don't have anything or at least nothing for an occasion such as this." He ripped off the tag and threw it in the basket.

Sipping wine, he was abuzz with the work they'd completed and the speed at which they did it. He was so enthusiastic about his work. I envied him. If I could work somewhere that left me this energetic at the end of the day, I'd be thrilled.

Reflectively, I said, "Are all your days like this because you've got me convinced that you do have one of the best jobs in the world."

"Most are like this only different. I had to do some pretty sweet jumps today. It's going to look incredible."

"Are you ever concerned for your welfare?"

"No. That wouldn't be acting." He reached into the basket and pulled out quite a spread—hummus and pita chips, olives, pickles, sliced turkey and some cheese and he piled it into his lap.

"Probably would work better if I put the blanket down first," he said ruefully.

I helped him put the stuff back in the basket and spread out the blanket.

"Who made you this blanket? When I saw it, I thought it had to be Grandma."

"Nope. My sister. She teaches school in Massachusetts. When she has breaks, she is a knitting fiend. I think she was hoping that it would be baby clothing a couple of years ago but she's gotten over that."

"It's really vibrant. I love it."

"Me, too." He began to arrange the food. We ate in silence.

"You're quiet," he said, finishing off some humus and pita.

"Soaking in the last rays of the day. And watching you eat. I don't know where you put it but you can really eat."

"Growing boy. Told you before." He winked. "And I don't do anything half-assed."

I put my glass down in the sand and tossed my plate back in the grocery bag. Lying down in the sand, I was in my glory.

"This is how I would like to spend every day. Can you arrange that?" I said, rolling on my hip to see him.

"You've got remarkable taste. I'm sure I can arrange more of this," he said, licking his fingers. "I don't get here often enough. How do you feel about swimming?" He chucked his garbage in the bag.

# PERFECT

"I love swimming. I used to take the Polar Bear Plunge in Matunuck. In the middle of winter when it's freezing outside."

"It takes a special person of fortitude to strip and dip in December," he said, giving me a once over.

"I am and always will be a special person."

He laughed easily. "You are."

"I like surfing, too. Not very good at it but I'd love to get better."

"Surfing!" he said eagerly. "The waves here are a little more intense that back East."

Appraising his face, I ran my fingers through his hair. "What's with the color change and cut?"

"One of the joys of being with an actor. You get to date a different look with some regularity. What do you think? I think this is closer to the natural color."

"Spikey, too. Will you still be spiking your hair when you're forty?"

"Let's not plan out my hair for the next ten years, okay? And what's wrong with spikey? If I don't put something in it, it stands up on its own. It looks fluffy, like a stuffed animal. Trust me, not a good look." He reclined next to me, watching the waves crash.

I grabbed the edge of the blanket and dragged it over us, resting my head on his chest.

"Cold?" he asked, covering my shoulders with the blanket.

"Comfortable," I replied, hugging him.

Time passed and we were quiet, watching other people pack up and go home. The sun was getting lower and I could hear the waves lapping at the shore. Too bad I didn't bring a suit. Or a tent. I was not interested in leaving.

"Sarah." He shifted. "Sarah," he said again. "SARAH!" He wiggled. "My ass is asleep."

"You don't sit still, do you?" I sat up, allowing him to stretch.

"Sorry." He put his arm around my back. I felt his hand creep under my shirt. And then the girls were free.

I slowly turned to him. Averting his gaze, he whistled.

"I'm feeling much more liberated, Mr. Sparks."

Leaning his face into mine, he huskily said, "How free are you willing to be?" His hand snaked around my chest and he pulled me flush against him.

We were alone. The last umbrella was heading home. My enthusiasm for this situation was growing exponentially. I loved screwing around outside.

"What are *you* thinking?" I whispered.

"Not thinking. Doing. Done thinking." He eased me down onto the blanket, pushing my shirt out of his way. As he was kissing my exposed chest, he stopped.

"How would you feel about getting rid of this?" He shoved my bra up and aside. He quickly discarded it in the basket. My heart was racing. As he pulled his shirt over his head, I was once again amazed at how lucky I had become.

~~

Wrapped up in our blanket burrito, we took turns looking at the moon and what one could see of the stars. The bright city light dimmed them but it was still an incredible vista. Eventually, I was cold and incapable of hiding it.

"You want to go home?" he asked, covering my body with is. "I can warm you up."

My body shook. "What time is it?"

"Are you late for another date?"

"There are no other dates that can compare to the ones I have had lately." I put my hands on his face, feeling his advanced twelve o'clock shadow. "I was just curious what time it is."

He rolled off and looked at his watch. "It's just after midnight."

"Time to go then. Nothing good happens after one a.m."

"Nothing? Are you *sure*?"

"It's my motto. It's proven itself true over and over again. So, yeah. Pretty sure we'll be arrested for indecent exposure or something if we hang around. What would happen to your All American image if you were tossed in a cop car with a naked girl at the beach?"

He handed me my shirt. "Nothing good." He found my skirt. "Nothing good at all."

"Ha! So you're not from the 'any press is good press' camp?"

"Definitely not," he said, fastening his shorts. "I wouldn't mind being taken off the 'hottest bachelors' list."

Finding my flip flops, I was surprised by his sentiments. "You *are* a serial monogamist! You need to be in a relationship!"

"I hope it's not a turn off because I am still *very* turned on." He finished putting the blanket back in its bag. "Seriously, Sarah. I am enjoying my time with you. You're just what I was looking for." He picked up the basket. "It's probably way too soon to say anything else. My mouth sometimes gets ahead of me."

Loping into the parking lot, he stopped. "Can we leave your car here and head to my place? I can bring you back for it tomorrow."

"I didn't bring a car. I don't *have* a car."

"Nobody walks in L.A. There's even a song about it." He put his arm around my shoulders, steering me towards the only car in the lot.

"With your bleak apartment, I can't believe you have a red sports car. I woulda thought you'd be driving something economical, like a Prius." I was teasing.

He raised an eyebrow, opening my door for me. "Do you think all six foot three of me would fit in that dinky, if efficient, thing?"

I scoffed. "Like this car is any bigger!" I said, marveling at how good his butt looked in his shorts. "This car is flashy."

"Am I anything less? Don't judge me based on my apartment!" he said, dropping into the driver's seat.

"I'll try, but that place is awful."

His eyes full of mischief, he revved the engine. "Tell me you like it."

"It has potential," I said, listening to it purr.

"Potential! Should I trade it in for a Prius?"

I turned on the heated seat, ignoring him.

"I'm gonna take us home. You let me know."

~~

I flipped on the light. "This place sucks the life out of me. How can you stand it? I'd have to keep the TV on just for some color," I said, looking for the remote.

"I don't spend much time here." He rounded the couch and sat.

"I wouldn't either. It's bleak."

"What do you think we should do to make it less terrible?"

"Leave it." I sat on his lap.

"I'm listening."

Craning my head around, I raised an eyebrow.

"You have plenty of good ideas. Where'd you like to go? We can't go too far tomorrow but I am game for anything. Want to go site seeing? Disney Land? Surfing?"

"What I want is for the location to match the rest of this experience. I am thinking something tropical with lots of water and fewer people."

"Unlikely to happen today but duly noted. You did give me an idea, however." He picked up his phone from the end table and started scrolling.

"How would you feel about going for a car ride?"

"Now?"

"It's just after one now so we should probably wait until after breakfast. I don't want anything *bad* to happen to us."

"Where?" I asked, scoping out his long lashes and well-manicured eyebrows.

"Not interested in a surprise?" he said, his eyes meeting mine.

~~

# 5

We actually slept. With sleep came the realization that I was no longer afraid that he was going to disappear like a fleeting dream. He was going to be around and things would happen in their own time and pace.

When I awoke, I was happy. His arm over me, I caressed it. Even sleeping, his face was addictive. He had such long, dark lashes for a blond guy. I snuggled against him and sighed contentedly.

Eventually reality called and I got up to answer it. He was still rock solid-asleep. I took a shower.

When I came back, he opened one eye. "Hey. Good to see you. I was having the best dream." He stretched and patted the bed.

I sat next to him, toweling my hair. He pulled me back into bed and gave me a bear hug.

"Ouch!" was all I managed to get out before his grip relaxed.

"I know we have places to go today but I wanted you to know how happy you make me. I could lie here all day and be content." He pulled the towel off my head. "Do you have clothes here or do you need some?"

"I have what I had on yesterday."

"How would you feel about keeping a few things here?" he asked, rolling me onto my back.

Words were failing me. I released my towel.

"Although not having any clothing has its advantages." Hovering over me, we marveled at each other.

I felt like a little kid with a new toy. I didn't want to let it go. He leaned down and gently kissed my neck. I could very easily stay here all day. I was curious what the other option was so I pushed up on his chest as hard as I could, dislodging him.

He fell on his elbow. "You're thinking about the destination, aren't you?"

I picked at my finger nails.

"Live in the moment, baby!" he growled.

I ignored him.

"You're incredible!" He circled his hand around my bicep, yanking. Falling onto him, his stomach let out another of its famous rumbles.

"Who's incredible? Your damn belly is *incredible*!" I pressed my ear to his belly. "Sounds like you swallowed a mountain lion. I don't think we can stay here all day."

Sheepishly, he put his hand on my butt. "I'd like to try—"

"I don't think so. I can do the new hair but I don't find the incessant growling to be sexy. That sound makes me want to get up and forage for you."

"Oh, don't do that. I don't think the choices have changed in my kitchen. Up it is."

I slid off his chest. He dumped some shirts out of a drawer. "What's your pleasure today? Probably not white, huh?" He picked up a few of the plain t-shirts and tossed them back in the drawer.

I selected a very tired super hero shirt. "Do they give you these when you work on the movie or are they from your own personal collection? You seem to have quite a few."

"I do but I don't wear them. If you like them, you can have them." After putting the remaining shirts away, he threw on a plaid button down shirt that brought out the blue in his eyes.

I pulled on my skirt and waited intently for him to finish in the bathroom.

"Where're we going?" I asked eagerly.

"Do you want to stop home before we go? It's going to be about four hours in the car." He ran his hands back and forth through his hair, the bed head falling apart into spiky strands. "Actually, let's just buy what we need. I'd rather set off."

"Where are we going?" I asked again.

"Just enjoy the ride," he said, leaning on the door jam.

"You're not going to tell me?"

"I'd rather not. Can you trust me?" He squinted at me. "Four hours' worth of trust?"

"Four-hours-*and*-new-panties trust? That's a lot to ask," I said. Buying all new clothing with him sounded doubly painful.

He coughed. "Yep. It's either that or go without."

"I have to say that I have never lived that way."

~~

Once we were in the car, he apologized for what was going to be a fast food breakfast. I didn't mind. It was a beautiful day and being in the car was strangely appealing. To feel the warm air on my face and know that he would take care of everything was blissful.

After we finished off our breakfast sandwiches, he finally told me where we were heading. "Vegas, baby!" He whacked the steering wheel.

"Vegas? That's four hours away?" I put the extra napkins in the glove box. "How did I not know that? I could have gone there by now." Vegas always seemed like a trashy yet exotic destination and being a mere four hours made it less than exotic.

"Yup. We can do anything."

"You're pretty incredible."

"Thanks," he said, winking at me. "I do, however, have a favor to ask."

"Sure."

"As we have four hours, can you run lines with me?" He motioned to his bag in the back seat.

"Ewww. I can *try* but it may be better if I drive."

He glanced at me, confused. "It shouldn't be a big deal. I read my part and you read the other lines."

"It's not a big deal and I would do it if we weren't in a car. I get dizzy if I read in the car. I don't know if it's my dyslexia but I've never been able to read in a car."

"Oh, wow. That sucks. I bet family trips were really long and boring." He paused. "*And* you're an only child? Jesus! What did you do in the car?"

"We didn't go anywhere. Well, we *rarely* went anywhere." I brushed a few crumbs off my skirt. "Do you want me to drive? I'd love to drive. I have never driven anything with horsepower."

"Do you want to drive? You look content as a kept woman. Maybe help me run lines later. It'll probably take an hour."

"I am not going to lie. I am diggin' sitting in the sun with no responsibility. Can I drive on the way home and you can run lines then? *Can* you run lines by yourself or do you need another person?"

"I can do it alone but I like having a helper." He changed lanes. "You have dyslexia? I don't think I have ever known anyone with it. Can you read for fun? Is there treatment for it, a cure?"

"I can read. I can do everything that you can do but sometimes, I miss words or make mistakes. Numbers are tricky. I have to go over them a couple of times to make sure they're right."

"Huh. Life is hard enough without something like that as a kid."

"Like anything else, you learn to live with it."

"That's a great attitude. You're no victim." His hand found its way to my thigh.

"Want some music?" he asked, turning on the radio. "What kind of stuff do you like?" As he was flipping, he hit an oldie but goodie by Dirty Charles, one of my favorite bands of all time.

"This is good!" I screamed.

"I guess so! You've got lungs, girl." His eyes darted to me. "Have you ever seen them in concert? We should go. Might even be able to go backstage if my people make a couple of calls." His eyes left the road as he waited to see if his remark had the proper effect.

I smirked. What a great life. Make a few calls and things happen just because people want to be around you and make you happy.

"Speaking of calls, where do you want to stay? Pull up some hotels or just pick one." He handed me his phone.

"Cool! I've always wanted to stay at the Pyramid."

"Sure. It has all of the Egyptian décor that your heart could ever desire."

Humming, I found the Luxor quickly. There were plenty of rooms. "What's better, the tower or staying in the pyramid itself? The Pyramid rooms seem to be more expensive."

"Unless we're talking thousands, pick what you like. Want to take an elevator sideways? Then we have to stay in the pyramid."

A few more clicks and we had a room. This was shaping up so nicely that I really wanted him to pull the car over so that I could properly thank him for being so thoughtfully unique.

"Stop the car."

His brow furrowed. "Stop the car? We're almost there."

I unbelted myself and maneuvered over so I could kiss him.

His face lightened. "You wanted me to pull over so you could kiss me?"

"Yup." I settled back into my seat.

Although he was shaking his head, he was grinning from ear to ear.

Time flew by. We talked music. We sang. I fell in love with the changing vistas, from the exceptionally flat lands to the mountains. The only thing that would have made it better is if I could have put my feet out the window.

~~

# 6

"Welcome to Las Vegas, Sarah!" he said, touching my shoulder as we ambled into the hotel. Las Vegas was just like the movies. Everything was much larger than life. People crawled over everything like an endless procession of ants.

The décor at the Luxor was so convincingly Egyptian that I wished I had more of a memory for the pharaohs. They were omnipresent. We meandered to an elevator, my body pulsing with excitement.

"Any idea what you'd like to do first?" he asked, hitting the button to our floor.

"Explore but more specifically, I couldn't say. I'm not going to lie. This has the potential to be very overwhelming."

He took my hand and guided me into the elevator.

Moments later, we were in our room. I thought it would be decked out in Egyptian paraphernalia but it wasn't. It was rather stately with hints of Egyptian royalty sprinkled throughout.

"The view is pretty amazing. How many times have you been here?" I watched the sign at MGM repeatedly advertise a Paul McCartney concert.

"A few but it's always a good time. You look like you're ready to jump out the window."

"I am. Can we just start walking? I've heard a lot about so many of these places."

"I will warn you that the Strip is longer than it looks. Your feet might be dead dog tired before you know it."

"Bah! It'll be great," I said, wondering if my flip flops were really up to the challenge.

We spent the next couple of hours walking around, making it as far as Treasure Island. While watching their show, I felt like a part of such a normal couple. All of humanity was focused on the spectacle and we were no different. No one was looking at us. We were totally anonymous.

We wandered into Caesar's Palace for a very late lunch. When we were done, we strolled around, looking at all of the stores. There was more crap in that place than there were tourists on the strip. Passing a jewelry store, Chris stopped. Talking to myself, I realized that I had left him behind.

"What do you think of that?" he asked me as I approached.

"It's pretty," I said noncommittally of the silver necklace with a turquoise charm.

"Do you like it?" He was fixated on the jewelry case.

"Sir—can I help you with something?" asked an older gentleman in a suit.

"Would you wear it?" He quickly appraised me. "Yes. I think I'd like to see that." He pointed to the piece.

"Very well, sir." He pulled out the velvet form with the necklace. It was really pretty, different than what I usually wore. Chris took it and put it on me as the jeweler pointed me to a mirror. After admiring it, I peeked at Chris. He was so pleased to see me wearing it. I no longer felt any hesitation. I wanted it. I wanted to wear it right now.

"I like it. I'd like to wear it." I gently rubbed the turquoise gem.

The dapper salesman smelled a sale. His eyes never left Chris.

"I think we will take this," Chris said, retrieving his wallet.

I appraised the necklace. The turquoise was moon-shaped, thin. It was delicately suspended in the middle of a larger silver circle. It was truly elegant.

How long had I known this guy and he bought me a necklace? No one had ever bought me jewelry before. Not even from a gumball machine.

"That necklace and your shirt seem to be at odds," he said, returning. "If you see anything you like, let's pick it up. We're both gonna need new clothes."

We were on our way shortly but I felt like we had more of a mission. We discussed all of the options from taking a gondola ride to a show and looped back around to a nice dinner and maybe dancing. I was turned on by the idea of dancing with him. I had never been the club girl who had guys all over her. It was usually me and my girlfriends. This had real potential. If he could dance half as well as he did anything else, he would be the center of attention.

We spent another couple of hours carousing for clothes. I hated shopping but he made it fun. He tried on just as many pairs of pants, shorts and shirts as I did skirts and tops. He repeatedly trundled out of the dressing room doing a little booty move. He played the hapless goofball with wild abandon. Once, he came out with fire in his eyes and singing a tune with such devotion that he must've been reliving a scene from a movie. When I didn't get it, he cartoonishly deflated.

In one of the stores, the clerk recognized him. They had a pleasant conversation over shirts. She kept checking me out as if to determine if I were a relative. He sought my hand and brought me into the conversation. The chit chat flowed easily, as if he'd known Demi for years.

She left briefly while Chris finalized his dinner attire selections. She returned with a manager.

"Mr. Sparks, this is Alasdair, the manager. He will finish taking care of you. It was very good to meet you!" She bounced in her little business-y suit jacket then disappeared into the store.

"Hello. It looks like you've made some decisions?" He picked up the pants and dress shirt.

"Yes. I don't think I really need any more help. We're ready to ring it up."

Alasdair smiled thinly, returning to the register. An excited entourage awaited. Pilar, another manager, engaged Chris in a brief conversation about Vegas. She was keenly interested in providing us accommodations at Caesar's Palace. When we didn't accept, she instructed Demi to give him the ensemble, free of charge. He was very gracious, making one more attempt to pay for his stuff.

She shook her head. "It's not every day we get someone like you here." Handing him her personal business card, she sweetly said, "Please give me a call if I can help you with anything."

We left. "Does that happen often?"

"Define often," he said, eyes flashing.

"If I have to define it, I have to imagine that the answer is yes. Yes, you get special treatment because you're cute and good at working a room full of people."

He untangled the bag handles. "I can't say that it happens often. I don't do a whole lot of shopping. Not my favorite thing to do." Moving the big bag to his other arm, he said, "But I must say that it's been fun today. I probably should have done my Christmas shopping today, too!"

"Are you sure you didn't? What's the necklace for?" I asked, touching it.

"The necklace is because it's pretty. I wanted to get you a little something other than an old t-shirt. Make sure that you're not still dreaming of Mike."

He jostled the bags again. "You know what we're going to do? We're going to find someone to get this shit back to our room. I don't want to carry it."

He pulled out his phone. "I am going to get someone from the hotel to come here and get it." And he did. We left our bags with the Caesar's front desk and they made it to our room without incident, all for a hundred bucks.

Back in our room, we went through our bags to find dinner wear. I had a flashy new skirt and a pretty, sheer blouse with a bejeweled pair of flip flops. He purchased a dapper grey plaid suit with blue pinstripes with an equally appealing blue shirt and tie.

Modeling our clothing for each other was enjoyable. His skin was shiny with perspiration, the new shirt adhering to his chest.

"I think we both need to hit the shower. I feel amazingly sticky from walking around all day," I said, pulling the tank off my chest.

"I am *always* game for a shower with you." He peeled off his clothing. Hopping on one foot to get the last sock, he added, "Look! I am going to beat you, too, even though I had more buttons!"

Grabbing his elbow, I steadied him. "Yeah, you did beat me but you would have fallen over, too, had I not stopped to help you."

"Sarah, my savior!" He slowly ran his hand down my cheek, my neck and to the turquoise. "Thank you," he said, fingering the jewel.

~~

# 7

By the time we were finally ready for dinner, we opted to stay closer to home. Mandalay Bay was buzzing with people who looked like they'd been dumped out of a San Francisco office building. I never went places like this but in my new high end duds, I fit right in.

Towards the end of our meal, Chris was deep in thought, eyes drifting into the distance. I savored my beer, enjoying the atmosphere.

His head rolled back around to me. "So. What have you told your friends?"

I raised an eyebrow. "What should I tell them?"

He bit his lip for a second and then smiled, "That you're involved with an incredible guy."

"Involved."

"Involved."

"How involved?"

"Quite," he whispered.

"Incredible," I added slyly. I was not expecting a 'Will you be my girlfriend' speech while in Vegas.

"I would like to call you my girlfriend." He squirmed, pulling at the cuff of his jacket.

"You're cute." Even though the restaurant was arctic, he had a fine layer of perspiration on his forehead.

"You're killing me." He fiddled with a fork, squinting at me.

"I have never seen you look so uncomfortable."

"Fear of rejection is a bitch."

"You've undoubtedly dated some amazing people and you're afraid of my answer? Seems a little unreal."

"Finding someone like you *is* unreal." He focused on my necklace.

I gazed at him, a bigger smile creeping onto my face. A drip of sweat ready to drip off his nose, I sat on his lap. I took his capable hands in mine. "Okay."

I felt his body relax. He rested his head on my shoulder. "I hope you know how much I like being with you."

I dabbed his face with the cloth napkin. "It's mutual."

A lusty growl rumbled out of him as he held me tightly.

"Too bad we're surrounded by all these suits. I'd really like to—" His voice trailed off as he played with my bra through my shirt.

Getting away from his fingers, I excused myself and went to the restroom. I was glowing as I fastened my bra. It had been awhile since I had had a boyfriend and even longer since I had one that held any promise.

I took an additional moment to send out a crazy text to Jess. I followed it up quickly with texts to everyone I could think of, knowing that they wouldn't make a great deal of sense. Most of my friends had no idea what I'd been up to. Since he walked into my life, I had dropped off the radar but I was sending one hell of a signal now.

He flashed me a toothy smile as I made my return. He met me, putting his arm around my waist. With our newfound status secured, we dropped coins into a few slots before heading back to our room.

"So, what's next?" he asked, taking off his jacket.

"Dancing."

"Dancing?" he said with a twinge of amusement in his voice.

"Yes, sir."

He walked over, took my hands and started a gentle slow dance.

"Dancing," he said softly. "Right here."

I stopped swaying and did my best to grind instead.

"No. Let's hit the club downstairs for a little while. It'll be fun!"

"'It'll be *fun*,' she said." He grimaced. "Any way we can stay *here* instead?" Picking up intensity, his eyes alternated between bedroom and unbridled energy.

"Nope. I want to dance!" I leered at him.

He groaned. "Then you've got to stop that. *Now*." He backed up a step and glared at me. "Dancing," he said, crossly.

"Yes, dancing," I said energetically.

"In Vegas," he added, drolly.

I was bouncing.

"Better get moving. It'll be one before you know it. I don't want you turning into a pumpkin." He pulled out a clean white t-shirt, plaid shirt and a pair of jeans.

"Would you still be going if you weren't my boyfriend?" I coyly asked, taking off my sheer blouse.

He ripped the tag off his jeans. "Are you saying that if I kept my mouth shut, this wouldn't be happening?" He zipped his fly.

Without the blouse, my orange tank top was spritely on its own. Checking out my reflection, I was ready to go.

Closing the distance between us, I said "We're going to have fun! Or at least I am going to have fun."

He was far from convinced but maintained his good humor. As for me, I was eager to get downstairs and see what Vegas nightlife had to offer me and my freshly minted boyfriend.

~~

The club was like any club anywhere except, borrowing from *The Lorax*, they 'biggered and biggered' everything—more people, more lights, more truss, more stages, more bars.

We had a few drinks and people watched. There were people of every kind. Some of them should have left hours ago instead of stumbling around the dance floor.

I tipped my bottle to Chris. He mimicked me, pounding down the end of it and banging our bottles simultaneously on the bar. I bounced my way to the middle of the floor, applying my best 'come hither' look.

I felt a little self-conscious at first but focusing on Chris was joyous. He was a damn good dancer for someone who didn't want to come. His body was athletic and moved with incredible grace and poise. He was hypnotic. The more I watched him, the less of 'him' it seemed to be. It was more like a performance.

I was in my groove, dancing with my eyes shut when I sensed that Chris was gone. Opening my eyes, he had been accosted by a small group of twenty-somethings who were on to him. Their leader was determined to make a play for my boyfriend.

As I made my way over, Chris helplessly shrugged but he was obviously enjoying himself. Who wouldn't enjoy nearly naked young girls?

When the saucy brunette put her hands between his legs, I couldn't help myself. I sandwiched her back and dug my nails into her dainty paw.

Her girlfriends doubled over in laughter. Still dancing, I shook my head at her and her crowd.

"What was that for?" she hissed.

"Exactly," I said as Chris put his hands around me and tried to pull me away from this little confrontation.

"Whatever!" she crabbed. She ran her hands through her damp hair, scowling at Chris.

I wore Chris like a glove, rejoicing in his obvious display of carnal grinding. I was confident that she was still staring, plotting her next move. I turned around and grabbed Chris's face, planting the biggest, most movie star kiss I could. He clasped his hands on mine, responding ardently.

When we came up for air, he said, "I think that worked. She's sulking by the bar."

"What time is it?" I asked, seething.

"Ah! Maybe it's after one!" he said lewdly, artfully dipping his fingers into my bra. I swatted his hand away.

"Actually, it's just about one," he amended, checking his watch.

"If it were after one, I would have hit her. It's time to go."

"If you say so. I was having fun." His eyes sparkled. "You sure you're going to let her chase you out of here?" He resumed his masterful performance.

"When you put it *that* way, no!" I bounced right along with him but kept a wary eye on those around us. He was just as alluring to others as he was to me. In a voyeuristic way, it made dancing with him that much more compelling. He was my boyfriend and come what may, they would watch us leave together.

~~

An exhilarated if drenched mess, we left the club. The slots were calling. I had never played dollar machines but Chris fed in the money and I pulled the lever. When another machine opened up, he settled in next to me.

An hour later, I was bored and broke. Hovering behind him, I noticed that he had quite a few credits piled up.

"Are you done? I just got $500!" He was juiced.

"Then *you* should be done," I whispered into his ear.

"I'm feeling lucky," he said, slapping the button authoritatively.

"Then you should *really* be done." I leaned in and nibbled his ear softly and insistently. I ran my hands through his hair, down his wet back.

He sighed and cashed out.

On our way back to our room, we ran into a couple of people who Chris knew. As they chatted, I scoped them out. Were they famous? I didn't immediately recognize them.

The tall, dark and smokingly handsome guy was Ian Hartlass. It had to be. I knew he'd worked with Chris more than once. If I was correct, the other guys were famous actors, too. Seeing them out of context and in civilian clothing, I couldn't immediately decide who they were.

Taking my hand, Chris introduced me. The eyebrows went up at 'girlfriend.' It being such a new term to me as well, I was just as startled. That little word also changed their focus. They checked me out more thoroughly, sweaty mess that I was.

Tom was very chatty. He wanted my life history on the spot. It's not every day that such a gorgeous, well-known celebrity hangs on your every word. The intensity of his interest embarrassed me. Colin Williams, a disarmingly charming British man, listened attentively. I had watched a lot of indi films in my quest to see more of him. He was a fantastic actor.

Lucas St. Martin, one of Hollywood's up and coming bad boys, stepped away from the group, more interested in their end destination. I couldn't think of any movie I'd seen with him in it.

Ian casually invited us to join their troupe. He was Jessica's favorite actor, bar none. If I could get just one picture with him and hide it in the apartment—I could already hear her shriek.

Chris looped his arm possessively around my waist and took a rain check. Spending any time with Chris could never be disappointing but I was bummed that he declined. Too bad we hadn't run into them before we went dancing.

When they took off, I said, "Earlier, I thought this was one place where you might be anonymous."

"Nah, anonymous is wearing a costume to Comicon." His eyes twinkled.

"Have you done that?" I asked, mouth agape. "You've fooled your fan base?" I ran in front of him, walking backward.

"What'd you wear? Did you go as Orion?"

He frowned at me. "That'd be original."

"Come on, tell me!"

He walked at a faster clip.

"Just tell me already, before I walk into something," I begged.

"You're not going to let this go."

"No! Were you another character? The Lieutenant—he had a sweet mask. Did you go as your own lieutenant?"

He stopped and grabbed my arm. Turning me around, he loosely gestured at a mob that I almost walked into.

"People see what they want to see," he said, steering me towards the elevator.

~~

It was now just after three and I was done. I wanted a shower and some sleep. Moseying into the bathroom, I wasn't alone in my desire.

"Don't know about you but I think I need a shower and some sleep!" He scraped his wet shirt off and tossed it on the floor.

"Amen to both," I said, tossing my shirt similarly.

"Good time so far?" he asked, stepping into the shower with me.

"Incredibly! Do we really have to drive home in a few hours?" I asked, rinsing the soap out of my hair.

"You never know. I am happy you're happy." He leaned in and gave me a gentle kiss.

"Oh, dear God. Don't start *this* now! I thought we agreed on a shower and sleep!" I squealed, basking in his attention.

"We are in the shower. Next up—sleep. Totally on task," he whispered, trading places with me.

Watching the water course over his body, I couldn't stand it. I moved in to share his space. Soaked, I made full use of the fact that it was a hotel. I hopped out, getting water all over everything and reached for two towels. As he turned off the water, I threw him one. He caught it and dropped it.

His hungry eyes bore into me as he peeled off my towel and pushed me up against the wall. My senses were on fire. I felt the extreme temperature difference between his skin and the cold tile. Every cell was alive, carrying mixed messages.

Mirrors covered the walls. Everywhere my eyes ventured, there was a lovely show to watch. Every muscle, tense. His face, gentle but deeply focused. When the phrase 'making love' was coined, this is what the speaker had in mind—beauty, power, passion and purpose moving in concert.

Exhausted, we fell into bed and so entwined remained for the better part of the morning. The incessant chirping of his phone woke us.

He squinted at me through one half-opened eye.

When he didn't make any effort to get it, I swung a pillow at him.

I hit him squarely in the head. "*Get that*, please." Rolling on to my belly, I growled. "It's not going to stop till you do."

He stretched over me to the nightstand and retrieved it. Reading his texts while flopped on my back, he chuckled.

"You can sleep in."

"I could have, you mean."

"Okay. We could have. I don't have to go in till—it looks like Wednesday at the earliest." He tossed his phone and kissed my back.

"What time is it?" I asked thinking that it had to be the middle of the day. As if on cue, his damn belly grumbled. "You can't be serious." I wriggled under him, turning over.

Sheepishly, he swept the loose hairs off my forehead. "Can't I get a pass? I was very active yesterday. And it is going on one."

"I suppose we have to get up anyway. I still have to go to work tomorrow." I ruffled his hair.

"Call in. You know you want to."

"Oh, there's no question I *want* to but I can't."

"Why."

"Two things—I don't like to call in at the last minute. It's not cool. Number two and most importantly—I don't work, I don't get paid."

He fell defeatedly on the bed next to me. "How well do you know Amy? Is she a friend?"

"Why?" I asked curiously.

"Where's your phone?"

I showed it to him. "Why? What are you thinking?"

"Say cheese" he said, taking a bed-selfie of us.

The picture was pretty damn hilarious. His hair was true bed head. He had the biggest, cheesiest grin. I had an eyebrow raised and appeared worried.

"Let's try that again. Say *cheese* this time!" He snapped another one. It was equally ridiculous.

"Maybe we should go for demure instead?" he asked, raising the camera again.

"Thaaat's a keeper." He handed me the phone. "Now. Send it to Amy."

"Say *what?*" I rolled on to my belly, staring at him. "What will that accomplish?"

"A couple of things, I bet. And it's fun. We could start a new trend!"

I sent it to Jessica. She'd get a kick out of it. Then, I had to send it to my other girls. I was still thinking about Amy. If I sent it to Amy, part of me was concerned that she'd try to do something with the picture instead of chuckle and delete it.

"Did you send it?"

"Yep."

"To Amy, I mean?"

"Nope."

"Do your friends know about me now?"

"Yep."

"Nice," he said, sweetly. "But what about work? Please call in, just for a day or two."

I was reading a text from Jessica along the lines of 'what happens in Vegas, stays in Vegas?' when he followed up his request.

"Or are you married to the Sandwich Shoppe? Maybe now is a great time to say goodbye to deli meat." He pulled himself up next to me. "Sarah? Opportunity is knocking and you're texting?"

I ignored him, catching Jess up. He read our conversation.

"Tell Jessica I said hello. Or hand me the phone." He reached for it.

"Why do you want it?" I asked, dangling it out of his reach.

"Because I could use her help!" He made another play for it and, pinning me, took it.

After a short wrestling match, I relented.

"Fine. You can have her!" I got up and went to the bathroom.

No matter what I thought of my new boyfriend and how much I wanted to leave the Sandwich Shoppe, was I seriously considering quitting just to stay in Vegas? What then? Wasn't I too responsible to consider something this unstructured?

I dug through a bag for something to put on. I threw it down.

"What the hell? You're still talking to her?" I feigned indignation.

"More like reconnaissance." He was intently texting away.

I found the other bags of new clothes and started pulling out shirts. Having found a cute yellow tank, I dramatically ripped the tags off. Getting no reaction, I threw the tags at him.

He looked up. "Oh, you're still here?" Holding my gaze, he sighed, put the phone down and climbed out of bed.

Watching the big, naked boyfriend approach was a nice treat. He had six pack abs and wonderfully sculpted legs. He was sinfully glorious. I dropped my act.

"What will it take for you to stay here. With me. For another couple of days? Is there anything I can say?" He reached out and took my hands, resting them on his butt.

"Or do?" I was enraptured by his exquisitely chiseled chest. It had the right amount of soft, blondish fuzz.

"You're impossible. The deal was that you look into other work for me, remember? And I move on when there's something worth doing!" My resolve was drying up. His insightful blue eyes were so damn convincing.

"Girlfriend. There's plenty worth doing. Please *think* about it. At least until we've eaten? No good decisions happen on an empty belly. That's my new motto." He gave me a warm hug then headed to the bathroom.

While he was indisposed, housekeeping knocked. I knew that there was a 'do not disturb' sign on the door but I went to get it anyway. Chris cut me off, wrapped in a towel.

The young girl on the other side was titillated. She offered him everything on the cart from razors to tooth paste. Chris barely whispered in response. She flushed and continued to offer him things in broken English. When he accepted clean towels, she took off.

He dropped the towels on the foot of the bed. "I think we have to extend our reservation. She was here to turn the room over and I am not ready to go."

He called the front desk. Although he tried to keep his voice down, I was certain that I heard him extend the reservation through Wednesday. It did make it easier when choice was removed.

"How long are we staying?" I asked, sitting down on the bed.

He returned from the bathroom with a Q-tip in his ear. "We have the *room* until Wednesday morning. Does that work?" Misreading my expression, he tossed the Q-tip and swatted me with his towel. "*Yo!* Does that work?"

Distracted by his naked body, I was inclined to say 'yes, yes sir. It does.' Instead, I shook my head.

"Honestly. What am I going to do with you?" I handed him his towel. "I'll call in."

"You'll feel better once you do. Then, food and run some lines by the pool?"

"That's quite the itinerary." I walked into the bathroom with my phone. I called Amy and loosely filled her in. She did a lot of girl-screaming. She was too excited for me and felt that I should follow him as far as he would take me. She was so supportive, I sent her the bed-selfie. After more crazed noise, she said she'd handle the shifts and saw no need to tell anyone else. She only asked that Chris come by the store upon our return and maybe bring a friend.

We went down to the buffet for lunch and then out by the pool. It being February, the weather was ideal for being near a pool but not necessarily in it.

We claimed lounge chairs near the hulking pyramid.

"What happens if you tan?" I asked, pondering what an afternoon of sun could do to his movie look.

Waving a bottle of sunscreen at me, he said, "I'd prefer not to. Would you be so kind?" He pulled off his shirt.

"You don't want to tan yet you're taking your shirt off?" I squirted the sunscreen in my hands.

"Better than having a farmer's tan," he said, over his shoulder.

I slathered him in the stuff, rubbing it into his skin.

"Do you want any?" he asked as I returned the bottle.

"Nope. My skin can be the canary in the coalmine. When I look rosy, we should get out of here."

"Awww. You'd do that for me?" He leaned over and kissed me.

"Alright. Let's get to this line business." I waited for him to hand me whatever I was to read.

He dislodged a tired, loosely bound script from his messenger bag and leafed through the pages.

"Let's start here," he said and then flipped another couple dozen pages out. "And maybe try to get to here." He dog-eared the page and handed it to me. Reclined in his chair, he put his arms behind his head.

"You look really comfortable. I take it you think you know this material already?"

"Hope so." He closed his eyes. I read a couple of the lines to myself and found myself sucked into the story. When I reached the dog eared page, Chris was asleep.

"Chris," I said humorlessly. I leaned over his chair. "*Chris?*" I said more forcefully. Nothing. I didn't like being ignored so I straddled him.

His body tensed and his eyes flew open.

"Hey, there, handsome. This is a good story." I set the script on his chest.

His hands on my thighs, he said, "Did you read the whole thing?"

"No, but I did read what we're supposed to be working on."

"Cool. Then you're ready for me."

"You're trying to tell me that you meant to fall asleep?"

"No, I didn't but I did think you should read it first so I intentionally tuned out."

"Shall we?" I asked, still sitting on him.

"Yeah, but I can't do it like this. You're much too distracting. I don't need to associate this scene with *this* scene." He patted my ass.

"Alright but let's get it done." I got up and moved back into my chair.

We went over that section at least three times. It was pretty boring by the third run because he had it. I didn't see the reason to keep going over it and finally said so.

Looking at his watch, he said, "It's only been an hour. Maybe we could run some other parts? Would you mind?" He was paging through the script.

"I don't think I can sit here much longer. I either want to get *in* the pool or out of the sun."

"Would you rather run lines in our room?" His tone was all business.

"If you promise me we can *do* something soon. This much reading is not my idea of a good time." I scanned the pool, amused by what people considered appropriate attire for public swimming.

He appeared chagrinned. "I'm sorry! Is it a dyslexia-thing?" Sitting up, he set the script down.

"Not really. I'm just ready to *do* something before it's time to climb back into bed."

He hooted. "Based on last night, we have another twelve-plus hours before we're back in bed. Plenty of time! But it's cool. Let's head back to the room for an hour or so. I think I can do it in an hour."

We gathered up our things and headed back.

"What did Amy say?" Chris asked, opening the door for me.

"She did a lot of screaming."

"That doesn't sound good."

"*Girl*-screaming," I corrected.

He laughed. "Big difference. You're off the hook then?"

"I am but you're not."

He raised an eyebrow. "Oh?"

"Amy wants you to bring in a boy for her, too. That's what she wants in return."

He cocked his head. "You're serious."

"Very."

"Huh." Approaching the elevator, he had an epiphany. "What if we were to include her in something and let the chips fall where they may?"

"That'd be incredible for her. What do you have in mind?" I asked, getting into the elevator.

"Not sure but that sounds easier than feeding her my friends."

## PERFECT

~~

I desperately wanted to be back outside in the sunshine. I leaned on the wall near the window, script in hand. I lost my place a couple of times. The activity on the strip was compelling.

Chris paced, crouched, jumped and strode purposefully around the room, delivering each line in a flat monotone. It felt like we went over some of it hundreds of times. As the afternoon wore on, I snarled my lines. It didn't seem to affect him. He forged ahead.

"Just one more time," he said, trotting over. He leaned over me. "Let's pick it up right here."

Annoyed, I scowled at him. He smiled faintly but was waiting for the line. I sighed. His smiled disappeared but he continued to wait. I sighed *loudly*, licked my fingertip and traced down to the line.

"For art," I said lifelessly.

"I got your art," he said, tantalizingly tugging and removing what little he had on.

He ran out of clothing a good page or more before we ran out of text. He shrugged and struck some ridiculous poses instead. When I could finally see the end, I pushed him on to the bed. Still reading, I climbed up on top of him. I delivered the last line majestically as he pulled off my shirt.

~~

# 8

"When was the last time you had a girlfriend?" I asked, straightening out my skirt.

"Is that really what you want to know?" he said, looking up from tying a shoe.

"As a serial monogamist, yes. I don't think you went around screwing different girls regularly. Am I wrong?"

"'Serial monogamist.' Makes it sound like there's a prison yard for men such as myself." He shook his head. "It's been a while."

"How long is 'a while?'" I prodded.

"I don't remember the last time I broke up with someone, how's that for an answer? It's been *a while*."

"Was your last girlfriend famous—would I know who she is?"

"Quite likely, yes. I don't get outside my circle much."

"Yet you picked up the Sandwich girl. Explain that."

"You were pretty. Funny. Alone. I saw opportunity." His eyes drifted to my bosom. "Is this when we discuss our sexual pedigrees?"

I wrinkled my nose. "Now it sounds like we're talking about dogs instead of girlfriends."

"Let's go get some sunshine and save this conversation for later," he said, unlatching our door.

Undeterred, I continued to pester him as we made our way outside.

"Who was she?"

He popped his neck before putting his arm around my shoulders.

"You don't let things go, do you?"

"Not this one."

"I really don't like thinking about her. Even mentioning her name makes me feel badly. It was just not the way things are supposed to go. I don't get played but I was."

"Oh. I'm sorry. It's hard *not* to be curious." I had relationships that I didn't remember fondly but they were also easy to gloss over as irrelevant. It seemed safe to say that his last girlfriend was not irrelevant.

Perhaps it's not possible to have an immaterial relationship with someone that everyone knows? I can talk about my past because there is a veil of secrecy. The likelihood of my current beau knowing anything about the previous fella is exceptionally slim enough to be zero.

We continued in silence for a couple of minutes before switching gears. It being seven already, we opted for dinner at the Bellagio. I felt out of place. It was many steps up from the Luxor in décor, guests and attitude. Dinner was a grand affair right down to the lack of prices on the menu.

"I have never been anywhere that didn't include prices on its menu," I said, trying to make sense out of the meal descriptions.

"Don't worry about it. It's not every day that I can do this with you." He unleashed one of his movie star smiles. Between his words and his heartwarming smile, I was at a loss.

"Thanks," I said, pleased. He made me feel valuable, comfortable and loved. It was as frighteningly right as it was refreshing.

"Thanks for changing your schedule." He caught the waiter's eye. "Have you given any more thought to quitting?"

I slouched. "I'd *love* to. I really would."

"What's holding you back?"

"You're infuriating. You have the ability to make me question myself in a way that leaves me feeling like anything is possible. Life is not that way." The waiter appeared with the dessert tray.

"Haven't you ever done anything on a leap of faith?" he asked, selecting one.

"No. Not in a long time."

"How'd you get to Los Angeles?"

"Jessica came out here months before. She was receiving some recognition for her writing and just moved. She's your leaper."

"Did Jessica hook you up? Give you some big reason to come out here, a safety net?"

"I moved in with her."

"Did she find you a job?"

I laughed. "No. She's a writer. She doesn't orbit this planet on a daily basis."

"*That* was a leap of faith. You came to L.A. because there was no reason not to. You just did it." He took a bite of dessert. "How's it working out for you?"

Taking a sinfully big bite of the chocolate mousse, I smacked my lips. "It's satisfying."

"Satisfying." He put his fork down. "Lovely. Then it's time for another leap. Last time, you had Jessica. Now, you have me. I'm not going anywhere." He reached across the table and covered my hand with his.

"If money were no issue, what would you like to do? What did you do back in Rhode Island—not another Sandwich Shoppe?"

"Believe it or not, I worked for the Freemasons," I said smugly.

He raised his eyebrows. "I thought that was a men's fraternity."

"You know what they say, 'behind every strong man is a stronger woman.'" I snickered. "So imagine how strong *I* am."

"No doubt! What the hell did you do for them?"

"Front desk stuff, mostly."

"Did you learn their secret handshake?"

I laughed. "No. I had access to their most sacred books, however, and heard some curious stuff." I loved that place and hadn't had a reason to talk about it in some time. "My first day of work, the phone rang during lunch. My boss got up and answered it. I could hear her half of the conversation and it was paranormal. When she returned to the table, she told me she was relieved that she answered the phone. Apparently, the caller had moved into a defunct Masonic Lodge in Massachusetts and had been experiencing paranormal events. My boss listened to her as she recounted bags being thrown at the new inhabitant—all sorts of stuff. My boss told her that she should really call the Grand Lodge of Massachusetts as the ghosts were in their jurisdiction."

Chris's eyes sparkled. "And you stayed there?"

"How could I leave? You get a ghost phone call on day one? Sign me up! Those guys are the most charming, the most gracious. They were good to me."

"Now you have me wanting to join."

"You'd fit right in. With their rituals, they all have a part to play. They're actors."

"Well, unless you're going to reach out to the Masons here, I ask again: what would you do if money were no problem?" He rubbed my hand gently and waited patiently for me to answer.

"Talk about uncomfortable! I don't know what I'd be doing. Money does matter. It has always mattered in a basic, take-care-of-myself sort of way. It would take a *major* adjustment for it to not matter."

"Here's your opportunity. Let's figure out what you want to be doing, what would make you happy, if money were something other people worry about—not you."

The table suddenly felt like a very small, very intimate place. My mind was flying through all sorts of basically untrue answers about what I could be doing. Finally, I settled on a truth.

"I would take some time and just be. I would travel. And when the newness of that wore off, I'd probably develop some hobbies or get a job to pay for all my credit card bills." I withdrew my hand and pushed myself as far back in my chair as I could go.

"Cool."

"Cool? It could be cool. It's about as likely as pigs flying."

"Did you ever think you'd be here with me having a priceless dinner in Las Vegas? Or would you have said that the likelihood of you walking through flying pig droppings would have been higher? Sarah, I think we have found your weakness." He crossed his arms. "You're too grounded by reality. You need to get up higher than them flying swine and let go."

"Right. Look out, below! Here comes Flying Sarah and *her* droppings!"

"Now that's gross."

I smirked. "Why do I feel like it'd be easy with you? Honestly. *Why*? I am thirty five years old and have never once thought of doing anything crazy. Maybe jumping out of an airplane. Even then, you have two parachutes."

"One of the benefits of being who I am is that I am not tethered money. The reality is that I have enough. It is likely that I will always have enough or more than enough. I don't know what to do with what I have. It sits, unsexily, multiplying in bank accounts. It would make me *happy* to see you doing something. I know you can do it. This is your opportunity."

"To what?"

"To what? Whatever you want."

"That's uncomfortable."

"You'll get used to it." He picked up his coffee.

"I'll think about it." Grinning wickedly, I said, "Can we talk about something else, your past girlfriends, perhaps?"

He stifled a laugh, nodding to the waiter for the bill.

~~

We casually strolled outside and were just in time for one of the fountain shows. Finding some open banister, we stopped. His arm around my waist, I felt at peace. The show was something I had always heard about and for good reason. What they were able to do with water and lights in the desert were really incredible.

This was another one of those moments where everything felt normal until I started analyzing it. Everything about this was not normal. This did not happen to normal people. This kind of experience was for people in Chris's circle, not mine. My friends would be the ones changing their sheets or selling them souvenirs. Yet here I was. Ruefully, I searched the sky for pigs.

Chris was developing a sixth sense. His arm tightening around me, he looked at me tenderly. He completely understood what he was asking me to do and he had faith in me. I wove my arms around his waist. Inhaling deeply, I allowed myself to consider that he could be right.

When the show ended, we waited for the crowd to disburse. He slid behind me and held me. He was my rock, giving me security and strength.

I turned around. Pressing my nose to his, I kissed him. His support and conviction were so sexy. I balanced on my toes and gave him the most soul searching kiss I could. Seeing a fire light in his eyes, his hands pulled at my hips.

He broke the embrace and chuckled throatily. "I offer you the world and you give it to me."

~~

Chris and I flipped on the TV and checked our phones. I had a ton of messages from people that I had not heard from in ages. Picking which ones to answer right now was challenging. While scrolling, I hit upon an old friend from Connecticut, Melissa, who was working as a pit boss. When I last saw her, she was working for Mohegan Sun in Connecticut and pining away about Vegas. Looks like she'd taken the leap.

"Tomorrow, how would you feel about going to Bally's? One of my girls from the East Coast is apparently a pit boss. She'd like to take us to dinner."

Texting away, he said, "Nice. When was the last time you saw her?"

"I haven't *seen* her in ten years. I keep up with her on Facebook." I started a response.

He moved a pillow up against the wall, leaning against it. "Oh, you really keep up with her. She's in Vegas and you didn't know it until minutes ago."

"I have been distracted."

"For years?"

"I don't know how long she's been here."

Chris set his phone down and picked up the remote. "Can we head back on Wednesday?"

"I'll check in with Amy after I answer a couple of these. People are suddenly very fascinated with my life." I scrolled and tapped, picking and choosing how to sum up recent events.

"Hey, Melissa would like to take us to dinner at the Tequila Bar and Grill after her shift ends tomorrow. Sound good?"

"Where's that?"

"Bally's. She's off at seven. She'd like to show me the house she bought about a year ago, too."

"And she's lived here long enough to buy a house, Sarah. How good a friend is this?" He tsked.

"Oh, it gets better. She wants to know if she can have some friends over."

"What would Vegas be without a house party? Ask her if I can invite the guys." My head whipped up. I wasn't sure if he was serious but I'd love to have a chance to hang out with his crew. If you're gonna dream, go big.

"Too bad Amy's back in Los Angeles! This would be perfect for her!" I leaned up against Chris. "And yes, she said you can bring your friends. Got any names you'd like to drop?" This had potential.

"Hand me my phone. No name dropping unless they're in."

As he texted, he looked jazzed by the idea of uniting our two circles. I set my phone down and flipped around for a movie. I chuckled when I saw *Enemies of Orion*. It was so close to the end, I had to watch.

Chris glanced at the TV and shook his head. "I texted them. Colin is usually on his phone. It won't be too long." He picked up my phone.

"Can I check out your friends?" He cradled my phone.

"Sure. Knock yourself out."

Before I knew it, I realized that he was texting.

"Who're you talking to?" I asked, curiosity piqued.

"Jessica."

"About?"

"Schedules."

"More specifically?"

"I thought it would be fun if she and Amy could get here tomorrow."

"Say what—what the hell're you doing?" He had my full attention now.

"Relax! Nothing *nefarious*, I promise! In fact, I'd call it tying up loose ends." I moved so that I could read his texts.

"Does she know it's you?"

"Yes. I would never masquerade as someone else." His eyes sparkled mischievously.

"Riiight. Give me my phone!" I launched myself at him.

"How did this work out for you last time?" He swatted me away and finished his conversation. I stared vacantly at the TV. As much as I wanted to see Melissa, I wasn't so sure I wanted other elements of my life to hone in on my Vegas time with Chris. He, and our relationship, were still too new to be shared.

When he handed me my phone, he apologized. "Sorry. You look stressed." He slid out from under me. I fell comically on the bed and continued to stare at the ceiling.

When he returned from the bathroom, his hands were on his hips. He climbed onto the bed and gently rolled me over on to my belly. He kissed my arms, placing them at my sides. He ran his hands through my hair, splaying it on my shoulders.

"What're you up to, Mr. Sparks?"

"Making things better," he said, lifting my shirt and kissing my back.

~~

# 9

Monday morning, we took our time getting out on the strip. We did all of the touristy things—from the roller coaster to the Eiffel Tower and a stroll through movie memorabilia lane. Although it was fun, it was anticlimactic. What I really wanted was to meet up with Melissa.

About an hour before dinner, we headed back to our room to freshen up for the evening.

Chris called from the bathroom, "Hey—can you check my phone? I never did get a response from the guys."

He had a slew of texts. Raising my voice, I yelled, "I didn't realize that you *text* so many famous people! Your phone is a goldmine." I scrolled. "Are these people what you consider your 'circle' to be?" There were multiple messages from the guys we'd met at the Luxor.

While I answered their texts, Chris asked, "Are they coming?"

"Looks like yes. I'm giving them her address."

"Cool. Amy might be very lucky tonight." He tapped his razor on the sink. "They don't fall into your 'serial monogamist' category."

"She'd like nothing less. Do you have someone in mind for her? Dear god, do you have someone picked out for Jess?"

"What do you think this is, Fiddler on the Roof?" He peeked out at me, shaving cream on his ear. "I think Jess has someone picked out for Jess." He turned off the water.

"Oh? What kind of a conversation did you have with her yesterday?" I was awed by the names.

"She's a straight shooter. I appreciate that."

I raised my eyebrows. "That's a weird response to my question."

He came around the corner, toweling off his face. "I had a brief conversation with her. She did most of the talking. She was very—*enthusiastic*—about this evening."

Sliding into my flip flops, I met him at the door.

"You ready?" he asked, looking me over appreciatively.

"Considering I don't know what I am getting myself into, yes."

~~

It didn't take too long to find the restaurant. Walking up to the hostess, I felt a tap on my shoulder.

A smile spreading across my face, I greeted Melissa. She hadn't changed much. She still had the mega-watt smile. It always put me at ease.

"Nice uniform," I said, checking out her casino-issued attire.

"Hey, thanks! You haven't changed!" She leaned in and gave me a big, heartfelt hug.

When we got our table, Melissa bubbled on. She loved her Vegas life as a pit boss. With the steady income, she purchased her house a year ago in a subdivision that has yet to be completed. It was an unlived-in foreclosure with a swimming pool. She couldn't pass it up.

"Chris, who can I expect this evening? Sarah said you were bringing some friends?" She flashed him a toothy smile.

He finished his tequila. "There're four guys that Sarah and I bumped into. You never can tell if they will have found anyone else to drag and for that, I apologize."

"Anyone I'd know?" she asked, sweetly.

"Lucas St. Martin, Colin Williams, Tom Warp and Ian Hartlass."

"Holy hell! Are they *friends* of yours? I know you're working on a movie with them. I saw that a while ago." Her eyes were wider than saucers. She downed the hefty remnants of her margarita.

"Yeah, they're friends." He flagged our waitress down for another shot.

"I suddenly feel very unready! Had I known you were bringing them, I would have gone out and gotten my hair done and cleaned the house." She threw herself back in her chair, eyes glazing over at the possibilities.

"You're fine, Mel. They really are just regular people who eat and sleep." Chris squeezed my thigh.

"Oh, you can say that. He picked *you* up! I am going to have these people whom I've never met *in my house*!!" She emitted a couple of ear piercing girl screams.

Chris shook his head like a dog. "Is that what you meant when you talked to Amy?" He frowned jovially at Melissa.

"Ian Hartlass. Is he really the womanizer he seems to be? That man is *hot*." She fanned herself.

"He hasn't found 'the one.' He does have discerning tastes, too, so you two ladies better stay safely away from him." He eyed both of us seriously.

"Sorry, guys, but this doesn't happen to me. It's crazy! My friends and I are the ones who provide *services* to you, Chris." She looked at her watch. "It's going on nine. I'm thinking we should get out of here. I gotta make sure that things are presentable! Do we need to pick up anything to drink?"

"You've got nothing to worry about." He handed the waiter his credit card. "They'll take care of it."

~~

Turning into her subdivision, we heard loud music.

"That's odd," Melissa said, rolling down the window to the cab. "My neighborhood has never been known for loud parties! They must know I have company."

She leaned further out the window. "Oh, my god! That's coming from *my house*!" she screamed.

Chris grimaced. "Sorry, Melissa but I think they started the party without us." He shook his head, "Animals."

The car wasn't even in park when she leapt out, running to the back gate.

In hot pursuit, we followed her into the backyard. Tom and Lucas were in the pool, fighting over the only float with a cup holder. We all froze when she screamed.

With perfect comedic timing, they turned around slowly. "Melissa?" they said, voices going up an octave.

Mouth agape, she spun and screamed again. Ian Hartlass was staring at her seductively from the hot tub.

"Evening," he said, tipping his non-existent hat. He stretched his arms out on the edge of the tub. "Care to join me?" he asked innocently, caressing the edge of the tub.

"You guys really couldn't wait? It's *early* by your standards!" Chris said, reprimandingly.

Lucas shrugged. "So, where are all the hot girls we were promised? Right now, this is pure sausage fest and I'm losing the one float to this guy!" he said, cupping his hands and spraying water in Tom's eyes.

Swimming under water, Tom came up at the edge of the pool by Melissa. "Thanks for having us over. You've got a really nice place."

He pulled himself out of the pool and picked up a towel. "Keg's over there."

Melissa looked dazed, confused and ecstatic. "A naked man—a Hollywood heart throb—just pulled himself out of my swimming pool." She pivoted, watching Tom towel off his hair, body glistening.

I raised my eyebrows and turned away. I had no interest in being around a naked Tom Warp.

Chagrinned, Chris said, 'Tried to warn you." He took my hand and guided me to the keg.

Tom ass-bumped me out of the way, swiftly getting his cup under the tap.

"Sorry love," he said, imitating Colin's voice perfectly.

Melissa giggled like a child as the banter drifted back and forth between them.

Finally, I interrupted, "Melissa, I think there's someone ringing your front door bell!"

Brow furrowed, she said, "How on *earth* did you hear it over the music?" She yanked open the sliding doors and flew into the house. I tagged along, eager to welcome Jessica and Amy.

Opening the front door, Amy tripped into the house.

"Didn't you hear us?" she demanded, weaving through us. "We've been out here for at least five minutes!" She quickly inventoried the house.

Jessica came in behind her, a glint in her eyes. "I told Amy that it sounded like the party was in the back. She told me, 'I don't do back door.'" Jess gave me a hug. "Good to see you." She peered around me. "This is nuts. Where's the music coming from? It's horrible."

I grabbed her hand.

"What's up?" she asked.

"Do you know who's out there?" I asked.

"Nope."

"Ian Hartlass is in the hot tub. Tom Warp is wandering around in a white bath towel. Colin Williams and Lucas St. Martin."

"NO SHIT." She did not look surprised in the least. "Ian Hartlass? I hope he's not a doucher." She craned her head toward the patio doors. "We're not going to stand here all night, Sarah dear." She ran her hands through her mahogany hair. "Hey—did you know your boy arranged for car service for us? He asked if we'd prefer to fly but I thought a limo'd be pretty cool. It was. I had no idea we were this close to Vegas."

We noticed that there were a couple of new faces outside. Women we didn't know had their toes in the pool. The boys were coercing them in with or without their clothing.

I commandeered a lounge chair. I was not getting involved if I could help it. Chris was sitting on a bench, cornered by one of the newcomers. With Jessica here, it seemed like a great opportunity to watch it all play out.

Jess noisily dragged another lounge chair over, thumping it into place beside me.

"Be right back. I gotta find that music." With a determined look on her face, she stomped off.

Ian Hartlass climbed into her seat, adjusting his white towel.

"Hey there, honey," he said, his towel split provocatively.

"Hi, Ian," I said reservedly. He was so pretty. My heart quaked.

"I don't think we've really met." He put his hand on my thigh, his towel splitting dangerously high.

"Biblically, no." I plucked off his greedy fingers.

He gazed at me calculatingly. "Hey, Tom! Bring the lady one over here!" He thumped the arm of the chair dramatically.

Tom gave him the finger.

He was definitely more attractive in person. His eyes were an unreal dark brown. He had a perfectly sculpted scruff of a beard to compliment a luxuriant mop of black hair. He had the body of Adonis. There wasn't an iota of extra anything anywhere.

Allowing a small smile onto his face, he said "Caught you looking."

I held his gaze. "You are better looking in person," I said thoughtfully.

"It's the lack of clothing. It has that effect on women." He winked.

"I can see that." I blushed.

"You're a great looking person, too."

I squirmed. I'd never considered myself to be anything special.

"Having fun with Chris?" he asked, scratching his chest idly.

"Yes," I responded, checking in on Chris and his admirer. I could feel Ian's eyes on me.

"You're his girlfriend?" he asked innocently.

"Yes." If he was willing to talk, I was going to enjoy his attention.

"Huh," he said. "That's a recent development."

He artfully stood, the towel barely enough to keep anything a secret. "Ready for another?" he asked, pivoting. The towel slit was much too close to my face.

"No, thanks." I wrinkled my nose.

"You look awfully cute when you do that." He completed a very thorough once over that left me feeling exposed.

He wasn't watching where he was going and collided with Jessica. She staggered backward. He reached out and supported her arm.

"Sorry, sexy." His eyes followed her heavily tattooed chest.

"You okay?" he asked, rubbing her arm.

"Unless you're contagious."

"Don't you use protection?"

"Do I need to?" Jessica quipped.

He smiled appreciatively, sizing her up. "I think it's time for a drink." His hand dropped to hers. She shot me a look like she'd died and gone to heaven. I didn't think I'd see her again for a while.

The activity in the pool was getting louder and more crazed. How long it would be before the cops were called? At least there weren't any houses in close proximity to hers.

Watching Lucas with my beer goggles on, he was actually not bad looking either. He was exceptionally tall and thin, probably a good 6' 2 or more. Wavy dark hair and brown eyes. He looked like a man-child in the pool, ducking under water and pushing women off the island raft much to their girlish delight. He'd never be my type.

Melissa made it to my chair. Her eyes were glassy.

"Thank you," she said, riveted by the antics in the pool. "This is a-mazing!" She was soaking wet, shirt stuck to her chest. She picked up my cup and headed back to the keg or more specifically to Tom. He was in his element, entertaining the ladies and filling cups.

Scanning the backyard, Jess and Ian were not in evidence. I knew she could handle herself but I felt abandoned. Where was Chris? Panicked, I went hunting for one or the other.

Tom accosted me by the keg.

"Hey, Sunshine. Mel was just telling me about life in Rhode Island. I've never been but am thinking that if the state produced the two of you, I've gotta add it to my agenda."

"We're from Connecticut," I corrected, inspecting him closely. He was cute, impish even, with a big dimple and a kiss-me chin. He was shorter than he looked in the movies but was well built with mischievous green eyes.

"They're both suburbs of New York," he declared, taking a gulp from his cup. "Where're you off to so fast?" He stepped in front of me.

"I was looking for Jessica." I peered over his shoulder into the house.

"Ah. If she's the girl with Ian, I'd stop looking." He coughed meaningfully.

Melissa squealed, catching Tom's eye.

"Oh. Well." My eyes widened. "That was quick."

Waving my hand in front of Melissa's face, I asked "Have you seen Chris?"

She blinked repeatedly. "Last I saw him, a friend of Heather's was with him in the living room. It looked like she was giving him a lap dance or something."

"Does 'friend-of-Heather' have a name?" I inquired.

"Most people do, Sunshine," Tom said, handing me another cup.

"I'm not going to lie. I think you've probably had enough, guys," I said, toasting them as I left.

Chris was on the couch. He had an indecipherable look on his face. Before I even rounded the corner, he knew it was me and made room. As I sat down, 'friend of Heather' said disappointedly, "Are you two together?"

We both nodded.

"Really?" she said, confused.

"Let me get this straight." She leaned in, across the coffee table, swaying.

"You." She pointed at me. Stabbing at Chris, she added, "and him?"

Chris pulled me into his chest and kissed my hair in response.

"Huh. That explains a lot." She got up from the coffee table unsteadily. "The offer still stands." She crossed over to him and put her hand under his shirt, raking her pink nails across his shoulder before walking away.

"Who's that?" I asked, watching her make her way outside.

"Kaylee. She's determined to be a rock star's girlfriend. I gather she'd settle for an actor."

"Dare I ask about her offer?" I scooted to the other corner of the couch so that I could look at Chris.

"Blow job."

"Ha! She propositioned you?"

"I was being a little evasive so she had to come out and say what was thinking."

"You call that lap dancing 'evasive'? Looked pretty cozy to me."

"Sarah, remember that she wanted to blow me. That was evasive."

Melissa and Heather sat down on the coffee table across from us while I chewed on that.

"Chris," Melissa said. "Heather's been dying to meet you. She's a *big* fan of yours. She works at Bally's with me." Heather hadn't had nearly as much to drink and honed in on Chris.

Heather extended her hand. "Hi, Chris. You brought the party?"

Releasing her hand, he fell back into the couch. "Having fun?" he asked politely.

"And then some!" she said, happy to chat with her long-time fantasy man.

"Good," Chris said.

Heather smiled grandly. "What's it like working with them? Is it incredible?"

Chris smiled. "It feels pretty ordinary. I guess I take it for granted. It's daily life." He rewarded her with his shy-but-alluring smile.

Heather swooned. When she regained her composure, she asked him all sorts of random questions. I hung on his responses as I hadn't asked most of them myself.

I excused myself to refill our cups when he gave her a day in the life.

Returning, I overheard Heather saying, "And Ella McBride—what the hell happened there? I thought for sure you two would land up married. You were such a beautiful couple!"

Chris shifted on the couch, looked for his cup. I stiffened, keenly interested in his reply.

Softly he said, "What happened? Life, I guess." He looked over his shoulder and caught my eye. He wanted to be saved.

"Do you know what happened to Ella?" Heather inquired as I rounded the couch. "She is so fabulous."

I shook my head. "Ella McBride was your last girlfriend?"

He cracked his neck and took a cup from me. "She is fabulous. Our schedules were not. She needs a lot of attention. And when she doesn't get it, she's less than fabulous." He took a healthy swig.

Leaning in, Heather added, "But I heard that she was pregnant, that you guys bought a house in the Hills."

He smiled weakly. "I bet you did. It's just not my style to kiss and tell." He patted my thigh, excusing himself. His departure was followed by a cry of 'cannonball!' and a giant splash.

Heather's brow furrowed. "You heard the same stories, didn't you? They were pregnant. They had a house. Then she wasn't pregnant and the stories ended."

"It's all news to me." I swirled my beer.

"Sorry. I didn't realize that past girlfriends were taboo," she said, tapping her empty cup on her palm. She fiddled with her hoop earring, picked up her cup and went outside.

"Yikes," Melissa said.

"Have you seen Jessica?" I asked, changing the subject.

"I saw a lot of her." Her eyes twinkled. "Most of her clothing is scattered down the hallway upstairs." She pointed in the general direction of the stairs.

"Oh?"

"Oh. YEAH. Ian was all over her before they closed the door."

"Are they in your bedroom?"

"No. They sort of fell into the master bath."

"Sorry."

"Don't be. As long as they don't break anything, I'm cool." She was jazzed. "Come on." She grabbed my hand and pulled me off the couch. "Let's get back out there and see who's left for me!"

Everyone was in the pool, clothing strewn all over the bushes. Out of the blue, Melissa took a running leap at the pool, cup still in hand.

She landed right beside Chris. Startled, he picked her up and threw her. She smashed into Colin, the lone Brit of the bunch who had been reluctant to get involved for most of the evening.

Disentangling, he made a formal introduction while getting pelted with water from some of the other swimmers.

I made my way over to my lounge chair and sat. I pulled my legs up and contemplated that Chris was supposed to be married with a baby. That was more information than I was able to process under the circumstances.

Chris was trying very hard to have fun and shake off that conversation. If that was the life he wanted, it was very different than where fate had taken him.

I zoned out, *You can't always get what you want* stuck in my head. I snapped back when Tom accosted me. He was bare-ass naked. He picked up my chair and easily dumped me into the pool.

When I bobbed to the surface, he said, "Sorry, Sunshine. You can't sit there all night!"

He jumped in, pulling down my skirt. I screamed as he came up in my personal space with my skirt in his hands.

"Feels better, doesn't it?" He had one of the most desirably maniacal faces I'd ever seen. As I reached for my skirt, he held it behind his back and kissed my neck, sending shivers down my spine.

"Can I have that, please?" I asked in vain, reaching around him to get my skirt.

"I would ask the same of you." His eyes darted under the water. One of his hands tugged on my panties. He kissed me, trying to work his tongue between my clamped lips. I pushed him away, my eyes zeroing in on Chris. He was happily engaged in a water fight and would be of no help.

"I would like my skirt." I smiled at him.

"I bet you would." He threw it over his shoulder into the pool. "Loosen up, Sunshine! We don't bite—unless you're lucky." He ducked under water, pinched my butt, and was gone.

Unable to find my skirt, I saw Ian and Jessica emerging from the house. They both looked incredibly satisfied. I wanted to offer her a cigarette. Instead, I frantically waved. She was thoroughly distracted. Ian embraced her with movie star aplomb. Their display was sinful.

I really didn't want to get out of the pool without my skirt so I hopped around, looking more seriously for it. I bumped into topless Amy. She was full of apologies but was overly eager to claw her way back to Tom. He closed the gap quickly, grabbing her with one arm and me with the other.

When I felt him gnawing on my neck, I yanked Amy closer. Before either were any the wiser, I made my getaway.

I surfaced near Chris. He was in good spirits. He gave me a big goofy kiss. His eyes widened when he discovered I had very little on down south.

Wrapping me around his waist, he waded over to the side of the pool. He picked me up and sat me on the edge before climbing out himself. He was down to his boxers which clung revealingly to his body. He helped me up, gathered me in his arms and swung me into the hot tub.

Having him to myself was refreshing. Sitting on his lap, life was very, very good. I discreetly removed his boxers. It was hedonistically easy to block out the rest of the party.

I had just collapsed into his arms when Jessica and Ian headed our way. I was about to be trapped, pants-less with them. So much for basking in the glow.

Next to the hot tub, they dropped their clothing. Jessica climbed in next to me, Ian to her left. I wrapped Chris's boxers securely over my lap. Ian coolly appraised me, eyebrows furrowing when he saw my plaid loin cloth.

"Chris, I believe you know Jessica?" Ian put his arm around her like a sign of ownership.

"Hello, Jess," he said, trying hard not to stare at her considerable chest.

"Chris," she said perfunctorily. "You are welcome at our house *any* time." She had her hand on Ian's tattooed chest.

He casually moved his arm to stroke the inside of Jessica's thigh. "Why so shy?" he asked lasciviously, eyes trailing down to my loin cloth.

Chris cleared his throat.

Ian pursed his lips and looked questioningly at Chris. "This wouldn't be the first time we've shared," he said, tugging on the boxers.

Uneasy, I reached for Jessica's hand. Ian intercepted, guiding my hand to his crotch. I twisted my hand away, repulsed. He may be gorgeous but I was more of a serial monogamist than I'd thought.

He smirked. "Always angling for the good girls, huh?" Running his hand through Jessica's tangled hair, he added "I thought we might be able to tempt your buddies into something but perhaps they'd prefer to watch."

He nuzzled Jessica. I scrambled out of the tub, inventorying the bushes for anything to put on. I saw my balled-up skirt in the rocks. I handed Chris his boxers as I rocketed past. I had never been so relieved to see such a dirty skirt. I would have hugged it were it not for my exposed ass.

Clasping Chris's hand, I said, "I bet it's after one."

"You sure? If were after one, wouldn't you still be in the hot tub?"

I screwed up my face. "No way in hell," I whispered, slowly passing in front of them. "And what did he mean, 'it wouldn't be the first time you shared?'"

"Factually accurate, I guess."

"But what did he mean?"

We made our way back into the house, collapsing on the couch.

"That anything goes in Vegas."

"Chris—"

"Would you believe I lost Ella to him?" he said, with a pained look.

"To *him*?" He gave a small nod. "That kind of turns my stomach."

"Imagine if it were you. It doesn't really begin to describe the feeling." Resting his head on the back of the couch, he closed his eyes.

As he slid further down, I draped his arm over me and burrowed into his neck. The party was quieting down and he drifted off to sleep. I listened as many of the others came in, scrounged for food or collapsed on the floor. The conversations were inane, the noises not necessary to explain.

When I was ready to drift off, I heard Ian's voice answering all sorts of Truth or Dare-like questions.

"You know your girlfriend is going to get bored and leave him," Ian drawled.

"No, I don't know that," Jessica answered openly.

"If she's your friend, she's got to be at least half as crazy, as intense as you are. She's gonna tire of him. He's very nice. And we all know how nice guys finish."

"He does seem to be a very nice guy. I like the way they are together."

"Mark my words—won't last. It's either sex or she's wife material. Our Boy Wonder doesn't do casual sex."

"Maybe that's what she's after, too? Then what?"

"Girls like you don't get married. Get as much as you can while you can. Expect nothing more."

"'Take what you can; give nothing back. How very Jack Sparrow of you," Jess said coolly. She repositioned, getting more comfortable. "I hope to get married."

"No-no. Don't change my sentiments. It's more Buddha than Captain Jack. I give plenty back. I like to satisfy my partners." There was a flurry of fabric rustling and she crooned.

"Are you willing to be Mary Homemaker? You are adventurous, daring, sexy and fun. You can't be those things when you're with the same person every day. You will lose your spark or your will to live."

"That's bleak."

"Accept it. Live with what's in front of you today. Relish it."

In an effort to keep it fresh, their conversation ended. I vainly wished they'd stagger off to a room for their continuing escapades. I really had to visit the water closet and I was not going to risk the possibility of drawing their attention. When they were finally quiet, I rolled off the couch and bee-lined for the bathroom.

Tom was leaning against the door.

"Some one's in there," he said in greeting. "How long you been with Chris?" he asked, eyes darting to the couch.

"Not long."

"I should have asked—how long have you *known* him?"

"A month or so, maybe."

"Huh. Did you know he gave up dating the famous?" He rubbed his back on the corner of the wall.

"He didn't mention it."

"Doesn't trust 'em." He smirked. "Your boy has no ability to tell when the opposite sex is acting."

"What does that mean?"

"He's too sincere. He expects people to respond similarly. He's gotten hosed a couple of times, big time." He crossed his arms. "He also seems bent on marriage. Are you the marrying type?"

"How's that?"

"Just curious. Here's my Sarah synopsis. Tell me where I go astray. You came out here to escape something—probably a guy—a bad experience? A bad marriage? Something. I'd also venture to say that you're not eager— willing, even—to commit."

"Can you pound on that door? I really gotta go."

"I bet that's what you told Rhode Island when you left." He rapped on the door. "Hurry up in there! She's really *gotta go*."

Leaning on the door, he continued, "When he scares you away, and he will, look me up." He took my wrist and rubbed my tattoo. "Anyone who can tattoo 'now' on their wrist is someone of character."

He was sincere. I also knew he would bring out the crazy, something that I hadn't been in a long time, something that I didn't think I missed. As we appraised each other, the door made an attempt at opening. Tom moved to the side.

"Later, Sunshine," he purred, wrapping an arm around Melissa.

I locked the bathroom door, musing about what other people thought of me. I had never considered myself to be hot stuff but I had had multiple offers in the last several hours for a number of different opportunities.

And why was it that I didn't look like the marrying type? Was I the marrying type? Could I envision being bored by Chris? It seemed unlikely. He was sweet and willing to do anything for me. On what planet could that grow old? I'd never have to worry about trivial details with him. Chris and I shared the same basic need. We wanted a meaningful, committed, long term relationship.

When someone started rapping on the door, I checked myself out. Why were so many guys eager to get in my pants? I looked happily confident, the exterior was somewhere between day-at-the-beach babe and drown rat. If I could get lucky looking like this, the world *was* my oyster.

Heading back to my sleeping bear, Heather apologized again for asking about Ella. She was another straight shooter. I liked her immediately. She did not look anywhere near as tired as I felt.

We went in the kitchen and made ourselves some coffee.

Heather told me a little bit about working at the casino and the famous people who'd lost big bucks there. The money amounts were staggering but I guess they're fallible, ordinary people. They simply have more to lose.

She was genuinely taken with Chris. She knew more about him than I did. She filled me in on his shockingly short list of lovers and headlines. She moved on to the other guys at the party. Some of these boys were dirty birds and my friends were all over them.

"How'd you get him?" she asked, intrigued.

"Fate?" I answered blankly.

"But how? I see guys like these all the time and I've never had one ask me out."

"Technically, I think I asked him out."

"You didn't!?!!?"

"I think I did."

She fell back in her chair, hands firmly around her mug.

"I don't think I could do that even if my job allowed it."

I smiled, reliving the first time he walked into the Shoppe.

"I'm not going to lie. I was pretty freaked out. I surprised myself."

"But *how'd* you do it?" Her eyes hungered for the secret.

"I think he asked me what my name was, or rather, what my last name was and I propositioned him. I said I'd tell him over drinks. The rest, as they say, is history."

"Damn. That's all it took? He must've really liked the cut of your jib."

"Is that a nautical reference?"

"Yes, it is. Thank you for noticing. I grew up around Gloucester." She glanced over at the couch. "Um... What's it like being in those arms? Is it as heavenly as I think?"

Even with his spritely eyes closed, he was beautiful. "He's pretty great. It was his idea to come out here for a few days. We dropped everything and hopped in his car."

"What do you think would happen if I were to take your spot on the couch? Would he notice?"

I raised my eyebrow. "That's just wrong."

"I *am* kidding," she said in a tone that didn't mask her disappointment.

"He is my boyfriend. If I'd had more to drink—nah. It still wouldn't be funny. His buddies might find it to be good sport."

"Yeah. It sure looked like Ian and Tom were kind of pursuing you. Do they know you're with Chris?"

"We ran into them at the Luxor. He introduced me as his girlfriend. I gather there's some kind of a competition. I don't really understand. I think Ian takes pride in landing other people's catch."

"Yeah. I wouldn't have minded if he'd reeled me in. Your girlfriend is going to have some stories to tell. Damn, she's gotta have some stories. I saw them going at it in the hot tub as if they were completely alone. That takes balls."

"I don't know what happened to Colin but I bet he's available *and* he has that killer British accent."

"Oooh, I do love the accent but he's never been my type. Gingers are not high on my list."

"Then focus on some other aspect. You never know. He may say something that you find attractive."

~~

Not one for sitting inside, I refilled my cup and made my way outside, past all of the slumbering party guests. I enjoyed mornings and this one was no different. I put my toes in the pool and watched the sun rise. It was brisk but at least my clothing was finally dry.

Melissa's yard looked pretty good all things considered. Most of the clothing had been retrieved and the cups dumped in the trash. Things were askew but no worse for wear.

I inhaled my coffee, set it down and stretched. The sun felt so good on my face. It didn't take long for thoughts grounded in reality to intrude. I liked this life so much more than what awaited me in Los Angeles. Returning to the Sandwich Shoppe filled me with dread for the first time. If I never touched deli meat again, I would feel blessed.

Of course, Amy was going to be riding high. I was eager to hear about her exploits. If I knew Amy, the world was going to know everything and know it within an hour of her being conscious.

Melissa, too, seemed to take full advantage of her houseful of guests. She hadn't really changed. She had always been vivacious and ready for anything. Nothing upset her. Nothing diminished her good time.

And Jessica! We'd talked about him so many times while watching his movies. She was more than warm for his form. She also made full use of any opportunity.

I sat, eyes closed, and basked in the early morning quiet. It was heavenly. A shadow falling across my face, Chris stood with two bagels in his hands.

"Melissa's quite a hostess. She's putting out a huge spread." He handed me a cinnamon bagel.

"Was Tom with her?" I asked, taking a bite.

He sat. "No. He's passed out in a chair. Why? Were they together?"

"Looked that way."

"Did you have fun?"

"I did. That was a little bit crazy."

He snorted. "A little. What would qualify as a lot?"

"If the cops'd been called. Or if I saw Kaylee blowing you."

"Both were possible."

"I know." I took another bite. "What is it like to be propositioned?"

"I think you know." He gazed at me intently. "I may have looked like I was off on my own but I was very aware of your—situations."

"You do have something weird going on with Ian and Tom."

"You noticed?" He broke a chunk off his bagel and shoved it in his mouth.

"Hard not to. I overheard some stuff last night that was food for thought."

"Don't eat anything they're selling." He ripped off another hunk.

"Why are they both so fascinated with your women?"

"Deep down, I think they believe all guys are like them. They're just more honest. Or maybe I'm some moral compass. If they can sully me or my ladies, it makes what they do more palatable, if we're going to stick with food euphemisms."

"You live an unusual existence, my friend." I patted his knee.

"*Boyfriend.*" He corrected, coiling his arm around me.

"Wouldn't want it any other way."

"You certainly had plenty of opportunities for 'any other way.'" He squinted at me, knocking his body into mine.

"I'm not going to lie. In the hot tub, I kinda thought that Ian was demanding that we trade partners."

"His predilection is for orgiastic sex. I believe he can really bring it."

"Oh, god! Don't tell me you pulled out the ruler with Ian!"

Chris doubled over with laughter.

"Don't ever get in a donger match with that guy. Don't you ladies talk?"

"You've met your match?"

"It may be the once place where I concede."

"That's nuts."

"No, but they're close."

I socked him. "Enough!"

We finished our bagels as some of the others started moving around inside the house.

"I'd like to get out of here," I said, finishing off my cold coffee. "I have yet to sleep."

"What do I do about Jessica and Amy? Leave them my card?"

"I'm sure they can text you if they need a rescue."

"Still. It doesn't seem right to leave until we know what their plans are. I don't want to presuppose anything."

"You *are* a nice guy." I started to get up. "Do you need anything? I'm going to get more coffee if we're going to hang around here."

"If you'd get one for me, that'd be good. See if there's anything more substantial to eat, too. I don't want my belly to scare you away."

"Will do," I said, walking back to the house.

Melissa was lingering by the dining room table. It was covered in every last baked good known to man.

"Where did all of this come from? You're always prepared?"

She rearranged the serving utensils in the fruit.

"I set it up last night online before calling it a night."

"Where *did* you call it a night? Last I saw, you were involved with Tom." I retrieved a cup for Chris.

"Even if I never hear from him again—I can relive it over and over. Damn fine time." She inhaled sharply, dramatically leaning against the wall.

"Wow. Was he that good?"

"I think that may have been the most fun I've had in a long time. He's got some hidden talents," she said mischievously.

"Let's keep them that way. I think I saw more than enough Tom to last me a lifetime."

"Oh, said the girl who's with Chris Sparks."

"That would be the one."

"They can't *all* be Chris Sparks. Some of them have to be bad-dirty-womanizing-wild men."

"Too much of anything is boring. I don't know that I *need* any bad-dirty-womanizing-wild men in my personal space, however."

"You can't tell me that you don't think Tom's smokin'. He's got incredible eyes and the way he looks at you? I feel dirty just thinking about it!"

Passed out in the chair, he looked cherubic underneath a puppy dog fleece blanket.

"Do you know where his pants are? I hate the idea of him strolling around without them."

"I wadded them up under the blanket just in case he doesn't feel quite so care free the day after," she answered joyfully.

"Good thinking." I loaded some cheese and fruit into a bowl for Chris.

"While I was tidying up this morning, I found their phones. I have to say that curiosity got the better of me." I stopped perusing the food and stared at her. Her cheeks were pink.

"I was curious whose was whose," she said lamely, "so I flipped 'em on and just took a quick look at their connections. Pretty interesting stuff. When I had Tom's, I sent myself a text."

"Clever."

"I hope it works. He could be so much fun. Knowing that he's a mere four hours away—too good to pass up!" She helped herself to a croissant.

"Thanks again for hosting, Melissa. We're hoping to get outta here as soon as Jess and Amy are decent." Jessica was snuggled into Ian behind one of the oversized chairs. Amy was – nowhere.

"Have you seen Amy?"

"Yeah, I went up to change clothes and she is in my room with Lucas. She kinda looked like she died and went to heaven. She is sleeping but her face is—you should go look. I can't describe it."

I raised my eyebrows comically. Amy would not be amused if she heard that she was anything other than desirable.

"Are they *dressed*?"

"Partially is about all I can say. My bed looks like it was used for Olympic competition."

"Okay, I will pass on that unless she's still in there when we have to go." Balancing the bowls and coffee, I trundled back outside.

"Hey, gorgeous. Amy and Jess up?" He retrieved a coffee and bowl.

Moving into the lounge chairs, I responded, "Nope. Jess's still cozied up to Ian. Amy apparently had Olympic sex in Melissa's bed and hasn't quite recovered."

"Think we can consider her debt paid?" He demurely sipped his coffee.

"Oh, I think we're off the hook. Don't know about Lucas." I popped a strawberry in my mouth.

"As you profess to staying up all night, give me the rundown. Who was with who?"

"You can be a girl, can't you?"

"Nah, more like fact checking."

"You say potato—" I offered, reclining.

"Potahto then. Maybe I am curious how things ended up, too."

I cracked an eye to peek at him.

"Now that we've cleared that up, I am aware of the following couples, Jess and Ian. Melissa and Tom. Amy and Lucas. Heather was going to hunt down Colin and see where the chips fell. I have not heard nor seen any other pairings but that may be because you so coolly rebuffed Kaylee that she didn't try again. You put her off her feed. The other odds and ends friends of Melissa took off hours ago."

As if on cue, Jessica and Amy came outside carrying coffee. Jess sat on the foot of my chair and Amy sat on the ground, leaning on Chris's leg.

"Morning, ladies," he said, looking down at Amy. "We about ready to get out of here?"

Jessica shook her head minutely while Amy groaned.

"Rough night?" I inquired.

Jessica's blank face was overcome with a devious little smile but she said nothing.

"Rough might've been the best part," Amy rasped, stretching. Catching my eye, I detected a very small, very personal thank you.

"I'd like to get out of here but this guy over here wanted to make sure you weren't stranded in Vegas."

"Penultimate nice guy," Jessica said approvingly.

"So, ladies—my girlfriend wants out. Do you need a ride or have you found other avenues?"

"I think I will hang around. I have nowhere I have to be," Jessica said, blowing on her coffee.

"Uhhhh—I have to go! Goddamn job!" Amy doubled over.

"That job got you where you are today, missy," I said, feeling hypocritical.

"That's true for both of us but someone has *your* ass covered." She frowned angrily at me.

"Yeah. About that—" I had half a mind to quit right there.

"Don't do it. Don't say you're done! I can see what you're thinking. Don't do it!" Amy was instantly energized, annoyed and scared that her party train could be derailing.

"Okay. I won't do it but I am thinking about it."

She smacked me, got up and shouted, "I am going back in there now to see if I need a ride. I won't make you wait more than another hour." She sprinted back into the house.

"Poor thing," Jessica tsked. "Best night of her life followed by the revelation that you might not be there to bring the bacon again. That's rough."

Chris got up, offering to take our trash. "I think I should go in there and just make sure that Amy isn't stranded. Jess—you sure you're all set?"

"Quite. Ian's not completely heartless."

Moving into Chris's seat, she looked satisfied with her lot.

She squinted at me. "Don't judge me, Sarah."

My eyes widened. "I would never do that! I was a little surprised but now I think I'm just jealous. You look so happy—like deliriously happy."

"Imagine. That's what I've been looking at for a few weeks now."

"Really? I don't think I could be glowing like you are. Not for weeks. You have that *new* glow."

She blushed. "Maybe it's that I haven't had that kind of romp in too long. Sarah, he's gorgeous. He's witty. He's deviant. He's *hung*."

"Listen to you! Do you happen to remember where we put his picture around the apartment?"

"Oh, I don't know that he will be stopping by. That's a conversation for another time but it's going to be fun while it lasts."

~~

# 10

It wasn't more than another hour before we were loaded up in a limo and headed back to the strip. Pulling up to the Venetian in a limousine turns heads. Between Tom and Ian, the gaggle of women grew to epic proportions. Jessica, too, had more pictures taken in the walk from the car to the casino than she had had since birth. For her part, she looked worthy of her entourage.

As they ducked in, attention turned to our car and I was startled by the hands thumping the glass by my head. Chris gave the driver instructions and we slowly inched away from the curb leaving those people to wonder who was left inside.

We had no such problems at the Luxor. We easily made it to our room where we remained for the rest of the day, lolling around and cleaning up for the drive home. I felt like the other girls—if this ended, I had such a wealth of memories that I would be comfortably living in the past for some time to come.

"Hey—what happens when we get back?" he asked, idly flipping through the hotel's binder of area attractions.

"Ug. Can I tell you I am too tired for this conversation?"

"No, I can tell you're thinking about it."

"How can you tell?"

"Just can."

"But how?"

"Haven't you ever been in a relationship where you can read your partner's language?" He set the magazine down and studied my face.

"I've made guesses but I have rarely been right." I folded my hands in my lap, determined to make him work for this conversation. "Maybe you developed that skill?"

"Or maybe we become actors because of our ability to read people?" he queried. "Truth is, I think it's just a skill. If you care for people, put in the time. Read the cues. It saves a lot of trouble." He reached for my hand. "I'm not wrong, am I?"

"Damn you. No, I am thinking about it. This has been so much fun. I feel rejuvenated, this moment notwithstanding, and ready to take on new challenges."

"Then *do* it, girlfriend. I've got your back."

I swiveled my chair away from the strip and studied him.

"But do *what* remains the question."

"Baby steps. First—quit. Then, take what time you need to let yourself figure it out."

"What happens to my bills? Like the big one, housing?"

"I have an idea about that. I do, in fact, have the house in the Hills." His shoulders tensed, poised for rejection. "What if you were to move into it *with* me?"

"The house for you and your 'family?' That exists?" He eyed me warily. "Holy shit. Why do you stay in that shitty condo?"

"It's easier."

"Than?"

"Being in that place of promise with nothing promising."

"Huh."

After an uncomfortable silence, he said, "Did my mouth get ahead of where we are?"

He swung his legs over the side of the bed, concerned.

"I don't know. I can't stiff Jessica."

"She looked fine to me." He raised his eyebrows suggestively.

"Not funny and not what I mean."

He moved over next to my chair.

"She could live in the guest house as long as she wants to. Does that help?"

"You have a guest house?"

"Doesn't everyone?" he smiled tauntingly.

My chest constricted. I stared at the strip. He reached over and took my hand.

"Sarah, think about it. It's a lot. I know. I'll tell you about Ella." His grip strengthened.

"Are you stuck on her? Am I your rebound? Because if I am, it took you a helluva long time to rebound."

He caressed my hand. "I am over her. I just—it's more like 'once bitten, twice shy.' I don't *ever* want to go through that again."

"See, I don't even know what 'that' was. I can see that it's very upsetting to you. I don't know what to make of it and now you tell me that you've held on to the *house* for *years*. That begs the question, why? Why would you do that and not live in it? You told me that the studio provided your housing yet you have a house. This is *not normal*."

"Bad economy?" he joked.

"Right."

"Sorry. I never lived in the house. I bought it. I thought we were going to live there like a family. It went to hell. I felt like a sucker. It was easier to just walk away from it than to deal with it."

"That, my friend, is really fucked up."

"It's not ideal, I'll give you that." He dropped my hand and sulked into the bathroom.

I thought about my reasons for leaving Rhode Island. Tom hadn't been too far off with his guesses. I was definitely looking for a new lease on life and distance from the man who made Rhode Island miserable. It was easier to leave than to be around all of the things that I associated with him.

I heard the shower running and used the time to work through many of the immediate 'what ifs.' I liked the idea of having a house and several less bills. If it didn't work out, I'd have to find another place but if I held on to the cash that was no longer the rent, it would be a lot easier. I really liked him but he'd been my boyfriend for all of four days. Even though our relationship was in its infancy, nothing felt phony or like work. This was easy, fun and held promise.

As I swung back and forth with the pros and cons, he came out in a towel. He looked resigned, like he expected me to be gone.

Inhaling deeply, I tiptoed to him. His faced betrayed his confusion. Seeing him at a total loss was so endearing that I couldn't help but smile.

"You're complicated," I said, giving him a hug.

"You're not leaving?"

"No." I released him and sat on the bed. "But you are asking a lot of your girlfriend of *four* days. FOUR DAYS. You have suggested I leave my job, figure my life out, move in with you—into a house that was purchased for your last perfect relationship. That is a lot."

"Told you I get myself in trouble." He sat down next to me. "This feels different to me. I have always taken many things on faith. Maybe it's that indoctrination of putting your faith in a higher power and having things work out. I don't know. I *really* like you, Sarah. I want your life to be as easy as it can be. I want to be a part of it."

"Your buddies told me that you're interested in marriage only."

"I have known since I was a boy what I wanted relationship-wise. I want to be happily married with a wife and children. I thought that this would happen by the time I was thirty. I am now *in* my thirties, by all accounts 'successful' yet I have an emptiness that I cannot explain. Most of the time, I don't think about it. Being with you has made this hole more prominent and hard to ignore."

"I don't think I have ever progressed to this conversation so quickly."

"Me neither and I have lost a lot of time because of it. I'm done wasting time, Sarah." He was twisting a hand towel mercilessly. Looking up, he said, "I guess I'd like to know if you're the marrying type—not that you have to commit to me by any stretch but is it part of your life plan?"

"Wow."

He raised an eyebrow.

"I was already asked that question. Tom snagged me and told me marriage was your end goal. How do you know these guys? Or how is it that they understand you so well?"

"I *lived* with Tom when we were both new to L.A. A couple of years ago, I shared an address with Ian. He lived in the same complex. We kind of grew up together. I like them. Particularly if they're not fucking my girlfriend." He clasped his hands. "At the same time, they're a good filter. I bring home a girl and they can quickly determine if she's serious or a strumpet. I should thank them. Ella woulda left me at some point because that's in her nature. I didn't see it but Ian did. He got her to act on it before I was—"

"Was?" I prompted.

"A father. A husband. Committed." He angled himself so that we were thigh to thigh, facing each other.

"What *happened* with her?"

"You're not getting off the hook—" he said, patting my knee fondly. "I was working in the UK and had been for a couple of months. She and I had been together for the better part of a year. I thought things were solid. She was working. I was working. Shortly after I got there, she was sick. She took a pregnancy test and showed me the results. We were both surprised and did some crying. I wanted to be a dad. I felt as ready as I'd ever be. I guess she didn't feel quite the same way. Our schedules were at odds with the time difference so face time became infrequent. I carried on thinking things were okay, headed in the right direction. I got a real estate agent and had them looking around for a house for us. It wasn't long before that house popped up. She seemed excited about it. Not long after that, I started hearing stories that didn't jive but you know how the media operates. I wanted the rumors to be disingenuous. I didn't let them bother me. What bothered me was when I came back to surprise her and was greeted by noises that she couldn't be making alone." He sighed, despondent.

"I know it sounds stupid but that was my girl, my baby—our apartment. I didn't need to go in there to know who it was. Ian's leather jacket was on the couch. I paced around for a minute or two and then took his jacket and left."

I wrapped my body around his back. He was still hurting and I ached for him. He put his arms on mine and squeezed me, leaning back into me.

"After I left, I headed back to work and waited to see what she was gonna do. I took Ian's jacket so I was confident he would say something. She was gonna have to fess up. It took her longer than I would have thought to tell me that she wasn't ready for the white picket fence and swing set. She never mentioned Ian. She made the discussion all about her needs—that I wasn't physically there for her and couldn't support her during a pregnancy, that she didn't want to do it alone and wasn't sure she wanted to do it at all—ever. In a lot of ways, it was the stereotypical 'it's not you, it's me.'"

"What happened to the baby?"

He sagged. "I couldn't ask. She must've taken care of it. She would've been more of a basket case if she *lost* it. She has a strong need to be in control."

"I'm sorry. That really sucks."

"I lost a girlfriend but got a really nice leather jacket. It's the one I wear to this day."

We sat there for another minute or two before he got up, repositioning on the bed so we were nose to nose. He propped himself up on his elbow, using his free hand to touch my hair. He was uncharacteristically vulnerable.

I couldn't get past his eyes. Although they were always an alluring blue, their intensity was heightened. He was magnificent. He was in a towel. And he was waiting for me to determine if I was going to stay. My smiled broadened. His eyes brightened and lightened. It was as if the clouds were clearing between us.

I leaned in and kissed his neck. The more relieved he became, the more demanding he was. He had me on my back, secured under his weight. His happiness and future were tied to mine.

~~

# 11

We headed home in the late morning, me at the wheel. Driving the Mustang was more power than this girl was ready for, the ideal complement to a full weekend. Chris ran lines. I perused stations.

Stopping for gas, we traded seats. I was pretty confident that he didn't want me driving into Los Angeles and I was okay with that. As we got closer to town, he turned the music down.

"Want to swing by the house?" he asked tentatively.

"We could," I said noncommittally.

"I'd like to," he added more urgently.

"Have you maintained it or is it going to be decrepit?"

"It's maintained like any investment. The gardens are one of the reasons I bought the place. I have never been much of a green thumb but someone was. Add to that the pool—"

We arrived at an impressive gate. Swiping us in, we started up a long and winding driveway. His face vacillated between nervousness and contentment. The car was barely in park before he popped out and ran around to get my door.

With the discreet fountain and endless flowering flora out front, it looked like a smaller version of a hotel. Thinking of this as a 'home' struck my funny bone. There was nothing homey about it.

At the front door, he stopped. "I haven't actually been inside."

"That's just weird." I reached for the handle. "Time to open the door, big guy."

The interior resembled a high end hotel. The foyer was bigger than my apartment with a sprawling staircase and open floor plan upstairs. Spanish in its influence, it was lovely. There were even cut flowers in a vase.

"Flowers?" I said dubiously.

"I have people taking care of the place. Maybe I should have paid more attention to their bill." He touched the peonies, knocking off a couple of petals.

"If I remember correctly, the yard's this way—through the kitchen." He walked through an archway to the right.

The house was filled with natural light. It was like no home I had ever visited. The kitchen was immaculate and empty. I could envision it filled with character and people. This kitchen could be ground zero for a good time. In addition to the full service island, multiple ovens, wine cooler and wet bar, the back wall was all glass.

I opened the sliding glass door and stepped out onto the patio. It was like a second kitchen with a built in brick-covered oven, sink and fridge. The patio furniture looked invitingly worn. Separating this area from the rest of the yard were trellises covered with flowering jasmine. Everything was so vibrant that it broke my heart to think all of this had gone unappreciated for years.

"How long has it been like this?" I asked, turning back to Chris.

"I bought it almost two years ago. I thought about renting it out but that was too much work. It's been here, like this, ever since."

"It's gorgeous. Did the furniture come with it?"

He touched my waist. "Some of it. Some of it I had purchased for me. My mom and sister were pretty excited about where my life was going. They picked out a few things that they thought I'd like."

Putting his hand on the chaise, he found the price tag tucked into the frame.

"See. This still has the tags on it."

"What'd they think about you *not* living here?"

"They were kind to me but I am sure there was a point where they were worried. They've stayed here a couple of times."

"Think they'll be pleased to hear you're back?"

"They'll be more pleased to hear you're here." He rubbed my back.

"How big is this property?" I took another couple of steps into the yard.

"Square feet? I don't know. What do you think?"

"I think it's amazing. Is that the guest house?" I said, walking on the grass.

"Uh, that's the pool house."

"You're kidding. A pool house and a guest house and a house-house?" He shoved his hands in his pockets. "This is an embarrassment of riches but it looks like you know that."

He saddled up behind me and put and arm around my shoulders.

"It's just a house."

"A *big* house. A *colossal* house! It's not 'just a house.' Not by a long shot." I mosied over to the pool. It was bigger than a lap pool, surrounded by huge tiles that were probably very slippery when wet. It was designed to be beautiful but not incredibly functional.

The pool house had a fantastic living room with fireplace, a bathroom, kitchenette and a bedroom. It was only marginally smaller than my apartment and felt like home. It would not take much for me to die and go to heaven right here.

Chris admired the fireplace and assorted prints on the walls.

"You know what would really make this place? Jessica's pictures."

"I *love* this place. I don't think you need to change a thing."

He chuckled. "Leave it to you to love the pool house."

"It's great! I love it. I do. It's got this great view of the pool and the mansion. All the flowering Jacaranda. I think that's a lemon tree? Pretty awesome. Smells good, too."

"So, you'd be willing to move in here?" He leaned against the door, hands behind him.

"I don't think I could leave even if I wanted to with you leaning on the door."

He pushed himself off the glass. "I would prefer that you stay, for sure." He hugged me. "I thought this'd feel really strange but I think it's strange for different reasons."

Craning my head, I said, "What's so strange about visiting a house you own, maintain and don't enjoy for years? Perfectly normal."

"Don't give me a hard time. I thought I would feel more of a negative connection to it and I don't. I still like this house. It's got an ethereal quality to it. You look—it looks like—you look like—" He was flustered. "The two of you belong together. There's a reason you like this little house. Because you belong here."

I had to agree. Everything about this place was ideal. I loved the fragrant, flowering plants. The fact that many of them produced food was cool, too. I'd never been a successful gardener but here I wouldn't have to be. I would still be rewarded with fresh fruits. The pool and this little house had everything I'd grown accustomed to in the right proportions. I did like it. A lot.

"Wanna see the guest house? You can see what you think of that before laying dibs on the pool house, okay?"

The guest house was a trek deeper into the property. The walkway was beautifully sculpted with trellised flowers to the right and expertly maintained flower beds to the left. Not a blade of grass grew between the pavers.

The guest house was a miniature version of the main house. The foyer wasn't nearly so grand but it was impressive. The kitchen, too, was more compact. Through its bay window was a mural of a woman framed by jasmine. She was whimsical, like a breeze would blow her away.

I wanted to take her with me to the pool house.

Talking over my shoulder, I said, "She's perfect. Who painted her?"

He pushed the curtain aside. "I have no idea. She wasn't a selling feature."

"Much better than having a view of your neighbor's wall. She's really cool."

"She reminds me of you," he said softly, putting his hand on mine.

"It's the sparkle in her eyes. She looks so serene."

"This place doesn't look like it was ever used."

"I got that feeling about the kitchen." I leaned on the sink. "So all of this is yours and it's amazing. I don't know that I could ever leave it if it were mine."

"That's the most promising thing you've said to me today."

He was disarmingly sincere. I couldn't look away.

"You call me unusual but I think you're just as weird."

"Hey, I never called you weird," he said playfully.

"Always thought it was implied," I said, bumping into him.

"As long as 'weird' isn't a bad thing in your book, then maybe you're right." He opened up the fridge. "This feels like home. It's empty."

"Don't tell me you're hungry?" I said feigning surprise as I walked into the living room.

"Afraid so. Would you be willing to get something to eat with me before I go in?"

"Can we order something and sit at the pool house?" I couldn't believe that I was seriously contemplating texting Jess to see if she'd move in here with me.

"If that works for you, sure."

"How does ordering food work here? D'you have to buzz the driver in?" I asked.

"Gonna have to find the intercom."

We went in opposite directions to find the illusive security system. With each turn, I was more intrigued by the house itself. You could have an entire harem in this place and never cross paths.

Upstairs, there were four bedrooms each with a bath. The rooms were nondescript, like no one ever committed to giving them a personality. The master bedroom was distinguishable by its enormous walk in closet. I had had apartments that were smaller with fewer cabinets.

Someone had a thing for shoes. The shoe rack was taller than I and had endless cubbies for shoes, boots and slippers. Someone was also a little OCD as they were labeled things like, 'glass slippers', 'bunnies' and 'Uggs.'

Having completed my survey, I trotted back downstairs, locating Chris in what appeared to be a mudroom-like space.

"I figured this out so it's time to figure out what we're eating."

"How 'bout Thai? That seems appropriate for crashing in this place tonight."

"You're willing to spend the night?"

"It's back to real life tomorrow so why not?"

He monkeyed with his phone. "Why can't *this* be real life?"

Once our food arrived, we sat outside by the pool. It was a lovely night with the jasmine heavily perfuming the air. I knew he was going to be leaving shortly and I wasn't so sure I wanted to stay in any of these houses alone.

"What is your plan? As far as work schedule?" I asked, polishing off my satay.

"I will text or call."

"You won't be coming to any of your addresses?"

"Unlikely."

"What do you do when you don't come home? Not sleep?"

"I sleep, for sure. They've got some sweet trailers."

"Are they as sterile as your apartment?"

"You'd probably say so. I have my stuff scattered all over it. I run and dump so it's a bit of a mess. You want to see it?" He stabbed his food with the chopsticks.

"Some time, that'd be cool. I don't need to follow you to the office right now. I already feel a little weirded out."

"Okay. If there comes a point when you want to go, say the word." He popped a piece of chicken in his mouth. "What are *your* plans?" He set his food down.

"I need to go home. My stuff is there. Jess is there. And you've just confirmed that you're going to be neither here nor there so I don't see a reason to be either."

"Okay." He handed me a card. "This'll get you in if you change your mind."

I ran my fingers over it repeatedly. "Thanks," I said quietly.

"Why do I get the feeling you want to hand that back to me?"

"Five days, Chris, and you're handing me a key. Not only a key but a key to the Magic Kingdom. That's a lot."

"I've known you longer than five days. This is how I make relationships. Like, when I am involved in a project, I'm with people very intensely for a short period of time. Things move more quickly. I make friends quickly. I proceed *quickly*. This isn't weird or fast for me. It feels normal except when you say that it's not. My feeling is that when you spend intense quality time with someone, the passage of time is different. You've been my girlfriend for five days but we were together for each moment of those five days, a luxury that many people don't have. I mean, what we've learned about each other in five days would have taken people in other circumstances far longer to learn. Does that make sense?"

"Yes," I growled, sticking the card in my purse. "Damn you again for making what is not normal feel right."

"Not your normal. Normal for me, though. Normal for others and certainly not 'wrong,'" he said, regaining his confidence.

"Ug. Okay."

"Do you really think it's wrong?"

"If not wrong, can we call it weird?"

"Is weird wrong?"

"Weird is weird."

"You did say I was weird."

"And I'm unusual so maybe this is my shortcoming," I said, pondering our little exchange.

"And by that, you are equating weird with wrong. You're not wrong. Maybe just need to be a little more 'fly by the seat of your pants?'"

Embarking on a nonsensical linguistic argument, our phones started chirping. It being as good a reason as any to get out of this conversation, I hunted for mine. I could feel him watching me, waiting for me to continue this thread. When I texted, he audibly sighed and picked up his phone.

It was Jess. She was on her way back and wanted to debrief each other. When I told her where I was, she was uber-enthusiastic. There was no explaining this place. It really did have to be seen to be believed.

"I can't believe I am saying this but can Jess come over and play?" I didn't look up from texting.

"Yes! Of course she can. Have her bring a few things and you ladies can have the place to yourselves. I should be outta here in an hour or so. Long enough to greet her if she hurries."

"Okay. She's still with Ian. He's willing to swing by our place and bring her here." I finished the message and perked up. His expression was pained. "What's up, weirdo? You asked me to stay. I'm staying."

"I'm not overly fond of him coming here. I'll shake this one off." He picked up our leftovers. "I can't offer you much beyond water but do you need anything?"

"I'll take water. Thanks," I handed him my trash. I took off my flip flops and walked into the pool up to my thighs.

He emerged with a red plastic cup. "Nothing but the finest."

"Classy!" I said, taking it.

"I've got to get going. You'll be okay?"

"Oh, I think this place is the epitome of secure. I'll be fine."

He took my hand, entreating me to the shallow step. He gave me a peck. "Don't forget to lock up," he said dryly.

"Will do. How do I let Jess in?"

"I'll let her in before I take off. See you later." He marched off across the grass.

With nothing else to do, I sat on the edge of the pool and kicked the water. With him gone, some of the pressure dissipated. I was just a girl sitting in a pool without a care in the world. And I wanted Jessica.

While I waited, I took a couple of pictures of my feet in the pool, the pool house and surrounding greenery for Amy. I knew she'd really like to see the main house and went to take a few more pictures.

I already felt out of place. I snapped a couple of pictures of the fountain, the drive leading up to the house and the house itself. It was magnificent. While I was thumbing through the pictures, Jessica came up the driveway out of breath.

"Holy shit, that's a long driveway!" she said, giving me a hug.

"You walked it?"

"I didn't think it would be such a hike."

"I thought you might have Ian in tow."

"Nah, he's got to get to work, too. Besides, I wanted to catch up with *you*!" She leaned over and smelled a daisy. "This really looks like one helluva place. Have you checked it all out?"

"More or less. I thought we could hang by the pool."

Walking in, she gasped. "My god. Did you get lost in here? This place is *cavernous*."

"You should check out the master bedroom's walk in closet. It's bigger than our apartment."

"I bet it is." Swinging her bag, she added, "I picked up a bottle of Jack."

"Sweet! I'll give you the two cent tour on the way. Do you have any interest in seeing the upstairs?"

"Is it amazing?"

"It's big but it's pretty vanilla."

"I'll pass."

"This way then." I took off for the kitchen.

We smelled just about all of the flowering shrubs, trees and vines. When we finally reached the pool house, we filled our red cups. As it was getting nippy, we plopped ourselves on an oversized couch facing the fireplace. I slid a table over.

"So—" we both said simultaneously. We hadn't had much to drink yet but both of us were laughing.

"How did we land up here, Sarah?" Jessica asked, pushing herself into the corner of the couch.

"I keep asking myself that. Pretty incredible."

"Yes ma'am, it is. You're happy?"

"I think so. I like him, probably a lot." I swirled my cup. "He wants me to move in here."

She leaned over. "Whoa. What are you thinking?"

"It's freaking me out just a little bit."

"Hell, yes. I'd be freaking out, too. What are you going to do?"

"Still thinking about it. I go from thinking it's totally batshit crazy to thinking that it could be great and that if it's not—no big deal. He even offered to have you move in to the guest house."

"This is a sweet little place."

"This *isn't* the guest house."

"You're joking. There's *another* house in here?"

"Nicer than this one. Or bigger, at any rate."

"We'll have to check it out later. Gotta see if I could live there." She winked.

"Right? Kinda hard to say no without thinking about it."

"It's funny. I came out to L.A. because I knew it would provide for me. And when you came out, it was the right mix of old and new. We haven't been out here too long and look at us! We're amazing."

"Amazingly *lucky*."

"Luck doesn't come out of nowhere. We *made* this luck. I would like to raise a toast—to us and our profound good fortune."

We both took more than a sip. Jack would not clear my head but it would help me to relax and think things through.

"Speaking of being lucky, you and Ian?"

"Wild, huh? Me and Ian."

"Chris hinted that you had someone picked out before you even arrived."

"I gotta say that I was intrigued when I heard he'd be there. God knows I love his movies. He's supernatural."

"He comes on a little strong."

"A *little* strong? I don't think he's intimate with the word no." She adjusted her glasses. "How could crossing paths with him be a bad thing? I've heard all the same shit that you have but have been through worse. He isn't going to hurt me. I was hoping that he'd be as interesting as some of his characters."

"And?"

"I can see a lot of those characters draw directly from who he is. I think being—friends? Is going to have its merits. He's gonna be around for some time to come." She raised her eyebrows. "It's not the Jack talking, I swear, so don't look so concerned! "Of course, he could have put on a really good act and I could be delusional and never hear from him again. Who knows? All I know is that I see no reason to change tracks. I'm going to take this one to the end and hope that it doesn't blow up in my face."

"That almost sounds like advice."

"We're friends for a reason, m'dear." We sat quietly for a few minutes, each in our own thoughts.

"Can you show me my house?" She batted her eye lashes.

"Absolutely!" I jumped off the couch, eager for the distraction.

Jessica was just as impressed as I was.

"If I were to move in here, I'd be living large. I have never lived in anything brand new. I think some of my pictures would liven up this living room. I mean, these generic prints are okay but—"

"Chris said the same thing about the pool house. We are not generic." She smiled crookedly and took off for the kitchen.

"Sarah! You saw this mural? It looks like the Birth of Venus! She's beautiful." She tilted her head. "Is it me or does she look a lot like you? Like the sun bleached out the Venus and added the beach-girl Sarah?"

"I love her. Beauty. Grace. Peace. Does she look like me?" I took a better look. "I think it's how the paint is chipped. She looks like she's got a stud in her nose. The added twinkle."

She laughed. "Yeah, that's it. The *added twinkle*."

"Well, were you to move here, you could have your coffee every morning with Venus-Sarah."

"Don't see how that's better than the current arrangement of coffee with the *real* Sarah-Venus."

I touched her arm. "Thanks, hun. I love you, too."

"Speaking of love, doesn't the two of us living here sound a little like sister-love? I want to scream *'winning!'*"

"Feel free but let's not digress to 'tiger blood.'"

I sat down at the island while Jessica continued her appraisal.

"Did you look at these bedrooms, Sarah?" she called from down the hall. "They're not inspired but they're *huge*. If we threw some paint in here, we could totally make it ours. String some Christmas lights. Add book shelves, I could do this." She poked her nose out. "But hey, whatever you decide."

"He said he's going to be working heavily for the next couple of weeks. I'd rather not move in until he's around. I don't wanna be sponging off a guy that's not even here."

"It's not an additional expense for him, keep that in mind. He's already footin' the bill."

"But still."

"Yeah, you're right."

She pulled up a chair next to me and we both admired the mural.

"Do you want to stay here tonight or go home? He left you the car."

"The Mustang?"

"No, the *other* car," she said teasingly. "He told me to let you know you could use the Mustang. Ian offered him a ride."

"I'm not going to lie— that is a fun car to drive!"

"Keys are on the counter."

~~

I felt like an imposter. I was leaving this grandiose house in an expensive car to drive to our neighborhood. If we weren't pulled over and arrested as suspected car thieves, I'd consider that another example of our luck.

Neither of us was ready to go to bed. We still had quite a bit of catching up to do. The more I talked, the more I pushed off thoughts about returning to work. I was in a period of transition. Jessica was great.

She and I spent an inordinate amount of time going through the pros and cons of moving in now as opposed to giving my relationship time. I wish I could say that I was ready to commit but I wasn't. I'd never had such an effortless relationship. I was used to providing for myself and wasn't ready to give up my struggles.

Jessica's willingness to come along was comforting. She said that there was more than enough space for all of us, that she'd miss me if I left her.

Our conversation dissolved when we received texts from our respective guys. Chris checked in to see where I was. I told him that driving the Mustang was too good to pass up. Thankfully, he let it go.

When our time was up, I realized that Jess was highly amused with her conversation.

"What's got your funny bone?"

"You want to see?" she asked, titillated.

"I'm not sure. *Do* I?" I cozied up next to her.

"Oh, sure. It won't bite you." She chuckled and handed me her phone.

"Dear *Lord*! Is that—he sent you a dick pic?"

She smiled. "I think that's his version of hello."

"That thing's a weapon!" I said in awe. "Chris said that he was impressive. He wasn't lyin'." I handed the phone back to her. "Why is it that guys know these things? Is that what they do at the urinal? Can you imagine women comparing boobs?"

"Lots of women do," she said, admiring the photo. "That's why there's plastic surgery available on every street corner."

"But it's not like we whip out our ta-tas and a tape measure."

"Another example of opposites attract." She set her phone down. "What time're you going to work tomorrow?"

"Noon. What're you up to?"

"Writing. I think I'm inspired."

"Inspired by a penis. I hope that's a first."

She shook her head. I shielded my eyes. "I don't want to know."

"Gonna wait for the movie?" she asked, getting up.

I squealed.

"Think we can meet up after work?" She stretched, cracking her neck.

"Yeah. I'll stop and get some groceries on the way home. What we have is probably a bit funky."

"Speaking of funky—Amy was a mess after you left. She wasn't getting the quality time from Lucas like she'd hoped. He barely said good morning to her."

"Ouch."

"Yeah. It was pretty uncomfortable. He simply didn't care. At all. It's like he flipped a switch and was someone else who didn't know Amy."

~~

# 12

In the morning, I slept as long as I could and still got up with plenty of time to get ready for work. I usually took a couple of buses. Today, I could drive. I wasn't really sure where I'd put the car but leaving the car here, unprotected, didn't thrill me. When I realized that I wouldn't have to tote groceries on the bus, the decision was easy. I wanted to experience that luxury.

It was definitely a different experience. I couldn't catch up on my friends. I couldn't zone out. The drive was disappointing. I never even made the car *move* like I wanted to. There's nothing like having access to zero to sixty and keeping it under forty.

I drove past the Shoppe, looking for parking. Amy was already there with a long line. She must've been turning over a new leaf to be there before me again. She said nothing as I tied my apron.

It wasn't until things really died down around three that she even looked at me. I used that as my opportunity to pry.

"Thanks again for letting me go for a couple of days. When Chris suggested you come to Vegas, I knew you'd be down. Did you have a good time?" I asked brightly.

"It was *great*. I had a *great* time."

The first time she said it, it was sincere. The second was filled with irritation.

"Good. I lost you right away so I was wondering."

"Lucas is pretty freakin' awesome in the sack. He had more moves than anyone I'd ever been with." She cracked a smile, her mind drifting back to Vegas.

"I don't want to make you sound like a whore but that's saying something, isn't it?" I went to the backroom to get more lettuce to chop.

"It's okay. I like to think I'm experienced." Saying nothing, I returned with more veggies and set them between us. "He's a lot thinner than I thought. And so tall. He's gotta be 6'3" at least. You know how I like my tall guys—at least as tall as Chris. I couldn't believe it when I saw him there. Jess had mentioned that he might be there. I thought she was full of shit. I was *hoping* but really, what were the odds that you could bring Lucas to a house party? No offense to Chris, but Lucas St. Martin is of a different caliber, you know?"

Amy could always find a way to make her lot in life better than anyone else's. There would be no point in debating this. What she needed was someone to listen to her adventures and confirm that she got the best of it all even if she were currently feeling otherwise.

"Did you see us in the pool? I couldn't believe how quickly my top came off! When I saw the other girls taking off their clothes, I didn't want to be the prude." She stopped chopping. "Tom really seemed into me. He told me how much he liked my rack. He's much too short for me but in the pool, I didn't really notice. He's good with his hands, too." She fondled a cucumber. "It's too bad that you're with Chris. I think Tom would've liked a threesome. I mean, with another woman."

I glanced at her, interested in her story.

"He asked me, you know, but when we got out of the pool—he was too short for me so I dumped him. Have you seen how short he is? I think he's actually shorter than Chris." She waved her knife. "Anyway! Did you see Colin? When he said my name, I knew he was the one. 'Amy,' he said. Oh, my! Just his accent made me wet." She threw her head back, eyes closed.

"He does have a great voice," I said honestly. I adored the guy.

"Colin must have a girlfriend or something. He wasn't into the party. He seemed to spend a lot of time chilling."

"To be fair, there was a lot to watch, Amy. I didn't want any part of it either."

"Yeah but, you know, you're kind of boring—you know that. And you have a boyfriend. I don't think anyone else has a significant other. It was a free for all." She stopped slicing. "You think I will hear from him again?"

"Beats me. What feeling did you get?"

"We had incredible sex. But, in the car, he spent most of the time on his phone." She shrugged, praying for a lifeline which I felt obligated to provide.

"Maybe he was catching up on his work schedule or god knows what. Chris has a lot of stuff on his plate. He spent our ride back running lines. Could he have been looking over his stuff?"

She set her knife down. "You know, that could be it. He did tell me that he'd be tied up for a while. I'd love to be invited to the premiere!" she gushed, latching on to my suggestion. "Can you imagine if we all went as a group, like reliving Vegas? I'd love to walk the red carpet! Do you know much about the movie they're working on, like when it will open?"

"I haven't gotten much into the details of movie business. I think it takes like, years, between when they stop filming and release. I'll have to ask."

"Do you know what they're working on? I mean, does it have a name? You might've told me. I don't remember."

"Chris gave me the script to read when we were running lines. It's called *'Out of Time'* and it's like a cops and robbers. Instead of just being worried about the 'where,' the 'when' is also important. It's confusing to me but I loved reading it."

She bit her lip. "That sounds like sci-fi. Bleh. I'd still go to the premiere, though."

She was looking much more upbeat and ready to divulge her sordid stories. Giving me far more information than I had any right to know, she detailed her first foray into truly rough sex. Kaylee walked in and peeled off her clothing only to be scared away by their activities. Amy was determined to be memorable even outside of her comfort zone. When she finished, I wanted to take a shower. She was a dirty, dirty girl.

By the end of the night, we were both in good spirits. I didn't have the heart to tell her that Chris had asked me to move in. She'd probably hear something *if* or when I moved in but it wasn't important enough to burst her bubble.

When I hit the grocery store, I was shocked to see pictures of Jessica and the guys piling out of the limo on the front cover of *The Rag*. It wasn't the cover story but still. Talk about recent news. There they were with the banner, 'Who's the mystery woman?' I picked it up and tossed it on the belt.

I exploded into the house, eager to show Jess how famous she was. She was sitting in her room, writing in the dark. I really didn't understand how she could sit in her little pit and create stories. She claimed that the darkness helped her to focus her energy on her characters.

Without flipping it open, I placed it on her keyboard.

"Holy shit!" she screamed, picking it up. Her head spun around. "D'you already look inside?"

"Nope, that's a good picture of you though. I think you look like royalty."

She pushed back from her desk and flipped madly through the magazine. Finding the page, she screamed. "Who the fuck took these?" she demanded. She shoved the magazine at me, then right back under her nose. "Just so you know—you look pretty good with a square on your ass."

"Say what?" I said timidly, craning in for a better view. Sure enough, there were a couple of photos from the party. They were hedonistic. "I didn't know they'd publish stuff like that!"

"Or sell it at the *grocery* store!" I tugged the page so that we could both read it. Someone made some money off the pictures.

My head was spinning. My mother was a subscriber. She lived for this magazine. And that girl in the photograph? She looked enough like the one who left Connecticut. I prepared myself for her call. There was little doubt in my mind that she'd be dragging my dad out here at the first opportunity to make sure I was okay. I wasn't named so that was good but this wouldn't be the end of it.

Jessica bee-lined for the kitchen, magazine in hand. "You bought booze, right?" She rifled through the two bags. "You did! Good girl." Cracking open the bottle of Jack, she said, "Honestly, who did this? I thought 'what happened in Vegas stayed in Vegas' and all that shit." She filled two beer steins and passed one to me.

"We could try and figure out who's *not* in the pictures but even then, Melissa had a few people over that I never met. This picture of my ass is from fairly late in the night. I think they were gone." I thumbed through the magazine.

"So if it wasn't them, then it had to be one of us."

"I'd put my money on Kaylee. She propositioned Chris and was pissed when she found out we were together. I'm pretty sure she didn't get laid."

"Do you *know* Kaylee?" Jessica asked, mildly perturbed.

"I met her and promptly found out she'd offer to blow Chris."

Jessica choked on her whiskey. "She wanted to blow him?"

"Yup," I said, over-enunciating.

"Huh. Out of all the things I could do at a party, I don't think sucking on someone's dick would be very high on my list—or that wouldn't be my 'go-to' move."

"Heh. Based on the dick pic, it wouldn't be mine either."

She rolled her eyes.

"How do you think they put this together?"

"Damned if I know." She closed it. She took a couple of pictures and sent them to Ian. "Can't wait to see what he thinks."

"He's already got the rep. I doubt he'll be worked up unless he's got another lady who didn't know about Vegas. That'd be funny!"

Jessica gave me a cold look. "Fucking hilarious, Sarah. I'm no home wrecker."

"Does he even have a home?" Still irked, she picked up the bottle and moved onto the couch. "Got any more crotch shots?" I said in an attempt to bring back the humor.

"No," she said tartly, "but he did send me a text. Want to see it?"

I laughed. "The *last* time you asked, I got an eyeful of shlong."

"I promise—nothing like that." She handed me her phone.

There was a cute little entreaty from Ian which was at odds with the guy I met. He was just as good at working the ladies as Chris, maybe better. I could tell his message tickled Jessica's fancy. I hoped for her sake that he wasn't a turd. As I read it the second time, he responded to the magazine clip she sent him.

"Hey, Ian just sent you a text." I dropped the phone in her expectant hands.

They had a little exchange which she read to me. They were both wordsmiths. I couldn't help but laugh. Ian was taking it all in stride, trying to diffuse Jessica's agitation.

"He *is* funny," I said.

"You sound surprised."

"I'm just happy that he's more than I thought he was, how's that?" Switching gears, I asked "What're they doing?"

"Good question. I'll ask," she said, furiously typing. "'Sitting around and have been for a while.' They're waiting for pyro."

"That makes me want to go and visit. I'd love to see how they put some of those scenes together."

"Me, too." I thumbed through the magazine. I'd never thought of it as trashy before. Maybe being in it personally is what made it feel trashy.

I sent the fine spread to Chris, curious what his reaction would be.

"Can you ask him what Chris's up to?" I asked, curiously.

"This feels like high school," she said, doing as I asked.

"He's sitting, too. He says 'hi.'"

"Hi!" I waved at the phone.

"You're a dork," Jess said, eying me over it.

"And you're my friend." I refilled her glass.

"We're gonna be hammered if we keep this up."

"Maybe. Are you going to return to writing or are we going to hang out?"

"I thought we were hanging out."

"Right now, you're texting and I'm hanging."

She set it down. "Okay. So much for that!" She padded to the kitchen for more ice.

"That was a lot of fun." She stabbed her cup at the magazine.

"Did you know that Vegas was so close? It seems like we should've visited there before now."

"Probably better that we *didn't* know. I wouldn't want to live there but it could be addictive."

"You stayed at the Venetian?" I asked, eager to hear her side.

"Yeah, the guys shared a suite. And it was *sweet*. I would have loved to spend some more time there. It had a *baby grand piano*. Did you know that Ian can play?"

"How would I know that?"

"He really did play in that movie a couple years ago. He picked it up for that part. He learns things very quickly." She was arguably impressed.

"That's cool. I'd love to learn new tricks for my job."

"Hey, I bet that you're cutting edge when it comes to spreads."

I rolled my eyes. "Very applicable to life, knowing what to put on salami."

"Heh heh. You said 'salami.'"

"Jessica! It sounds like it may be time to put the bottle down."

"Oh, but why. Sausages are fun!" She tipped her glass.

"What was it like hanging out with all of them? Learn anything interesting?" I curled my legs under me on the couch.

"Tom's like my little brother. He's got a bit of the devil in him. I think the other guys keep him from going to the Dark Side. Lucas is all about Lucas or so it seemed. I didn't spend a great deal of time talking to him. I didn't like how he treated Amy." She turned off the lamp. "It wouldn't have taken much for her to have been riding high when we left. She definitely knew that she'd been used." She kicked off her sandals.

"Colin has a girlfriend. I did get him to talk about her. It's a relationship that he's not sure he wants to continue. He hasn't seen her in over a year. These people lead intense lives! I'm not sure why you'd choose to be in a relationship with someone you never see. What do you get out of that? It's not even 'roommate' status. It's more like familial. You get all the crap and none of the perks."

"Not that I will know her but, who is his girlfriend?"

"I didn't recognize her name. She's in a popular television show in Great Britain. I bet we could Google the show. I'd recognize her name if I saw it."

"Did the guys give you any warnings about Ian?"

"No. Should they've?"

"Just curious. Tom and Ian seemed to have plenty of thoughts about my relationship with Chris."

"Ian did?"

"I wasn't sleeping when you two came in."

"Ohhhh."

"Funny thing is that the guys *know* him. They're absolutely right that he's after a wife."

"That's noble."

"I don't know if it's noble but it is part of his life trajectory, where he wants to go."

"What did Tom have to say?"

"Something similar. He's convinced that our relationship won't work out. He sounded like Ian—like I'm after adventure instead of a peaceful home life."

"Do you prefer one over the other?" she asked, taking another swallow.

"I'd like to have a peaceful home life that allows me to adventure."

~~

# 13

The ensuing days were bleary and boring. Time crawled by, making itself known by the minute. I tried to remember what I did before Chris. I must've been going through the motions without really getting much out of life.

Being with Chris was the first time I'd had fun, pure and simple, without Jessica figuring into the equation. I don't recall being unhappy but life had been a lot more vibrant in the last couple of months. I had so many memories that colored my day. If I was feeling bummed that he wasn't around, it was easy enough to pick a moment when he was and daydream about it until I felt better.

I longed to have some quality time with him but refused to demand it in a text. Being in his life meant allowing him to be elsewhere. I was going to have to figure out what the hell to do with myself when he was not available. I spent over a week contemplating my options. Jess suggested that we put a bunch of paper on the fridge and use it for brainstorming. So far, it had things like 'become a yogi' and 'make hats.'

One night when I was really lonely, I added everything that would make me happy to my list. It was loaded with stuff—vacation, Chris, celebrate birthday with Chris in Vegas? Hawaii? See Chris, visit Chris, move in with Chris. The spiral tightened around his name. Chris was woven into the path I wanted to take.

When Jess came home from a writing group, she brought some hot tea over and sat down.

"Looks like you've been busy," she said, rotating the paper to read it more easily.

"I feel like I am ready to make some commitments," I said firmly.

"Oh?" She scrutinized me. "I think I've seen that coming for a while. Maybe there's no point in dragging this out. *Are* you happy?" she asked empathetically.

"More or less. What makes me unhappy is waiting for him to materialize. He has been so kind and cute, texting me and calling me basically daily but we're living different lives. I *miss* him—his body, his voice—HIM. I can hear his voice in the texts but it's not enough. I need *him* here."

She sat up. "Are you talking about breaking up with him?"

"No. But I question how I am going to get through a relationship with a guy who's not around. He said something about Ella not working out because of her need for attention. I don't want to be *needy* but I don't want to be the weekend getaway, either."

"That's fair. Have you talked to Chris?"

"About this? No."

"You should."

"I know."

"You're hiding."

"Am I? I think I needed this—introspection? I am glad, I guess, that we had to part ways for what has now been weeks."

"Time to poke out of your shell. Chris should know what you're thinking and I doubt he has a good idea. He seems to read people in person."

"But what if I bring it up and I get denied? What do I do with that?" It was my greatest fear. What if he shut down or withdrew?

"He's going to do what he's going to do. You can't change that. You should talk to him. At least he can *know* what you're thinking."

She was right. She usually was. "How do I start this conversation? I'm stuck on that part because I am not sure what I want so much as I know what I don't want."

"Start with that. Sounds like you've got direction." She tapped her mug. "He's really good for you. It will turn out. Even if you can't tell, I've known you long enough that I can. You've gotta go for it or you will regret it." She got up. "I'm going to my room to write. It's too light out here." She tossed me my phone. "Start now, now m'dear."

I unlocked the screen. I read some old texts. I checked in on social media. Annoyed with myself, I set it down and refreshed my tea.

I watched the steam come off my cup. My phone chirped. Sweet, I thought. He's coming to my rescue.

'Hello, gorgeous.'

'Hey. I was just talking about you.'

'Good things, I hope?'

'Always.'

'Cool. What's on your mind?'

'You.'

'I like that. What, though?'

'I miss you.'

'Miss you, too.'

'A lot. I am lonely.'

'You want to come here?'

'To the set?'

'Sure.'

'Wouldn't that be weird?'

'Oh no! Not weird!'

'Do other people visit?'

'Yes.'

'I want to see you.'

'Come here.' I didn't respond but drank my tea, my phone idling in my lap.

'Please come here,' he added. 'I miss you, too. There's nothing like being with you. I have been as cautious as I can be because of how we left things. I am trying to let time pass.'

'It *is* passing. It's excruciating.'

'Time is different in different circumstances, huh? You've come around to my way of thinking.'

'Yes.'

'When can you come?'

'This weekend. I'll drop a shift. We have a newbie who is trying to pick up hours.'

'How's the Shoppe? You've seen Art?'

'He's a nice guy. He's no you.'

'Thanks. You've got wheels. Details to come later when you're sleeping.'

'Cute.'

'How've you been?'

'You have time to call? I'm tired of typing. I want to hear your voice.'

'Will do.'

My phone didn't even ring before I heard his voice in my ear. I sighed. That was so much better.

"Hey, you sound a little sad."

"From my sigh, I sound sad?"

"Am I wrong?"

"Melancholy, perhaps."

"And how do you define that? I always think of Shakespeare's 'sweet sorrow.'"

"Sweet sorrow is about right. I *miss* you."

"I can hear it in your voice. It sounds like a new concept for you, like you're surprised that you miss me."

"I have spent a good deal of time trying to figure out what I was feeling."

"And?" he prodded.

"And I realized that I like my life a lot more with you in it. I have been going through the motions for a long time now. I've been responsible and comfortable."

"There's nothing wrong with those," he said amiably.

"I haven't stopped to smell the roses. Hell, I don't even think I knew Los Angeles had them!" I'd made my life about paying the bills, nothing more. I hadn't added to my life in any profound way in years.

"Years ago, I was focused on things that were not in my control. It was bad. That's when I got my now tattoo. I needed a reminder, something to anchor me to this moment. *Now*, I'm at a point where thinking about the future may be more important." I waited for him to offer a plan or a rescue. He did neither.

"Chris?" I ventured.

"Mm-hmm," he whispered.

"I thought I'd lost you."

"No. I am enjoying listening to your voice. And your train of thought. I want you here. Now," he added huskily.

"Is that possible?"

"No."

"So I am stuck with my now for now?"

"We both are."

~~

With my sights set on Saturday, time moved at a more reasonable pace. I went out and got myself new undergarments. I picked up some food. I didn't want to leave his trailer until I'd had my fill of him. I added a knitting project to my bag and was good to go.

Opening the door to his pod, it was as he described—strewn with stuff. Out of place, however, was a little bouquet of peonies sitting on the table and a note.

I picked it up. 'Thinking of you. Longing for you. Wanting you – Chris.' I blushed as I read it.

There wasn't much to explore. I shot him a quick text thanking him for the flowers. I didn't really expect a response. He came flying in the door like a giant puppy who'd been left alone for too long.

"Nice spandex!" I said. He lifted me off the ground into a bone-crunching hug.

"Thanks. It's extraterrestrial! I gotta go but feel free to push things out of your way. The PA who brought you here, Trinity, she can take you to the craft services if you get hungry."

He set me down. "I'm so glad you're here." He squished me again.

"Me, too."

He backed out the door, overflowing with positivity. With a wave through the window, he trotted back to wherever he'd come from.

I was instantly more content. I had nowhere to go and that was okay. This tiny space was filled to the gills with Chris— miscellaneous clothing, books, fan mail. With little to do but knit, I took a couple of the open letters out of their envelopes.

They were cute. One had a picture of him from a previous movie for him to sign. The second envelope contained quite a missive. This woman went on and on about how amazing Chris was and her desire to run into him. She wanted to say hello. Based on the Arkansas post mark, we all knew how unlikely it was. I'd have to get him to send her something to brighten her day.

As much as I wanted to read more, it appeared that he hadn't even though they were open. Every corner of the earth was represented. All of them said 'fan mail' and bore the name of his talent agency. That's one way to avoid stalkers—have your mail prescreened by your agency.

It surprised me how much of regular life these people didn't have to experience. No one screens my mail. God knows it would be nice for someone to provide me with housing and a top notch chuck wagon.

I retrieved a bottle of water and sat down to knit. I debated a small project or a blanket, opting for the blanket. This would not be the last time I was left to my own devices.

I ran out of yarn before I ran out of time. Idly flipping through my phone, I was hungry. There was no chance I was going to wander down to the food and risk explaining who I was and why I was there. To distract myself, I cleared off the bed and generally neatened things up. When I finished, I ripped into the pretzels, pining for my extraterrestrially-clothed boyfriend.

A couple hours later, I awoke to a cacophony. The boys were returning en masse. The trailer bounced as Chris bounded up the steps and flung the door open.

"They're going to a bar. Wanna go?" he asked, bursting with energy.

"Uh, not really," I mustered.

"You look sleepy," he said, sweeping the hair off my forehead.

"I fell asleep. I wasn't sure what else to do with myself."

"Sleeping is good. You want to stay in?"

"How long are you here?"

"Five and into makeup," he said, grinning.

"Listen to you talking about makeup. I may need a support group for women who date men who wear more makeup than they do." I smiled, scouring his face for any trace of makeup.

He sat on the edge of the other bench. "Did you get something to eat?"

"No."

"Why not?"

"I didn't want to go out and have to tell people why I was here."

"You wouldn't have to. There're always some people around that none of us know. And some of the people here know about you and were looking forward to meeting you, making you at home."

"Good to know but still. I'd prefer an escort."

"Beyond Trinity?"

"Yup."

"I am *very* glad to see you." He deftly pulled me out of my seat. What started off as a peck became a hungry battle between two people who missed each other deeply.

As we were lying in bed chatting, he mentioned that Colin's girlfriend was in town. He sent Colin a text to make sure Nicola sought me out in the morning.

"She's really a nice person," he said by way of introduction.

"From what Jess said, it sounded like she and Colin hit a rough patch."

"Oh, yeah?"

"They haven't seen each other in a long time." I stuck my needles back in the bag. "Anyway! Meeting her should be more interesting than trying to knit without yarn."

"You're outta yarn? I didn't know you knit."

"And you want me to move in. Think of all the things you don't know about me!"

"If knitting is as bad as it gets, that's fine by me." He folded his arms behind his head.

I propped myself on his chest. "I have been giving your offer a lot of thought."

Opening one eye, he said quietly, "And?"

"I think I can do it. I think you're right about time and maybe more so about timing."

~~

He was gone and I never heard him leave. Getting up, I was grumpy. Being in a different bed with less sleep and no particular reason to get up was unpleasant. I threw on clothes, made coffee and snuck a peek at my phone. When I had almost finished my second cup, there was a knock on the door. Voilà!

I opened the door to an exquisitely manicured woman. Nothing was out of place. She was a beautiful blond with hazel eyes and flawless skin. She was rockin' a sweet pair of flip flops.

"Nicola?" I said, extending my hand.

"Sarah!" She took a step up to shake my hand.

"I'd invite you in but it's a disaster."

"Not surprising. How about breakfast?" She smiled warmly.

At The Whole Schmear, we ordered coffee and one of their famous bagel sandwiches. What they brought was disgusting in its size but excellent otherwise.

I poked my breakfast, not sure what we had to talk about.

"How long have you been with Chris?" Nicola asked. She had such a crisp, British accent.

"A couple of months."

"What do you do?"

"I work downtown."

"Is that how he met you?" I liked her. She didn't push too hard.

"Yes." I took another wedge of my sandwich. "How'd you get involved with Colin?" I ventured.

"Worked together on a film years ago. He is such a gentlemen," she said pensively.

"I heard that you were working on a television show in the UK."

"I am and it sucks," she said, unabashedly irritated. I raised an eyebrow. Hearing a British woman use the word 'sucks' was funny.

"Beware, Sarah. Getting involved with actors sucks." She drove her knife through with such force that it squeaked on the plate. "I heard that Colin went to a party in Vegas. A *house* party. A drunken, dirty party." She wiped her finger tips daintily on her napkin. "That wouldn't happen if we were together. He'd never have gone."

I shifted uneasily in the booth. "I was at that party. One of my friends called him boring because he just sorta sat there."

"Your friends? You had the party?" she asked in disbelief.

"Sort of. Chris and I ran into the guys in Vegas. We invited them to my friend's house."

"I don't like hearing about stuff like that, feeling like I should know more about it than I do. I shouldn't be the odd man out."

"Have you talked to Colin about it?" I internally reviewed what he'd told Jess.

"No. I shouldn't have to. He should tell me about it."

"Do you talk?"

"What do you mean?"

"In my very short experience, it's been hard to *talk* with Chris. I hate it." I spooned some sugar into my coffee.

"We text. We talk. And I'm here," she said defensively.

"How long's that gone on?"

"About a year. But it's not by choice."

"Maybe it's time to talk with him about it. I wouldn't be surprised if he had some misgivings about how things are going."

"That sounds too much like *the talk*. I don't want to break up with him."

"What is this relationship giving you?"

"When we're together, he's everything that I want. I love him." Her eyes teared up.

"Coming to visit was the right thing," I said resolutely. I didn't want her to cry. I didn't know what I'd do if she did.

"Of course it is," she snapped. "I got the feeling when we were talking recently that he was slipping away."

"Talking or texting?"

"Same thing," she said sharply.

I was desperate for a change of subject. I had never been one to give advice on romance.

"Be careful with him. He really likes you," Nicola said. She reapplied her lipstick. "He didn't come out to the bar last night because you were around." Her eyes flirted with me over her compact. "He chose *you* over his friends. Keep up with him. Stay connected." She tossed her makeup back in her enormous purse. "I know distance is killing us." She delicately placed her silverware on her plate.

"To answer your question, I don't get anything out of the relationship right now. It's like a lead weight of obligation. I feel obligated to text or call and that sucks. What sucks more is getting a response hours later when you're busy and don't see it. It's missed opportunity on a daily basis. I've gotta make this work and get through it."

"Sounds like you have a plan." I pushed my plate away. "How long are you in town?"

"Flying out tomorrow. You?"

"Later today or tomorrow. I don't know. I don't want to sit there all day and wait. I fell asleep last night waiting."

"Hope you had sweet dreams. Sometimes sleep is the only answer. It's not something you get used to either," she said ruefully.

After breakfast, she wanted to run a few errands. We did some shopping or in my case, window shopping. The stuff she bought cost more than my weekly paycheck. The retail therapy worked wonders on her mood. Seeing her happy, I could understand her appeal.

While she was paying for a new pair of shoes, Chris texted. I couldn't help but ask if he'd be around later. I was disappointed to hear that he was around right then. Colin, too, was putzing around. I hoped that this would help Nicola to wrap up her shopping and get us back in time to see the guys. It worked.

Nicola took us to craft services. I was glad that she was there. I wasn't much for stumbling around blindly. With her, I felt like I belonged.

The spread was amazing. There were tables of beverages, baked goods, hot foods and snacks. Just about any craving you might be having could be answered by one of these tables. Chris was standing at the end of the hot foods, getting what had to be a second helping. Colin hung by his side, holding a paper coffee cup.

As I approached, Chris lit up. "Hey! It's good to see you." He juggled his heavily laden plate, bumping my butt. "Do you want anything?" he asked conversationally, walking towards an empty table.

"Nothing. I had a nice breakfast with Nicola."

"Where'd'ya guys go?" He greedily attacked a sausage.

"The Whole Schmear. I've been by that place a million times. I never thought I'd pay fourteen bucks for a bagel sandwich. It was good but way too much."

"What do you expect from a place with *that* name? It's gotta live up to being the whole schmear!"

"It was an experience. Good coffee, too." I sat across from him. "We did some shopping. How you people spend money is incredible. I watched her pick out footwear that cost more than I make in a week."

"It's all relative."

"You can say that. You relate to it. And to think she's probably got a closet full of shoes just like that."

He sliced off another bite. "No doubt. But if it weren't shoes, it would be something else and if it weren't something else, what good is it?"

"I guess I'd like to find out. Do you get *used to* spending bucks like that, without thinking about it?"

"Yup."

"Must be nice."

"It is." He patted my hand. "Hang around me long enough and you just might find yourself debating whether you should get one pair or another—or both."

I picked a piece of cheese off his plate, sniffing it.

"What're your plans?" he asked, wiping his hands.

"I think I'm going to head home."

"Bored here?"

"I don't like waiting for you. I feel like a house pet with nothing to do."

"You make a nice pet." He gazed at me warmly. "We should be wrapping this up soon."

"What do you mean by that? You'll be done filming?"

"Mm-hmm."

"Then what?"

"I go home."

"Is there anything else lined up after this?"

"Not until August, I think."

"What do you do in the meantime?" I asked intrigued.

"I guess that depends on you," he said eagerly.

"What would you have done if I weren't in the picture?"

"Probably'd go home and visit the family. Chill out. Maybe go somewhere and hike."

"And that would fill your *months* off?"

"It could. I'm good at finding stuff to do with my free time."

~~

Returning home, Jess was in the kitchen making dinner.

"Hey, how'd it go? Was it cool?" she asked, stirring some noodles.

"I met Colin's girlfriend, Nicola."

"No way! She's in town? That's probably a good thing. What's she like?" she asked, getting us each a beer.

"She's okay. I think she and Colin have a lot of talking to do. She was pissed about our party in Vegas." I took a drink.

"Vegas? That's awesome. News made it all the way across the pond. Sarah, you have a well-traveled ass!"

"Thanks for that. I told her that she had nothing to worry about, party-wise. I felt like I harnessed my inner-Jessica. I tried to offer her some advice. Like, maybe they should talk to each other in person about her concerns and stuff."

"How'd that go?"

"She got pissy."

"You hungry?" she asked, putting some pasta on a plate.

"Not really. The way the talent is fed, you'd think that it was their last opportunity to be near food. I have never seen so much fresh, good food."

"Did you eat?"

"I had a piece of cheese. I had a *huge* breakfast with Nicola at the Whole Schmear. Have you ever been there? What they call a sandwich has got to have enough calories for the whole week. It was good but way too big." Sitting on the couch, I added, "I think I agreed to move in."

"Oh?" she said, slurping up a noodle.

"You want to come?"

"I've been thinking about it, m'dear and I am not overly attached to this place."

"I'd love to keep you as long as I can. You're my security blanket!" I picked imaginary food out of my teeth.

"We do cover each other's asses pretty well, huh?" She smiled, digging the parsley out of her teeth.

"Ug. The idea of moving—we're lucky our house is so small. I hate moving."

"Me, too. You sure we won't be moving again in another couple of months? Maybe we should hold on to this one just in case?" she asked seriously.

"I've never lived with him so I'm not making any promises."

"What's your time line?"

"Let me get ahold of Chris and see if he can help us. That'll decide the time line. I don't want to carry furniture if I don't have to."

I sent him a lengthy text loaded with moving-related questions. My fingers typed 'love you.' I didn't send it. I'm not sure why. I spent the rest of the night wondering if it was love and if so, why couldn't I say it?

~~

# 14

'Why don't we wait until I'm done so we can do this right?'

My heart fell. I knew it made the most sense. I knew it would give me time to get stuff in order. It still hurt.

Jess and I started sorting through accumulated piles of crap. We tossed so much stuff that it looked like we were being evicted.

Some of our trinkets were going to be hilariously out of place. From the strings of Christmas lights to the endless boxes of books, we would transform the austere hotel into a home.

At the end of another week, Chris dropped by. He looked pleasantly exhausted, like he was glad to be here but ready for some R&R.

"This is impressive," he said, looking at all of the boxes by the door. "I can see why you didn't want to move by yourself. You need an *army*!"

He opened the top box. "Are these *all* books? Have you heard of a library?"

"There's nothing like owning a book," I said. "They're my friends. I don't like the idea of other people putting their hands on 'em." I lifted a book out of the box. Coincidentally, it was written by Jessica a couple of years ago. I would keep till death do us part.

I tossed it to him. "You should read it during your time off."

Reading the cover, he whistled. "I recognize the cover. Ian's reading this." He lit up. "Jessica's a published author in addition to being a photographer and artist?"

"Yes, sir."

"I never knew her last name." He set the book down with his jacket on the couch. "Listen, I have an idea—how about we get a moving company and we take a break and go somewhere? I'd like to get out of here even for a few days."

"That sounds incredible! I *loathe* moving with every ounce of my being."

"So do I. I haven't had to do it in a long time. We can be gone and when we get back, it'll be done. You can see if Jess wants to tag along or we can give her a key. Speaking of—she liked the guest house?"

"Who wouldn't? It's a lot of space for her. It's going to be the end of an era for us! I'm just glad she's going to be so close."

He gripped my shoulder. "You really find her comforting, don't you?"

"She's been there for me for a really long time. We've seen men come and go but we're always there for each other."

He pulled me into an embrace. "I am not going anywhere. There just may come a time when you don't *need* her."

I kissed him. I already needed her less. She was more of a comfort than a necessity.

"Where're we going?" I inquired.

"How long do you have?"

"Depends on what you want to do."

"How's that?"

"I could quit if the offer were a 'once-in-a-lifetime' kind of event."

His eyes widened. "What happened to my Sarah? You're ready to move in. Your house is packed. Now you're ready to quit your job? I think I need to sit down!" He skittered to the couch and dramatically collapsed.

Reticent, I said, "Your Sarah realized that she missed you and would prefer to see more of you if at all possible."

"How would you feel about taking a nap instead? I could really use one." Through closed eyes, he added, "Or are you more interested in planning our getaway? I could stay awake for that—or a late lunch."

"You can fall asleep in any position, can't you?" I asked, looking at the unnatural position of his neck.

"Another acquired skill."

"Why don't you go rest in my room?"

"Are you coming?"

"Are you resting if I do?"

A slow smile spread across his face. "Eventually."

As he lay sleeping, I admired him. His spikey hair was no longer jet black but had the beginning of light brown roots. His face showed signs of aging, like the schedule really took it out of him. And then there was his body. How he ate like he did yet had this body, I couldn't understand. Maybe he really required all those calories to work the hours that he did. He must. There was nothing extra anywhere on him.

I sent Amy the pictures of Chris's house and told her I was moving in. I knew she was working. She wouldn't be able to respond so I also mentioned that I was going to need some time off. I enjoyed envisioning her reaction to my messages. She was going to lose it.

In the time since Vegas, she hadn't heard from Lucas. She asked me about him in a back-handed fashion so that she never appeared to be really interested in the answer. I pitied her. She envied me my life in a way she'd never admit. There was a lot to envy considering that my deli days were now numbered. I pondered whether we'd stay in touch. I never disliked her but would never have sought her friendship.

While checking in with a couple of other friends, my mother called. I sighed. About the last thing I wanted to do was talk to my mom but if I didn't answer, she'd leave me a message that would make me feel guilty. She was good at that. I willed myself to answer.

"Sarah!" she said brightly.

"Hi, mom." I tried to match her energy.

"I have been thinking about you, honey." I could already sense that I wouldn't appreciate her agenda.

"Oh, yeah? What's up?" I asked noncommittally.

"I haven't heard from you in a long time. What have you been up to? Are you seeing anyone?"

"It's that time difference, Mom. When I get off work, it's too late to call you." I ignored her real question.

"Honey, you've always managed to call before. If you're seeing someone, that's great. I want you to be happy." I believe my mom'd always harbored thoughts that Jessica and I might be a couple.

"Thanks, Mom. I am happy."

"Good. Good." She rustled some paper. "Your father thought he recognized your girlfriend on the cover of *The Rag*. Was that Jessica, on the cover? I told him that it couldn't be but he's convinced." That's my mom—steamrolling ahead.

"Oh? She may have mentioned something about that."

"Oh, Sarah! Is that *you* in the magazine? You two have been peas in a pod for so long!" She was brimming with excitement.

I grit my teeth. "Which picture are you talking about, Mom? I heard that there were a few."

"Oh, honey. I can't—want me to send it to you? I can put it in the mail. We bought one at the grocery store before ours arrived. Better yet, your dad and I were talking about coming out there for your birthday. We haven't seen you in so long and we could really use a trip."

"It's expensive out here, Mom. And I was thinking I'd try to get home later this year."

"Well, we've already purchased the tickets, Sarah," she said haughtily. "They were expensive, too! We thought we'd stay with you to make the trip more affordable." Gaining traction, she continued, "I am so excited! I have never been to Los Angeles. I was wondering if you'd be able to get us in to one of the shows they tape out there. Maybe we could do some of the touristy things as well. You know, it's hard to say if we will be able to come to Los Angeles again so I'd like to fit in everything that we can. Dad is interested in checking things out, too. I hope you have a car. That's another thing that we're going to need. Dad doesn't like to walk around. Is there anything you'd like me to bring from Connecticut? Do you want any of the stuff you left here?"

This was just like my mom to inform me of her plans instead of including me in making them. It had always been this way from the time she threw me out of the house when I was seventeen. Her behavior would be very surprising if her methods were not so consistent. As I had gotten older, I realized that the only control she had left was forcing her agenda on others. Also, if she forged ahead without me, I couldn't say no. It was a win-win for her. It's not that I didn't have a soft spot for my parents but it was hard to say that I wanted to be around them. They were extraordinary and that was not a good thing.

I took a deep breath. "When are you coming?"

"For your birthday, honey. We arrive the Tuesday before and leave the Monday after. You're so lucky that your birthday falls on a Saturday this year! You don't have to work and that's always nice, isn't it?"

"Yes," I whispered, resigned.

"You think you will be able to take some time off and show us around? We'd really like to meet the person you're seeing. How'd you land up at a party with Ian Hartlass anyway?" she asked curiously.

"It's kind of a long story, Mom."

"I've got all day and I would really like to know. Is he handsome? Are you involved with Ian? He looks like such a dish but you know he's not a nice guy, right? He's a bad boy. It looked like he might've been there with Jessica. Did you tagalong with her? How'd she meet him? Oooh! Is one of her books being made into a movie? I always knew she could write. It's not my style, I mean, but I can see why it'd be popular with young people."

"I wish Jessica's book were being made into a movie!"

"Oh, well. I thought that would be good for you if she made a name for herself. You'd get to go to a premiere!"

"Could still happen."

"Alright, honey. Well, I have to go. Your dad's ready to go to dinner but I need your address! Can you pick us up at the airport, too? How much are cab—oh! Your dad's in the car. I gotta go. Talk to you later, honey!"

My parents were some of the only people who still used land lines. Dad was not going to wait very long before peeling out of the driveway without her. He was another one who took control with his actions. No conversation. You were either in the car or you were eating his leftovers later. Sometimes, I really wondered why they stayed together. It couldn't be love.

If the Captain could survive my parents, he could very well be *The One*. My parents had scared off or influenced every relationship I'd ever had. I couldn't think of one person who really meant it when they said, 'they mean well.'

He had no idea what was coming. There was no good way to warn him. Watching him sleep never grew old but I was itching to do something to take my mind off my parents. When I couldn't stand it anymore, I nibbled on his ear. It took longer than I would have thought but he ensnared me in one of his signature hugs.

"Morning, gorgeous," he said, opening his eyes.

"Hello, sleepy head. Sorry to wake you but life's calling." I stroked his bare shoulder. "I get the feeling you could sleep straight through."

"What time is it?" he asked, rolling over.

"Dinner time. Your belly will confirm it. Wait for it, wait for it!" I leaned over to listen more closely.

"You're cute," he said, pushing me out of the way and sitting up.

"It's time to find food and have a chat. My parents are coming out here."

"Oh?" He put his pants on.

"They saw the magazine and already booked their tickets. They're convinced that they're missing out on something or that I need to be rescued from drugs and prostitution."

"Yikes. Do your parents know about me?" he asked innocently.

"Ha. You've been my best kept secret. Had they known about you, they'd already've visited!"

"Do they know you're a grown woman?"

"I don't think they see me as grown *up*. Probably never will. We've got a strange dynamic."

He yanked a shirt over his head. "Well, they can't be *all* bad. They did a great job raising you."

I scoffed. "They didn't raise me. They threw me out when I was seventeen."

"Trouble maker, huh?"

"I don't think so. My mom is nuts."

"I was out of the house at seventeen. Maybe it was just time for you to get up on your own two feet?"

"Right. And that's why she chose Thanksgiving Day to give me the boot—so that I could land on my own two feet. Yup. There's no spinning this into gold. Trust me. Everyone tries."

"On Thanksgiving? What'd you do to deserve that?"

"Who knows? I've been independent ever since." I retrieved my purse. "You see why moving in with you is a big deal?"

"Does this change our getaway plans?"

"Maybe. They're coming for my birthday in two weeks."

"Your birthday! When's that?"

"Ah, something else you didn't know. April twenty-fifth."

"You're a Taurus!" he exclaimed with childish delight.

"Correcto! When's your birthday?"

"No, no. You're going to be thirty six, right?"

"Whoa. Good memory."

"Thanks," he said. "Hey, where d'you want to eat? Or can we order in? I'd be down with some TV time and takeout."

"I was hoping we'd go out. Looking at the boxes makes me want to pack or clean—or both."

"But if we stay here, we can get a jump on an excursion before your parents descend." He nodded his head like he knew he got me.

"I sent Amy some pictures of your house. I told her I might need some time off. I guess I'd rather not waste it."

"And that's why I love you," he said, enveloping me in his arms. It was the first time anything along those lines had been said and I heard it. It was ringing in my ears. It had a sweet, sweet sound to it.

I looked into his eyes and watched the smile fill his features. He was confident.

"I—" I stumbled, blushing. "You're making me horny," I said slowly processing his proclamation.

"Dear girl, I love you and if you're not ready to say it—that's the best possible response you could give me." He kissed me in a way that awoke every sleeping portion of my being. I wanted to strip his clothing off and throw him on the couch. I wanted to spend countless days with this man and this man alone. I wanted to be with him now and always.

I put my arms around his neck and jumped into his arms. "I'd rather stay in, please." I traced my tongue around his ear, goose bumps marching across his shoulder.

"Oh, Sarah." He shook his head. "You're something else." He strode to my room, knocking me into the doorframe.

"Ouch!" I cried, banging my elbow.

"Sorry. You do make a better door than a window." I buried his face in my cleavage.

"At least there's a great view." He kicked the door shut. "I'm going to waste away to nothing with you, you know that? All these calories out and no calories in. My mom's gonna be all over you!"

"If you ever mention one of our parents in our bedroom again, that'll be the last time!" I said, dropping onto the bed.

"Too much?" He tore his shirt off with a vengeance.

"Much too much," I replied, guiding him on top of me. My legs encircled him. He was trapped.

He was poised for the perfect push up, his face inches above mine. I wanted to touch him badly. It was as if we were memorizing each other's every last laugh line; maybe doing a little soul searching.

When I couldn't hold it any more, I screamed girlishly and looped my arms loosely around his neck. I loved this guy.

Grimacing, he slowly leaned in and kissed me lightly on the lips. Opening his eyes and lowering his weight on to me, he kissed me again. It was rare for me to let someone else control everything in the bedroom but this once, I let him.

~~

We were like an old married couple who no longer needed to speak to communicate. He turned on the TV as I warmed up Jess's leftovers. I knew I was glowing. Had Jessica been awake, she would have retreated to her bat cave.

"Is this how you decompress after a rigorous shooting schedule? By living by no schedule at all?" I asked during a commercial break. "I should be getting my beauty sleep."

"I have never spent more time in bed, personally," he said, his eyes glinting. "Consequently, I have never been more relaxed. You've brought me peace."

I warmed with his unsolicited praise. Our relationship was the best he'd ever had. This was heaven on earth.

He rubbed his belly. "Jess is a damn good cook. Do you ever return the favor? I get the feeling she's the maid in this relationship."

"Ha. She *never* cooks. She usually consumes my leftovers. What you've experienced is an anomaly." I took the plates back in the kitchen. Getting a glass for water, I screamed. Jess had found a place for her dick pic, right next to the glasses.

"Did you forget Jessica's sleeping?" Chris asked, bringing the bottles to the kitchen.

"Serves her right if she wakes up!" I closed the cabinet. "She put a dick pic up instead of Mike. What the hell? Where'd she put Mike?"

"Hopefully where he belongs." He craned his head to catch a glimpse.

"Holy hell! You're curious! No dick pics for you—to the couch, sir!" I said, pointing.

Bowing his head in mock shame, he shuffled back to the couch, picking up Jessica's book. "*Twisted River*—What's her book about?" he asked, checking out the back cover.

"Zombie apocalyptic love story. It's a quick read."

"I'll have to check it out. How long has she been writing?"

"As long as I've known her. That is the first one she published. She's got another two out now in the same series. My mom was just telling me that she's expecting one to be made into a movie so I can go to a premiere with Jessica."

"She'd take you?"

"Until recently, I'd've said unequivocally, yes. Now, I don't know what she's got with Ian."

"It's a wonder if she's got *anything* with Ian." He snorted.

"What do you give their friendship, what odds?"

"For long term success? He's not built for endurance. I can say that he's been in more contact with her than I would've thought so who knows."

"I wonder if she gave him the book. I'm gonna have to ask her."

"I bet he found it on his own. He has an intrinsic need to understand motivations, people. She probably doesn't even know that he's read her book."

"Why wouldn't he tell her?"

"That's who he is. He's a collector of information. If you don't need to share it, if you'd gain nothing from sharing what you know, why would you?"

"Because it shows that you're interested in someone."

"Bingo!"

"That's a bad thing?"

"Could be for him."

Reading her book had to be a good sign. He was curious about her and must've found her worth his time. I was looking forward to talking to Jess, maybe surprising her with this revelation. It was rare that I surprised her with anything. She was always one step ahead of me.

With the credits running, I switched gears. "Hey, what is your next project?"

"Work?" He patted the couch next to himself. I cracked another beer and sat.

"*Tall Lara*."

"What is it about?"

"Cinderella love story."

"Are you the lead?"

"Yup."

"Who's the girl?"

"Imogen Simmons."

"Whoa, she's beautiful. Is there a love scene?"

"Yes."

"More than one?"

His lips curled into a smile, he licked the edge of the beer bottle.

"The whole world is going to watch you making love to an amazingly beautiful woman."

He set the beer down. "The whole world is going to watch me *act* with a beautiful woman."

"Come on! She's stunning. You can't tell me that you don't get turned on."

He laced his fingers through mine. "Haven't you ever been in a situation where you've kissed someone, or been in bed with someone, and you've phoned it in? And that person has no idea? Think of it like that." He stared at me, gauging my expression. "It doesn't *mean* anything to me. There's no boner." A smile spread across his face, "Are you—*jealous*?"

"Um. I'm not sure I buy it." I climbed into his face. "Knowing that my boyfriend, who is devoted to me and me alone, will be with another woman? Everyone I know will see it. They'll come to their own conclusions." I settled into the couch. "It's a little disturbing."

Snaking his arm around me, he said, "Don't be disturbed. I won't be 'with' her. It's a job. It's a *great* job but it's still a job."

"But it's a job where you don't come home. You're with her."

"I'm not sleeping with her extracurricularly, dear girl. I do go to *a* home."

"Will you be naked with her?"

"She and I were talking about that."

"*WHAT!?!?!*"

"When they were thinking of casting her, I talked to her about the project. I wanted to get a feeling for her."

"Yeah, I bet you did," I scoffed.

He scowled. "Do you think we all just show up on the day of filming and get naked?"

"I don't know what to think."

"It's not like that. I like to know people beforehand."

"Are you still talking to her?"

"Like on a daily basis, no. She's in a relationship, too. Really—no big deal."

"Who's she with?"

"He's not in the talent-side of the business. It's my understanding he's a writer."

"That happens? I always think of you guys staying with the pretty people."

"Why can't writers be pretty? You're gorgeous and you've been hiding in the deli."

"You're odd, you know that?"

"Why? Because I can see past the apron?" he said, pulling at the front of my shirt.

Swatting his hand, I lamented, "Do you know how hard it's going to be to be away from you this fall knowing that you're lounging around with another woman?"

Staring at him, I watched his features change from amusement to seriousness to something in between. "What will be harder? Being away from me or thinking of me working?"

"Being naked with another woman, you mean."

"*Acting* with an actress."

"Too bad you won't be acting like you're naked instead of being naked."

"That'd make a difference? No one said we're going to be parts-on-parts, Sarah. It's a *movie*. Maaaaake believe."

~~

In the morning, I stumbled out of the room while Chris and Jessica were sharing some coffee.

"Don't you ever sleep?" I groused, rubbing the sleep from my eyes.

"Just hungry," he said apologetically.

"Morning, m'dear," Jessica said, getting me a cup of coffee.

I pulled up a stool. "Hot!" I screeched. "Did you eat?" I asked, eying the plates near the sink.

"I had a snack," Chris said. "I'll be ready to eat when you are. We were talking about going out to breakfast."

"I need a shower," I said, blowing on my coffee.

"Coincidentally, so do I!" He sat up ram rod straight.

Jessica laughed. "You two are something. Can you do *anything* alone?"

"Hey, she makes sure I don't miss a spot," he said with mock defensiveness.

"Whoa, what she must've scrubbed off when you two met! Years of filth." She smirked.

"I'm not gonna lie. Those were some *dirty* showers." Seeing these two interact confirmed that things were good, that I wasn't delusional. They enjoyed each other as much as I enjoyed them. I hastily finished my coffee and slid off my stool.

"I'm gonna shower. When're we leaving?"

Jess smiled. "As soon as you two are decent."

~~

Jonesing for their French Toast, we went to the Sunrise Café. The waitress, Gloria, was so happy to see Chris. He regaled her with a few stories that had her tittering. When breakfast arrived, we started kicking around ideas.

"I'm a big fan of going to a National Park," Chris declared, cutting into his toast. "I haven't been in a couple of years. We could take tents or get a cabin near the park."

"I went to the Grand Canyon ten years ago. I'll never forget the vault toilets without doors. It's weird being exposed to the elements. I saw the sunrise while perched on the can," I said, thinking about the last major trip I took with my ex.

"Sounds like a vote for a cabin. Jess?"

"Pooping out in nature or being responsible for the move? Thanks, guys. Great choices." She stuck a forkful of French toast in her mouth.

"Sounds like another no vote to being outdoors. You are coming?" he asked, finishing his orange juice.

"No, I don't think so. You two should get away. I will occupy myself—but thanks," she said definitively.

"Okay. Sarah! You call it." He pointed his knife at me.

"I was pulling for beach. I love the water. How long, d'you think?"

"Your parents are coming in two weeks so how about a long weekend?"

"Wait. Your *parents* are coming?" Jessica almost spit her coffee at me.

"Exciting, isn't it?" I said, smiling and batting my eye lashes.

"Oh, Chris—has she *told* you about them?" Jessica inadvertently knocked her plate.

"A little. I tried to tell her that they can't be all bad," he said tentatively.

"Ha. I—when're they coming?" Cutting me off, she said to Chris, "You do know that they always stay with her? That means they're going to be under *your* roof!"

"It's a big roof," he said undeterred.

"It's about to get *a lot* smaller, m'dear," she said with a snort. "A lot smaller."

"It's only a week. I can handle anything for a week," he said pleasantly.

"You're a Riley virgin. Sarah, this is awesome. If he survives—" Her eyes said what she did not. If he were to survive a visit from my parents, he really would be someone worth keeping around.

"He's gonna be a great lifeline. He's very good at working people," I said supportively.

"You better take her to the beach. She's going to need all the good juju she can get to make it through. Maybe you do a National Park once they've left." She paused, deep in thought. "This means they're here for your actual birthday?" She frowned.

"Yes, ma'am. Mom saw the magazine. She's not sure if she's coming to save me or to indulge herself. She thought I might be riding your coattails to stardom, that maybe one've your books was becoming a movie."

"I wish," she said longingly.

"A beach, huh?" Chris said, staring intently at me. "How do you feel about planes? We could hit Hawaii for an extended weekend. They're the best beaches anywhere."

"You've been?" I asked, envious.

"A couple of times."

"I'm not gonna lie, I hate planes. My anxiety is huge." My stomach twisted at the mere mention of flying.

"It's not that bad from this coast. We could do first class. You could have a couple of drinks and you'd have me to hold your hand. Come on. You know you want to," he said reassuringly.

"I dunno. That's adding anxiety to my anxiety. Maybe staying local is better? And we do something after they leave? That sounds pretty good to me," I said, convinced.

"Okay." The resignation in his voice was evident. He flagged down the waitress and paid our bill, leaving her a generous tip.

~~

During the week, the moving company came. With no active role to play, we hung out at the pool. It was relaxing but I still felt like I should help, hold a door or something. These professionals were really sweating by the time they toted the last items all the way to the guest house.

Once they left, Jess decided to attack her place and make it her own. I followed her briefly to help her hang assorted strands of lights and to feng shui her furniture. Once she was down to the details, I lumbered back to the big house. I wasn't at a place where I could call it *my* place. Everything about it was foreign to me.

For starters, it was enormous and new. It was breezy and clutter-free. All of my stuff fit neatly into one of the spare rooms. It kinda looked like the kid's room in mom and dad's house.

Chris was in the kitchen. He was opening drawers and cabinets, checking out what we still needed.

"Can opener, huh? Sounds like we're going to be cooking," I said, rubbing his back.

He stuck the pencil behind his ear. "You laugh, but if we're going to live here, we need this stuff. Have you looked at how far the walk is to borrow sugar from a neighbor? Unless you climb privacy fences. And then you're taking your chances."

"Who *are* your neighbors?" As the house was palatial, the idea of neighbors was comical.

"Haven't lived here. Don't know. Want to bake some cookies and walk 'em over?" he asked, finding the thought humorous.

"Not today. D'you think that'd work?"

"Nope. Our home is our castle. We don't want any riff raff coming up the driveway."

"I think I could easily be mistaken *for* the riff raff! Better meet the neighbors so they don't call the cops on me or Jess." I sat down at the island, surveying the surroundings. "We're really going to stay here?" I asked, incredulously.

"My sources say to yes." He pretended to consult a Magic 8 Ball.

"All this space is overwhelming. When I went upstairs, they packed all my stuff in one bedroom. There's even plenty of room to spare!"

"It doesn't have to stay there. Bring a blanket down. Throw it on the couch. Or a pile of books. It'll make it feel more lived in."

"It's funny that you're inventorying the kitchen when I don't see a single TV. There are so many things that you don't have. Maybe that's what we can bring down here is my little old school TV. I can't miss some of my shows!"

He started another sheet of paper. "The TV drops down from the ceiling in the living room," he said pointing his pencil in the general direction. "So cross that off your list. You want to take a tour together and get the big things jotted down? I hate shopping. You want to do it?"

"Sure, but don't expect me to know how to pick the best TV or whatever. I've never looked at new electronics of the magnitude that this house requires."

"I know you think this house is overwhelming but it won't be long before it feels right. Trust me."

We spent the next couple of hours, going room to room. When we returned to the kitchen, we finished it off with a grocery list.

"You know what's even scarier? Grocery shopping. I don't do it," he said, looking in the fridge at the miscellaneous condiments and beer that made it from my apartment.

"I noticed. I like to shop and cook. That's my first priority—going out and bringing home the bacon!"

"Do you *eat* bacon?" he asked, curiously.

"I love it. I don't eat it all the time but once we get some pans, I'ma cook me some bacon." It wouldn't take a whole lot of bacon to make the kitchen look lived in. It's such a dirty, oily, nasty food and this kitchen was pristine.

"What're you thinking about?" he asked, watching me intently.

"Bacon air freshener."

"Whaaat?" he said, not sure if I were serious.

"I was wondering if I am going to be responsible for cleaning this place. It could be a full time job." I quaked at the thought.

"Whatever you want. If you want me to keep the service, that's cool. If you're particular about your cleaning, you can do it or you can just get particular with the cleaning crew. I'm *sure* we can find more interesting things to do with our time than clean." He leaned over and kissed me delicately on the lips.

"What I want right now is to figure out food, maybe check on Jess."

"Why don't you send her a text? She can come up here when she's good and ready. I'd like you to myself for just a little while." He kissed me again.

"Are we going to make out in the kitchen?" I asked breathily.

"Nothing to stop us," he whispered, kissing my neck.

"How d'you ever get anything done?" I whined, goose bumps rising on my skin.

"Priorities. One must have priorities," he purred, pulling me into an embrace. He was really good at adjusting my priorities.

~~

Later, my mom called again to give me flight details and a hard time.

"Sarah, your dad pulled up a satellite image of the address you gave us. It's a funny joke. That place is *huge*."

"Really?" I inquired. "You looked at satellite images?"

"Honey, Dad was curious so he put in your address. Up popped this enormous Spanish castle that appears to be gated with multiple other houses. Your Dad thought it was a pretty good joke. He was looking forward to staying in the one with the pool."

"Ah—of course. Does he know he could fall in if he's drinking?"

"Oh, honey. That's not very nice. Can you give us your real address? It'd give him something to do, to find your real house."

"Sure," I said, giving her our last address.

"That one sounds familiar! That's what I have in my address book. We're really looking forward to seeing you. Have you had any luck getting us tickets for any of the shows that record out there? Dad was watching a Food TV show and has a list of restaurants he'd like to find. I can't remember them but one of them was a Coney Island! He was so surprised that you have a Coney Island in Los Angeles. Of course, I was telling him I'd rather eat Mexican food. There're so many Mexicans out that way, it's gotta be good stuff, right?"

"I don't eat out, Mom."

"I thought Mexican food was cheap. It's just rice and beans and aren't they all illegal immigrants, anyway? That's the place I want to go eat—the dirty dive that's in a gas station!"

"I'll have to ask around. I'll meet you at the baggage claim, okay? I really gotta go."

"Sure, honey. Oh, your dad found your house. Do you share the house with another family? It looks like a duplex."

"The house is a duplex."

She giggled. "We promise we won't be too loud. See you tomorrow."

~~

# 15

In the morning, I was a nervous wreck. Seeing my parents was never easy. My dad already had plenty of time to be drinking. I never knew what he was going to say and he eagerly shared his opinions. Mom could be a callous Negative Nelly. I usually felt all my goodwill dissipate within an hour of her presence.

"You going to be ready to go soon?" Chris asked, massaging my shoulders.

"As ready as I will ever be. Are *you*?" I asked, turning around.

His smile was reassuring. "We'll park the car and go in together. It'll be *fine*, Sarah." He kissed my nose.

"You have no idea what it's like to bring them around a new person. I never know what's going to come out of their mouths. It wouldn't surprise me if they're all nice around you. But I'll get an earful about the color of the paint in their bedroom or something as soon as you leave the room."

"Then I won't leave you alone with them."

"I love the sound of that but it'll happen."

"What'll happen?"

"Me being alone with them. We can't plan out bathroom breaks that closely."

He laughed. "Well, I will do my best to be on guard."

"What are we going to do for wheels, cram them in the Mustang?"

"It'll be a tight squeeze but they're not moving in. It'll be okay."

"Do you want some?" I asked, refilling my travel mug.

"Sure, then we should get going. We don't want them to think we're lost."

"Or not coming. They might grab a cab to my duplex."

"You didn't tell them you moved?"

"I gave them the new address. Dad went online and found the satellite images. He decided there was no way I could live there."

"Did you explain the images to them?"

"No, there'd be no convincing them. Besides, I like the idea of how surprised they're going to be when we pull in over here. That should be enough to throw them off their game for a while."

~~

We walked into LAX holding hands. I was jittery. Coffee was the worst thing I could have done this morning. Finding the baggage claim, their flight information was on the board but no bags were zipping around. I paced. When I came to a standstill, Chris moved in behind me. Within moments, I leaned into him, his calm demeanor soothing.

"I am surprised by how keyed up you've been today," he said, resting his chin playfully on my head.

"I don't see them very often. I have a lot of 'what ifs' that I can't control."

"If you have no control, don't fixate. Que sera sera." He chuckled. "Sounds a lot like your name," he added, hugging me.

As the baggage carousel began moving, I stiffened. This shit was about to get real. Sensing the change in my posture, he kept his arms loosely around me and put his head on my shoulder. He alternated between rubbing his face on my ear and whispering sweet nothings into it. Both were blissfully distracting.

Passengers began rounding the corner. I took a step out from Chris's arms, craning to see if my parents were in the first wave. The more folks who rounded the corner, the more I suspected that my parents missed their plane. It wouldn't be the first time my dad had inopportunely passed out.

I called them. Mom answered just as she came into view. I hung up without speaking, relieved.

Mom was still struggling with her phone when she locked her eyes on me.

"Sarah! Oh, it's so good to see you!"

"How was your flight?" I asked, giving her a one-armed hug.

"Fine. There was a kid kicking your Dad's chair but—"

"I got the flight attendant to bring me another beer," he said amicably.

My parents simultaneously turned to scan the belt for their bags.

"Are you going to introduce us," Chris whispered, as they pulled Mom's bag off the belt.

"Sorry. Just wanted to see if they'd notice you."

"They look like good old New Englanders."

As Mom lugged her bag back towards me, Chris intercepted her. Before anyone said a thing, Mom's eyes grew nine sizes. Her knees buckled and she dropped her bag. Chris grabbed her arm to steady her.

"Mom, this is Chris Sparks."

"Oh, I *know* who this is, Sarah!" She put her hand on his. "Hello, Chris! I am—what are *you* doing here?" she asked, fluttering her eyelashes.

Chris smiled and deferred to me as my Dad joined us.

I blushed. "Mom and Dad—this is Chris Sparks."

My mother rolled her eyes. "*Of course it is*, Sarah. You just said that! Are you two together?" she asked, her voice going up an octave.

I nodded, embarrassed by her reaction. "Chris, this is my mom, Lucy."

Dad clapped Chris on the shoulder and chuckled loudly. "You're her *boyfriend?*" He extended his hand. "Carl. Carl Riley." He shook Chris's hand firmly. "When she went out to Los Angeles, we thought she'd be dating women." He rolled his bag over. "How'd that happen?"

"Listen, are you hungry? We can pick something up before we head to the house," Chris offered, taking the handle of Mom's bag.

"Oh, well. I'd like to get something to eat. Sarah always makes elaborate meals. I want to eat *now*, not five hours from now," she said as a backhanded compliment.

"Great!" Chris took my hand and steered us out of the building.

# PERFECT

When he triggered the alarm system on the Mustang, my dad hooted.

"That your car? D'you like how it handles?" He only drove older foreign cars. He was obviously impressed.

"You can drive it later if you like," Chris said, opening the door for them to pile in.

"I'll get in the back," I offered, sliding in behind Chris's seat.

"Dad, you sit up front," Mom said, climbing in the back next to me.

Watching us jockey for space, Chris smiled apologetically. "Sorry, but I think you're going to have to keep the bags on your lap."

My mom giggled like a school girl. Nothing Chris could do would be wrong and for that, I thanked Allah. Dad eagerly climbed into the front seat, studying the instrument panel.

"Why'd they put seat warmers in a car in Los Angeles? Don't they know it's warm already?" He chortled self-importantly.

"You'd be surprised at how cool evenings can be," Chris said.

My dad harrumphed. It wasn't long before we hit the drive through for a couple of Double Doubles and some Fries Animal Style.

While we waited for the bag, Mom said, "That wasn't on the menu. Why're you ordering things that are not on the menu?" She was baffled.

"Welcome to Los Angeles," Chris ventured. "This is just one of the off-the-menu-but-always-available-to-those-in-the-know items." He handed the bags to my dad.

"Don't make much sense to have items not on the menu. How'd we know to order them if they're not on the menu? They covered with grasshoppers? Extra lettuce?" Dad opened the bag and peered inside. "Smog makes you people crazy."

I strained around a suitcase. "No, the 'Double Double' has extra meat and cheese and 'Animal Style' takes fries to a whole new level. You'll like it."

He buried his nose in the bag. "Smells good."

Closer to the house, Mom was overwhelmed by the west coast greenery and palatial homesteads. She asked Chris who lived behind each gate.

"I told Sarah we should walk around the neighborhood with cookies to meet our neighbors," he said, pulling into the driveway.

155

"Is this *your* house, Chris?" my Mom asked, mouth agape.

"Welcome!" he replied as the gate swung open.

"Sarah Elizabeth Riley! Why didn't you tell us you—" My mom couldn't even finish her thought.

"I tried to tell you. I gave you the address," I offered weakly, as we pulled up by the fountain.

Mom flew out of the car, forgetting all about me under her bag. She walked around the fountain slowly, taking everything in. My dad was awestruck, staring at the house itself.

Chris pulled the bag off me and helped me out of the car. He gave me a reassuring smile before letting me join my folks.

"It *is* something, isn't it?" I asked, stepping beside my Dad.

"There are three houses on this property?" he asked, incredulously.

"Yes, sir. Come on. We'll give you a tour," Chris said, opening the front door.

I dragged their bags.

"Wow. This is amazing. It's like a five star hotel!" my mom said, loudly. "I expect to hear my voice echo… echo… echo…" She made herself laugh.

"I think it did echo when we moved in. It was pretty empty."

We followed her into the living room. "It's pretty empty *now*. How long have you lived here?" she asked Chris as she admired the patio.

"We moved in just the other day. We've tried to get some stuff in so you'd be comfortable. There's still a lot to do," he said, taking my hand.

Dad dropped the bag on the island and pulled up a stool. "You gonna eat?" he asked, ripping open a burger.

Mom couldn't help herself. She wanted the full tour right away. So much for not leaving me alone, I thought. She went through every closet and was as impressed by the master bedroom's closet as I was.

"What on earth are you going to do with this closet?" she asked while checking out the shoe tower.

"Wouldn't you like to have one?" I mused, looking out the front window.

"Oh, Sarah! How did you meet him? I still can't believe you didn't tell me. I'm your *mother* for crying out loud! What if something'd happened to you?" She emerged from the closet. "I wouldn't have been able to find you!"

"Jess always knows where I am."

"Oh, Jessica! How is she?"

"Fine. She's living in the guest house."

"What? Why is that? I thought she was a successful writer!"

"She is but it's sort of—"

"Temporary? I understand. Nice of you to let her live with you. She'd do it for you."

I liked when my Mom filled in the blanks that really didn't matter. It made my life so much easier when I didn't have to explain.

She sat on the bed and felt the comforter.

"He's your boyfriend? Is he a good boyfriend? Is he like the movies—more like Captain Orion or that goofy little detective? He was so cute with that big mustache." She tugged suggestively on the bedding.

I wanted to die. "Honestly, Mom. We never had The Talk when I was a kid and you want to—" I stuck my tongue out at her and left. Whatever scenario she was working out, she needed a minute. I did not want any follow up questions.

With a deep breath, she followed me downstairs. The guys were polishing off their burgers.

"Do you want a glass of water?" I asked, as my mom sat down and opened her food.

"So, what'd you think? Want to stay upstairs or in the pool house?" Chris asked, passing the glass down to my mom.

"This is a very nice house, Chris. Does the pool house have furniture in it or is it empty?"

With an indecipherable look on his face, he responded, "Like this house, it has a lot but is missing some things. I think you'd be comfortable there."

Taking a bite of her burger, Mom frowned. "This is cold. D'you have a microwave?"

Chris tossed it into the microwave. Waiting for it, he said, "Would you like to see the pool house once you've eaten?"

She spit out an Animal Fry. "Yes. I would. If the bedroom is complete, that would be a nice place to stay for the week. Does it have a coffee pot?"

Chris brought her burger back. "I believe that it does. I can't swear to it. You could always come over in the morning if it doesn't."

"Oh, I'd hate to bother you. I get up so early. Maybe we should go buy one?" she said eagerly to me.

"Let's *eat* now and then go check it out, okay?"

"Those fries are really gross. How did you eat them, Carl?" She put another one in her mouth.

"If they're so bad, don't eat them! I thought they were great. More for me," he groused, jamming in a fistful.

"Sarah, honey—aren't you going to eat something?" Mom asked. She swished the water around in her mouth.

Rummaging around the bag, there was nothing left but empty wrappers. Meeting Chris's gaze, I said, "Nope. Looks like you guys finished it off. That's okay. I wasn't really hungry."

This was textbook parents. They eat when they're hungry. They eat till they're full. They don't make sure that there is some for everyone. Dad must've had multiple burgers. Whatever the case, it was okay with me. Having them around upset my stomach.

When they'd finished, we took a brief tour of the rest of the property shy of the guest house. Looking at its landscape, Mom fell in love with the mural. She spent several minutes taking photos from every angle.

When we made it to the pool house, Dad declared he was done. He was not leaving the pool area for any reason. He very much wanted to take a nap. Chris returned to the house to get their belongings.

"This is a nice bed," Mom said bouncing on it. "Is everything here new?" she asked, looking around.

"It's never been lived in, is what I understand."

"You mean he—he's been traveling? Is that it?"

"His work does take him away from home."

"How'd you meet him, honey? He's such a gentleman!" she cooed.

"He came to get a sandwich and we started talking. That's it."

Mom glared at me, figuring out how to get more of the story out of me.

"He's friends with *models*, honey. He has had some of the most beautiful costars, too." She fixed her cold little eyes on me.

"He's going to be costarring with Imogen Simmons later this year. It weirds me out that my boyfriend is going to be in love scenes with another woman."

"Oh, you better hold on tightly! You be memorable, Sarah dear. You know that's how I got your Dad. He was a catch when he was younger and had a full head of hair. I made sure he wouldn't forget me," she said reminiscing.

"He says I'm memorable," I said firmly.

"Sure, sure. He's such a gentleman!" she said dismissively. "I would hate for this house to disappear. You know what I'm saying. Hold on. Hold on *tightly*." She walked past me into the kitchen. "There's no coffee pot. Is there coffee? I'm gonna start a list. We can go to the store. Dad sounds like he wants to stay in tonight. I'm tired, too, so let's go get the coffee pot—"

Mom was one of those people who quickly comes in and takes over. She has her own way things must be done and it is the only way things *are* done.

As we were getting ready to leave, Dad shouted, "Make sure you pick up some beer—not that microbrew-Weird Coast-stuff. Get me something I'll recognize!"

~~

The cart rapidly filled with all sorts of odds and ends that she felt we must have. I questioned who was paying for it—the underemployed daughter, the moocher or if said moocher thought that I had Chris's bankroll behind me. I frowned. I did not want to ask Chris to pay for all this crap. Did we really need a palm tree soap dish?

"Mom, I think you're going crazy. You don't need all this stuff. We came here for a coffee maker, Dad's beer and some food," I whined, putting a toothbrush caddy back on the shelf.

"Honey, the house is half empty. As a housewarming gift, here's $50 towards the bill." She rifled through her purse.

"I don't want fifty bucks. I think we should put this stuff back. I won't feel right bringing this stuff into his house."

"I thought you lived there, too? Don't you want your parents to be comfortable?"

"If you'd be more comfortable in a hotel, I am sure we can find one," I said passionately.

She glared at me, trying to break my will as she did when I was ten. I held fast. She muttered something under her breath and forcefully strode to the checkout. As she put stuff on the belt, she was sweet as pie to the cashier. She refused to look at me. With the last items on the belt, she pulled out her wallet and swiped her credit card.

She did not say one word to me on the drive home. She jumped out of the car as I was putting it into park. Chris met me at the door.

"Your mom almost ran me over in her haste to get to Carl," he said, taking the bag.

"She wasn't running *to* anything so much as away from me," I said sweetly.

"Oh, yeah? Why's that?" he asked, as we returned to get the rest of the bags.

"She was filling up the cart with crap, home furnishing stuff, that we don't need. She felt that I was paying for it and by 'I'—I mean you."

He chuckled, closing the trunk. "Good stuff, I hope?"

"If you like palm trees. Lots of palm trees and sea shells. But I told her to put it back. I didn't think we should be choosing décor on this trip."

"We've got enough bathrooms. We could have found a place for it."

"That's not the point. She used to run over me when I was little but I didn't let her today. She's *pissed*," I said as we carried the bags back.

He grabbed my bag, stopping me. His expression was warm and understanding. I relaxed. "Sarah. I know how hard it can be to stand up to your folks." He kissed me and took my bag. "Don't let them ruin your vacation."

"Is that what this is? My vacation time spent moving and dealing with my parents?"

"Depends on if you go back to work. It could be a mere hiccup as you coast into what's next."

I opened the door to the pool house and held it for Chris. Depositing the bags in the kitchen, he pleasantly addressed my mother.

"Looks like you and Sarah did a great job getting some things for the house. Thank you. I hadn't had a chance yet to think of things like a soap dish."

As he spoke, Mom's face contorted. Her internal struggle to hold onto her rage was faltering. She, like all women, couldn't ignore Chris's charm. She didn't even realize that he was intentionally laying it on pretty thickly.

He helped her unload the bags on the counter. They sorted them into piles for the different rooms. He complimented some of her selections, commenting on others. He diffused a smoldering situation completely.I knew that she would be nice to me now.

When she left with a pile for the bathroom, I flitted over to Chris. I put my hands in his pockets.

"*THANK YOU*," I said, pulling myself in closer.

"You bet," he replied, giving me a passionate kiss.

"You're really very good with difficult people."

"She's not difficult. She wants to be appreciated and now she is," he whispered, giving me a hug.

"You make a charming couple," Mom said appraisingly from the doorway.

"Thank you," we replied in unison.

"I'm tired. I think Carl and I will have dinner by ourselves. Tomorrow, why don't you come here when you're ready to go and show us the sites?" she said pleasantly.

"Sounds like a plan, Mom. What're you thinking about for tomorrow?"

"Coney Island!" Carl yelled from the bedroom.

"That's easy. We can do that," Chris said loudly for Carl's benefit.

"What're you thinking, *MOM*?" I asked again.

"Oh, I don't know. Maybe the Stars on the sidewalk? Or that garden-park thingy we passed? That looked very pretty."

"Well, give it some thought and we can pick off a couple of things, okay?"

"Great," she said, coming over and giving me a hug. "I am so glad that we made the trip out here. I was worried, you know, that maybe you needed something but now I can see you've landed on your feet." She was proud of me. "You will take care of my little girl?" she said, scrutinizing him.

"Yes, Lucy. I hope to take care of her if she will let me."

My mother blushed and giggled like a girl. "Oh, she better! You're so charming! Just like your movies!" She leaned in and hugged him closely.

As they separated, Chris was in high spirits. He thanked them again for coming out to visit. Carl poked his nose out and saluted before returning to the bedroom.

I had the door open and was halfway out before my mom let go of him. "Goodnight, Mom," I said leaning on the doorframe. "You gonna let go of him?"

She held onto his arm. "You are so muscular! I never knew how much of it was real but you're very muscular!"

For her amusement, he flexed. "Oh, my! Sarah, have you—of course you have, never mind," she added, clasping her hands in front of her.

"Before you say anything else—Chris, let's get out of here. *Please*," I whimpered, stomping my feet.

"Good night," he said, meeting me at the door.

Clutching his arm, I hurried him out.

"My mother's in love with you," I said, holding on to his hand possessively.

"She did take a shine, didn't she?" he said happily.

"If you're not careful, it will be hard to get them to leave. Did you really see all the stuff she bought? She's setting up *shop*."

"She's just getting comfortable."

"I'm glad that they have return tickets. I could see her staying past that ticket if there's any indication that we'd let her. She is really good at having other people do everything. I think she sees you and your dollars."

"You *really* don't like her, do you?" He put his arm around my shoulders as we approached the patio.

"I know her and 'to know her is to love her' as they say."

"Why don't you relax and I'll get us a beer?" he said, pausing by the lounge chairs.

"Why don't you bring them all?"

I collapsed into a chair. What will we do with them for an entire week? We had six more days to go. Dropping them off for a taping was sounding better and better. I wouldn't have to stay and I certainly wouldn't have to talk to them for hours on end. What else would necessitate silence— a movie? A performance? Maybe a tour of Warner Brothers or Paramount Studios. That'd eat up time.

Chris waved a beer in my face. "You didn't even hear me, did you?"

"Sorry, just thinking about what we can *do* with them this week. Are you willing to be the tour guide?"

"Of course. It's not every day I meet the in-laws. You thinking Santa Monica Pier or maybe Muscle Beach? I bet your mom'd get a kick out of Muscle Beach."

"I hadn't thought of that! That's a great idea. I was thinking of maybe a studio tour or a taping. Do you think we could get them in to see something?"

"Absolutely. It's easy to get into a lot of them—Wheel of Fortune, Jeopardy, Let's Make a Deal." He pulled his phone out. "Let me ask around and see what we can do."

"You're great, you know that? You took my shrew of a mother and made her smile. You let them decorate your house. Now you're going to use your connections to entertain them? Awesome."

Glancing up, he said, "You're welcome."

I took a couple of hearty gulps. "My parents aren't going to last all week in there without a TV either. That's one thing we probably should have picked up for my sanity."

"We can take your old TV down there. Plug'er in and they should be good to go."

"I can't go down there again today," I said, finishing my beer.

"Yeah, I can see that. You *drained* that thing!" He leaned over and took my empty.

"Any more of those?" Jessica asked, coming up from her house.

"Hey, Jess!" I said, about to get up. Chris put his hand out to keep me in my chair. He opened another and handed it to her.

"Thanks," she said, getting comfortable. "Your parents make it in okay? I thought I'd've heard them by now."

"Mom and I did some shopping while Dad waited for his beer."

"Good ole Carl. He doesn't change, does he? Did you find him something 'he'd' recognize?" she asked sardonically.

"Sure did. He was explicit—no weird coast microbrews. I was very thoughtful. I got him a case."

"The best beers come in cases, don't they?" she said ironically, savoring her Scrimshaw microbrew.

"Quantity over quality. Oh, yeah." To slow down my own consumption, I set mine down.

"We were coming up with the list of things to do with them. Got anything to add, Jess?" Chris put his feet up.

"For your discerning parents? I'd say—game show, studio tour, Walk of Fame. Maybe Muscle Beach? That's pretty hilarious." Jessica knew my parents all too well.

"I thought the same thing. Dad wants to hit a Coney Island that was featured on some food show, too."

"More importantly, do you have birthday plans? Chris and I have been stirring up some stuff." A devious smile flitted across her face.

"Awesome. What are we doing?" I asked, pleased that my birthday wouldn't be ruined by my folks.

"A party. Famous people've said they'll come."

"Really?" I asked, eyes wide.

"They *are* my friends." Chris shared a knowing smile with Jess.

"Now I really feel left out! Are you going to tell me anything?" I said, feeling my anxiety rising higher than my curiosity. "You do realize my parents will still be here. It can't be like Vegas. I'd never live it down. I don't want to see my parents engaging in that either. Kinda makes me ill to think of them without clothing." I shuddered.

"Touché. 'No naked parents'—great rule." Chris pretended to write it down.

"Oh, laugh it up! I'm telling ya, the potential for disaster with them is high. Could we get them out of here, like to an event for the evening?"

"What fun would that be?" Chris asked. "Your parents are charming people. They'll get a kick out of hanging out with us. I can't imagine they will be anything but pleasant."

"For an actor, you sure are limited in your vision!" I scoffed. This party would provide an opportunity for Chris to really understand at a fundamental level what he'd gotten involved with. My parents were not normal in so many ways.

While we were catching up, we heard my father bellowing. He realized that there wasn't a television in the house. As he got louder, I shrank into my chair. When it continued, Chris offered to take my TV down and see if he could do anything else to appease Carl. Beer and TV was really all he needed to be content.

"Can you please tell me what you've got cookin'?" I pleaded with Jessica.

"Just a few people more than you met in Vegas. I will tell you that you can count on seeing his costars again."

"How's Ian?" I asked trying to sound like it was the most normal question in the world.

"Good."

"Do you hear from him?" I prodded.

"Shockingly, I do. He friended me on Facebook. I can tell when he's posting stuff specifically for me. It's cute, another game to play."

"I always wondered if those Facebook accounts were manned by lackies or the real people."

"I'm sure it's both. He swears that he's behind his stuff." She picked at the label. "He found *my* profile. I tend to believe him."

"Did I ever thank you for putting the dick pic in the cupboard? I screamed when I found it. Chris wanted to check it out."

"Did you let him?" she asked, sipping her beer coquettishly.

"No! I sent him back to the couch. Rumor has it that he cannot compete in that arena."

The hint of a smile crept onto her face. "They say size doesn't matter. It's how you use it." She measured the beer bottle, driving the neck through her finger and thumb pornographically. "I dunno if I believe that any more."

"Jesus. Every time you put that to your lips, I'm gonna think about your great problem." I folded my legs under my chair. "When I was shopping with my mom, I overheard an older dude—he must've been in his 60's—he was giving advice to his son. And I quote, 'Don't ever give them the last two inches. That's what they fall in love with.'"

Jessica spit her beer, narrowly missing my face.

"Can't make that shit up," I said, smiling. "Have you gotten the last two inches, Jess?"

She sucked on the bottle in reply.

I nodded. "I think it's about time for me to go to bed. I need all of my regenerative sleep to deal with Lucy and Carl tomorrow."

"Before you go, are you working these days? Amy sent me a text. She mentioned that you'd asked for a sandwich sabbatical."

"Ha! I'm not gonna lie—I like that phrase. I have the next two weeks off for 'personal issues.' I think the idea of going back is harder with each passing day."

"Did you know that ninety five percent of our thoughts are not original, that thoughts recur day after day? Talk about wasted energy." She read the label on her beer. "What'd happen if you just didn't go? After a while, they'd *know* you quit."

"True, but I also want to leave open the possibility of returning if I need it."

"You will never *need* it. Jobs are everywhere and you're a great person. You will have what you need." She patted the beer off the chair with her scarf. "Don't worry about it!"

"How are things going for you, anyway? Professionally, I mean."

"Good." She felt her scarf, dabbed some more. "Out of the blue, I received an inquiry about *Twisted River*. I don't know if it will go anywhere but the inquiry said something like, 'Jessica St. Aubin, this is your Faery Godmother and today is your lucky day!' I haven't gotten back to the lady yet but she's with an agency. It sounds like they're interested in developing it."

"Say what? How'd that happen? Have you been pushing it?"

"Uh, no. I've been working on another series all together. I haven't thought much about my zombies."

"You'll have to keep me posted. I hope it goes somewhere!"

"I know and if it does, I can get my own place! Do you know how long a walk it is to get back there? I need a golf cart!" She polished off her beer.

"I bet there is a golf cart." As Chris came into view, I said, "D'you have a golf cart? Jess is tired of the walk."

Chris was shaking his head. "Your parents are funny. When I got down there, your dad was sitting by the pool making up his own dialogue. I had to ask him to repeat himself. Lucy was making a faery circle out of stones. She had a little door that she brought from home." He paused and asked earnestly, "Does she *really* believe in faeries?"

"It shouldn't surprise me that she brought a door. It's probably to help her little people find her out here. When I was a kid, she talked to tree stumps. No lie. I don't know if they responded but she could have some detailed conversations."

"Huh. Well, in any case, she said the door is ours to keep. She said they will bring us good will for years to come. I like goodwill, so let there be faeries!" he shouted, extending his arms to the heavens.

~~

In the morning, I made us a quick breakfast before checking on my parents. With the pool in view, I was startled by the number of beer cans stacked up on the table. Dad had been up late.

Knocking on the sliding glass, I announced myself and walked in. Dad was sitting at the island, beer already in hand.

"Morning, Dad. Where's Mom?" I asked cheerfully.

"Showering. That's one old TV you brought down here. I am surprised it didn't have a dial to turn," he grumbled, draining the can.

"Sorry. We just moved in. It did work though, didn't it?" I asked, looking at the TV precariously balanced on an end table in the living room.

"Oh, it works. It's a dinosaur. You can't kill those things." Out of conversation, Dad went out by the pool and put his feet up.

I was tempted to pick up the cans but my mom quickly appeared.

"Morning," she said pouring herself a cup of coffee.

"Good morning. It looks like Dad was up late," I said pointing to the pile of cans.

"Oh, gosh. I don't think those are from last night. He probably couldn't sleep. You know how early he gets up."

I raised my eyebrows but didn't pursue it. "Do you know what you want to do today?"

"I thought you were going to put it together. I don't know what there is to do," she said, her voice full of exasperation.

"Okay, Chris was looking at getting you in to a taping of a game show like Wheel of Fortune or Jeopardy. I was thinking we could find Dad his hot dogs. Maybe hit Muscle Beach or the Walk of Fame. That's a neat area. Maybe we can figure out what appeals and loosely plan the rest of your stay?" I said, hopefully.

"You do the planning, sweetheart. I don't know where anything is. Just take me in the car." She removed a price tag from the kitchen towels. "We just want to see Los Angeles and live the life."

~~

# 16

The day of my birthday, my parents were coerced into keeping me out while Jess and Chris got things squared away. We went to Griffith Park and the Observatory, two places which I'd never visited. All day, I was antsy. I wanted to be home. We were *not* to go home until they were ready.

Dad was a grouse almost as soon as we left the house. He had no particular interest in where we were going after he took the obligatory pictures of the Hollywood sign. He turned his camera on unsuspecting tourists, plants and a dog relieving itself.

Mom was enraptured with both the Park and the Observatory. She could have spent the entire day at the park installing faery doors. She informed me that there was some imbalance. The park needed healing. I could sense that she was getting closer and closer to talking to the shrubs.

When the call finally came to go home, I was overjoyed. The day hadn't been too terrible. I could have enjoyed it thoroughly had either Chris or Jessica tagged along.

Dad drove us home. He was in his element. Dad rarely let people see him excited but driving the Mustang in Los Angeles rubbed him just right. In his desire to be seen, he honked at trees and people, waving enthusiastically at his target.

Getting home, there were balloons everywhere. It looked like the circus had exploded. Nearing the pool house, there were two huge bounce houses in addition to a DJ and lots of lights. We were going to party like it was 1999.

Jessica and Chris were jumping around foolishly in the castle bounce house. It was hard to believe they'd been working on anything.

"Hi, guys," I said, peering through the mesh. "Having a good time?" Chris swung his arms, bouncing higher and higher. "I thought you were putting a party together? How come you're in the bounce house?"

"We're done." Jess landed on her butt, riding the wave of Chris's jumps. "It was more orchestration than manual labor."

Chris took one more impressive leap before coming out to hug me. "You have fun today?" he inquired, lifting up my chin.

I bit my lip. "It wasn't horrible. The Observatory and the Park are beautiful. Without the smog, I think I saw the ocean!"

"Probably did. Do you like it?" he asked, pivoting me around to see the craziness.

"Your friends are going to get down with this, really?"

"Hell, yes! The DJ will be back in a couple of hours. Food should be here any time. Beer's already here. Bounce houses, balloons—good times."

"I'd love to see you plan a kid's birthday party," I said offhandedly, admiring the princess bounce house.

"Me, too," he said a little too earnestly.

"What is the game plan?" I asked, climbing into the bounce house.

"Any time after six and they're welcome to stay the night," Chris said, gaining height with each bounce.

"Melissa's coming, too." Jessica bounced over to me. "Surprise!"

"Cool! The last visit was too short."

"You know what? You look like you could use a beer!" Jess angled her way out.

With a giant leap, Chris landed in front of me. Losing my balance, I fell on my butt.

"Happy birthday'" he said, pulling me into him for another spine tingling mini-make out session.

"Is it like a water bed, guys?" Jessica said, returning with beers.

Lying flat on my back with Chris perched over me, I blushed.

"I'd be more than happy to give you the full report if we could have a little bit of alone time. What'd'ya say, Jess? Can you be a sport and make sure Lucy and Carl are occupied?" His hair was standing up from the static.

"I'd do it for you," I said sweetly.

"You're lucky it's your birthday." She licked her lips. "You've got an hour. I've got an hour or Carl and Lucy." She set the beers down. "I'll leave these for you. I'm sure you'll be parched after your workout." She took off for the pool house, calling loudly for Carl.

His chest heaving above me, I said "I love you." I was surprised at how easily the words came out. They'd never been easy before.

A satisfied smile spread across his face. I put my hands on his biceps, feeling them harden as he lowered himself.

"I love you, too," he said quietly, returning my gaze. He rubbed his stubbly chin on mine. "Have you ever wanted to do it in a bounce house?"

"How d'you know I haven't?" I whispered, looping my arms around his neck.

~~

I tried vainly to pat my hair down. It had such a charge to it that I knew I was receiving radio signals from other planets. Chris looked much like I did—hair out of control, clothing rumpled and his face flushed. Holding hands, we went to save Jess. She had done us a solid.

"Are you playing cards?" I asked incredulously. They were engrossed at the living room coffee table.

"They're trying to teach me Kanasta," Jess said, dryly. "I've never even *heard* of Kanasta." She rolled her eyes. "They said it's easy to learn." Jessica had never been a fan of cards beyond poker. She excelled at Texas Hold'em.

"I'm stunned you're not playing poker," I said to Dad. He loved poker even though he wasn't very good.

"I said no to poker," Mom responded. "Your dad gets too competitive. I can't be around him when he loses. He's just mean."

"It's not that I'm 'mean' Lucy. It's just that I hate to lose." He played another card.

"What time are your friends coming over?" Mom asked.

"Probably in another hour or two. It's like an open house," Chris said.

"I see. Jessica was saying some of your costars are coming?" Mom dropped her cards, done with the game.

"Yes. I'll introduce you."

"Oh, that's just wonderful. Are they are charming as you are?" she asked cloyingly.

"What d'you think, ladies?" he asked, including us in the conversation.

"I'd say so," I said. "And more."

"Hey, now. More than me?" Chris asked flirtingly.

"They're charming," Jessica said. "They can get a little wild. You'll be the talk of Connecticut when you get home and tell people who you met at your daughter's birthday party!" Jessica dropped her cards as well. "Looks like you won, Carl."

He slapped his knees. "And that's how you play Kanasta!" Getting up, he asked, "Keg's ready to go?"

"Yes, sir. Can I get you something?" Chris asked from the door.

"You can drop the 'yes, sir' bullshit. I don't piss in my top hat, son." Dad headed outside. Chris just shook his head, following Dad.

"Jessica!" my mom said, clapping her hands. "Does your mother know about you and Ian? When I saw that magazine, I thought it was nice to see that you have a boyfriend. You should have kept your clothes on though, honey. The people back home, they talk. You know."

Jessica got up from the table. "Oh, I know Mrs. Riley. That party was a little out of hand. At least I know you're back there to defend my good name. I appreciate that." She patted my mom on the shoulder.

Jessica gave me a knowing look. If anyone knew about our escapades, it was because my mother was pedaling her conjectured details all over town. She had the ability to take three pictures and narrate a novel full of flavor.

Mom was flustered. "I don't know much about the other two in the movie. They're handsome! Honey, I thought you had a thing for British accents. You could have had Colin Williams!" Envisioning him, she shook ever so slightly. "He's such a dish!"

"Um, Chris came into the deli, Mom. That's how I know any of these people. Chris. There would've been no knowing Colin without knowing Chris. Chris is amazing—look at this birthday party! Talk about memories. You're gonna be talking about his for *years*."

Mom was already rewriting history for delivery back home. I could hear it in her voice. Her daughter had plenty of paramours lined up. The good news for me was that she was taken, smitten even, with Chris.

Cleaning up the cards, Mom reiterated, "I know, honey. You are one lucky girl. Hold on *tightly*. He's got such good looking costars. You better be memorable, right Jessica?" she said, sweeping into the kitchen. "You knew how to get Ian's attention! He hasn't forgotten you either. I can tell. He's a wild one and yet he thinks about you. My two girls!" Her eyes misted over with pride.

"I'm gonna go change clothes," Jessica said leaving. "By the way, Melissa should be here any time."

It was time to freshen up and text Melissa. No sooner had I sent her a text than Chris was coming up behind me.

"Melissa's here," he announced. He opened the gate for her.

"Talk about timing. I just texted her," I said, stowing my phone and heading to the front door.

"Your dad's funny. I can see some of your facial expressions when I talk to him."

"Well, I don't piss in my top hat either, Mr. Sparks," I retorted, doing my best Carl impression. My dad was an overweight, balding older man with a mottled complexion and excessively wrinkly skin. The last thing I wanted to look like was an alcoholic old man.

"When he smiles, I catch glimpses of you. I didn't say you *look* like him. You share some of the same *expressions*. That's all." Passing by me, he added, "I'm gonna have her park in the garage. Be right back!" He took off down the driveway.

Sitting by the fountain, I waited for them. The house was beautiful. The fountain was a waste out here in front of the house. Other than looking at it upon arrival, who really enjoyed it? Why put it out here instead of in the backyard?

When Melissa came out of the front door, she was squealing.

"Happy Birthday, Sarah!" She hugged me energetically. "This is incredible! What have I been missing?"

"I'm so glad they invited you! Come on inside. You're the first one here so I can give you the nickel tour. You can stake out a bedroom. I am assuming you're staying here tonight?"

"God, yes! Jessica and Chris were kind enough to share the guest list with me and I gotta say—awesome!" She and I cruised into the house. "Did they really get you a bounce house? I couldn't tell if they were joking."

"They sure did!" I responded, climbing up the stairs. "When I got back—I was exiled today—Jess and Chris were jumping like little kids in the castle. I don't know how they got anything done."

"All work and no play—" she said.

"I get it, trust me, but when you see all the effort—the millions of balloons—" I paused at the top of the stairs. "Feel free to check it all out. Nothing's sacred," I said, moving aside.

"Is this the master bedroom?" she asked, entering the room we'd set up for Mom and Dad.

"Nope. It's nice though. Great view of the fountain."

"Holy shit. I can't wait to see the master bedroom if this isn't it!" she said, coming out. "Do they all have their own baths?" She ducked into the second room.

"That one's even got a bath tub. I like to think of it as the kids' room. They put all of my earthly belongings in it and it really made it feel like the kids' room."

"Kids?" she said demurely. "You thinking *kids* with this guy?" The intensity of her gaze made me squirm.

"Let's not put the cart before the horse! I meant that it looked like a kid's room with all my stuff in it. I didn't mean that—" I stumbled over myself, mortified that anyone would think I was that far down this path.

"It's okay. I'm giving you a hard time." She touched my arm lightly on her way to the master bedroom.

"Holy shitballs! Well, this is obviously the master. I love the shoe tower of power! Nice to see your variety of flip flops elevated to their queenly position!" She chuckled. "Honestly, who builds a skyscraper for shoes and leaves a spot specifically for 'Bunnies?'" Emerging, she stopped in front of the windows.

"Those the bounce houses?" She glanced at me. "You weren't kidding about the balloons. There's a small fortune in helium out there."

"I know. I would've liked to see the elves who blew 'em all up." I joined her at the window.

"You were out?"

"Yesiree."

"I'd be tickled if someone did this for me."

"I am. Today's been great, and I say that even though I spent a lot of it with Carl and Lucy."

"I can't believe you *live* here. How'd I fall off that memo?"

"Sorry. The last couple of weeks've been intense."

"I'd say so!"

"Wanna go and say hello to my parents? I don't think they know that your house featured so prominently in the magazine. If it comes up, Lucy may never leave you alone. I think my mom is in love with my boyfriend."

Melissa laughed. "What? No! She can't be! She's *OLD*."

"He's a movie star. That transcends age."

"Eww. You might be right." She bounded down the stairs. "This place is huge!" she yelled, checking out the empty dining room and another room of unknown purpose. "What the hell're you going to do with this room? Looks like it should have a grand piano or something!"

"That's a thought. I'm having trouble taking care of the immediate needs like the living room."

"I can tell. How long've you been here?" she said, coming back to the living room.

"You can count the days on your hands."

"*And* your parents descended? Are you nuts?"

"I'm not the one who's nuts. You haven't seen Lucy in a while, have you?" I said, tsking.

"Charming as ever, I hope?"

"She even brought us a faery door and put it in the yard. Decorated and everything."

"What'd Chris say?"

"He picked a daisy for them. He still believes 'they mean well.'"

"Ah. Well, we've all been there. Did you tell him that you were tossed out at seventeen?"

"I didn't mention that I lived with you and your family though."

"That's just a detail. Not important. Any one of us would've helped you. On Thanksgiving, for God's sake!"

"Thanks, hun," I said, opening the door to the patio.

"Whoa! Booty tunes!" she said, busting a move. Chris came up the hill doing likewise, complete with a comical white man's overbite.

"DJ's here!" I said, stating the obvious.

Putting his arm around me, Chris said, "DJ's here!"

"It's hard to hear you!" I screamed. "Did you say the DJ's here?"

"I'm headed in for a few minutes. They're getting the grills going!" he added, giving me a quick peck on the cheek.

"Who is?"

"The party planning pit crew. We *all* get to have fun." He ran into the house.

"What're his flaws, Sarah, because I gotta say—they're not obvious," she said watching him retreat into the house.

"Still looking for them. Maybe his lack of vision in regards to my parents. I'm still anxious about how tonight's going to turn out. The old fogies and all of us? Beyond that, he's pretty much the ideal."

"Damn, girl. That's great. You deserve it! Can you believe that it's all because of a sandwich? What're the odds that someone like that'd walk into *your* shop and leave with your number?"

"I know, I know. If you had asked me a couple of months ago what I'd be doing, I would've said that I'd be making sandwiches and maybe waiting for divine inspiration."

"Something *divine* intervened, for sure! Is Jessica around? I want to thank her for thinking of me."

"Yeah, I'll show you the rest. We'll find her around here somewhere."

As we approached the grills, Dad was talking shop with the chef. I pitied the guy. My dad considered himself to be a Grill Master. He was explaining how to build a hot fire to someone who was trying vainly to be polite.

"Hey, Mr. Riley!" Melissa waved.

Looking up, Carl frowned, non-plussed by the sight of Melissa. Going for broke, Melissa gave him a one-armed hug. His face contorted like he'd just been accosted by a leper.

"Oh. Hello, Melissa," he said coldly. "I didn't know you were still friends," he added for my benefit.

"Tight as ever," I said, attempting to pull her away.

"You helping to get the grill going?" She admired the foot-high flames. "Looks like you used a lot of gasoline!"

"I was just explaining to this young man that he's gotta wait until that burns off or the food's gonna taste like lighter fluid."

Eyes sparkling, she looked at the well-dressed twenty-something. "Hope you've got the time for that."

He smirked at her before answering professionally. "We've done this just a few times."

"Good man!" she said, trying to find a place to high five around the fire. My hand closed around her wrist. I dragged her towards the guest house.

"He's cute!" she said, glancing over her shoulder.

"And he will be here later. Let's find Jess!"

Arriving at her door, we saw movement inside. Neither of us was prepared to see Ian when he opened the door.

"Afternoon, ladies," he said affably. He had a fine layer of sweat on his bare chest, the button to his jeans undone.

"Hi, Ian. I didn't know you were here. Is Jess around?" I asked nonchalantly.

"She's getting dressed," he said, resting languidly on the door.

"Wow! You don't waste any time, do you?" Melissa said slyly.

Turning his head ever so slowly, a smile playing on his lips, he purred, "Waste not, want not." He opened the door further. "Please come in."

"Just looking for Jess," I said, embarrassed.

Melissa took a step inward. "You alone, then or did you bring your buddies?" she asked snooping around expectantly.

"They're coming but were not as motivated," he drawled, smiling deviously in turn at each of us.

"Nice place!" she cooed, walking into the living room.

"For a guest house, it's not bad," Ian said, leaving the door open for me.

Melissa waltzed into the kitchen, checking everything out. "What a cool painting! So much nicer than the privacy fence, huh?" she said to no one in particular.

As I took another step into the living room, Ian reclined on the couch like the sexual god that he was. How he could make the act of sitting that inviting, I'll never know. He held my gaze, a thoughtful smile lighting up his features.

Trying to get control of my internal thermostat, I called for Jess. Ian snorted, like an announcement that I'd just lost a game of chicken.

"Moved in with the big guy, huh?" Ian said, scratching his chest. "Nice place."

"Yeah."

"He's on track."

"Huh?" I asked.

"He's focused in one direction," he said, extending a leg out on the couch.

Coming from him, the concept sounded like a death sentence. I felt otherwise the rest of the time. I looped behind the couch on my way to the kitchen.

"I think I will be seeing more of you." Ian absently reached for my wrist.

"Oh?" I rocked on my heels.

Patting the couch, he beckoned us to sit. Internally, I whined. He made me very uncomfortable at such close range.

Melissa, however, saw an opportunity and would have sat right between his legs had he not repositioned himself at the last second.

Grinning at him, she said, "How are you? It's good to see you!"

Regaining his composure, he chuckled. "Well. I'm well. And you?"

Melissa had endless energy and confidence. Sitting that close to Ian, she found multiple reasons to touch him. Each time, she looked electrified by her success.

When Jessica emerged, I excused myself. Trotting back towards the big house, I noticed Tom. My mother had her camera out and had my dad taking pictures of her standing between the two actors. She looked a good fifteen years younger, youthful enthusiasm radiating from her features.

"Why don't you get in this picture with your mom?" Tom said gesturing to me.

Mom was so giddy that she didn't even mind when Tom pulled me into the picture, smashing my face up against his for a very goofy, overly friendly photograph. With my head pinned to his, I crossed my eyes and grinned toothily. I received a huge, on-the-mouth kiss for my efforts.

"That's a fun one!" My dad chortled.

"Hi, Tom," I said, disengaging.

"Hello, Sunshine!" he said, draping his arm around my mom's shoulders.

"Oh, Sarah! Tom and Chris've been so kind. Carl, show Sarah the pictures!" she said, vibrating.

"Lucy, later! Sarah, smile! Come on, Chris. How about a picture of you and Sarah?" He motioned to us.

While my dad took one of us embracing, Tom sprinted off and came back with a couple of flowers for my hair.

"It's not quite a lei but really what is?" he said mischievously.

Looking bemused, Chris asked, "Tom said Ian's already here. Is he with Jessica?"

"That's a good way to put it," I said quietly for his ears alone. Cocking his head, he raised an eyebrow. "Melissa's down there now. I told 'em that they can come and get some food when they're ready."

"Not a bad idea." Chris took a kebob off the nearest pile and handed it to me.

It smelled fantastic and my mouth watered.

"You *can* eat it, birthday girl," Chris said getting another one for himself.

Flowers in my hair, kebob in my mouth, he led me to a throne. It was oversized, purple and covered in jewels. Once I was perched, everyone got something to eat. Moments later, the guest house gang joined us at the buffet.

Jessica was in her element. I didn't realize how much she had invested in Ian, but at some level, she had. Ian appeared to be attached to her as well. He allowed Melissa to touch him but his response was markedly cooler.

As soon as Tom saw Melissa, he ran up and gave her a boyish hug and kiss. Turning a delighted shade of pink, she responded to his advances fully. I watched the color drain from my mother's face. It appeared that she felt like her chances had just been greatly reduced by the other young women in the yard.

Picking Melissa up, Tom fell back into my lap. Although it may have looked accidental, it wasn't. He craned over his shoulder and winked at me before making all sorts of noises for the benefit of his audience.

I eased my way out from under them. My dad, the unofficial photographer, showed me the picture of me getting squashed. He thought it was hilarious. The look on my face was priceless. I was going to have to relax if I was going to enjoy myself.

It wasn't long before we were all done munching and surrounded by more people—unknown friends of Jessica's, Melissa's, and Chris's. Poring over the assembling mass, I didn't see Amy.

As night fell, I was introduced to several other well-known actors and actresses. I didn't have much of an opportunity to have more than quick conversations with them. It was hard to hold a conversation when bouncing.

I was tickled by the number of adults who were willing participants, jumping their brains out. At one point, lounging and chatting women filled the princess bounce house. Out of the blue, Tom appeared, naked and leaping. Melissa took control, barking a game plan.

Pretending not to hear, he continued jumping, flopping and gyrating. Getting really wound up, he made us an offer, "Ladies! You take your clothes off and I promise I will put mine on!" He pinched the front of Melissa's shirt, animatedly peeking at her cleavage.

With no one else eager to lose their clothing, she whipped off her shirt, hurling it at him.

"There! Put *that* on!" she screamed.

The opposite of a strip tease, he sensuously guided it over his head, slowly poking his arms through. He looked ridiculous, like a magenta sausage in her tight v-neck. Extending his arms like a top, he spun. Verifying that he had an audience, he began his version of the Russian hat dance, jewels a'jangle. His agility was remarkable even if he were playing the fool.

"Why couldn't he wear it like a sarong?" I whined, laughing. My dad hovered with his camera, snapping pictures through the netting. Chris, Ian and Jessica were laughing hysterically.

I pulled the netting back at the exit.

"Hi, honey!" Mom said, scrambling past me.

I wiggled over to Chris. "Anyone know where his clothing is?"

Jessica stretched her hands out, depositing it in my hands.

"Oh, *God*! Why'd you have 'em?"

"He threw 'em at the grill and I caught 'em. He doesn't need any excuses to be naked *all* night!" she added, conspiratorially.

"You're a savior!" I shouted over the chaos.

"Happy birthday, darlin'!" She beamed.

"Have you been in one yet?" Ian said, bumping into Jessica. "The castle's looking a little unloved."

"If there's anyone who can add some love, it'd be you two." I cleared my throat.

"You can be the king of my castle," Jessica said suggestively, jogging over to the castle.

"You don't know what you're missing," Ian said to us. "But you are welcome to find out." He kissed my hand. "M'lady."

"D'you think he's serious?" I asked Chris. He seemed far less creepy chasing Jessica into the primary colored castle.

"Absolutely." After a few minutes, he said, "Hey, there's someone I want you to meet!" He took my elbow and steered me over to the pool. Imogen Simmons was holding court. I was filled with dread and intimidation. I really had no desire to meet her at all on my birthday and so I shuffled.

"Come on, silly. It's Imogen! She came here with Julian, her writer-spouse. They're even *married* so you have nothing to fear. *Nothing*!" he said reassuringly.

Rounding the fence, her eyes lit up when she saw Chris. Immediately, she was out of her chair and striding towards us.

"Chris! Thanks again for the invite!" she said, leaning in and giving him a peck on the cheek. Expectantly, she looked at me.

"Imogen, this is my girlfriend, Sarah Riley. Sarah—Imogen Simmons." Shaking her long, lean fingers, I sensed a kindred spirit.

"Sarah! It's good to meet you," she said, clasping both my hands like we were old friends.

I looked questioningly at Chris, wondering if he'd mentioned me.

She continued, "I'd like to introduce you to Julian." Pointing in his direction, he was engrossed with his phone. She chuckled. "I leave him for moments and he uses that as an excuse to write."

Julian was dressed in black, ash blond hair falling in his youthful face. Fingers flying, he didn't look up until Imogen touched his shoulders. Recoiling, he guiltily stuck his phone in his pocket.

"Busted!" she said affectionately.

"So busted. How long you been there?" he asked, squinting up at her.

"Moments. Julian—this is Christopher Sparks and his girlfriend, Sarah Riley."

I enjoyed talking to them. Julian was working on a new script. And if I followed Imogen's complaints, he was incapable of anything else right now.

He was engagingly funny. If he wrote anything like he spoke, he had to be great. I instantly thought of Jessica. It would be great if we could get their heads together. It was only my dad's guffaws that jarred me from the conversation.

He'd started a poker game and was pulling a huge pile of bills towards himself. On my way in to the bathroom, Dad called out to let me know how well he was doing against these 'West Coast weirdos.'

Inside, Mom was rummaging through her suitcase for her Tarot cards. Not only was Mom into faeries and Mother Earth, she'd also picked up Tarot card reading when I was little. She used to terrify me with her readings. They tended toward the negative. As her daughter, I didn't want her to tell me the sky is and will always be falling.

On my way out, she'd found her first victim—Imogen. God bless her heart, she appeared invested in my mom's reading. Creeping up behind Chris, I put my hands on his shoulders. He took my hand and absently kissed it. Giving my mom an audience, he was listening intently to the reading.

I had to get away from Mom, the woman who would forever seem crazy to me. I leaned over and told Chris that I was going to do a little dancing.

Although his head was bobbing, he hadn't heard me. I was pleased by his desire to make my mom comfortable. The goodwill garnered would last him a lifetime. I'd given up on those ambitions long ago. She could do whatever she wanted to do as long as it didn't hurt me.

I walked up to the DJ who promptly put a 'birthday girl' tiara on my head. It complimented my flowers nicely. After requesting a number of songs, I boogied my way onto the spacious dance floor and closed my eyes. I was ready to shake my money maker.

The dance floor filled in before my second song finished. I was aware of someone in my space, someone who was getting a little dirty in their dancing. Going with it, I performed my part as the dance pole for the better part of a song until I was forcefully spun around. Lucas had come to wish me a happy birthday.

With recognition spreading across my face, he asked, "Where's your beautiful trollop of a friend?"

"Amy?"

"Blond hair. Wild child—yes. Amy!"

"You didn't remember her name?"

Smiling wickedly, he said, "Sure I did. I haven't been able to find her. I thought you were tight."

"I don't know if she's here," I said as he snaked his arms around my waist, lifting me off the ground and into him.

"You can dance, girl!" He swung me like a ragdoll. I enjoyed my willing dance partner. The return on my effort was tenfold.

Several dances later, Lucas took my crown and stuck it in his own hair. He was adorable and knew it. Teasing me, he sauntered away and sashayed back, getting close enough that I could almost grab my crown. His towering height, however, made success unlikely.

When the novelty wore off, he grabbed another gal and spun off with her leaving me to once again wonder—*was* Amy around? And if not, why not?

~~

# 17

As the night wore on, many of our guests left. The core remained, playing poker with my dad. I was in Chris's lap while he played several hands. It wasn't long before Dad was losing to Jessica. To lose was one thing but it was entirely worse to lose a *man's* game to a woman.

After losing three hands in a row, he was enraged. He screamed and ranted about her in such a personal way that the rest of us were shocked into silence. Mom, beer in hand, ended it. Like a controlling mother, she handed him a beer, told him to get up and pulled on his ear when he did not do as directed.

He knocked the chair backward and rose unsteadily to his feet. "Watch *this* one" he said to Ian, pointing to Jessica. "She's a witch."

Wobbling and almost poking Melissa in the forehead, he added, "And you can't trust *this* one either."

He stared at Ian. "You're gonna lose. *Big time.*"

"Same old Carl," Jessica said undeterred.

"Nice ear move," Melissa commented with an embarrassed chuckle.

"Are you a witch? I would have thought you more queen of the faeries," Ian said, waiting for more cards.

"No, that's Sarah. She's my Titania," Chris said. Reaching around me to pick up his cards, he added, "Did you notice our faery door? It already looks lived in."

I poked him. The last thing I wanted to do was discuss my Mom's tight kinship with sprites.

"Did you get a reading?" I asked, changing the subject.

"Yes," he said, arranging his cards.

"Readings? Your *mom* pulled out her Tarot cards?" Melissa asked incredulously. "She's still doing that?" I nodded. "Are her readings any less caustic?"

"Chris, are you going to live to see next year?" I asked sarcastically.

He set his cards down. "Lucy says the coming years are going to bring me everything that I've been looking for." Kissing my neck, he added, "So far, she's not wrong."

"Oh, God. You two are predictably *boring*," Tom said, dropping a chair by the table.

"Hey, thank you for putting your shorts on," I said eager for the distraction. "That magenta really brings out the green plaid in your shorts."

He pulled at his chest hair tuft ruefully. "Melissa, love—any chance you want to trade shirts? Darlin'?" His eyes did not leave her ample bosom.

"Maybe after this hand," she said tartly. "It's not strip poker. You'll have to wait."

He threw himself back into his chair, whacking the arms. "I hate waiting! I don't *wait* well!" Grabbing my wrist, he modeled my tattoo for the table. "It's all about the NOW, people!" He massaged my tattoo.

"Easy, boy. *Easy*," Chris said, removing his offending hand from my arm.

"Speaking of waiting, when're you going to give her the present?" Melissa asked, peering slyly at Chris.

"Present?" I inquired, twisting around to see him.

"I did get you something," he said cautiously. Staring at him, I was waiting for a clue. "Something you need," he offered.

"Oh—out with it already. What'd you get her?" Ian said, tossing his hand down in disgust.

"Can I show her?" Melissa asked, reaching for her phone.

"You've got a picture of it?" I asked, curiously.

"Mm-hmm," she said, scrolling on her phone.

"We're trying to play poker, ladies!" Jessica said. She was anything but poker faced. She obviously had another winner.

"You know what'd be inspiring? Strip poker. You'd have my attention for that," Tom said lewdly.

"Don't get too excited, cowboy. She's winning," Ian said.

"Quite likely you'd see more of us than the ladies," Chris added, tossing in his hand.

Revealing her straight flush, Jessica wrinkled her nose. "Playing for money's a lot more fun." She stared lustfully at Ian. "Why mix business with pleasure?" She swept the cash into her lap.

"Ooh, found it!" Melissa shouted, handing the phone to me.

With Chris's permission, I looked at the picture and went white as a ghost.

"You—you got me a Jeep?" I asked, astounded.

His whole body was tense, his eyes searching for approval.

"And yes, it *is* orange!" Melissa added enthusiastically. "Do you know how hard it is to get an orange Jeep?"

"What's on the roof?" I asked. The picture looked like it was taken in our garage.

"Surf board!" Jessica said, absently shuffling the cards.

"You were all in on this?" I asked, staring at my car. "I'm not gonna lie—this is perfect." Setting her phone down, I wrapped my arms around Chris's neck and kissed him repeatedly.

"If I buy you a Jeep, can I get some of that?" Tom asked, whimpering. Opening one eye, I swung my arm out and knocked him soundly in the head.

"Heeey! That wasn't very nice," he said, feigning indignation.

"I think she liked it," Ian said, putting his hand on Jessica's thigh.

"Get a room!" Dad bellowed from the living room.

Turning scarlet, I rubbed the lipstick off his cheek. Leaning back into Chris's chest, I asked "Where're you guys staying tonight? We have some extra rooms at the big house."

"The 'big house'—isn't it *your* house?" Tom asked, needlingly.

"Still getting used to that," I said sheepishly. "Anyway, you're welcome to crash anywhere. I wouldn't recommend getting any closer to Carl and Lucy than you have to."

Jessica got up and stretched. "That castle's pretty comfortable, too." She shot Ian a come hither look.

Tom moved into Jessica's seat and immediately tried to reclaim his shirt.

"Hey!" Melissa yelped, letting him get the first couple of buttons open.

"You *are* welcome to join us." Ian looked meaningfully at Melissa and Tom. "You two, too," he said putting his hand on Chris's shoulder.

"Titania," he crooned, dragging his fingers across the back of my neck. "Happy birthday," he whispered.

I shivered and pulled my hair back into a ponytail, letting it go slowly. Chris gathered my hair and nuzzled my neck. "You ready to call it a night?" he asked lovingly.

Putting my hand on his scruffy face, I was more than ready. I stretched animatedly to get Melissa's attention. Although she looked perfectly content, I didn't want to make any assumptions.

Tom's hands on her chest, they froze like they'd forgotten we were there.

"Good night?" I said, trying to avert my gaze.

"Oh, yes. Very good," Tom answered. "Don't wait up."

~~

Once we'd safely crossed the threshold, Chris stopped me.

"Happy birthday, Sarah," he whispered, leaning into me.

"Thanks. This makes up for so many birthdays' past."

"I'm glad." He put his arms snugly around my waist. "Making you happy makes me very happy. I love you."

"One thing though—" I put my fingers to his lips. "I only saw one surfboard. It'd be better if there were two."

Taking my hand, he led me to the garage. In addition to the one on the Jeep, there was another propped up against the wall.

"Great minds," he said, lifting it away from the wall.

I circled the Jeep repeatedly. "You have the keys?"

"They're in it." He opened the door for me.

I slid into the driver's seat. "What time is it?"

"I have no idea but I'm sure it's well past one."

I caressed the wheel. "Nothing good will come of a ride." Sighing deeply, I hopped out.

"Thank you," I said, feeling incredibly lucky.

"You're welcome." He pushed me up against the hood. "I gave you a Jeep. Will you come to bed with me *now*?" His fingers curled into the hem of my skirt.

"Sounds better than screwing in the garage," I said, kissing his lips, his cheek, his neck. As he responded, I slid my hands up his shorts, feeling his body tense. His muscles engaged, he pushed with such force that I thought we could very well dent my brand new wheels.

With his hands in my skirt, I relaxed onto the Jeep. "Take me to bed." I released the death grip my legs had on his waist.

Breathing hard, he maneuvered me on to the hood. "Too little too late," he said, lifting my shirt.

With him kissing my breasts, I vacillated between 'let's do this' and 'let's-do-this-somewhere-else-before-we-ding-up-my-new-car.' Allowing a little moan to escape, I pushed back on his shoulders.

"You're worrying," he whispered, rubbing his bristly cheeks on my hand. "It's a JEEP. Its brothers have been through worse." His weight pinned my hands. Getting rid of my skirt, I was thankful that we'd already warmed up the metal.

I peeled his shirt off, balled it up and turned it into a pillow. Chris smirked, amused by my need for creature comforts. He mirrored me, pulling my shirt slowly over my head. He delicately folded it and placed it underneath my head.

"I love you, Sarah," he whispered, inches from my nose. He expertly removed my bra, covering me in lustful kisses.

He was a long drink of water. Finding his shorts was no short order. As I wrestled with the button, he snorted. "Need some help down there?"

"Unlike you, I don't have lots of practice. And why're you so long-chested? I can't even *find* your shorts!"

"Now is not the time for practice," he said, guiding my hands.

~~

We didn't emerge from our burrow until noon. I was prepared to do a great deal of cleaning up but was pleased that I didn't have to. The same crew who put it up were already half done taking it down. They'd also brought a breakfast spread that surpassed Melissa's.

Making my way through the buffet, Melissa and I kept conversation to a minimum. We sat by the pool, enjoying the midday sunshine.

After my first cup of coffee, I felt more human.

"Where'd you crash?" I asked.

"I was going to ask you the same thing! We came into the house and didn't see you anywhere."

"Must've been checking out the Jeep," I said, reminiscing.

"Oh, my god! That was *you*?" she said, lunging out of her chair. "We *heard* you upstairs! I was wondering who would be in your house but it was a party! I thought someone found a secluded spot." She tore into her Danish. "I'll spare you what we heard but damn, girl—I thought I had it good."

"Marvelous," I said, inhaling deeply. "Where is your paramour, anyway?"

"Still sleeping. Too bad he's not boyfriend material. He's a lot of fun—I mean, *a lot*." She shook the last drops of coffee in her mouth.

"It looked like you were having a really good time. I'm sorry that I've been out of touch—did you hear from him before today?"

"He asked if I'd come here and he sent me some selfies. Nothing that makes me feel like we're going to be a couple. More like he's poking around to see what kind of response he's gonna get. I don't think he really cares either. He has a healthy ego."

"As strong as his libido?"

"Ha! He almost had me convinced to stay in the castle with Ian and Jessica."

"Oh?"

"Yeah, I've never had a threesome. Have you?" She scooped some of the apples out of the pastry, licking it off her fingers. "I've never known anyone who was okay with multiple partners. And a shot at Ian and Tom at the same time?" She started fanning herself, tossing her head back on the chair. "A girl can only dream."

"So, what stopped you?"

"Who said we stopped?" she said, color sweeping over her cheeks. "They were just as interested in seeing me and Jessica together and I have never had a thing for girls. No curiosity. Nothing."

"Me neither."

"I don't think Jess was turned on by the idea." She tapped her empty mug. "But she seemed open to whatever."

"She was blinded by your beauty."

Melissa rolled her eyes. "I think it was the booze. That, and the company."

"She doesn't shy away. She had some crazy experiences and knows what to do with all of them."

"I wish I could say the same. I wish I had that kind of drive—or had had a *lot* more to drink."

"I don't know how—I gotta know—how far'd you go?"

"Jealous? Or just insanely curious?" Melissa said, eyes twinkling.

"Would it be wrong if I said both? I adore Chris and I am totally happy but those two are—they intimidate me and excite me at the same time."

"Yeah, exactly," she said, exhaling. "Clothing was off. The castle was groovin'. I've *never* had that kind of attention from guys—not one-on-one and I never thought I'd have the option of two at once. And two? Where they can—explore different areas simultaneously? I thought I might explode."

"Ooh! The big 'O'?"

"Big would've been an understatement. Is it getting hot out here?" she asked, looking around. "Suffice it to say that, if an opportunity presents itself and you can, you should."

"Damn." Having Chris as a boyfriend pretty much negated the 'can' part. On no planet would he be interested in that scenario. Only in my other lifetime would I have relished that kind of adventure. I'd put myself in some unique situations before but had never followed through.

"Mmm. We're a good match. Too bad he doesn't live in Vegas," she said ruefully. "Or looking for something steady. I'd love to get a steady piece of—"

Tom snuck up behind us. He playfully pulled her head back, giving her a face-devouring, soul-eating kiss. He was such an imp. It was easy to see why she'd be interested in a relationship with him even if his proclivities were wildly impulsive.

As they made out, I took my time getting up and refilling my coffee cup. I noticed that my parents were intently watching the shenanigans outside their windows. I was instantly embarrassed by my parents and for Melissa. What voyeurs.

I marched right up to the glass before they noticed me. Mom immediately picked up a crossword and pretended to be engrossed. Dad, however, was non-plussed by my interruption. He cracked another beer, acknowledged me and then returned his attention to them as if they were a television show.

Tom was sitting on her when I returned, clearing my throat. "Hey, my parents are in there. Why don't you take this—"

"Your parents are cool," Tom said, giving the thumb's up to Carl.

"Eww. I don't need them watching us. That's gross!" Melissa screeched, straightening up her shirt. "Get *off* me!" she yelled, shoving him.

"Aw, darlin'. That's a bummer." He rocked his hips. "You're hot," he added, springing off her lap.

Melissa's face lit up. My guess was that he'd never acknowledged her in such a way.

Tom tapped on the glass and invited my parents out. "No sense hiding in there," he said, as they emerged.

"Oh, we weren't hiding, honey," Mom said, getting herself something to eat. "We were—" she stumbled.

"No worries, Lucy." He took her plate so she could sit down more easily.

"Oh, you're just so handsome!" she blurted out, getting ahold of her plate.

He rewarded her with a mega-watt, heart-stopping smile. "Odds are two to one that you go home and tell people that I'm shorter in person."

Mouth agape, Mom tried vainly to come up with a cover but Tom was astute. My mother had sized him up, commenting on his looks rather than his shorter stature.

"That's not what I'm going to tell *my* friends," Melissa said, piping up.

He grinned and sat down on her chair, rubbing her thigh.

"You've got *plenty* of insider information," he said covertly, sliding his hand between her thighs. His eyes sparkled, daring her to continue the conversation. "And you don't have to steal my phone this time. I've got your number."

"You took his phone?" Mom tsked.

"More like borrowed. And *briefly*," Melissa said firmly.

"No harm, no foul," Tom said smoothly, grinning impishly at Lucy.

"No one should take your phone," Mom said, miffed.

"Lucy, drop it," Dad said. "Kids and their phones—it's no big deal."

"Is that a short joke, Carl? Because I've got more experience than you'll ever have," he said challengingly.

It was unlike my father to be at a loss for words. He clamped his mouth shut, working hard to come up with a witty rejoinder.

"You *are* a shortie. There. There's your short joke, you cocky son of a bitch!"

"Carl, we'd be buds if we were neighbors!" Tom grabbed one of Carl's beers, cracked it and toasted him.

Picking up the rest of his case, Dad grumbled. He fled into the house, hiding behind the tube.

"Think Jessica will join us?" Tom asked eagerly. "She's a neat lady."

"Hard to say. She's got everything she needs where she is," I replied wryly.

"Awww, come on. That's only a guest house. And some of the entertainment is out here—or wait, are we the guests to be entertained?" He crushed the beer can against his forehead. "Either way, let's flush her out," he said energetically.

"Don't you *ever* rest?" I asked.

"Hey, I don't know when you'll invite me over again. So, I'm making hay while the sun, shines," he added, batting his eye lashes clownishly.

"You certainly have a way with words."

"I have a way with more than words," he said suggestively. Under the intensity of his gaze, I dropped my eyes. "I heard you," he said kissing

Melissa's throat. He closed his eyes and inhaled deeply, his lips curled in the hint of a smile. "Just loosen up before you're tied up, ball and chain-style."

He straddled my chair, locking his arms on the back of my chair.

"Do I make you horny?" he said, mimicking Austin Powers.

His eyes less than an inch from my own, I squirmed. My mother retreated into the house.

He studied my face. Though he wasn't touching me, all of my personal space was gone. With the heat he was generating, I willed my body to relax completely, puddling into the fabric.

His eyes narrowed, a smile spreading across his face. "So, do I?" he whispered.

I idly wondered how long he could hold the squat before he'd sit on me. He leaned further in, drawing my attention back to his face. His green eyes were amazing, uncharted waters. He would have been a lot of fun had he walked into the Shoppe.

Having witnessed enough of this, Melissa grabbed a fistful of his hair and bent his face upward, planting a big unexpected kiss on him. He dropped all his weight onto my lap, creating his own threesome.

His hands fell from the chair and down my chest exploratively. When his hands slid between my thighs, I drew the line. I shoved them in his crotch. With a jolt, he broke from Melissa.

"Totally unnecessary, Sunshine," he said, covering my hands with his. "Totally. Unnecessary." He stood effortlessly, swinging his leg over the chair. In one fluid movement, he took Melissa by the waist and swung her into his lap as he sat down.

Quietly but intentionally loud enough for me to hear, he whispered into Melissa's hair, "What's it gonna to take?" His calculating green eyes wandered over my face. His hands on her hips, he slowly stroked Melissa, teasing and tempting me with his behavior.

I couldn't handle it and excused myself. I needed a moment to clear my head. The bounce houses, DJ and lights were gone but the balloons were tied to everything—trees, bushes, trellis and glinted in the sun. I was ready for my guests to leave and to reconnoiter with Jessica.

I rapped hesitantly on her door. As much as I wanted to barge in, I knocked once more. Jessica waved at me through the window. She and Chris were having coffee, sitting at the island in the kitchen.

"Hey," I said, giving Chris a kiss. "I didn't know you were up."

"Morning. I haven't been here long," he said with a perplexed look on his face.

"Ian's still sleeping?"

"In the shower," Jessica said, finding a cup for me. "Want some?"

"I'm coffeed out." I slid a chair up next to Chris. "Thanks again, guys. It's been a birthday party for the record books."

"D'you like the surf boards? It was my job to pick them out. I thought the one looked like the Rolling Stones album cover. When you're in the water, it's gonna be like you're surfing a giant tongue!"

"Think we can try it once my folks leave?"

"Isn't that tomorrow?" Chris asked, tired.

"Yes, thank god. You've survived the inaugural Riley visit. I wish I could give you a commemorative t-shirt!"

"I've got something better," he said, gazing at me intently.


"Ah, you brought your protector and savior," Tom said, saluting Chris. "I keep trying but she's a tough nut."

"Morning, Tom," Chris said unenthusiastically.

"I'm taking Melissa home so we're gonna abs-quat-u-late." He offered his hand to Melissa, helping her to her feet.

I looked at Melissa quizzically.

"Oh, he's gonna drive me home," she said euphorically.

"I'll catch up with you later. Are you working this week?" I asked, pleased for her.

"Yeah. I'll give you a call though." She hugged me. "Happy birthday, Sarah!"

"Thank you," I said, taking a step back.

"Happy birthday, Sunshine!" Tom chirped, getting an opportunistic hug before leaving.

"Thanks. Good to see you." I wove my arm around Chris.

"I'm going to walk them out," he said, walking out of my arms.

"Okay. I'll see what my parents want to do with their last day." I trudged over and let myself in. I was pleased that both of my parents were wiped out and had no inclination to do anything other than pack. My day had just improved a hundred fold. As I felt similarly, I made myself comfortable on the patio, rejoicing in the solitude.

Much later, I awoke to laughter. Jess, Chris, Ian and my mom were playing badminton. They had incredible energy reserves. Wielding a racket was about the last thing that I felt inclined to do. I wanted a waiter to refresh my drink and bring me a pillow.

"We have a badminton set?" I asked, stepping around their impromptu game.

"You do now. Consider it a housewarming gift," Ian said, swatting at the birdie.

"Just what I always wanted," I said, bemused.

"Sometimes, you don't know what you need. It was either this or croquet," he added, twirling his racket.

"And I told him that I already had that." Jessica whacked the birdie at my mother.

"Where's Dad?" I leaned on the split rail fence. "I still can't believe you're playing badminton!"

"Resting. That was a long night for us, honey." Mom ducked under Chris's swing.

"Anyone have their phone because I have to get a picture."

Chucking me his phone, Chris jumped right back into the game.

"Oh, honey! You're going to have to send them to me. It's not every day you play a lawn game with two hunky stars!" Mom gushed, putting up her racket defensively.

"Are you keeping score?" I inquired.

"No," they answered simultaneously.

"How d'you know when it's over?"

"When we put our rackets down." Ian saluted.

I rolled my eyes and got comfortable. With his phone, I posted a couple of the pictures to my page. These pictures were going to make my friends crazy. After sending the pictures to my mom, I noticed that Chris had a couple of conversations with Jess and Melissa. I read through Melissa's and was shocked by the volume of personal questions she asked and his willingness to answer them.

These were a beautiful insight into a mind that I knew too little about. Melissa asked about how he met me, why he pursued me, and what his intentions were. God bless her heart. This was a goldmine!

I read that exchange over and over again. He was in it for the 'long haul.' If he were willing to answer these questions so openly, it had to be true. I desperately wanted everyone to leave. Looking up, it appeared that the game was coming apart. The boys were hitting the birdie back and forth between them. Mom and Jess were sitting, drinking bottled water.

It was impossible to figure out Chris' relationship with Ian. There was so much history. Some sounded so unpleasant yet here they were, grinning foolishly and swatting the birdie like little boys.

~~

# 18

After sorting out departure details with my parents, I joined Jess and the boys for some R & R, which turned out to be a zombie movie and leftovers. Sharing an oversized chair with Chris, I marveled at my new circle of A-list actor-friends. Gone were the days of pseudo-solitary confinement. Between this realization and the imminent departure of my parents, I was content.

As Jess returned from the kitchen with more snacks and drinks, she said, "Is anyone going to ask Sarah?"

"Hola," I said, with a wave. "Ask me what? Is it my turn to choose a movie because I could think of a few from our collection that'd be fun."

"No, but that is a great idea." She scooted down the couch next to Ian and the guacamole.

Dead silence. "What's up?" I asked, clueless.

Jessica squinted at each of the boys, prompting them to say something. When she failed, she sighed. "They've got a benefit to go to and wanted to know if we'd go." She popped a chip in her mouth. "I said yes."

"A benefit? For what?" I asked, startled.

"It's to benefit a group like the Make-A-Wish Foundation. One of the A.D.'s on the set asked us to go," Chris said.

"*When* is it?" I asked, thinking about my lack of wardrobe and social experience.

# PERFECT

"This coming weekend," Ian said, smiling. "We're going but it would be a lot more palatable if we had dates. If, for once, I could go with friends—well, raising money for childhood cancer would be a lot better."

Raising my eyebrows, I gaped at Jess. "You're going?"

She nodded her head vigorously, swallowing her chip. "Yep."

"Yep?"

She winked. "Yep."

"That's all I am going to get out of you is 'yep'?"

"Yep," she said, grinning.

"Incorrigible!" I said, wrinkling my nose. "Chris—how am I—*what* am I going to wear? Is this one of those things where people are wearing designer everything, because I shop at Target. I don't have even have knock offs that'd fly."

"Whatever you want to wear. If you want to shop around town, go. If you want a professional to help you put together a look, cool. Whatever," he said. "And if you both want to do something together—great! Have fun with it. It's never inspiring to buy a suit but you ladies—you've got so many shiny accessories and shoes. You will look incredible." He devoured a heap of guac.

"I'm not gonna lie. I thought that we were gonna have some time to relax. I'm freakin' out a little bit."

Jessica poured a whiskey shot and slid it to me. "It's gonna be great, Sarah. And yeah, let's do it right. You send a designer over here and we'll figure it out. We can surprise you, like a wedding."

"How will we know what color tie to wear if it's a surprise?" Chris asked in mock horror.

"Oh, I think we can give you the palate. You'll just have to wait to *see* us," she said smugly.

"Dare I ask where this is?"

"Like you'd know if we told you," Jessica said sardonically.

"Hey, I bet I could search it."

"Would it make you feel more or less anxious?" she asked, pouring herself a shot.

"Depends on the answer," I said truthfully.

"It's at Pardo's. Supposed to be a really elegant place. Big, too. I think they're expecting several hundred."

"Of Hollywood's finest?" I asked.

"Thank you," Ian said, deferentially.

"How do these things come about?" I wanted details.

"In this case, the A.D.'s nephew has cancer. He was frustrated by his inability to *do* anything for his sister's family. So, what do you do? Have a benefit and invite all the people you know. The more people with connections and money, the better," Chris said. "This ain't my first rodeo. I've gone to a dozen of these."

"Combing for dates?" Ian asked cynically. "Lots of good girls at a kid's cancer benefit," he added haughtily.

"That's low." Chris frowned.

"Ha ha! But true! I told you—this boy here—he's been hunting for the perfect girl for a long time in some atypical locations."

Chris sighed. "Who made you Sherlock?"

"Not Sherlock, old chap. You're transparent, an easy read."

"Thanks."

"Could be worse. You could be trolling strip joints. At least you've done your charitable giving while in pursuit of a higher goal." He downed a shot. "You've got appeal. God knows girls go crazy for a sharp dressed man."

"Now, play *that* on the piano, Ian!"

"ZZ Top?" Ian laughed heartily. "Have you had any luck? That's the *real* question."

"Only you could make attending a benefit sound like a trip to the brothel," Chris said, laughing.

"But, am I right?" He slid Chris a shot.

"Why am I friends with you?" Chris asked, emptying his glass. "Yes," he said looking at me. "Yes. There was a point in my life when I was after an easy mark—someone who was pretty, well off and available. It was always an ego boost to leave with someone."

"Always? Like you've done this hundreds of times?" I asked, slack-jawed.

Ian hooted. "Always," he mimicked.

Chris shifted. "Not hundreds. A couple, tops." He glared at me. "You know me. Do you really think that I've misled you and now you're going to find out that I'm a gigolo?"

"There's a lot we don't know about each other."

"I'm gonna get you for that," he said, lunging for me. I hit the floor.

"And you picked them up as an ego boost? For real? You need ego boosts?" I asked, nudging him with my foot.

"Yeah, I do," he said, grabbing my calf. "Look at the competition over there. He's always got multiple girls on his arms, in his bed—" he said, looking pointedly at Jessica.

Ian was gazing intently at Jessica as well, gauging her reaction. When she didn't react, a satisfied smile crept onto his face. Not privy to their conversations, I was curious if Jess was as cool with this as she seemed to be or whether he'd cleaned up his act.

"Chris, you're not fooling anyone. You could be swimming in girls if you'd open up your search criteria." Ian poured himself a shot. "Sarah, you are the first really interesting girl he's dated." He glanced at my dreads and leather choker. "Wouldn't you agree?" he said, gliding back into the couch.

"Hey, now," he said, bristling. "Probably why I'm not with any of them," he grumbled. Clapping his hands, he added, "So, Sarah! Did you pick out the next movie?"

"What constitutes 'interesting' to you?" I asked, enjoying my impromptu leg massage.

"Outside of the norm," he responded shortly.

"I am outside of the norm? Me?" I considered myself to be right down the middle—normal.

"How about a movie?" Chris asked again, releasing my leg.

As I hopped up to find one, Ian went through the stack on the end table. "You really have a thing for the undead."

"I do. They may be dearly departed but the effect they have on the living is enervating," Jess said, staring intently as he rifled through them.

"Do you think there's room for another zombie movie?" he asked, sweeping the hair from his eyes.

"It'd have to be a great story. Seems like most of it's been done," Jess said. Poking the top disk, she said, "This! Sarah—I know what you're looking for and it's here." She put on one of our favorites.

I recognized the opening credits. "Cool. *Gruel*! Have you guys seen it before?" I asked, pretty confident that they hadn't.

"Never even *heard* of it," Chris said, taking the case from Ian.

"No matter how many times I watch it, I still need a pillow for the kitchen scene. I can't watch it. God, it's horrific," I said, scouting around for an appropriate pillow. Moving Chris's arm, I nestled into his arm pit. "This'll do but you can't leave me."

"No problem," he said, kissing my head.

Taking the hint, Ian grabbed the throw off the back of the couch and spread it over himself and Jessica, giving her butt a pat.

"I didn't realize that you need a solid story if there's solid gore," Ian said.

"Stories are the backbone! Why make something that's already been done?" Jessica said earnestly.

"They do it all the time. Just with new pretty faces," Chris said. "Imagine if you could do a movie with a good story, gore and the two of us!" He stuck his tongue out, crossing his eyes. "I'd love to be in a quality flick loaded with dead things."

"Maybe you should start a production company," Jessica said, rearranging herself, reclining on Ian.

"I've thought about it," Ian said. "Don't know that I want to *take* direction forever. What about you, Chris?"

"I'd like to think my acting days are numbered." He put the case down. "Directing'd be a good way to spend another twenty years."

"What would that do to your social calendar, compared to acting?" I asked, plotting my future.

"More work—or more intense work," he said, glancing at me.

"I really don't want to see less of you." I cringed as the first zombie was liquefied.

Chris chuckled. "It's been *a long* time since I've been the protector of innocence during a gory movie."

Ian was staring intently at the back of Jessica's head, oblivious to our continuing conversation. When she sighed, I realized that there was some activity going on under that blanket. As hard as I tried to focus on the movie, I was overly aware of her toes curling. A tiny piece of me was jealous that she was having a fuller, remorseless undead experience. When she leaned back and sank her fingers into his hair, demanding to be kissed, I shrank into the couch.

Chris snickered. "Any more blankets around?"

"I'd be more than happy to go look."

"And leave me alone with the flesh-eating crew on the couch? No, thanks."

"I think if we left, they wouldn't even notice. Wanna go?" I asked quietly.

"Relax," he said, petting me.

"Are you kidding?"

"Are you?" he asked mischievously.

"Is that something else you've learned, to go for it in front of an audience? I gotta say, even in high school, there had to be a dark closet for me to kiss someone."

"Sounds like you missed the best part of school!" he said, gently taking my chin and turning my head. Under his ministration, I lost track of the death count.

Pulling my skirt over both of us like a blanket, I fumbled with his button. I heard his soft laugh and became more determined. I was going to master buttons if it killed me. When he sighed, I knew that my efforts were paying off. Concerned about me, he managed to move me in such a way that I was shielded from their view before his hand slid under my skirt.

I felt exceptionally dirty but in good company. The noise coming from the couch was building, adding to the eroticism of the moment. I loved having a talented, courageous, willing boyfriend.

~~

# 19

After seeing my parents off to the airport, the following days were bizarre. Jess and I visited a couple of high-end shops with designers and image consultants. After the second day, I was done. I felt like a manatee squeezing into floor length chiffon. When we came home thoroughly disgusted, Chris brought a new team to the house.

In the pool house, the fitting and fabrics were a joy. The team brought music, aromatics, sketch books and tons of photos to peruse on their tablets. Within a couple of hours, we'd selected our looks. We were told it would take about two days before we'd be asked for a fitting. I was so happy with the emerald green flapper-style dress that we'd designed. It was something I could rock and be true to me. Even the headband, if it came out as illustrated, would be elegant.

Staring at my head, Tilda questioned if it might be time to lose the dreads. I'd had them for years and hadn't thought about life without them. When she pointed to all of the hair that wasn't dreaded, she suggested that I do something. She had no experience with dreads and wasn't sure who to recommend if I wanted to dread the newer growth. I knew how to do it myself but hadn't had the time. My ex had always helped me in the past.

This seemed like the perfect time to cast off one of the remaining vestiges of Old Sarah. She enthusiastically agreed to cut and style my hair on the day of the gala. Goodbye, dreads.

When the dresses came, we were giddy. It was like playing dress up as a kid but this time, everything was stylishly built to fit us. Slinking into my dress, I swiveled my hips, sending the 5-inch fringe flying. I was gorgeous. When Tilda handed me the gold headband embellished with green Fibonacci spirals, I was delirious. I had drawn this headband a million times and never could get it to look anything other than silly. Created by professionals, it was a show stopper and a piece that would be incorporated into my daily wardrobe.

Jessica was going to be eye candy in black. She was so pleased when they presented her with a stylish pair of Fluevogs. They would peek out from her floor length dress. Like my headband, those shoes were a nod to her personality and underestimated ass kicking qualities.

I was also introduced to a clutch purse. As a human being, this little device struck me as contrived and inconvenient. Was it to keep my hands busy? Why on earth would I want to hold a little purse all night? Who invented these stupid things and why was that considered more in keeping with fashion than anything with a strap? I had to admit that my little gold bag was exceptional but would an additional length of fabric make it less so?

Jessica welcomed her clutch as part of the costume. Covered in crystals, it shone gloriously between her fingers. As she modeled it for herself, her assistant, Leif, pulled out a selection of rings from which to choose. She picked out an opal ring that was as mysterious as it was beautiful. I went with a large cat's eye-like emerald set in a thin gold band.

As soon as we'd firmed up our choices, they slipped off our gowns and took off, promising that they'd be back tomorrow morning with the finished products. I wanted to dance around the house in it and see what it could do.

~~

When Saturday arrived, I happily dolled myself up with Jess. I didn't know how many events I'd be asked to attend but I was going to play my part. Already, this benefit qualified as a real learning experience. I now felt more comfortable talking about fabrics and accessories.

I carried my heels as I walked to the house with Jess. She snickered at me but then she'd always worn heels.

Chris had gotten a limo for us. We were to meet the boys at the benefit. Apparently, their role in the affair was larger than they'd let on. Ian was the entertainment, playing piano and singing. Jess had said he was good but I didn't realize 'good' was good enough for hundreds of people. Chris was the emcee for the evening. They couldn't have picked a better one.

In the car, I came to appreciate my clutch. It gave me something to hold very tightly without looking like I needed a security blanket. Jessica pulled a flask from hers, shaking it in my direction.

"I know you're not fond of carrying a purse but it's all about what you put *in* it!" she said, uncapping the delicate flask and handing it to me.

From the whiff, I knew it was whiskey. God bless her and her friendship! Feeling the heat course down my throat, I instantly felt more in the moment. Her eyes sparkled as I handed it back to her.

"Stick with me, kid, and you'll be fine," she said, taking a swig.

"Oh, trust me. I intend to. Did you know they were invested in this thing?"

"I knew Ian was playing the piano. He never mentioned that Chris was the emcee. Probably figured we knew already."

"You look amazing." Her dark hair was pulled up, a few curls falling haphazardly from the pins. The plunging neckline exposed more than her tattoo. She was very well endowed. I hoped the dress was secured with super glue because if she leaned, just a little, she would suffer an extreme wardrobe malfunction. "Do you feel as glamorous as you look?"

"I could say the same. I always loved your dreads but you look regal. Very refined. I love the new you," she said, cocking her head.

"I'm not gonna lie. My head feels so light without my hair helmet." I tentatively touched my hair-sprayed coif. It was quite short. I was curious what Chris would say.

"I could get used to this," she said, putting the flask back in her purse. "I even like this up-do. I never know what to do with my hair. I was tickled that Leif was able to spend the time on it."

"You have a personal assistant!"

"No, but I want one. Badly."

"Think there're more events in our future?"

"Good things are coming our way, Sarah. This is the beginning of greatness. All we have to do is be willing to embrace it." She glanced out the window.

"I think I've always believed in the law of attraction. I just got a little lost there for a second." I followed her gaze. "How's your book coming?"

"Ha! Nice segue. Just about finished with it. You're welcome to read it if you have the inclination!" she added, glancing at me.

"I love how you write. It's engrossingly fast paced. Perfect for me and my ADD!"

"Oh, stop. You're not ADD. We both just like to get to the nitty gritty, I think. Never hurts to stop and smell a few flowers on the way, though. This book takes a little more time. I like to think I painted a few extra pretty pictures."

"Can't wait! Have you ever considered writing a screenplay?"

"Some of my books could be translated into screenplays easily enough. Might have to think more about it because I'm still talking to a group who wants the rights to *Twisted*. I don't know how I feel about that yet. It's *my* material. God only knows what it would become!"

"But I gotta think the reason they're after it is because they want the nuts and bolts of what's there. Would they really option it only to decimate it?"

"What if they like it but hate the ending or think it'd end better if Rory didn't die? That's what gets me. It feels like I'd be giving it up completely and I'd have to be satisfied with the paycheck."

"Huh. I met Imogen's husband. He's a writer. Maybe he could talk to you about how to maintain some level of control?"

"I never did get that chance to talk to him." She reapplied her lipstick. "Imogen sure is beautiful."

"She's really cool, too. Knowing that Chris is going to be doing love scenes with her in a couple of months is still weird but I think I can handle it. She really seems in love with Julian. She seems so genuine!"

"Refreshing, isn't it? Once again, I cannot tell you how happy I am that you ever got involved in making sandwiches. God bless deli meat!" she screamed out the window.

"That's gotta be a first—the blessing of deli meat."

"Won't be the last. That should be our first toast of the evening! Hey, look! We're here." The limo slowed down, pulling over to join a long line of limousines.

When the door didn't open immediately, I began to go for the handle but Jessica swatted my hand away.

"We're at least a city block from the door, m'dear. Hang in there. He will let us out when we're at the door."

"I'd almost rather get out here. Less ostentatious."

"Mmm. But think about your heels! Less walking this way."

"Dammit. You win."

"We *both* win, dear," she said, as we continued to plod along.

I took a moment to inventory my purse for the umpteenth time—lipstick, gum, driver's license, my phone and a handful of bills. I wasn't going to get very far on the contents but then I wasn't expecting to MacGyver my way out of here either.

"Well, you ready?" Jessica asked as we came to a stop.

I closed my purse. "This is going to be fun, right?"

"Yep! Relax, hon. It's going to be unlike anything we've ever done before."

"I just realized that we're with the two most eligible bachelors here this evening."

She stepped out. "That we are, m'dear. Try to be memorable."

I laughed uncharitably at her use of my mother's quotation.

People were milling around, catching up. I was fairly certain that we passed Julian, who was tapping away on his phone, blond hair in his face.

Once inside, we saw Chris and Ian standing back to back, like they were protection for each other. Jessica walked right up next to Ian's glad-handing target and introduced herself. The gentleman's eyes widened as he absorbed her audacity and beauty. He was momentarily perturbed by the interruption but drawn by her magnetism. It appeared that he was trying to get a read on her availability. Ian must've felt the same thing because he possessively put his arm around her waist and introduced her as his girlfriend.

Score one for Jessica, I thought. I neared Chris.

He dropped his conversation and spun around.

"Wow. Look at you!" His eyes were fixed on my hair. "You look gorgeous." He gave me a once, twice and thrice-over.

"Thank you," I said with a quick curtsey.

"You look like you're at a loss for words!" his companion said, laughing.

"You have no idea." He leaned over and gingerly touched my hair. "Sarah, this is Stefan. He's the one who put the benefit together."

"It's so good to meet you," he said, shaking my hand very firmly. Stefan looked like my kind of people. He was a little older than myself, rail thin and sporting long, stringy ultra-black hair. In addition to his shiny suit, he had oxblood Doc Martens.

"You, too. You worked with Chris, right?"

"Yes. And I have to thank you again, Chris, for emceeing. I hate talking in front of people. I got cold feet."

"No problem."

He clapped Chris on the back. "If you need anything, I'll be around. Meet me by the dance floor around eight!" he said, nodding deferentially to me.

"So we've got an hour before you have to do anything?" I asked, checking out the room.

"Sort of. I've got a lot of talking to do." He took a couple of champagne flutes. "Want to check out the silent auction?"

Juggling my clutch and the champagne, I said, "I've never been to something like this before but it's oozing money."

"That's what you want at a benefit. Add free booze and the charity does very well."

I was astounded by the high-end jewelry laid out on the tables. Some of the necklaces, brooches and rings sported Everest-sized rocks. Moving along, I found a ring that I really liked. It was an emerald or emerald-like stone on a white gold band. It had a vintage styling that made it really unique.

Cruising through the tables, I lost Chris a couple of times. He had a lot of connections and, as he said, a lot of conversations to complete. I looped back to that ring repeatedly, watching the bidding go up significantly each time. I was curious what the ring was really worth and what it would bring by night's end.

Closer to eight, I found my table. We were seated to the left of the dance floor-stage in proximity to the piano. There were a couple of purses and suit jackets on the chairs so I knew our table was full. I put my purse down next to Jessica's. I felt an arm around my waist.

Thrilled that he was going to take a minute for me, I pivoted and came face to face with Tom.

"Sunshine! So good to see you," he said, giving me a kiss on the cheek.

"Good to see a familiar face," I answered winningly.

"I'd say the same but you look incredibly—different." His eyes wandered over my hair. "I didn't know you could look even more riveting but you do."

"It's just hair," I said, embarrassed.

"Oh, it's a lot more than the hair, Sunshine." He fondled his tie. "Hey, look. We match. It's like you were *meant* to be my date!"

It was a very close match to my extremely vibrant green dress and a compliment to his eyes.

Very pleased with himself, he said, "Tilda took good care of you. I love that woman. You look like a jewel—multifaceted and beautiful from every angle."

"Wow, that's some serious cheese. You been sitting on that one or did you just come up with it?"

"If I sat on it, it'd be di-a-mond," he said, drawing out the word. He gave me champagne.

"How'd you know Tilda was over?" I asked, perplexed.

"Chris thought that she was great and asked me for her number."

"Which you just happened to have."

"She's one of those great ladies. You just never know when you might need her—and for once I don't mean as a partner. She's a sweet girl that I taunt and tease for target practice." He swapped his empty for another full glass, spinning skillfully in a circle. "She gets so bothered. I love her reactions but I'd never do her," he said, eyes twinkling.

"There's someone you wouldn't hook up with?"

"If she were one of a tag team, maybe. She's inexperienced." He shrugged. "I like my women to know their way around. So much better if you don't have to teach."

"Why'd you need her? Can't you put on your own make up?"

"I can do *everything* for myself. I could handle you, too. No problem." Leaning over, he said, "I'd love to see you first thing in the morning. I bet you're a natural beauty."

Taking my hand, Tom guided me to the dance floor.

"Your dress *is* spectacular. You are the only woman here with balls. Have you noticed how much attention you've drawn?" he asked as we slowly twirled around the floor. "More than half these women think you're the entertainment. The other half want to know who your designer is."

I wasn't sure if he was laughing at me or with me. "I'm sure you brought some one. Which camp does she fall in?"

"Ah, Angel. I will have to introduce you if you haven't met her already."

"That's quite a name."

"Don't call her an angel. She doesn't have wings nor heavenly ambitions. It's *ahn-GEL*."

"Sounds like a model."

"Good call."

"She is?"

"She was."

He stopped moving. Taking my hand, he pointed. "That's m'lady." It was easy to pick her out. She was statuesque, dressed in an elegant if daring white form fitting dress. My jaw dropped. If ever there were a perfect woman, she had to be it.

"If you're with her, why're you dancing with me?"

"Ah, but I'm not *with* her."

"Okay. Well, she *came* here with you. I am sure she can dance."

"Ha. You haven't met her, have you?"

"No."

As the song ended, he said quietly, "Mmm. She's Ian's little secret."

Before I could ask another question, Chris had a microphone and directed us to our seats. Tom walked me back to mine, pulled it out and hovered, looking around. "Where's Jessica? I know she's here."

Looking over my shoulder, I asked, "How's that?"

"Angel wouldn't ask me to take her if Ian were available."

"Playing second fiddle? I didn't think that was your thing."

Leaning into my ear, he said huskily, "Have you *seen* my fiddle? I'll take it out. All you need to do is play it."

Taking my purse, I swung it haphazardly over my shoulder, clipping him. Straightening, he massaged my shoulders until Angel was en route.

He extended his arm and guided her to their seats—which abutted my own. At least he was going to keep the night interesting.

Backing out my chair, I pretended to be hunting for something in my purse. Closing it, I scanned the room for Jess and saw them by the doors. On the way to the table, she discreetly pushed her hair back into place. Ian nonchalantly straightened his pants.

After pushing her in, Ian gave my shoulder a squeeze in greeting.

"Hi, Ian," I responded as he pulled out his own seat next to Jessica.

I sat patiently, waiting for her to acknowledge me. After she had spoken to everyone at the table, she finally met my gaze.

"Don't judge me," she whispered, smiling.

"Oh, I'm impressed. *Here*? You've been busy—*here*??"

Her face, still flushed, deepened to a crimson. "Limo," she uttered under her breath.

I couldn't help myself and started laughing. Tom bumped into my chair, "What's so funny, Sunshine? Care to share?"

I shook my head. He slid out of his chair and stood behind Jessica, engaging Ian in conversation. Ian answered monosyllabically. Although he was smiling grandly, he was obviously annoyed with Tom.

Chris came trotting over and stood behind my chair, shaking Tom's hand. Offhandedly, he asked Tom who he was with. Chris's eyes widened considerably upon hearing the answer. Chris quickly sat down with Angel, making things right for her. When her laughter drifted over, Chris excused himself and sat down with me.

"Nice save," I said. "I don't think she was in a happy place."

He draped his arm around my chair when dinner was served. "It's hard to be when you're always the bride's maid, never the bride."

Leaning into him, I had to ask, "Is she an *ex*-girlfriend?"

Shaking his head, he said quietly, "She's the one who stays. She's been around forever. She watches the new flavors come and go but he always goes home to her."

"Literally?" I asked, irritated.

"Think so. Haven't been to his crib in a while. I don't know."

"As in, they *live* together?"

"I wouldn't go that far. More like she's got a few things in a dresser drawer."

"*Really?*" I said, incredulously. The idea that my Jessica would be involved in a triangle bothered me. If she were unaware of the other point, that would be worse.

"Another time, okay?" Chris said, accepting his plate.

After dinner, Chris apologetically departed to remind people about the silent auction items and to introduce Ian.

While he was talking, my irritation grew. How could Ian double dip? Why was it okay? I didn't realize that I was fixated on him until he returned my gaze. His eyes burned under an errant lock of hair. I was annoyed with myself. I was falling under his spell. There was a good reason the world was fascinated by him. He was a thing of beauty.

As a cover, I asked, "What're you playing tonight?"

"The piano," he cooed.

"Jessica, hit him for me!" I crabbed.

As she wound up, he apologized, shielding his face with his hand. "Don't hit me. I've gotta get up there in a minute." She put her purse down. "They want me to do about five songs. You should recognize them. They're all favorites although I don't think they're regularly done with piano accompaniment. I get my kicks trying to figure out the arrangement for piano."

"That's fun?"

"Mental gymnastics. Except for the last song—that's just icing. Pure candy."

Jessica asked, "What *is* the last song?"

"A surprise," he said, kissing her.

Hearing applause, Ian was on his feet with a quick wave to the crowd. Jogging up to Chris, he shook his hand before sitting at the piano.

Tom turned his chair around and kicked my chair repeatedly.

I glared at him. He took that as an invitation to pop into Chris's seat.

"Have you heard about the finale?" he asked.

"Have you?" I threw back at him.

"Ooh, you don't know! What fun!" he said, with a goofy little golf clap.

Ian was remarkably good. His voice was sultry and deep. He filled the hall as few could, saturating the silence with his golden voice. As soon as he hit the keys for his last song, I realized that Chris was behind him, microphone in hand.

As they both started to belt it out, it took all of a nanosecond to place the song, *Great Balls of Fire*. Chris was Goose to Ian's Maverick! Sporting Ray-Bans, they brought the crowd to their feet. Ian was stuck at the piano but was sending his performance to Jessica. Distracted, I jumped when Chris was at my elbow, singing to me. I was overcome by the energy of the moment, delighting in the spotlight. It was the sweetest thing anyone had ever done for me. Giving me a quick kiss, he retreated, finishing the song with Ian at the piano.

"I didn't know you could dazzle any brighter, Sunshine, but he must be your guy. You're radiance in blinding!" Tom said, slipping back to his table.

When the applause died down, Ian returned, leaving Chris to work the crowd.

"That was *incredible*," Jessica said, weaseling her way into his lap. Very pleased with himself, he kissed her cleavage.

"You're still the center of attention!" I hissed, jerking his arm.

Rocking the chair back, he took a peak behind him. He got Jess to her feet and spun her out onto the dance floor.

Knowing Chris should be done soon, I took another trip past the remaining auction items. My ring was up to $57,000. It was worth every penny. Angel crept up behind me and introduced herself. She was awesome, a real specimen, and I had nothing to say to her.

"That's a really pretty piece, isn't it?" she asked, touching it.

"I like it."

"It'd match your dress. Which is phenomenal. Who's your designer?" she asked, scrutinizing my accessories.

"I didn't really have a designer; more like a friend."

"Talented friend," she mused, fingering the fringe.

"I wasn't sure I could get away with it, but I knew I couldn't pull off anything like what you're wearing," I said, checking out her glass slippers. "You are as your name suggests."

"*Don't* say it. I'm tired of being compared to a heavenly body. Did you see who I came with? I think he's made it his mission to come up with every possible compliment based on the ethereal heavens." She pouted, looking furtively for her date.

"Tom's a visitor to earth himself," I said, commiserating.

"Yes." She zeroed in on me. "I hear you're friends with Ian's date—Jessica?" She pursed her lips. Her expression was chilly, like she was having some internal debate.

"Are they—together?" she blurted in a tone reserved for grossly unpleasant topics.

"Honestly, I don't know." I started perusing the items again.

"Okay. Sure," she said, tucking her hair behind her ear. "You and Chris, huh? That's something," she said, trying a different tact.

I smiled.

"He's smitten."

I tripped on my own foot. "Smitten?"

"Can't you tell? He's all about you, dear. If you gave the slightest nudge, he'd put a ring on it," she said smoothly.

"How do you know?" I asked disbelievingly.

"I've been around for a long time. I've met their girls." She tugged on my fringe. "Besides your wild fashion, there's something else that's got him hooked. You're here to stay."

I smiled. "Wild fashion. That's the first time I've ever been mentioned in the same sentence as fashion!"

"Beware. Your dress and headband will be all the rage at the next social event. Anyone young enough to wear it will be."

"Bullshit," I said, laughing.

She sniffed. "Would you introduce me?" She looked at herself in a mirror. "To Jessica?" She eyed me in the mirror.

If a super model could be insecure, I was witnessing her meltdown. She was fragile. I felt the need to reassure her but of what?

"Sure," I said. "She's a writer, you know."

"Oh?" she asked politely. "How'd they meet?"

I read a certificate. I didn't want to implicate myself. Unfortunately for me, the section had closed and a gentleman swooped in and took it. Straightening, I heard her ask again.

"Oh, through friends," I offered. It was a white lie but it could be good enough.

"*Whose* friends?" she asked, edgily. "I *know* their friends."

"Chris."

She slowly nodded her head. "I see," she said connecting the dots. "And how'd you meet Chris? You don't look like—" She trailed off instead of insulting me.

"You're right, I'm not. I was told that some people thought I was the entertainment today." I shook my dress, fringe flying.

"Mmm." She pursed her lips. "So, how'd you meet him?"

"At work." Ian was closing in on us. I wanted to disappear into the carpet.

"Hey," he said, coming up behind her. "Angel. You've met Sarah."

She looked at him coldly, pushing out her lower lip in a sultry frown.

"You look incredible," he said, putting his hands in his pockets.

If it were possible, Ian looked like he was at a loss for words, too. Under her breath, I thought I heard her say, 'how could you?'

About to walk away, Ian took my elbow. "How about a dance?"

He guided me to the floor, my hand on his bent arm. "That was painful," I said.

"It's just Angel." He put his hand on my waist. "To know her is to love her," he added noncommittally, watching her over my shoulder.

Coming around, I saw her. She was rooted to the spot, pouting.

"Do you?" I asked. "Do you *love* her?"

Holding his gaze, the hint of a smile graced his handsome features.

"Not everyone operates by your tight standards."

"Is that your answer?"

"Sarah, Angel is Angel. She knows as well as anyone who and what I am. I spend time with her. She likes it. She likes me. It works."

"Where does that leave Jessica?"

He sighed.

"She's my best friend. No one likes to share."

"How do *you* know? Have you ever had that conversation? Ever? Even once?" He stared at me. "Don't assume, Sarah. It's not attractive."

"I don't need to assume. I *know*. Intrinsically. I know. As a *woman*, I know."

"Oh, Sarah," he said, tightening his grip on my waist. "What you *know* could fill a thimble. Relax. Allow people to be who they are. I'm not a bad person just as your chosen attitude doesn't make you anything less than adorable."

I stiffened and slowed my feet to a crawl.

"I'm sorry," he said, spinning me out and watching my fringe fly. Pulling me back in, he added, "That was unkind. I adore you. I think you know that. I would love to—I would enjoy a change in your—restrictive—beliefs."

Color suffused my face and I swallowed nervously.

He inhaled deeply, rubbing his stubble on my cheek. "There are plenty of dark corners," he said enticingly.

A chill running through my body, I grimaced. "Yeah, you and Jess found one."

His eyes narrowed. "She knows who I am, Sarah. She doesn't need you to save her."

"I'm not trying to save her," I said, my voice rising.

"She's a grown woman and a *very* capable one." He cocked his head and took a deep breath. "Your body gets so stiff—"Another circle and we saw Chris deep in conversation. Ian's grip on my hand tightened. "You're the one, aren't you?"

~~

## 20

While at the grocery store, I saw pictures from the gala in another tabloid. They made my day. Of the many pictures, there was a really good one of the guys at the piano, as well as my impromptu serenade. I photographed nicely. And my new do was so shapely. I was a new woman. They put a picture of Angel next to me. She was beyond compare.

It was then that I decided I was going to have to get a subscription to some of these magazines. They'd never interested me before but it was like thumbing through a high school yearbook, trying to pick out the faces you remembered.

I hadn't seen Jessica in days. She'd disappeared, leaving me with little other than vague texts. When she surfaced, I was going to give it to her. In our relationship, I had always been the over-sharer but this was low flow even for her.

Chris was busy reading scripts and getting stuff 'lined up.' He was always lining something up. We finally had the house under control and I was comfortable thinking of myself as retired. He, God bless him, hadn't asked me what I was going to do.

Instead, we had jointly focused on getting our affairs in order. Although he was still going to be around for a couple of weeks, I was already anxious about him leaving. Even knowing that Imogen would be on the receiving end of his affections didn't assuage my fears. I really didn't want him to go. We were better together.

With that percolating in the deep recesses of my mind, I mentioned my anxiety to him as we were getting ready for bed.

"You worry too much, Sarah," he said, nestling into the bed and crossing his legs. "I don't know what else I can say."

"I don't know what I want you to say," I grumbled, wrapping my arms around a magazine. "Actually, I do. I do know. I want you to say that you're not going or that I can go with you." I looked at him, pain etched on my face.

He rolled onto his hip and rubbed my cheek. "I'm sorry. Perhaps you wouldn't feel so bereft if you had something concrete to do? Have you considered that?" he asked gently.

I flopped lifelessly on my back, croaking, "Of *course* I've thought about it."

He wiggled over to me, hand on my belly.

"Okay. Sorry. You do know that you can visit, if that helps?"

"It's just unfair to have you so fully to myself and then let you go." I flicked his hand. "Hardcore. Blows chunks."

"Distance makes the heart grow fonder?" he asked meekly.

"Not possible."

"You could always go back to Amy. She'd welcome you with open arms."

"Speaking of—why wasn't she at my party? That seemed like a no-brainer to me."

"Believe it or not, she had a mental breakdown and was not available."

"You've got to be joking."

"No, I would never joke about institutionalization."

"How'd you find out?"

"When you're Chris Sparks and you show up on someone's phone, people answer you. Her dad sent me a note asking if I was really me."

"So the apple doesn't fall far from the tree?"

"Guess not. He was quite willing to tell me her troubles. I just asked him to pass on my well-wishes. You haven't spoken to her?"

"No. Probably guilt stopping me."

"That's not cool. She's a friend, isn't she?"

"Um, I don't think so. I *never* would have chosen her as a buddy. She was a good coworker though. I'm sorry to hear her cheese slid off her cracker." She reminded me of Angel. She so wanted what she was unlikely to ever have. That had to be heart breaking.

"Oh, to suffer the slings and arrows—" I whispered.

Without prompting, Chris popped up and continued, "The slings and arrows of outrageous fortune, or to take arms against a sea of troubles, and by opposing end them? To die, to sleep; No more; and by a sleep to say we end the heartache and the thousand natural shocks that flesh is heir to, 'tis a consummation devoutly to be wished—" He paused, a satisfied smile on his face. "I love Shakespeare," he said wistfully.

"You're a nerd!" I patted his hand lovingly.

"Hey, you started it. I bet you could've given me another line or two."

"Probably not but—"

He leaned over and kissed me passionately. "I love you," he said, dropping his head on my belly.

Petting his hair, I felt a lot better even if it was temporary. "I love you, too."

He lifted my shirt and kissed my belly.

"How much do you love me, Sarah?" he asked keenly.

"How much?" I repeated.

"Yeah. How much?"

"Do you mean 'how'?" I pushed him off me, ready to disrobe him.

He sighed. "I know *how* you love me." He guided my hands to the edges of his boxers. "What I asked was more pressing—how *much*?"

"There's a children's book about that. 'I love you right up to the moon,'" I said, tugging on his drawers.

"Cute, do you love me that much?"

"How much?" I queried, getting them off.

"Enough to have—you know, kids."

I froze. His blue eyes wavered. He knew he was making a giant leap. I climbed on top of him and sat down. I wanted to say something but there really wasn't anything to say. Instead, I pulled off my pajama top and bent down to kiss him. I didn't see this coming but it was the natural progression. Deftly, he removed my bottoms. Birth control aside, we had baby-making sex. It was an entirely different thing from anything I'd ever done before.

For the third time in our outrageously oversexed relationship, we had taken it to another level. I thought about giving this up, even if only while he worked, fake-banging other girls.

As happy as I was, I was crying. Chris melted, like he thought he'd hurt me.

"Hey, hey—" he said soothingly. He scooped me up, tucking me against his chest. "You okay?" He kissed my forehead.

"Just having a dumb girl breakdown."

"Is that what it is? I thought—I think that was the best sex we've ever had," he said, twisting my chin to face him.

"No lie." I sighed. "Tell me again—*why* are you leaving?"

"I'm not *leaving*. I'm not in the military. I will be back. Without doubt." He kissed me again. "Especially if *that's* in my future. I may use it for source material."

I recoiled. "Are you suggesting you might think of *me* when you're rolling around with Imogen?"

With a look somewhere between confusion and incredulity, he slowly nodded. "Is that the wrong thing to say? I told you my mouth betrays me."

"That's a very wrong, or at least weird, thing to say."

"Ah—good old 'weird' equated with wrong again."

"It's a hard habit to break. You know, Ian suggested to me that my self-imposed rules were too strict."

"They're not *rules*. Think of them more as your moral compass, something Ian has pointing in another direction." Rubbing my shoulder, he chuckled. "You wanna talk about things that are inappropriate in our bedroom? I nominate *any* and *all* conversation about that guy."

"Good rule."

"I don't want there to be any doubt who you're thinking about because that—that could break me."

~~

When the day finally came, it didn't matter that he was only headed to New York and only for the better part of four months. There were so many things that we hadn't done yet and were unlikely to do for some time.

Giving me another hug, Chris said, "Haven't you ever heard the phrase, when a door closes, a window opens? Maybe this is something like that. I know we were supposed to take a trip but now you'll have to make the trip to New York. Swing by, see your parents—maybe meet mine? Come to the City." He gripped both my hands and pulled me into a tight hug.

Silently crying, my body heaved against him. He set his bag down. Snot running down my face, I whimpered and clung to his hand.

"I can't even look at you. You're killing me," he said into my hair.

"Sorry," I sobbed. "I hate good byes."

"This isn't good bye. Save good byes for people that you don't like and won't see again. We're just—this is. This is tem-po-ra-reeeee."

"Doesn't *feel* temporary to me," I sniffed again. He wiped my nose.

Meeting my gaze, he said, "I have given you everything I can to ensure that you're happy and comfortable. I have to go. I will return. You can come *and* go as it suits you." Bumping noses, he added, "You know, you *can* do this." I raked my hand across my face, rubbing my tears in. "Take a deep breath."

I did as instructed. I furrowed my brow, pouting. "I'm done. Done crying."

"Listen, I will give you a call when I get in. You can come any time. Don't sit around here and get worked up. Bring Jess or Melissa or even Amy. Be a tourist," he said, picking up his bag again.

"Kiss me," I demanded, closing my eyes. I couldn't look at him and I couldn't let go. I dropped my head, leaning against his chest. "I can't look at you. I'll start again."

He chuckled. "You want me to walk away, leaving you with your eyes closed? That doesn't seem right. Talk about love 'em and leave 'em."

"Okay, how about this—you kiss me. I keep my eyes closed for a count of thirty. I will open them and you will have gone as far as you can go in that time? Okay? I will find you but it will be the break I need."

"You are ridiculous," he said lovingly. He leaned down and kissed me again, a real soul searching, I-don't-want-this-to-end-either smooch.

And then, he hugged me and backed away. With my eyes shut, I counted Mississippi-style until I got to twenty and opened my eyes. He was in the security line, fumbling around for his pass.

He handed the agent his boarding pass and ID, smiling grandly at her. Recognition dawning on her, she stood a little straighter and returned his grin. I shook my head. He was mine but I had to share him.

~~

At home, I made myself a quick cup of coffee, grabbed my phone and sat on the patio. I was going to find someone to talk to if it took me the rest of the day. Starting with Jess, I went through my all-star line-up wishing that I had a sister or a close relationship with my mom. I wanted someone who was going to listen, tell me that everything was going to be fine and that they'd be right over. When I continued to strike out, I texted both Ian and Tom to see if they'd seen Jess.

Finally, a response! Jess had Ian's phone.
'What's up, m'dear?'
'He left this morning. I'm crying.'
'You home?'
'Yes.'
'Want company?'
'Yes.'
'K. See you soon.'

Only after I'd sat there for a few minutes did it register that she had Ian's phone and that I was now dragging her away from him—wherever that was. Given my anxiety issues, I was confident that she'd understand but I was disappointed in my own shortcoming.

Taking another sip of my sinfully hot coffee, I started a list of things I could do, should do, during the next couple of months. I should go through my stuff and throw out whatever was still in boxes that didn't mesh with this house. I should make a decision about birth control. I should see who could come with me to New York and when. Actually, that was a good one because it led me all sorts of follow up questions—where'd we stay? Should we take in a show? Visit Connecticut?

It was at times like this that I really appreciated Jess. She took a little longer than I would have liked but she had a bottle of Jack and some cups when she rolled through to the patio.

"Hey," she said, setting the bottle down next to me. It took all of my willpower not to whimper.

"Hi," I said, misty-eyed.

She poured me a cup. "How long's he gone?"

Willing myself to answer, I said, "Several months—but he said I could visit. D'you want to go to New York?"

She laughed and handed me the cup. "He's been gone less than a day and you're already planning your trip? Gonna see Lucy and Carl while you're out there?"

"I'm pathetic." I rubbed my snotty nose on my hand.

"Yes, but you will be okay. Look around you. He didn't exactly kick you to the curb."

"Yeah, I know. I should be grateful, right?"

She got comfortable in her chair. I watched her wriggle in an attempt to get my mind off my questionable man troubles.

"You had Ian's phone," I said curiously. She poured herself a shot. "Where were you?"

"His place."

"I've missed you," I whined.

"I'm never far," she said, swirling her cup.

"But you haven't been around as much."

"True. Thinking of getting my own place."

"Or moving in with Ian?"

A smile crossed her face. "I don't think so."

"Oh? You had his phone."

"He doesn't have any secrets."

"So why not?"

"Why not move in? I like the way things are. I don't know that they'd be as good if I lived with him."

"Do you have *stuff* at his place?" I asked.

"A few things."

"In a drawer? Next to Angel's?" I said, thinking about what Chris had said.

She smirked. "No, her stuff isn't in the same room. It's down the hall."

"Does she live there?"

"Not really."

"But she's still around?"

"Sort of, yeah. She's more like a sister than anything else. I think she's Ian's me. Or rather, she is to him what I am for you. She's just around and takes care of him."

"Oh, I bet she *does*."

She refilled my cup. "I don't know. I'm not his keeper."

"Are you *okay* with it?"

"Their relationship?" She picked at the label on the bottle. "It is what it is. He's been very open with his lifestyle and I can take it or leave it. Right now, I am choosing to take it. He's really bright on top of being hot. I've let him see some of my stuff and he's given me some thoughtful feedback. He also has connections that he's offered to introduce me to."

Huh. He'd found a way to keep her. It wouldn't work for me, but she didn't seem to be upset in any way with their arrangement. In fact, she seemed more grounded and happy than I'd seen her in a long time. If he were using her, it appeared to go both ways.

"What're you thinking? A screen play?" I asked, enthused. Anything that'd get her writing and her work before the masses, I supported. If she could just get a break, she'd be famous.

"Thinking about it. It looks like *Twisted* will get picked up. I did talk to Julian and he gave me some advice as well as a lawyer. I haven't called her yet but I think I will. It's not *huge* bucks but it's enough that I am excited."

"That's amazing!" I squealed. "You're going to be famous and not because you met some guy. It's your *ability* that's gonna take you there."

"Thanks," she said pouring another hearty shot for me.

Feeling the whiskey sear my throat, I asked, "And you're leaving me?"

"Never," she said, staring at me.

"But you *are* thinking of moving? Already?"

"We both knew I wasn't going to stay here forever. You're going to have a *life* with this guy. There will come a point when it's just weird for me to be here all the time."

"You haven't been here much lately," I said morosely.

She dramatically rolled her eyes. "Ian took me on a vacation. Okay? We went on a *plane* to Hawaii and it was awesome."

"Seriously!?!?"

"I would never joke about Hawaii." She paused, reminiscing. "It. Was. Glorious."

"How cool! What'd you do?"

"Ian. In the sand, the ocean, the pool, the elevator—"

We always did have a thing for sex anywhere, any time. "Guess you don't need me to hide pictures around the house any more, huh?"

"I will miss those," she said piningly. "But it's a price I'm willing to pay, given the circumstances."

"Is he all that?" I asked, squinting.

"*And* a bag of chips," she answered with an explosive puckering noise. She gripped the bottle. "I should put this in the house. We're drinking it like it's water."

I put my hands on the bottle. "No, it's okay. Leave it."

"Okay, but I'm taking it with me when I go. I can't leave you a drunken wreck with the bottle. You can have your little pity party but then you've gotta get back on your feet, deal?"

"Deal."

"What are you going to do with yourself besides plan a trip to New York?"

I handed her my phone. "I've produced a list!"

She casually read it. Eyeing me over the phone, she said, "Birth control?" I blushed, already haven forgotten that it was *on* my list. "What're you up to?"

"Well, you're not the only one who's moving forward."

"With?"

"Life."

She flipped the phone around and around, staring at me. "Say it. I dare you. I *double* dog dare you."

"I—think I'm thinking about not taking another shot." I snatched my phone. "Not that it matters. He's not here anyway."

"That's colossal news, Sarah! You're thinking about having babies?"

"I always knew I wanted them. I just didn't think it was going to happen for me."

"But now?"

"He's made it very clear that he wants a family and I'm—I'm thinking that I'm as ready as I will ever be." I set my phone down and scooted my chair closer to Jessica. "I haven't felt this content possibly ever. I love him and love how I feel when I'm with him. I think—"

"You think he's the one?" she asked so sweetly, a hint of jealousy in her voice.

"Yeah, I do. I really do. I've never felt like I was just something to do. And he's really been good to his word, letting me figure out my life."

She hugged me. "Great things, Sarah. I'm so happy for you." She sat on the edge of my chair. "Babies. Wow." She poured us each a shot. "I would like to offer a toast to you and your offspring." She gave me the glass. "May your loins be fruitful."

One look at her face and I burst into laughter. "Fruitful loins? That's what you've got?"

She grinned. "It seemed appropriate. And, hey—you're really smiling now. You feel better, don't you?"

~~

## 21

Over the next few weeks, I helped Jessica look at new places and generally encroached on her space. She was generous, allowing me to follow her around like a puppy, until she wasn't. I had forgotten how to do my own thing around her and sucked up all of her time. When she gently pushed back, it was time for a trip.

In one brief conversation, I mentioned this to Chris. He thought this was serendipitous. His sisters were coming to New York for the weekend and he felt that it would be a great opportunity for me to meet them. Nights, he promised, were for me alone. I'd go for an extended weekend so I could have some 'just us' time.

Although I hated flying, I was enthusiastic about trying first class. At the first opportunity, I did as Chris suggested and asked for a cocktail. I'd had two by the time we took off and had struck up a friendship with the gal sitting next to me. She worked for a day time talk show and had been in Los Angeles filming a segment. She was relaxed, yet spoke animatedly. I enjoyed her stories thoroughly.

At Laguardia, Chris had arranged for a car. He planned everything out so that I didn't have to lose any sleep over the details. Instead, I was fretting over meeting his sisters. Susan was three years my senior and Mary was six years my junior with Chris sandwiched right in between.

Although Chris spoke lovingly of his family, I knew little about them. Susan was an elementary school music teacher who only recently married. Mary had finished up some degree at Rhode Island School of Design and had a live in artist boyfriend named Todd.

Just like Los Angeles, Chris had an apartment and the car dumped me at the curb. The doorman had been expecting me and easily picked me out as 'the one.' Charles was a charming fellow who decided he should accompany me all the way up to the door just to make sure I got in. When I had successfully unlocked it, I wondered if I was supposed to tip him. He seemed to hang on just long enough that I had the uncomfortable impression that I owed him money for his kindness.

Thanking him profusely, I closed the door and hoped that I hadn't just stiffed him.

Other than the view, the apartment looked like a more cramped version of his previous digs. He'd brought his blanket and thrown it on the couch. He had another pile of books developing on the end table including a heavily dog-eared copy of *Twisted River*.

Setting my bag down, I thumbed through the marked pages. He'd high-lighted sections and underlined names. It looked like a high school reading assignment gone awry. He'd created the *Cliff Notes*. He certainly didn't read it for enjoyment.

As I hadn't read it in years, I got more comfortable and began to read it in earnest. I was totally engrossed when Chris called.

"Howdy, gorgeous!" he said, energetically.

"Hola," I said, looking for a bookmark.

"Everything go alright? I thought you'd call when you got in."

"I thought about it but knew you'd be busy. Thanks for everything. First class was cool. I had several cocktails before we even took off. Met a cool lady who works for a TV show. You'd've liked her."

"What'd you think of Charles? I'm sure he took good care of you?"

"He brought me up to your apartment to make sure I got in. I wasn't sure if I should tip him or not and I felt really bad when I didn't."

He laughed. "You don't have to worry about it. He's fine. I took care of him."

"But should I have?"

"He would've *taken* it, for sure. But don't feel bad. There're enough of us here that he's doing just fine."

"Other actors?"

"And a couple of other people who're working on the project."

"Cool. Have you made new friends?"

"Of course."

"Oooh—is Imogen here?"

"Just got in."

"In my head, she'd be here at the same time you are."

"She's here to shoot *our* scenes but she had something else going so she's a little late to the party."

"I'd like to see her again."

"She was asking about you last night when I was hanging out with her and Julian."

"He's here?"

"Yeah. He's staying with her."

"That's an option?"

"Sure. Why, d'you want to stay?"

"No, I don't think I could."

"Now, why's that? Before you came out here, you sounded like you were lost with nothing to do."

I was quiet. I'd *love* to stay.

"Bueller?" he said into the silence.

"Sorry. Are your sisters here yet? Where're they staying?"

"They're coming in on a train later today and going straight to their hotel. It's a couple of blocks from my apartment. Walking distance."

I hadn't been on the West Coast for too long but my sense of geography had morphed. Taking anything other than a plane to New York sounded wrong, but from Boston, it made sense.

"I told them that we'd catch up with them tomorrow. I thought it'd be nice to see you tonight when I got home. It's been a long, long time," he added longingly.

"My dirty texts weren't enough?" I asked saucily.

"Ha! You could've sent more any time. They'd never be a replacement though." He paused and I heard him chewing. "What d'you think of the apartment? Nice view, right?"

"It looks just like your last place. I wondered where that blanket had gone."

"It's like my good luck charm. I always take it."

"Chris has a security blanket!"

"I called it a *good luck charm*, Sarah."

"Same thing."

"Really?"

"Has it brought you any outstanding luck?"

"You're here."

"I would've come even if the blanket didn't."

"Oh? What if I'd left it and it was enough of a token that you didn't need me?"

"Now you're being ridiculous."

"Hey, if it's a *security blanket*, it might've worked on you and you would've stayed there, contentedly, until I returned."

"Whatever! I also noticed that you've completely marked up Jessica's book."

"Going through my things?"

"No, I haven't made it past the couch yet. I saw the books and opened hers. I was trying to figure out your madness and then I just decided to reread it."

"She wrote a great story," he said, taking another bite.

"Are you on a lunch break?"

"Sorry. You can hear me eating, huh?"

"Yeah, but that's okay. Why'd you write all over her book?"

"What, you don't do that?" he asked, deflecting my query.

"I *did* that, past tense, for writing assignments. Do you have an assignment?"

After taking another bite, he said, "You promise not to tell?"

"I'm not fond of promising anything unless I know what you're after."

"Smart girl! But I was sworn to secrecy."

"Damn you. I thought that spouses had legal coverage for things like this."

"That may be but you, my sweet, sweet, Sarah are not my spouse!"

Even though he said it lightly, I was surprised by how much it stung. Short of the actual ring, I felt married to this guy and didn't think that there was anything he wouldn't tell me.

I got up and carried the phone to the kitchen, saying nothing.

He sighed. "Fine—" I cut him off.

"There's a remedy for that, you know."

It was his turn to remain silent. I wanted to pound my head with the phone, Steel Magnolias-style. The last thing I really wanted to do was ask him to propose. Pulling a cold bottle of water from the fridge, I switched topics.

"When you get home, you're gonna have to tell me more about your sisters. I realized that I don't really know much about them and I'd love to find some common ground."

"You do have something in common—probably many things."

"Besides being women from the East Coast?" I asked, wondering what connections he made.

"Me!"

"Ug. I'd love to have other things to talk about than you, if that's reasonable. I want to get to know *them* and be able to hold a conversation without hiding behind your muscles."

"I get that. Don't worry is really what I meant. They're my friends. I was hoping to take you to Massachusetts to meet the whole family before coming here. Sorry that didn't happen."

"I was wondering when I'd meet the family, or if I was to remain the best kept secret in town."

"You were *never* a secret to my family. My sisters have radar for my personal life, like a sixth sense."

"So they outted you?"

"Noooo. I offered you up to them."

"Like a sacrifice?"

"Ha—no. I was answering some texts and delicately slipped you in there."

"When was that?"

"*Ages* ago. I don't even know when. I know that they've been chomping at the bit to meet you but after having your parents out, I thought you needed a break. I told them that you'd all meet in good time."

"So they know about me and I know nothing about them."

"As much as I'd love to continue this, I gotta go. I should be home by ten. Want me to bring something home?"

"Having just been in your fridge, that'd be a good idea."

"Hey, there's juice, water. I think there's some cheese sticks in the drawer."

"Mmm, delish! That'll be lunch."

"Alrighty then," he said finitely. "I love you and will see you soon."

"You better," I said ruefully. "I've got some things I want to do to you."

"You're such a tease," he whispered.

"Bye." I hung up. I picked up the cheese and my water and poked my nose through the rest of the apartment. It had a bedroom but other than that, it was a studio apartment.

I picked up her book and read for a couple of hours. If I pushed just a little bit harder, I'd be able to finish it. The further I read, the more of the story came back to me and I started to dread what I knew was coming. I grabbed my cheese and ripped it open, prolonging the inevitable.

Checking the time, I knew I didn't have much left, so I prepared myself for Rory's death. Killing off a strong character was a shame. I loved my foray with her and wanted her to succeed. Her impending demise was spectacular and unforgettable. She'd soon be just another zombie casualty.

I heard the door unlocking when I had only pages to go. I winced. I'd abandoned my plans for wearing nothing more than the lucky blanket hours ago. As much as I wanted to jump him, I also wanted to finish the book. With the door opening, I closed the book and tossed it on the table.

I took a running leap. When he caught me, the surprised look on his face was priceless.

"And good evening to you, too," he said, lightly kissing my lips.

I wrapped my hands around his head and fervently returned his greeting. It had been too long.

Coming up for air, we both heard his stomach growl. I poked him the chest, "Not *now*, boy!" I scolded his belly.

"I left the food in the hallway. Chinese from across the street."

"I don't care," I said insolently. "I want something else inside of me."

His eyebrows raised, he smirked. "Wow, that really gets lost in a text."

He bounced me in his arms into a more comfortable position but remained stationary.

"If you get that bag, I will scream," I said. Without another thought, he carried me into the bedroom.

He wasn't nearly as muscular as he'd been when we met. He looked more like a man than an action figure. His hair was jet black, making the intensity of his blues eyes insufferable. I crawled across the bed, waiting to pounce.

Tossing his remaining sock, he met me at the edge of the bed and kissed me long and hard, pushing my body backward onto the bed. As we got reacquainted, I knew there was a discussion that we should probably have before things went any further. I chuckled to myself when I realized that this must be what it's like for guys when they have to stop what they're doing and reach for a condom.

"Hey," I said, pushing on his chest. "I—uh—"

"What?" he said, intently kissing my neck.

Putting my hands under his armpits, I shuddered. I did *not* want this to stop. As I tugged, his concentration broke. Making eye contact, he pitifully asked, "What?"

"How we left things—I. I haven't taken—I'm not on anything. So you might want to wrap that up."

I watched his face move through acknowledgement, understanding and finally to concern.

He rocked onto his elbow and pushed a lock of hair behind my ear. "What do you want to do?" he asked quietly.

"Do you have anything here?"

"I know every guy's always prepared but no." He shook his head, a look of panic setting in his features. "No," he added resolutely.

I caressed his shoulder. "You know what? There's a reason I stopped." I kissed him. "I just felt that you should have the option."

Rubbing his whiskers on my face, he softly said, "Thank you." Staring into the depths of my soul, he added, "I know what I want, too."

~~

With his belly screaming for sustenance, we devoured cold Chinese food on the couch. Between bites, he filled me in on his family. Susan had always been into children and had been disappointed that neither of her siblings had reproduced on her timeline. Of course, she took her own sweet time in finding the ideal mate and only recently was working on starting her family. Her husband, Daniel, was a product design engineer. He'd married young and had been divorced for many years before meeting her at a school function.

Mary was the free spirit in the family. She was an artist in search of adventure. She'd never had much of a plan but had finally decided to finish her education at Rhode Island School of Design, where she'd met her boyfriend of the last two years, Todd.

Mom was an indomitable force. She'd never worked. She married her high school sweetheart, Jonathan. For them, the most important thing was that she stay home and raise a good, Catholic family. She had strong opinions about what kind of girl was right for Chris and they rarely saw eye to eye.

Setting my chopsticks down, I rearranged myself under the blanket. I had an insatiable urge to touch my stomach as if to say, 'are you in there, buddy?' I knew I'd completely tuned him out when he started tickling my feet.

"Hey, stop!" I said, kicking at him.

"I thought I'd lost you!" he said. "You looked like you were deep in thought."

"Just thinking about family," I said sheepishly.

"You'll meet them soon enough *if* that's what you meant." Pushing the blanket up, he rubbed my foot.

"God, that feels good." I ignored his comment.

"How'd you feel about meeting my parents?" he asked, moving the massage up my leg.

I nodded, closing my eyes.

"Maybe we can squeeze in a quick trip later this month. I can't see waiting," he added under his breath.

"We are overdue, aren't we?"

He snorted. "That's what I'm afraid of. My mother'd be pissed if she found out she was going to be a grandmother and she'd never even *met* you."

~~

In the morning, his sisters came to get me and we walked over to a breakfast spot that Chris had talked about on more than one occasion.

Both of his sisters seemed really jazzed to meet me. Mary wanted to hear everything from my angle, exclaiming, 'We all know how guys tell stories!' which I took to mean lacking in detail. Over a lengthy breakfast, I did my best to fill in what they already knew. When Mary got up to hit the bathroom, Susan eyed me keenly. She'd developed bullshit detectors over time and I could sense that she was going to grill me sooner or later.

"You better not break his heart," she said matter-of-factly.

Taken aback, I blurted out, "I don't intend to."

"And I hope you're not some kind of baby-mama. He's been so careful—"

Interesting how families spun things. I wasn't so sure he'd been particularly careful so much as unlucky in getting what he wanted. I wanted to defend myself but instead, I returned her steady gaze.

"Wow, you haven't thought much of his previous girlfriends."

"Chris's a bleeding heart. No offense. I just don't want to see him hurt again."

"Well, that makes two of us," I said, spotting Mary.

Reaching the table, she picked up her purse, "You ready to get outta here? I thought we could check out the MoMa."

Sliding out of the booth, I couldn't agree more. "That sounds great. How d'we get there from here?"

~~

The Museum of Modern Art was the perfect destination. Conversations were brief and non-intrusive. Stopping to take in one piece, I considered how different these two sisters were. Mary was short, slight, and dark haired with blue eyes. If Chris were here with his dyed black hair, he'd look like Mary's taller twin. Susan was taller with mousy brown hair and hazel eyes. She looked like a teacher. When she smiled, she looked infinitely younger than her thirty eight years.

Later in the afternoon, Mary noticed a text from Chris. He'd offered to meet us at a bar. She lit up with the news.

"Oh, Sarah. I haven't seen my brother in ages," she bubbled. "And I've never met his girlfriends—well, not since high school. Throw in a trip to New York, the MoMa and this is stellar!"

"You don't see him much?"

"There's that East-West Coast thing and schedules. I just got out of school and have been busy trying to find a job."

"Anything promising?"

"Job-wise? I don't know. If I could be a student forever, I think I would. What do you do?" she asked casually.

"I'm looking for something myself," I demured.

"Yeah, I hate job hunting but whatever. It'll work out." We caught up to Susan. She was fiddling with her phone, she said, "Chris taking you to meet the folks any time soon?"

"Funny, we were talking about visiting them later this month."

"Huh. The way he'd been talking, I got the feeling he didn't have any chance to get away between now and Christmas."

"He said it'd be a quick trip," I replied, wondering if Susan was going to actually look at the art.

"Hey, Suzy-Q! Wanna go find Chris? Looks like you're done here."

She smiled apologetically. "Sorry. I'm not into art like you are. If I had my munchkins with me, it'd be fun to watch them, but just looking at art? Not so much."

~~

Chris was already at the bar, deep in conversation with a well-endowed woman sitting coquettishly to his right. Mary ran ahead and attacked her brother with a big bear hug, almost plowing down this woman.

Bouncing, she turned to the trollop, engaging her in conversation. As Susan and I approached, Chris was out of his spot like his pants were ablaze. Susan glanced at me and back at Chris.

"It's so good to see you," she said, hugging Chris tightly. Separating, she added, "Mom says hi."

He offered his seat to Susan. "Glad you guys were in the area. I know how much you like this place."

"Good memory. I haven't been here since your opening night after party in—that had to be ten years ago?"

Chris smiled. "Guess good memories run in the family."

"Back when you still took family to those kinds of events," Susan said.

"Did you *like* going? I never got the feeling that you had a great time."

"Oh, it was quite an experience. Too bad the me-in-my-thirties can't go. I'd love it now."

I kept glancing at Mary and the interloper. Chris was usually so good at introductions. When I couldn't stand it any longer, I asked, "Who's the broad?"

"'The broad?' Is that jealousy talking?" He gave my hand a squeeze. "Her name is Alicia."

"Is there anyone you won't talk to?" I was certain the answer was a resounding no.

"No, probably not." He pecked me on the cheek. "What'd you ladies do today?"

"Wait," I said. "Shouldn't we rescue your sister?"

"Nah," Chris and Susan said in unison. Chris added, "She makes connections wherever she goes. Watch. Alicia will either be looking for an art installation or will know someone who has a gallery. Mary's got great karma."

Susan agreed. "She is always willing to sit next to the crotchety old man on the airplane, too. She's had all sorts of offers over the years on her trips to and from Los Angeles." She shook her head ruefully. "A couple of times, I thought we could've lost her, but no. She always comes back home."

"I never would've thought you'd meet people worth talking to on a plane, but I met a woman on my flight out here who works in television. She was pretty cool," I said, thinking about Sylvia.

"While I was waiting for you, I heard from Imogen. She's going to meet us." Looking at his watch, he added, "Any time now."

"Julian, too?" I inquired. I was looking forward to spending some time with them.

"No, he's holed up in their apartment. I think that's one of the reasons she's coming out. She gets a little annoyed when she's ignored after a long day at the office."

"I would think it'd be nice to come home and have a little peace and quiet," I said.

"Maybe a little, but don't you find that you, as a woman, want to talk about your day?" He looked from me to Susan. "You ladies do like to talk." His eyes lit up. "A lot. Imagine coming home to someone who's lost to their own world? Julian's very single-minded when he's working on a deadline."

"As are you!" Susan chided. "You haven't talked to Mom in weeks. She keeps calling me to find out what's up with you."

Chris cringed. "Will *that* ever change?"

"I don't know. Are you going to settle down and move back home?"

Although it was dark in the bar, I think he blushed.

"Unlikely, appealing as that is," he said, rubbing my back. "You want anything?"

I shook my head as he asked his sisters.

"Took care of that! Thanks, big brother, for starting a tab!" Mary raised her half-empty beer.

"Least I could do," Chris responded, happy to be surrounded by all these women. As if on cue, Imogen appeared at my elbow.

"Hi, Sarah. It's good to see you again. I've gotta tell you—"

Chris interrupted her to introduce his sisters. Perhaps it was because they'd been in these situations before but they both pulled off the right amount of awe and normalcy easily. Even though I thought I was developing nicely, I wasn't sure that I'd ever look that blasé.

~~

We shared a cab home with Imogen who continued to prove herself a lovely lady. Arriving at our building, she said, "I almost forgot to thank you for introducing me to Lucy. She gave me quite a tarot reading."

I blinked. "I'm glad to hear that. She's been doing it for a long time, since I was a kid."

"I could tell. I've had lots of readings but hers felt like she was channeling," she said, pushing the elevator button.

"What're you looking forward to, if you don't mind me asking?" I said, following her in.

"It feels like it should be a secret," she said, debating. "But Chris was there so there's no real secret—" The door opened. "Oop. It's my floor. Have a good evening. See you tomorrow, lovah," she added, touching Chris's cheek fondly.

I turned, expecting him to fill in the blank. Chris leaned on the elevator jam.

"Well?" I said, waiting.

"Well, what?" he asked, basking in my torment. The elevator started beeping.

He gestured for me to get off. I was ready to pop him in the nose. He still hadn't answered. "Is this *another* secret only a wife'd be privy to, cuz if it is, I'm gonna—"

With his hands on my arms, he backed me out of the elevator, Frankenstein-style, rocking my stiff-legged body. "Oh, I'm sorry I ever said that." He was grinning like a little kid.

"I'm getting mixed signals down here," I said, growling.

"Sorry." He hugged me. "It seems baby brain is going around."

My body stiffened. "Come again," I said, perturbed.

"Your mom saw all sorts of fertility in her readings. That's all." He grabbed my hand and dragged me the final couple of yards to our door. "Babies! Babies for everyone!"

~~

## 22

He was gone before I awoke. There was something deflating about waking up in an empty bed. I had my doubts that I would grow accustomed to it any time soon.

I put on some coffee and found his note.

'Morning, Sunshine. Thinking about having and holding you. Love you, C.'

I read it over and over. I took my phone and sent a picture to Jess before tucking it safely in my purse. 'Take *that* world!' I thought. As much as I loathed sitting and waiting for him, this note was pure gold. Nothing was going to irritate me today.

I texted Mary to see what was on today's agenda. She gave me two options—she was going to go meet up with Alicia-from-the-bar and check out her gallery, maybe visit a couple of artist-friends or I could hang with Susan on the set.

I chose Mary. Dressed in black, she was ecstatic to be showing me around New York. It took some effort to find Alicia's gallery. It was in the basement, the only streaks of daylight coming from the open door. She had loud modern art on the walls, chaotic paintings that shrieked at me like tortured souls. As interesting as they were, this was not my bag. She also had display cases of unusual jewelry made out of found items. There was a necklace with a captivating bottle cap charm.

"You like that one?" Alicia asked, rounding the counter.

"I've never seen anything like it," I responded, standing up.

"You can have it. It's one of the first things I made. It's been here too long." She opened the case and took it out, squeezing it in her hands.

"Do you want a box?" she asked, admiring her work.

"I'd rather wear it."

"Cool," she said, sliding it onto a leather cord. "I'm glad to know it's going to someone who appreciates it."

I pulled off the $200 price tag. "I'd like to make things like this. I used to make hats for all occasions—little hats on head bands. I have some real classics."

"Hey, I could sell those here. Do you have any pictures?" she asked, intrigued.

"Sure do." I scrolled through my photos.

"Did you make that?" Mary asked, peeking over my shoulder.

"Uh-huh. I love getting my artistic groove on." I handed Mary my phone.

"That's *awesome*! That's Gotham City?" She passed it to Alicia.

"I made it for a friend who was going to Comicon."

Alicia flipped through a couple of pictures before handing the phone back. "If you'd do maybe five to ten of those for me, they'd be easy to sell. Are you interested?"

I'd thought about opening an online store. My hats were always well-received. Until recently, I hadn't had the time to make any, let alone mass produce them.

Mary nodded her head vigorously. "Come on, Sarah! What've you got to lose?"

~~

Mary and I grabbed some hot dogs and headed for Central Park. I fell in love with her. She was vivacious and charming and funny and clever and talented. I was ready to bring her to Los Angeles with me.

Laughing, she said, "It feels like you could be my sister."

"I feel the same way. I was a little nervous yesterday. I got the feeling Susan didn't approve of me."

"Oh, Suzy-Q! She takes after my mother when it comes to matters of the heart. No one can be perfect enough for her little brother. And, truthfully, she thought that Ella was *the one*. He dropped off the face of the planet when he was with her."

"That's hard to believe. Your brother is such a big talker. Sometimes, between his makeup and desire to gossip, I think I'm dating a girl. I can't imagine him disappearing."

She bumped me with her shoulder. "I gotta confess. I think you see a side of Chris that we don't. He's always a gentle giant but very guarded when he's at home. Which is rarely."

"Is that why you made so many trips to Los Angeles?"

"No, I made all those trips because my bro is a rock star. I want to live that life! He was kind enough to remember the little people on his way to the top."

"He is generous, kind. A good guy," I said thoughtfully.

"I'm overdue for a trip out there. *You* put a halt to my frequent trips. Not that I couldn't go on my own dime, but I'm still counting those. Besides, I *love* hanging with my big brother. I've met so many cool people. I just wish I had the talent to do what he does!"

"It does seem like a great lifestyle, doesn't it?" I said, finishing off my hotdog.

"Word. Has he taken you to an opening? I got to go to an awards ceremony with him and the people-watching was outstanding!"

"I went to a fundraiser. I didn't recognize most of the faces but I think I was just overwhelmed. He was the emcee. Ian Hartlass played the piano." Gauging the change in her expression, I asked "Have you met him?"

"Oh, I more than met him," she declared proudly. She took a long drag off her straw.

"You were a conquest?"

"God no! I don't think anyone knows." She looked panicked. "*Don't* tell Chris—*PLEASE!*" she said, putting her hand on my thigh.

"You've got it. Wha—I probably don't want to know." I desperately wanted the details.

"I've never had a chance to talk about it, really. I told a friend back in the day but I really don't think she believed me." She smiled. "It is hard to believe."

"Why's that? He's got quite a rep."

"Yeah, but this was *ages* ago. He was barely a somebody. He was *hot* but not a household name."

"I can't even picture a young, innocent Ian."

She guffawed. "I don't think he was ever innocent! I learned a lot, quickly." She said, meeting my gaze.

"I'm not sure if I should offer you a cigarette or—"

"I'd take a cigarette, if you have one," she said, cutting me off. "That's another one of my dirty little secrets. And damn, thinking about him makes me really want one. Thanks, Sarah!" She stomped her feet.

"Tell me about Todd. He's gotta be pretty cool. Chris said you've been together for a couple of years?"

"Todd. He's a graphic artist with a great deal of tattooing experience. If you want to add to your collection, you should talk to him! I'm sure he'd extend the family deal to you," she said pulling up her shirt to reveal a sleeve tattoo that culminated in a dragon.

"That's some serious art on your arm!" I admired the lines. Todd had a deft hand with detail.

"That was his final project when I met him. It's *how* I met him."

"Sounds like a story."

"Not really. I heard he was looking for someone to tattoo as kind of a performance piece. I thought it'd be one way to get a tattoo for free so I brought my drawing to him and asked if he could do it. He said yes and showed me some he'd done already. I was convinced."

"Why'd you call it a performance piece?"

"Oh, because he tattooed me in front of an audience. Don't ask why, cuz I don't know and I don't recommend it." She absently rubbed her arm.

"Do you have any more?"

"You know what they say—once you start you can't stop. I've got sleeves and another on my back and ankle. I'm trying to stop but Todd's got a few, too so— " She shrugged. "I love your 'now' tattoo. If I hadn't seen it on you, that'd be my next one. Simple and poignant."

"I still like it."

"Hey, what has Chris told you about dear ol' Mom and Dad? If you're coming, I think you should be warned."

I snorted. "He survived *my* parents. My mom believes in faeries and tarot cards. Dad's a drunk. Your folks sound normal in comparison."

"Nothing wrong with—does she *really* believe in faeries or does she have a *fondness* for them?"

"No, I think she believes in them or maybe that fondness is so deep I can't tell the difference. She's always making and installing faery doors and leaving them tithings."

"Well, there are worse things. My mom is very religious. That's worse, trust me." I waited for her to continue, putting my trash in my cup. "I think her tenacity is one reason that Chris bolted as soon as he could. He left for New York in his late teens and rarely comes home. He says it's his schedule but I think it's that distance allows his heart to grow fonder. She was a great mom when we were little but as soon as we discovered the opposite sex, she went on lockdown. You'd've thought she never wanted us to grow up and get out."

"But you and Susan didn't go far?" I prodded.

"True. Susan lived with them forever. I think she was afraid of Mom. Her husband, Daniel, is stronger willed than my mother so that's a good thing. He wormed his way in and is her beacon now. I hope that she gets to have babies soon. They've been trying since their honeymoon."

"And you?"

"Like I said, I tried to move to L.A. but Chris kicked my ass back here. When I got back, I fell in with the wrong crowd. I've since gotten myself together, but I was definitely the black sheep."

"Well, I'm looking forward to meeting your family. I haven't been back to the East Coast since I moved to L.A. and that was years ago."

"I'll make it a point to be there. Todd and I are very distracting," she added, grinning. "Personally, I'd like to welcome you to the family. You and I are going to get along just fine."

~~

That evening, I was chilling on the couch, reading when Chris walked in. He took a stage dive over the couch, smashing me and my book. Nuzzling my nose, he put his arm securely around me and he shoved me to the edge of the couch.

"Welcome home!" I said, returning his enthusiasm. "To what do I owe this pleasure?"

Kissing me again, he said, "Imogen."

It was such an unexpected response that I stopped mid-kiss, holding his lip between my teeth.

"Say what?" I said in horror.

"I spent the last several hours rolling around with her. It was— " He stopped, looking for the right word. "Something."

"Something? 'It was something.'" I laughed. "Yeah, that's my big fear—that it'll *be* something for real!"

"No, no, no. This was different. I know I was joking about using you as source material but you live in my head. I—" He blushed. "I should stop. I know. Nothing good will come of this!"

"It *is* after one. And you can say anything if you like, but I like this lusty Chris who walked in the door. You've got *one* thing on your mind, huh?"

"Oh, I've got a couple of things on my mind but they all involve you. I *need* you. *Badly*," he said, weaving his arm behind my head and pulling me in for a passionate kiss.

As he continued kissing down my neck, I put my hands in his over-styled hair. Whatever product they threw in it, as soon as my fingers cleared, it stood right back up. I could've continued to play with it but as he unbuttoned my shirt, he forcefully shifted my focus.

We were both so tightly wound up that what used to be a ripple now caused a cascade of sensation. Every caress, every kiss—I felt his presence both physically and mentally in a way I'd never experienced.

I knew what he wanted and met him at every opportunity. Hearing little noises escape him only goaded me on until I was on top, his hands on my hips. I had no idea what their scene looked like but I was doing my best to be memorable.

~~

The remaining two days passed in the same way. When I went to the airport alone, it felt like my little foray to New York never happened. The memory had a dream-like quality. I felt warm, maybe melancholy, that it was over. I didn't feel the need to cry but I felt like a used rag, limp and lifeless.

Before I drove home, I hit some craft stores to get supplies for my new hat making endeavor. Toting the bags upstairs, I quickly turned the bedroom overlooking the fountain into my impromptu studio. With a new sense of purpose, I went through my remaining boxes hunting for my glue gun.

Sitting with a pile of paper, cardboard and fabric in my lap, I wrapped and unwrapped the same headband multiple times. Just as I hit upon a winning design, I saw Jessica and Ian heading up the driveway with boxes. I froze, the significance of the boxes apparent. I wanted to scream and stomp my feet. The tip of my finger turned purple around the tightly twisted ribbon.

I tossed my stuff down and jogged down to the guest house. Inside, they'd thrown the boxes down and were getting something to eat. I knocked, opening the door as I did so.

"You're back!" Jessica said, surprised. "I thought you were out till tomorrow?"

"Nope. What're you up to?" I asked, aware that I sounded desperate.

Ian handed me a beer. "Packin' her up."

"Did you find a place?" I asked cautiously.

"She's moving in with me," he said, using his most sultry tone.

I took a heavy swig from my bottle, eyes flashing. "You are?"

Jess set her bottle down. "I'm *thinking* about it." Her eyes darted between us.

Hungrily kissing her neck, he said "You were doing more than thinking about it even ten minutes ago." Shaking her hair, she swatted him away. "Consider the not-so-fringe benefits," he said silkily.

"Hello? I'm standing right here," I responded loudly.

"*Un*invited, I may add." He reached out and put his hand on mine. "If you change your tune, you're welcome to stay." He gently brushed my hand with his fingertips.

I picked up my bottle, ignoring him. "Is your departure imminent?"

"No, I've looked at a couple of places."

"Which are ultra-conservative," he implored.

"Two places that would need a little Jessifying," she corrected.

"And too small—unimaginative," he declared.

"They are small. No getting around that," she agreed.

"Move in with me. You're better than a guest house, babe," he entreated.

"Is Angel still around?" I fired off.

"She's not dead," he answered darkly.

"Jess?" I said, expecting the worst.

"She hasn't been around. I think she got tired of being an addendum," Jess said unemotionally.

"She was *never* an addendum. She is a collection of exclamation points," he said, savoring a memory.

"How 'bout an ellipsis?" Jessica said through a crooked smile.

He shook his head.

"I'm glad you've met her. I hear there's a lot of Angel-related history," I peppered.

"*Everyone* has history. There's a lot about your life pre-L.A. that would be informative. The best of times, the worst of times?" he challenged.

"But it's ancient. There's no one who keeps things in my drawers."

Ian choked on his beer. "Oh, really?"

Jessica snickered.

"Both of you—you deserve each other!" I huffed, defeated. "Back to the original question—"

Jessica gave me a hug. "I'm collecting boxes. That's all. I have seen a few things but I'm still looking. I want to stay in the area. Obviously, I won't be your *neighbor* but I don't want to be too far away. It is time for me, time for you, to go forth and prosper."

She was right. That became clear as soon as I told her I wanted babies. Though Jess liked kids, it was probably time to find a new crib.

I picked up a pita chip and scooped some hummus, inviting myself to dinner. As we ate, I mused. What would they look like when they grew up? Would this be their lot in life or would either of them outgrow his predilection? He viewed women as consumables, but he had it bad for Jess. Perhaps he'd be satiated by one high caliber partner before she moved on.

When they put on another horror flick, I commandeered a pillow and buried myself in the oversized chair. I contemplated the other relationships around me, from Melissa's failed marriage to her toying entanglement with Tom; Amy—willing to go the distance but unable to find the track; my parents and their warped mess of a partnership; me and Chris.

Our relationship was solid and yet not seeing him on a daily basis was a chronic problem for me. I couldn't see giving him up permanently but the temporary breaks were no less painful. I wanted to be watching stupid movies with Chris. He was halfway across the world with a beautiful woman while I was hunkered down with a smelly old pillow.

Signs were pointing to a proposal but I wasn't convinced that marriage would remove the aforementioned white elephant. A ring was not a noose—he was still free to move around the globe with or without me. Chagrinned, I had to admit that I was more than a serial monogamist. I was a concentric circle and without him in my space, the definition didn't work.

Halfway through the movie, I left and sat on the patio. The stars were out in spades. Jasmine hung heavily in the air. It was a perfect night for a romp in the hammock. I kicked it and watched it swing.

Digging out my phone, I gave Chris a call. It was no surprise when he didn't answer. I knew his hours were irregular at best and he did like to hang out after a full day.

I imagined him rolling around with Imogen, going out to the bar—with Imogen. Taking the same damn cab to the same freakin' building—with Imogen. Had I not met her, I would be hellaciously jealous, but instead I was envious. She didn't even care for what she had. How could anyone take him for granted? 'Just a job' did not sum up this situation. The job was part and parcel of my existence and I resented it.

I sent him a couple of texts. I wanted to be playful but I also wanted to convey my dislike of mandatory separation. Rereading my own texts, I sounded manic even to me. Not a good realization.

~~

## 23

I booked a ticket. Instead of having Chris take care of everything, I dreamt of a big reveal. I was going to surprise him. I already knew the lay of the land so it would not cause me undue anxiety. With this plan, I arrived in New York mid-day Monday.

Letting myself into his apartment, I was giddy. I poked my nose in his fridge to make a list of essential food stuffs that I should acquire. A few computer clicks later, I'd placed an order for delivery. That was one thing I really liked about this city—the ability to pick out groceries and have them delivered to your door the same day. When I'd introduced Chris to the concept, he'd been receptive but his fridge belayed his antipathy. Beyond snacks, the guy did not eat here.

Today was the day that I would do the lucky blanket surprise, my version of 'nothing but a trench coat.' Looking at the clock, I knew it'd be hours before he was home but even so, I was jumpy. If I could have arrived on the set dressed as I was, I would have. Instead, I showered and rubbed essential oils into my skin. I was going to look and smell good enough to devour.

As I was finishing up, I heard the door unlock and voices. Standing there au natural, it sounded like Imogen had followed Chris into the apartment. As the door latched, I was positive. I was stranded in the bathroom with a towel and the blanket.

Trapped, I painted my toes. When I finished one foot, I heard him in the kitchen. Mid laugh, he stopped. I set the polish down, eager to understand the pause. Moments later, he returned to Imogen. Strangely, they spoke more quietly. I was having a harder time hearing them. I finished my other foot and reveled in their beauty.

I folded the towel and made a little throne out of the toilet seat. If I was really going to have to spend much more time in here, better to be comfortable. I pulled the blanket around me and started counting wall tiles, looking for patterns in the dirty grout. The longer I sat, the more annoyed I became with his ability to talk.

When their conversation tapered off altogether, I had an overwhelming feeling of dread. What if they'd brought their project home? What if they were snuggled on the couch, practicing? All one had to do was pick up a tabloid to see onscreen romances blossom before your eyes. I thought I was going to lose my mind, when there was a tap on the bathroom door. I pulled the blanket more snugly around my body.

"Sarah?" he said buoyantly. "Open up."

Relieved, I did as instructed, standing against the bathtub. He walked in and latched the door.

"How long've you been holed up in here?" he asked, giving me a hug.

"Feels like forever," I groused. "Imogen in there?"

"She fell asleep on the couch," he said, kissing me. The first kiss was a simple, reassuring hello but when I dropped my blanket, we almost fell into the bathtub.

"You smell outstanding," he said, licking my ear. "Don't taste bad, either."

"I wanted to surprise you," I sniffed.

"Oh, you did. I've spent the last hour trying to figure out how to get her to leave. As soon as I opened up the fridge, I thought you could be around—not *holed* up in the bathroom. I thought you might be downstairs at the bar or something."

I crossed my arms. "So," I said conversationally. "How was your day?"

He started chuckling. "Not bad, not bad." He rubbed my arms. "Is that my lucky blanket?"

I snorted. "It's *certainly* not mine!"

"To be fair, you called it a security blanket." He eyed me hungrily. "Are you feeling secure?"

I glanced at the blanket ringing my feet and bit my lip. "Better now that you're here."

"See, it's better to call it a *lucky* blanket," he said, kicking it out of the way.

"Duly noted. What're we gonna do now?"

"I think we *both* know what we're going to do," he said, kissing my throat. "The question is *where*."

"And how. I'll raise you a how."

"Ooh," he said, licking his lips. "Want to discuss the *how* or shall I—" He cupped my breast and played with my nipple. "Show you?"

~~

I chose the right day for a surprise. We were given the luxury of rolling around in the morning until there was a discreet knock at the bedroom door.

Imogen quietly opened the door. "Chris?"

Yanking the blanket up under our noses, we peered out like naughty children. Watching the color spread into her cheeks, she dipped her head.

"Well, good morning, guys," she said, leaning on the door frame. "I never heard you come in!"

"She was trapped in the bathroom," Chris said, sitting up.

"Hi, Imogen." I saluted.

"Silly girl! Why didn't you come out?" she said, adjusting her purse.

"I—uh. I froze. I had this great plan and you weren't a part of it," I said honestly.

"Ah, I see. Well, I thought we could go in together. Why don't you come and get me when you're ready to go?"

"Sounds like a plan," Chris said.

"Good to see you again, Sarah," Imogen said, making her exit.

"That felt too much like college, 'the walk of shame,'" I said, eyeing Chris.

"I didn't realize you went. I didn't," Chris said, inching back into the bed.

"I wasn't there long. Didn't even finish my first year."

"What happened?" he asked.

"I found out I really didn't like school." I scoffed. "I wish I could say it was something else. It was too much work and I didn't know why I was there. It's not like I was going to be a doctor or something."

"Mmm," he mused, playing with my hair. "What'd you do instead?"

"I traveled a lot. I held jobs just as long as I had to in order to eat and have a car."

"No roof?"

"Not *my* roof. I always had a place to crash. Lots of good friends."

"How long you staying under *this* roof?" he asked, tickling my arm.

"I brought some stuff to do and thought I'd stay for a while."

"No end in sight?"

"Not right now. I am getting better at leaving things open-ended."

"That's great news. Did you bring some stuff for the gallery? Mary sent me pictures of your hats and necklaces." He smiled. "She said that she really likes you." He fiddled with my fingers.

"I like her, too. She feels like a kindred spirit."

"I think she *is*. Mary wants you to meet the folks," Chris said, eyes dancing. "She said she's eager to run interference so that you stay."

I rolled on to my hip, facing him. "I'd love to meet them. She did warn me that mom can be a bit of a religious zealot."

"Ha! She would say that. She's just kind of a controlling person by nature. She's afraid that some bawdy lass is going to come in and steal my money. That was one thing that didn't bother her about me and Ella. She never felt that Ella was going to take me to the cleaners."

"What does she know about how you two separated?"

Chris looked at me thoughtfully. "You know, it isn't nearly so painful to talk about that part of my life now, and I have you to thank." He traced my jawline with his finger. "It's true." A smile spreading onto his face, he answered, "Everyone knew that I wanted a family. When things started creeping into the tabloids, Mom got concerned that 'where there's smoke, there's fire.' She told me that I should drop what I was doing and address it which—I sort of did. I guess I can thank my mom for that. It was her nagging that made me drop by unexpectedly." He paused. "I've never really thought about that series of events."

"And when the baby disappeared? How did the family matriarch take that?" I pursued.

Chris's handsome face contorted. "None of us were happy. You don't get raised a Catholic and then 'lose' a baby. Mom crossed her off the face of the earth and never mentioned her again." He frowned, staring at the blanket.

"Well, I've got that on her. I'm *interested* in procreating!" I moved his hand to my butt.

He brightened. "You've got *a lot* more on her than that. I love you," he said huskily, massaging my cheeks.

I rolled him onto his back, lying across his chest contentedly.

"How long d'you think we've got before you're pregnant?" he mused.

"I dunno. I was on birth control forever. It can take a long time," I said matter-of-factly.

"How long is 'long?'" he asked, tickling my back.

"Like I said—I didn't go to school to be a doctor, and I have been running from pregnancy forever, so I don't know. More than a few months, I'm guessing."

He kissed my hair. "Cool. Lots of practice!" he said, lazily.

I propped myself on my forearms. "You're goofy."

"Whatever keeps you coming back for more," he answered.

"Back to meeting your parents," I said, staring at him.

"Another topic that should be outlawed from the bedroom!" He slid me off his chest.

Before he could get a controlling position, I sat up. "We can get something to eat, if you like, and talk about it? I'd love to meet them while I am on this side of the country."

He grabbed the pillow and hit me with it. "How about we make sweet love and *then* eat and *then* make our plans?"


Taking his sweet time, there was none left for planning much of anything. I was intrinsically happy, lying in bed watching him get ready to go to work. He was grinning from ear to ear as he toweled off his hair.

Because he was going to be rolling around with Imogen again today, he fastidiously took care of the details right down to a good Q-tip ear cleansing. His primping solidified my notion that I was dating a girl. He spent more time in front of the mirror than I ever did.

While he was digging for a shirt, I got up and hugged him. Between the wonderful scent of his aftershave and shiny, clean torso, I wanted to pull him back into bed.

Peeking over his shoulder, he stopped. "I'm so glad you're here."

"I wish you could stay," I said brusquely.

"Trust me—me, too." Pulling a shirt over his chest, he stopped to kiss my hand.

"What're you gonna do today?" he asked, wrapping my arms around him.

"I think I'll see what social media has to offer, visit Julian and see if we can eat together and then take my stuff over to Alicia's gallery. I told her I'd be by today or tomorrow."

"Sounds like a full calendar," he said approvingly.

"Should keep me sane while I wait." I gave him a hearty squeeze.

"Imogen's gonna be knocking. I gotta go." He bent down and kissed me lightly on the lips.

"Parting is such sweet sorrow," I cried.

"Do *not* say good night till it be morrow!" he added, disentangling himself. "I will be back at a reasonable hour. If we can sneak in a trip to my parents, we should. Short and sweet is the best way to go."

I followed him into the hallway, "Hey! Which room is Julian's?"

"End of this hall on your left," he said, disappearing into the elevator.

I went to see if Julian was ready to eat something. I was ravenous. Knocking on the door, Imogen yelled, "I'm coming!"

"Hi, Sarah," Julian said opening the door and looking for Chris.

"Chris is already downstairs. I came to see if you're interested in getting something to eat."

Julian swept the hair out of his eyes. "We just had something to eat, but you're welcome to come in if you'd like?" he added, throwing the door open.

"Chris, I'm coming—I'll meet you downstairs!" she yelled.

"Looks like you guys had a morning like ours," I said, noting his bare chest and lounge pants.

He looked like he'd been caught red-handed. "I don't know about you but there's something about knowing your partner is going to, you know, work—"

"I get it. It's hard to let them go."

He had a charming smirk. "Yes. It is," he said as Imogen bowled into him.

"Hi, Sarah," she said gliding through the door. "I'm sorry about last night. Hey, you guys should get something to eat!" She kissed Julian on the cheek. "Make sure he *eats*, would you?" she commanded, sprinting to the elevator.

"Shit." He grimaced. "I don't have long," he said, watching her get on the elevator.

"You do have to eat," I said sounding more like a mother than I liked.

"Rumor has it you were stuck in the *bathroom*?" His eyes twinkled. "Bet that was fun."

"Far from ideal. But anyway—food! Want to get something downstairs or do you want to come over? I did some shopping."

"You bought groceries? Endless restaurants in New York and you're cooking." He snorted. "That'll change if you hang around us long enough."

~~

While eating, Julian was more than willing to talk. I got the feeling that perhaps Imogen felt ignored because maybe, just maybe, she didn't want to hear about his writing when she got home. Given the opportunity to talk about his project, the floodgates were open. It was hard to keep up with the onslaught of detail.

Interestingly, he assumed that I knew about his latest project that Ian and Chris'd roped him into. Hearing that I wasn't any the wiser, he looped back and filled me in on their latest conquest, a zombie thriller written by some unknown author that he was now adapting into a screen play.

Although he'd talked to her on the phone, he hadn't made the connection.

On Jessica's behalf, I had to ask one question. "What do you think about the ending—you gonna let Rory die?"

His eyes widened. "You're familiar with this book."

"You could say that. I'm surprised that they didn't tell you that Ian's girlfriend wrote it."

"I never would've believed them."

"Oh?"

"Angel couldn't string together a complete thought."

"That's not the girlfriend I was talking about."

He smirked. "Only with Ian would you have to clarify *which* girlfriend." He gazed at me intently. "He doesn't date women with brains."

"That may be true, but Jessica is a writer."

"A long time writer or a long-time girlfriend?" he asked disbelievingly.

"Long-time *writer* and by Ian's time line, maybe a longer-time girlfriend," I said uncertainly.

"Why wouldn't he tell me that he'd optioned his girlfriend's material?" he said, perplexed. "It'd be helpful, really, to talk to her; maybe work with her to see what is possible with Rory."

"Eww. So you think it's going to be hard to have her die? That's Jessica's biggest concern—that Hollywood doesn't have the balls to let her go."

"Nobody wants her to die. She's a great character—strong, compassionate, an ass kicker. It's also hard to have a sequel if you've killed off the only reason one would happen."

I raised an eyebrow. "Did you know that there are more books in the series? It does continue even without Rory."

"I'll have to get my hands on those."

"But if you think *Twisted River's* worthy of a sequel, that might get her attention."

Sweeping the hair out of his eyes, he said, "Never hurts to plan for the future."

~~

Seeing Alicia made my day. The best part of my visit was getting paid for doing something that I really enjoyed. After giving me some walking around money, she warned me to cover my eyes as she affixed the prices. Comparing what I was paid to what she thought she could get, I did suffer sticker shock.

She briefly showed me her website as she uploaded pictures of my hats. Her website was polished. She could sell anyone a bridge and profit mightily at the same time.In awe, I asked if I could work for her in exchange for an introduction to what she does and how she makes it work.

As the afternoon faded away, I had a new job and a sense of purpose. I was going to rock New York!

On my subway ride back, I texted Mary. If there was someone that I wanted to thank, it was she.

'What'd Alicia think?'

'Loved it. She's great. I left with a job and a problem.'

'Problem?'

'She says I need a website and I don't know anyone who does them.'

'Todd can do it.'

My luck felt endless. To be dropped into an artistically-inclined family was exactly the kick in the supportive pants that I needed.

'He's good at them. Check out his website.'

'Thanks! Wish you were here.'

Looking around the subway, I would have loved company. Although I feared flying, I could now add a distaste for traveling underground as well.

'Won't be long. I'm dragging him out to look at some places.'

'Exciting!'

'And about time.'

'Makes me wish that our home was New York."

I hadn't thought about living anywhere but Los Angeles, however, having her around made New York more attractive.

'No. You belong out there. You can *visit* here. BTW, Mom says she's meeting you later this week! We'll be there.'

'Cool. That must be hot off the press.'

'Whoops. You didn't know? Damn Chris and his schedule. Sorry.'

Getting a text from Chris, I let Mary go. Chris wanted me to be ready to go out on the town when he got home. Looking for a clock, I was pretty sure that I was going to have to move faster to be ready. Finding one, I wasn't going to make it. He'd be home in the next couple of minutes and I still had at least another twenty to go.

I also had texts from Jess. She had, in fact, sold the rights to her book to a production company called Doppelgänger Films for a pretty penny. She was likely moving and wanted my help. Amidst the upheaval, she also finished her most recent book. I whipped out a couple of congratulatory notes to her.

Checking in online, I was confused by an off-handed tweet from Chris. I'd been a follower long before I met him and usually his tweets were work-related. I wasn't sure what to make of 'Let It Begin.' It had already garnered quite a few comments which seemed to sum up an overall 'huh?' from his fans. I added, 'hope I'm not late!' before stowing it and heading into our building.

Opening the door to our apartment, I heard the muffled sound of the shower under the upbeat music filling the apartment. He was obviously in good spirits, I thought, setting my purse down on the couch.

"Chris?" I called, walking towards the bathroom.

Peeking out, the color drained from his face. "You're late," he said, an unfamiliar quality in his voice.

"Sorry," I said, stopping at the door. "Wow, it smells *good* in there!" I inhaled deeply. It smelled like my body butter, full of sweet orange and lavender. "Is it you?" I asked, coyly.

He shook his head, opening the door. "Change of plans." He took my hands in his and pulled me into the cramped bathroom. "The bath's for you."

"Instead of going out, I'm taking a bath?" I eyed him quizzically.

"We can still go out but I thought, I thought—" he stuttered. Regaining his composure, he said, "I had one of those days at the office. I want to see you, *be* with you, before anything else." He put his hands on the edges of my shirt and slowly lifted it over my head. "Has anyone ever given you a bath?" he asked, dropping my shirt on the floor.

"Not in more than twenty years," I said, as he spun me around and removed my bra.

Kissing my back, he whispered, "It's about time."

"'To begin?'" I asked, referencing his tweet.

He took a deep breath. "Yeah. To begin." I danced out of my skirt. One hand on my waist, he tested the water with his other. He guided me into the tub, putting a towel behind my head.

He lit a couple of candles and disappeared. He changed the musical selection to something softer before returning with a couple of my favorite beers.

"You have no idea how hard it was to walk in here with beers when the scene demands wine," he said, handing me one.

"Thanks," I said, confused.

He was jittery and my Spidey sense was tingling. He took a sip of his beer, started to set it down and then belted more down.

"Sarah," he said, dropping off the toilet onto his knees. "I've been thinking a lot about us, our future and doing some planning—"

A knot was forming in my throat. I felt my humor succumbing to his jitters.

"I've had some *amazing* ideas." He snatched a washcloth, dropped some soap on it, and half-heartedly took a swipe at my chest.

I smirked. Thank god I wasn't filthy. I watched him squeeze out the water and submerge the washcloth over and over again.

Letting go, he traced my collar bone. Wriggling in the tub, I was torn by the urge to pull him in and the desire to get out and tell him everything was okay.

"I know I've told you that I'm done—" He trailed off. "Dammit! This is what I should have been rehearsing." He ran his hands viciously through his own hair, staring at some indeterminate place on the ceiling. He stood and jammed his hands in his pockets.

"You are everything that I've been looking for. You're the face I want to see before I go to bed, the person I want to hear from—be with. I think about you constantly—when I'm working, eating, sleeping. You color every moment." He pursed his lips. "I love you, Sarah. Will you marry me?" he said, choking up. The words ringing in my ears, he fell to his knees and popped open a pretty little green box to reveal the ring. It was the most exquisite piece of jewelry.

His eyes overcome with tears, I gasped and slid a little further into the bubbles. Although it may have been nothing more than seconds, I felt my entire life flashing before my eyes. I saw all the other paths that a 'yes' would create or that a 'no' would make necessary. Always a practical person, I saw no reason to leave him, and for that, I grinned and nodded my head wholeheartedly.

"Yes," I whispered, sitting up and proferring my hand.

His hands shaking, he hadn't thought through the wet-girl-in-the-bathtub part of the equation. He reached around for another washcloth. Setting the box on his lap, he delicately dried off my hand and slid the ring on.

I admired it. It was brilliant if unconventional. Sitting up, I held his hand. Were he smaller, I would have pulled him into the tub. Instead, I used his arm for support and pulled my dripping hulk out of the suds.

Standing in the tub, I leaned over and pressed my wet body to his. Forcefully, he wrapped his arms around me. It was hard to breathe. He kissed my wet head and sighed. I returned the favor, soaking his shirt.

We looked at each other in silence. His face was content, his eyes filled with excitement. "You have no idea how hard that is," he said softly.

Puzzled, my brow furrowed. "Hard?"

"Yessiree. I wanted it to be memorable. I wanted to know you'd say yes—I was pretty sure you'd say yes but damn—" He shuddered.

Putting my arms around his neck, I gazed at my ring.

As he kissed my neck, I said, "What a gorgeous ring. Where'd you get it?"

He eyed me closely, "You know where I got it. You picked it out."

"Oh, I did?"

His head bobbed vigorously. "Yeah. You did. If ever a girl salivated over a ring, you did. I heard about it from everybody who crossed paths with you at the benefit. It was quite a conversational piece—you, our relationship, that ring!" He continued to squint at me. "You *do* like it," he said authoritatively.

"I love it!" I squealed. "You're really cute when you're operating outside your comfort zone. I thought you were gonna lose it."

"Hey, that's what was going through my mind, too. I could be going too far and you'd have nothing left to do but peel outta here." He slipped his arms loosely around my waist.

"Is *that* why I had to go in the tub? To slow down my exit?" I laughed loudly.

He bowed his head. "Maybe. Subconsciously."

"I'm so happy. No one can say no to you, Christopher Sparks," I whispered, kissing him.

He laughed sharply. "I don't care about anyone but you. Your 'no' is the only one that matters."

~~

"What *are* the dinner plans?" I asked, finding some shoes.

"I thought we'd go out with Imogen and Julian. We're actually right on time. We're supposed to meet them in about forty five minutes," he said, rooting through the closet.

"Where?" I asked, startled that there were plans at all.

"Down the street at Onyx. Some celebrity chef opened it a couple of years ago."

"Who?"

"I don't remember. It was Imogen's suggestion. She knows the woman."

"Does Imogen *know*?" I asked, thinking he'd roped in another conspirator.

"'Fraid so."

"I'm getting tired of being the last to know!" I said, swatting him with my purse. "This'll change when I'm Mrs. Sparks, right? In fact, there are a lot of things that I think you should come clean about."

His shoulders tensed. The longer he went without so much as a twitch, I became convinced that he was opening closets and examining his skeletons. He was waiting for me to give him direction so that he could leave some of them undisturbed.

Fingering my ring, I volunteered, "First off—what the hell're you doing with Jess's book? It really pissed me off when you wouldn't tell me."

He relaxed. "I'm sorry. I thought I was being coy."

"I didn't like it," I affirmed. "I felt like you didn't trust me."

He rotated my ring. "I *am* sorry."

"Is it something we can discuss over dinner or is it a big secret?" He cringed. "What? Do *they* know about that, too?" He winced. "Jesus! I am the last to know *again*!?!"

He bristled, a look of mea culpa on his face.

"Is there anything else in the works that I should know about?" I crossed my arms. "Anything? Anything at all?" I scrutinized his face, taking pleasure in his discomfort.

"Um… We're meeting my parents on Friday?" he said under his breath.

"That's a good one!" I stomped to the front door. "Hadn't we better get going? I'd hate to make 'em wait," I said tartly.

A smile spread across his face. "You were jerking my chain."

Feigning shock, I cocked my head and eyed him.

"You were. You little funster. Julian told you about the book." My eyebrows went up. "And you know about our trip to Newburyport!"

"What are you insinuating, Mr.Sparks?" I asked, knowing that the jig was up.

He crossed his arms. "You're not much of an actress, Miss Riley."

~~

## 24

We couldn't get to Newburyport fast enough. Seated in first class, I told Chris how Mary had volunteered to get us at the airport. She was hell bent on being around for the introduction. She also seemed over-eager to spend the night at home.

"The house is big but not *that big*," Chris said, getting a beer from the flight attendant.

"What d'you mean?"

"Mary's giving us an out. There are only so many bedrooms. If she stays, we have a built in reason to get a room."

"Would your mom let that happen? You're the guest from out of town!"

"Mom doesn't like unmarried couples to share a room. It might be easier for her to look the other way if we were to stay elsewhere."

"I guess we won't be telling her of our baby-making efforts."

He gagged. "Yeah," he rasped. "No."

"Do you—*how* do you intend to share out engagement?"

"After dinner. Mary already knows so she's going to be shaking all night until it's announced." He put my hand in his lap, twisting the ring.

"Ooh! What happens if they ask about how you proposed?"

His head thumped against the seat. "That's one good reason to have an orchestrated proposal." He bared his teeth. "Unless you have a great idea that doesn't involve a naked woman in a bathroom, I'm gonna have to think about it."

I leaned forward. "You're gonna *lie*?"

"No, I'm going to evade just like people who hook up online. There's gotta be a tasteful response." He scrutinized me. "What have you been telling your friends?"

"Sorry. Those who asked, know."

"You told them that you got a ring in the bathroom? There goes my good name."

"Nobody cares. I got a proposal from *you*. They're all insanely happy about my good fortune. All of 'em would take a proposal from *you* in a bathroom any time."

"So being me gets me out of the troubles associated with being me?"

I bobbed my head. "Yeah! You shot yourself in the foot but you're pure gold. It doesn't matter." Poking him, I giggled. "You're like Teflon!"

When he was silly, I couldn't get enough of him. I loved each laugh line, every hair on his head.

"You look pretty wound up—is this what happens when you visit your folks?"

"Not generally," he said, pausing to get another beer from the flight attendant. "I've never made this kind of a visit before. I've never, not since high school, brought a girl home. I guess I have a better appreciation for how you felt when your mom told you they were coming."

"You survived the Rileys, though! This should be icing. You're doing what your mom and your sisters wanted you to do. You're getting married and starting a family. That's pretty awesome. I'm sure they'll see it that way, too. Maybe they'll even get misty."

"How do you want to tell your parents?" He shifted in his seat. "Should we have them over? One big happy family?"

I cringed, shrinking into my seat. "I'd rather not."

"What're you going to do when they find out that we came to the East Coast and told my parents but didn't do anything for them? Your mom's gonna be *pissed*."

I sighed. That was true. Seeing them would do more than engender good will. It would avert a major malfunction.

"Could we *invite* them to your folks' or maybe just to dinner in Boston? That'd give us another reason to get away from your parents."

"I think we should have them over. Let *all* the old people get to know each other."

"This is very last minute. I don't know that they'll come."

"I met Carl. You know as well as I that he'd be in the car and to Boston immediately. Call your mom or text her. They could come over tomorrow and show up when they show up."

I stuck out my tongue then finished his beer. "This is going to be one *hell* of a weekend, buddy."

~~

When Mary pulled into their neighborhood, it felt homey. The gorgeous houses were large, but nothing like our *home* in Los Angeles. They were delightful wood shingle representations of East Coast architecture, nestled amidst the lush, green grass and framed by old trees. I was looking forward to inhaling the smog-free coastal air more than I'd realized.

It wasn't long before she pulled into the lengthy driveway of a stately, manicured home. I'd never put much thought into what kind of place created Chris, but this made sense. The trees, like the house, had been there forever yet were maintained and thriving.

Putting the car in park, Mary tooted the horn. "We're here!"

Chris was out of the car in a flash, opening my door for me. Mary caught my eye and grinned. Her enthusiasm well outpaced her typically high spirits. As she bounced to the front door, Mrs. Sparks opened it.

Nothing could have prepared me. She was beautiful and looked like she belonged in Los Angeles. Small, like Mary, she had beautiful blond hair pulled back in a loose bun. Her makeup was understated but accentuated her obviously-radiant skin. Dressed in a simple black shirt and jeans, she was a proud mother. Laying eyes on Chris, her face erupted into an enormous, satisfied smile.

Stepping out onto the porch, she stretched her arms out as if to hug him long distance.

Chris dropped the bags and walked into her mama bear hug.

"Hi, Mom," he said, kissing her cheek.

"Oh, honey. It's been too long!" she said, giving him a loving pat. "Sarah!" she said, jovially. "I've heard so much about you!"

It was hard to read her face, but I gathered that she didn't know nearly as much about me as she would have liked. Taking a step closer, she wrapped her arms around me and hugged me as if I were her own.

"Mrs. Sparks, it's so good to meet you." Patting my back, she released me. She gave me a barely-disguised once over, her head bobbing ever so slightly. Having made the grade, she grabbed the door knob and threw it open.

"Welcome!" she said, motioning us inside. "And please, call me Leah."

In the foyer, Mary snatched me for an impromptu tour of the house.

"That's wasn't too bad!" she mused once we were upstairs and out of earshot. "She can be very harsh but that wasn't too bad." She turned on a light at the top of the stairs. "Just wait till she sees your tattoos!"

She leaned against the wall. "She used to associate tattoos with drug use. I was on a trip with my mom years ago and totally forgot about a tattoo I had on my back." Mary lifted her shirt to reveal a vibrant phoenix on her shoulder blade. "I was changing my shirt so we could go out to dinner and all I remember is my mom gasping and the freaking out and asking if I was on drugs." She straightenedns out the hem of her shirt. "It was so uncomfortable and hilarious all at the same time. My mom saw me *all* the time. She would've known if I were on drugs."

"Yikes."

"Yeah, Todd's covered in 'em. Mom likes to say, lovingly I hope, that 'he's a piece of work.'"

"I don't think she's gonna see more than the one on my wrist. I'd have to change my shoes and socks." Framed Christening clothing hung over the bed in the last bedroom. Above the dresser were individual pencil drawings of the kids.

"This is most likely your room. You have been warned that it's unlikely you'll be sleeping together? Mom has a real problem with unmarried cohabitation."

"I did hear that. Even though he's a grown man?"

"'He'll always be my baby,' she says." Mary rolled her eyes. "Moms never stop being moms, do they?"

"Some are *never* moms," I said, thinking of my own.

She turned off the light. "They all have flaws. They're human. Come on, let's go find 'em." She flew down the stairs.

I shuffled along, looking at all the pictures on the wall. It appeared that they had portraits done every year, right through high school. Each picture had a glowing little face in it, something that I don't think held true for many families, my own included.

I followed the voices to the kitchen. It was no surprise that Chris was leaning on the island, pulling apart a cheese stick.

As I joined him, he winked and handed me a piece of his cheese.

"This is a great house. I love all of the pictures," I said, taking in the kitchen.

"Thank you, Sarah. Chris said you're from Connecticut?" Leah said, stirring the world's largest crockpot.

"Yes, from Prospect—it's near a water preservation area—but I also spent some time in Little Rhodie before heading west." I inhaled deeply. "What *are* you cooking? It smells outstanding!"

Putting the lid back on, she said, "Pot Roast. It's one of Chris's favorites." She beamed at him. "I wanted it to be ready for your arrival. He's always hungry!"

Chris stuffed the rest of the cheese in his mouth.

"He sure can eat. I always wonder where he puts it! The rest of us would be enormous," I said.

"Hey, it's tough being me. Don't forget that." Throwing out his wrapper, he cracked the pot. "I'm sure it's done. Mom, pass me a plate?"

"Honey, wait for your dad. He's getting mower blades and should be back soon," she said, reaching for the dishes. He reached above her and took a stack.

"Got any more cheese sticks?" he asked, opening the fridge. "Hey! Mary, did you buy these?" He pulled out a couple of Newport Storms. He opened one and handed it to me.

Taking the next one from Chris, Mary said, "Let's make a toast!" Her eyes twinkled as she handed one to her mom. "To a lost brother and his newfound lady-friend. It's good to have you home!"

Leah set hers on the counter. "You know I don't care for these—or has it been that long?" she asked, a calculating expression on her face.

Chris sighed and wrapped his mom in his arms. "You know that I come home when I can. Aren't you supposed to be happy for me, that I'm so successful?"

"Of course I'm happy for you. Sometimes though, it feels like you're on another planet and that's not the one where you were born. I miss my only boy!"

"Throw in a DVD, Mom. That's what I do," Mary said jokingly.

Leah scowled at her then returned her attention to Chris. "We thought you'd be home over the summer. Didn't you have a break?"

He nodded, draining half his beer. "I did and I thought I would but—" He put his arm around my waist, dragging me to him. "Sarah came into my life. I got delayed."

"Well, Sarah. You must be really special. He hasn't brought anybody home in over ten years." She smiled warmly at me and pinched Chris. "And we *know* there've been girlfriends, right Chris?" Petite though she was, her imposing demeanor filled the kitchen. She was not to be trifled with.

"This is fun. Can we stop? How about we focus on That Todd for a while?" he asked, catching Mary's eye. "Will we be seeing Todd? Does he have any new art?"

Sitting at the table, Mary said, "New body art? No. He's got one that he's thinking about but he's runnin' out of real estate and it's a big sucker. It's Steampunk and really cool. Other than that, we're getting ready to move to the Big Apple."

"Is he coming?" Chris asked again.

"He wouldn't miss an opportunity like this. It's not often that the prodigal son returns!" Kind though she was, she was mischievous, needling Chris about his lengthy absence. "When this one's over, are you gonna change your ways and grace us more often, or do we have to move all the way to your coast?"

"You could do that. I don't know that you'd see *more* of me." He was quiet for a moment, playing with my fingers.

"Yeah, I had to come to New York to see him and I *live* with him." I joined Mary at the table.

"I didn't know you lived with Chris, dear." Leah's eyes bored into her son.

"You shoulda known. I'm sure I sent you a text." His eyes danced.

"And I'm sure you didn't. I'd remember it," she said coolly.

"Mom! I know Chris told you. And if he didn't, I did! I've been hanging out with Sarah."

Leah brought over a bowl of carrot sticks. "I hope she's not like the *last* one," she said, sitting.

"She's *nothing* like the last one," they responded.

"I'm certainly not famous," I offered meekly.

"Famous is overrated, Sarah. All I want is for my son to be happy with a nice, strong woman. He could stop acting tomorrow and move home. I'd be happy."

"Is that all?" I asked with a chuckle. "I think I've got that covered."

Leah's eyes lit up. "You're going to move back here and get him to stop acting?"

"I don't know about *that* but anything's possible."

Chris picked up a carrot. "Anything *is* possible. Who knows? Maybe I'll go into directing or something. I am lining up another project."

Leah growled. "You're always lining something up. I'd give anything for you to be *home* for the holidays."

He clamped his lips tightly around a carrot, eyes flashing. This was a sore spot.

"Hey, I think Dad's home!" Mary jumped up and ran to the front door.

Quietly, we waited for them to return. Mr. Sparks was almost as tall as Chris, athletically built with a full head of brown hair. In his clean jeans and Red Sox t-shirt, he looked like he stepped right out of a catalog. His energy grew exponentially as he rounded the kitchen and saw his son.

"Chris!" he exclaimed as Chris pushed out his chair.

The two Sparks exchanged a tight hug. It was a relief to be amongst a family that found joy in each other's company. When they separated, Mr. Sparks acknowledged his family.

"Saaaaaraaaaah," he said, more warmly than anyone had ever said it.

I stood, anticipating another familial hug. Instead, it felt cursory.

"Sarah! It's so good to meet you. Mary's told me so much about you!" He glanced at Chris.

"I hear you're selling stuff at the same gallery that Mary found? In New York? We'll have to check it out, Leah, the next time we're in the City." He stole a carrot. "Todd coming?" he asked, looking for dip.

"Yeah, he sent me a text. He should be here soon."

"What about Susan? We could have the whole family together and pretend it's Thanksgiving!"

"Dan's working late today. They were hoping to join us for dinner tomorrow," Mary added, getting up for more carrots.

"Oh, are we doing something tomorrow, too? You're spending the night?" Mr. Sparks asked happily.

"We're here for the weekend. A quick visit but long overdue," Chris said, nodding to his mom.

"Well, I'm glad you're here. We're overdue for a trip to L.A. I can't remember when the last time was. Oh. Right. I've never been." He offered me some dip. "Pitfall of starting your own business is that it's hard to leave it. And with no one in the family there to step in, I never step out."

"Don't let him fool you. He wouldn't have it any other way. Raising these kids, we never saw him." Leah said, setting the table.

"Hey, I took the kids to see the Sox," he said emphatically. "Gotta raise 'em right."

"I think we did alright," Chris said, opening the silverware drawer.

"Atta boy. See? He's got my work ethic!" Mr. Sparks took the roast out of the crockpot and began slicing it.

"Aren't we waiting for Todd?" I asked, surprised that dinner was in motion.

"Todd's *never* on time," Mary said. "He'll be here when he gets here."

"So, you eat without him?" I asked.

"Todd doesn't *eat*," Leah clarified. "He sits at the table and picks. I've never seen him really eat a meal. He's all skin, bone—and tattoos."

"He does eat, Mom. He's a vegetarian. When we start having vegetarian food, he'll start eating it."

Leah waived her arm dismissively. "There're always things for him to eat—mashed potatoes, green beans—"

Mary cut her off, irritated. "That's not *dinner*, Mom. That's why he picks."

"Maybe you help me next time, okay?" She smiled apologetically at me. "It'd be much easier if he'd just eat meat."

"Or you could make a veggie meal, Mom. You eat pasta but you seem to save the big beefy dinner for when we're coming over."

"Oh, I'd never do that!" Leah responded, defensively.

"And welcome, Sarah," Chris said, gesturing at their futile argument.

"I was a vegetarian for a while," I said. "My mom didn't cook for me either." I put my beer next to my plate. "I got used to it."

"See, Mary. She's not a vegetarian any longer, are you? I bet you feel better. Everyone needs red meat."

Mary frowned. "I think Todd's here," she said leaving the room for an imaginary car.

"Let it go, Mom," Chris said. "It'd make Mary happy if you'd treat Todd like family."

"But we *do*, honey. I—"

"Chris's right, Leah. Maybe 'Todd Nights' should be synonymous with pasta."

It appeared that a breakthrough was in sight. She acquiesced to her husband, the only person who had more control than she.

She pushed her chair away and threw on a pot of water. As she rummaged to find pasta and sauce, Chris and his dad caught up—Red Sox, how the Patriots would fair this year. Once there was nothing left to discuss about New England, Dad got a brief rundown from Chris.

Eyes wide, Mr. Sparks smiled broadly. "You are a machine. Look at you!" His face full of pride, he marveled at Chris. "How do you keep that *size*? To think you never even played football!"

Chris glowed under his father's praise. "Yeah, that's never been my sport."

"Well, whatever you're doing—it agrees with you. You look great."

"Jonathan, he has to. He's in a romance. Ladies across the globe will be swooning over him," Leah said girlishly.

Chris bowed his head. "Enough!"

"You know it's true, honey. Every time you take your shirt off, your net worth goes up." She cupped both hands around one bicep.

"We're just jealous," Jonathan said. Washing his hands, he continued, "Don't know that I'll see *this* movie but your last one—what'd'you call it? The time travel thing—that sounds like one I might go see."

"Imogen Simmons is in Tall Lara," I offered. "Is that worth anything?"

"She is a pretty lady, isn't she? But I'll catch that chick flick with Leah when it's on TV." He brought the roast to the table.

While we had our salad, Todd arrived. Like the others, he warmed up when he saw Chris. I was beginning to wonder if there was a soul alive who didn't find him engaging.

"Hey, Todd!" Chris said, shaking his hand. "Good to see you."

Todd was gangly. In his late twenties, his face was lined with life. Hair buzzed, he resembled a heavily inked Auschwitzian. He had amazing sleeves, stylized writing on his fingers. He was a work of art.

"Chris! Long time, no see. Lookin' good," he added, checking out the muscle-bound boy.

"Good to see you, too. That new ink on your hand?" Chris asked, taking a better look at the hand he shook.

"Probably since the last time I saw you, yeah."

"Hi, Todd," Leah said, plating up some pasta. "We've got some pasta, if you're interested?"

Todd's eyes bulged. Befuddled, he looked around the table. His eyes narrowed in on me. "*You*'re a vegetarian, too," he said confidently.

"Me? No." I smiled. "Leah made it for you."

He pulled up a chair. "Thanks, Leah. I am hungry." His smile grew when she set a big bowl of spaghetti in front of him. "That's really nice of you. Thanks again." He stuffed a big forkful into his mouth.

Mary beamed and picked up her fork.

After dinner, the guys went into the living room and put on the Sox game, while I helped Mary tidy up the kitchen with Leah. The kitchen had been remodeled at some point within the last twenty years. It was stylish yet unassuming, ideal for their historic home. With cupboards all the way to their sixteen foot high ceiling, I wondered who put away the dishes. Not one of us ladies could reach the higher shelves.

As I cleared the rest of the table, I felt at ease. The Sparks family operated like a family should. Everyone had their job and they did it without complaint. Thinking about how the menfolk cleared out of the room, I smiled. I wanted their job.

"What's so funny?" Mary asked, ringing out the sponge.

"I was just thinking about your family. You seem to get along so well." I handed Mary a fistful of dirty silverware.

"Most of the time, we do. But that's not funny. What's funny?" she asked again.

"I was thinking about how the guys cleared out of here, like their job is in the living room. And your cupboards are so high! How are we going to put the dishes away?"

"They're responsible for putting it away when it comes out of the dishwasher." Leah put the leftover pasta in the fridge. "You're definitely from this coast. It's nice that he found a hometown girl, isn't it Mary?"

"Let's not go *that* far, Mom," Mary said dramatically. "She's from Connecticut. I bet she's not a Sox fan."

Both of the Sparks women slowly pivoted, eyes on me.

I squirmed. If there's one thing that divides New England, it is the hatred between Sox and Yankees fans.

Mary clapped her hands loudly. "Ha! I *knew* it! You're a Yankees fan!"

"Sorry. I hope it's not a deal breaker for family peace."

Leah counted out dessert plates. "Sports are sports. They're not nearly as important as a good, grounded woman with faith."

Giving me a warning look, Mary interjected, "So—who wants coffee with dessert?"

"There's dessert?" I asked, taking a seat at the table.

"In this house, there's *always* homemade dessert," Leah said. "Tonight, it's cheesecake in honor of Chris's visit." She took it out of the fridge. "Do you have a favorite dessert, Sarah? Or are you on an L.A. diet?"

"*Mom!*" Mary screamed, swatting at her mother.

"I didn't mean it *that* way, dear. I meant—Los Angeles is a strange place and people develop strange eating habits. It's a wonder Todd isn't from that area."

"If he were, he'd be a raw eater—but thanks, Mom, for making him dinner. I can't tell you how much I appreciate that." Mary placed some coffee mugs on the counter.

"A 'raw' eater? What the heck is that? You mean he'd eat raw meat? Like beef?" Leah's face contorted with disgust.

"It tends to be veggies, I think, but I'm sure somebody'd eat raw meat. Isn't steak tartare raw?" I asked, not being much of a culinary visionary.

"I think *all* cultures serve raw meats. It's just us Americans that have developed an attitude about it." Mary snorted. "But we have attitudes about everything. Why is that? Why can't we celebrate our differences, or at least be open-minded about them?"

She added water to the coffee maker then joined me at the table.

Wiping down the stove, Leah said, "Oh, Mary. It's not that we're not open-minded. It's that your elders have been around. We have more experience. Some of the things you choose to do in your twenties do not work in your favor later in life." She leaned against the counter and wiped her hands on a towel. "Like Todd's tattoos. You think it's cool now but Todd's tattoos will keep him from ever being a successful business man. Or banker. Or doctor! Can you *imagine* going to an OBGYN who was covered in tattoos?"

"God, Mom. I don't want to think about going to an OB *period*."

A smile playing on her lips, Leah replied, "That is precisely why you see an OB."

"Gross!" Mary kicked her feet under her chair.

"I've had blood draws from people who are tattooed," I said mildly. "Tattoos are so common today that I don't think they're a deal-breaker like they used to be. My tattoos have not kept me from a paycheck."

Leah pursed her lips. "You're tattooed? I thought I saw something on your wrist under that bracelet. Is that your only one?"

I moved the bracelet further up my wrist. "No, I've got a few others. Nothing big but I'd get another."

Leah brought us coffee. "Are you ready for dessert or should we give the guys a few more minutes of the game?"

"I'm stuffed," I said honestly.

"I can wait," Mary added.

"May I see your tattoo?" she asked, reaching for my arm.

I moved the bracelet.

"It says 'now'? How peculiar, Sarah." She rubbed my arm as if she could erase it.

I retracted my arm. Mary was ready to jump in and save me, but I felt I could handle this one.

"Tattoos help me work through things. I've never had a solid support system. My parents were not helpful. I've had to figure a lot of stuff out on my own. So, this tattoo helped me focus on the present. I had a hard time for a while." I wrapped my hands around my coffee.

Leah's face softened. "I'm sorry that you had a tough time. The Lord is always there to see you through."

Mary craned her head toward the living room, "Dessert's served!" She tapped her coffee mug. "Can I refill you?" she asked, getting up.

"Hey, we're going to have to ask Todd about your website!" she said, bringing cream and sugar to the table. "I bet he could get it done in a week or so."

"I thought they were complicated," I said, thankful for her redirection.

Thumping the table, Mary added, "Mom! There's another profession for you that could care less about tattoos—anything computer-related. Ha!"

"I guess I'm from a different generation." Leah retrieved the cheesecake.

"Yeah, you are!" Chris said, walking into the room.

Leah shuddered. "When you say it, it makes me feel *old*. Am I really that old?" she asked plaintively.

"No, you're only as old as you feel!" Jonathan said, eyes still on the TV as he walked to the table.

"In that case, I'm not a day over forty," Leah said, hands on her hips.

"Forties were good. The kids were all in school. You had more time to yourself. We refinished the bathrooms and the backyard, right? Business was good. Yes, I could do those years again." He pulled a piece of chocolate cheesecake over.

"D'you like cheesecake, Sarah?" Jonathan asked, taking a forkful.

"*Anything* chocolate is great. Anything homemade is even better!" I said, taking a plate from Leah.

"You a Sox fan?" he asked, attempting to check in on the ballgame from his seat.

I slowly rolled the cheesecake around in my mouth.

His eyes narrowed. "Chris! Did you bring home a *Yankees* fan?" He looked furtively at the rest of the table while Chris smiled and waited for my response. "Somebody gonna answer me?" he asked again, glaring at me.

"Mom always said if you can't say something nice, not to say anything at all." I dabbed at my face with my napkin.

Jonathan slammed his fork down. "Chris, did you *know* she was a Yankee's fan? Out of all the fish in the sea—"

Todd smiled broadly. "Sarah, welcome to the family. I've never been much of a sports fan but you, you root for the enemy. That's gotta be worse than indifference?" He tried to catch Jonathan's eye.

"Do you think those dating websites screen for Yankees fans?" Jonathan asked, inhaling his dessert. "I've never understood a need for 'em but if you can prescreen for like-minded sports fans—"

Finishing his dessert, Jonathan got up and put his plate in the sink. He put his hands on my shoulders, "I am kidding, Sarah." He squeezed my shoulders and then left the room.

"Your family takes its sports seriously!" I said, watching him settle in front of the tube.

"There is no other way in New England," Leah said, clearing the plates. "Coffee, Todd?"

He nodded. "Mary mentioned that you need help with a website?"

"She does! Alicia, that woman I met in New York? She's selling Sarah's stuff and so she really needs her own website. Just the basics— information about the artist, a gallery, places to get her stuff, contact her information."

Todd grinned. "Is that what you're after? I can do that. D'you have pictures?"

As my mouth opened, Mary resumed. "I've got some good pictures. We need to take one of Sarah but I think we're in good shape."

Todd put his hand on Mary's. "Are you her translator?" he asked. He put his finger to his lips. To me he said, "So— is that what you're after? What functionality do you want the site to have?"

My eyes widened. "I— " Mary responded simultaneously. Her mouth shut when Todd affectionately glared at her. "I've never thought about it so I dunno." Chris put his arm around my chair.

"How 'bout this—I'll play with a few things during the week. You can see it and tell me if it's headed in the right direction and we'll go from there?" Todd took another slice.

"That'd be great. Thanks, Todd."

Chris knocked his shoulder into mine. "Want to watch the game? There's only another couple of innings left."

"Sure," I said, polishing off my coffee.

Cozied next to Chris on the couch, I was instantly bored. Although I was a Yankees fan, I wasn't a baseball fan. With coffee coursing in my veins, I wasn't able to get comfortable. I kept fidgeting.

Chris ran his hand idly through my hair. I loved when he did that but I couldn't sit still. During a commercial break, I started poking around for Mary.

She and Todd were building a bonfire in the yard. They had a fire pit ringed with an assortment of comfortable-looking swings, chairs and logs. Bonfires appeared to be a popular family activity if the number of seats were any indication.

"Tired of the game?" Mary asked, tossing in another handful of pine cones.

"You could say that." I admired their fire building prowess. "I take it you guys do this often?"

Todd threw on one more log, forcing it into teepee position. "Yeah. It's beautiful out here."

"And it's a good place to be with the family but not have to keep up conversation." She wiped her hands on her pants and climbed into Todd's lap.

He put his arms protectively around her, two peas in a pod.

Mary caught me looking at them pensively. "How long have you two known each other?" I asked, curious.

"Known each other or dated?" Mary asked. "Because I knew Todd long before we dated. We've been dating—" Her eyes rolled back in her head as she tried to come up with the most accurate response.

"It'll be two years next week," Todd answered authoritatively.

"Next week?" Mary stared at him. "You know the *date*?" She was incredulous.

"I don't think there's any question about what the first date was."

"I don't think I know." She nestled back into his chest. "Go ahead. Tell us."

"I consider our first date to be shortly after I gave you your tattoo. Remember? We went to see your brother's movie."

"That doesn't count! There was a horde of people that went!"

"Yeah but only one came home with me," he said, kissing her passionately.

"Okay. If sex equals 'date,' then you win."

Todd's brow furrowed. "What do you think our first date was?"

"Not *that*!" Mary spat. "I was gonna say probably two weeks *after* that. You took me to Tweets for pasta, just us."

"I didn't realize that you had sex with random dudes that you weren't dating."

Mary's eyes lit up. He didn't know about her forays to Los Angeles. She laughed it off.

"Well, I don't make a *habit* of it. You were just lucky."

He coughed. "I'll say."

"Do you guys live around here?" I asked. I had forgotten just how lovely New England was.

"Close enough for government work," Todd replied.

"We still live in Rhode Island, near RISD," Mary responded. "It's close enough, but not too close. We're not driving home tonight, that's for sure."

"How far's the drive? Two hours?" I'd never driven up this far north of Boston.

"Good guess, but probably closer to an hour-and-a-half unless traffic is stopped," Todd said, shifting in his chair.

"Mom seems to like you," Mary said pensively.

"I have to agree. She made pasta on meat night." Todd was genuinely impressed.

"That was for *you*," I said. "I had nothing to do with it."

"Oh, yeah you did. I've been around this family for almost two years. Friday nights are beef nights. Always have been, always will be." Todd pushed Mary out of his chair so he could stoke the fire.

"You're welcome, then. I was surprised when we sat down to dinner without you. I thought all families ate together."

"They used to wait but I've never been overly fond of pushing meat around my plate. Shit. I meant that traffic's always worse than anticipated. I've never been intentionally late, I swear!" Glancing at Mary, a smile spread across her face.

"Right. And we never ditched classes either. Goofball." She scooted a tree stump closer to me and sat. "*So!*" Mary squeaked. "When's he gonna do it? I've been very patient," she added conspiratorially.

"Why're you asking me?" I stared at her.

"Ooh, I could text him!" She reached for her phone.

"Don't do that!" I said, knocking her phone. "I think he's waiting till tomorrow night. We invited my parents to come up here."

She sat bolt upright. "Do what?"

Biting my lip, I curtly nodded. "Chris thought it'd be best if all the parents heard it at the same time."

"Your folks're coming here?" Todd restocked the pile of logs. "That's cool."

"Not cool. Probably necessary, but not cool. They're not cool."

Todd looked at me knowingly. "Sarah, I think you and I should swap stories some time."

I snorted. "What d'you want to hear? About how they threw me out on Thanksgiving? Maybe about the time my dad burned his flesh right off his torso? Ah—you think I'm making it up?" I flicked off a mosquito. "He had too much to drink and stumbled into the potbelly stove that we used to heat the house. I don't know how but he made it to bed, burnt to a crisp. Mom said she smelled bacon." Their eyes widened. "No lie. She said she smelled meat cooking and thought that my dad did something stupid. She landed up taking him to the accident room." I rubbed my bare arms. "Thankfully, I didn't see him that night so I can only imagine what it looked like. Even days later, it was grizzly."

"Wow, that's something you don't hear every day," Todd said, envisioning the scene. "Holy hell, that must've hurt!"

"He didn't get out of bed without a bottle for at least a week afterward." Thinking about my dad, it was surprising he was still above ground and taking nourishment.

"Why don't you tell her about the time your parents took off for your sister's wedding? That's a good one."

"You just have the one sister?" I asked.

"He didn't *know* he had a sister," Mary exclaimed, eager to tell the story. "He went home from college to do some laundry and his parents were getting ready to leave. So, he asked them where they were headed. Getting into the car, they said, 'To your sister's wedding.' *That's* how they told him he had a sister! By saying that they were going to her wedding!"

"Did you go, too?" I asked. Todd was staring off into the dusk.

"No, I wasn't invited." His smile was forced.

"And that was the first you'd heard of a sister?"

"It was the best kept secret that everyone but me knew." He glanced at me. "Families are fucked up." He rested his shoes on the fire pit ring. "Well, *my* family is."

"Do you have much of a relationship with her?" I asked softly.

"No, she's older than I am by about ten years. I've yet to *meet* her."

"The first time that I heard of her was at a *funeral*. I saw a name on his grandpa's tie that I didn't recognize. It was covered with the grandchildren's names. I had to ask who 'Linda' was. I'm standing there, looking at Dead Grandpa with Todd and it felt like the world stopped when I asked. There was radio silence and then Todd says, like I should know, 'She's my sister.' Honestly! I'd met his parents dozens of times and never once had I seen or heard of a sister!"

"I'm not gonna lie. That's pretty weird," I said, picturing the funeral.

We were all quiet, reminiscing, when Chris arrived with a six pack.

"Evening, guys. Sox won," he said to Mary.

"Score?" she inquired.

"Nine to six. Good game. The next time I'm in town, we should go to Fenway."

"Right. Like there are ever tickets," Mary said.

Handing her a beer, he said, "Don't forget who your big brother is. There'd be tickets for me. Guarantee it."

"You'd play that card?" she asked. "Don't you ever want to be just a normal human being?"

"I am a normal human being. I just—there are perks to being me."

Chris passed a beer to me and Todd. He sat down in the glider, rocking it backward so hard it lifted off the ground.

"Forgot your own strength, huh chief?" Todd asked, amused.

"I need more ballast!" Chris patted the seat next to him.

I moved into the glider. "How're you?" he asked serenely.

"Good." Everything about this trip was on target. "So far, so good."

"Parents haven't scared you off?" he inquired analytically.

"No, it's cool to see where you came from. You make a lot of sense."

Chris laughed. "After meeting my parents, I make a lot of sense? I don't know if I could say the same to you."

"God, I hope not." The idea of Lucy and Carl adding clarity to my character was terrifying. They were the opposite of everything I strived to be.

"Hey, I'm gonna duck inside and get the bedroom arrangements." Mary set her beer down and trotted back to the house. Glancing at us, she added, "Takin' one for the team!"

"How long are you in town, Chris?" Todd asked.

"Sunday," he said strongly.

"Your mom's gotta be tickled."

"Hope so. I don't get home as often as I'd like." Chris took my hand and put it in his lap. "I miss this. I don't have time for this—and I miss it. Mom always says she'd be thrilled if I just stayed here and some days that's pretty damn appealing."

"What's stopping you? You've got more money than God." Todd got up and moved closer to Chris.

"I *like* what I do. I like what it's gotten me. I love the creativity, meeting new people." He paused. "But it does affect living a normal life. I didn't realize how much of a normal life I wanted until recently." He gazed at me with such intensity that I felt myself blushing.

"While we're alone, congrats. Mary told me that I couldn't be late today because of the big news."

I laughed. "But you were still late."

"Yeah, well, it was the traffic." He cocked his foot sideways, ogling the sole. As he yanked it away from the fire, I saw that his Doc Marten had melted.

"It's *always* the traffic, isn't it?" Chris said, getting up to throw on another log.

Mary joined Chris at the fire. "It's settled. Todd, you get the basement bedroom. The rest of us are upstairs."

"There's another bedroom in the basement?" Chris was surprised.

"Mom and Dad decided to convert the gym into another bedroom. I think they're hoping to turn one of the upstairs bedrooms into a nursery."

Chris's eyes widened. "Do you know something I don't? Is Suzy pregnant?" Chris sounded so hopeful.

"It's just a matter of time. *Someone's* gonna make a baby!" Mary said, poking the fire.

"I hope for Susan's sake that she goes first!" Sitting back down, Chris almost tipped the glider over again.

Mary whipped around. "You got other news, big brother? That sounded like news."

"I'm not getting any younger," Chris answered cryptically.

"I've *never* heard that said by a guy. Ever. That's doctor-speak to women!" Sitting down, Mary continued, "Did you know that they consider you high risk at thirty six? Susan told me that she's gotten a lecture about her 'advanced maternal age.' That's freakin' crazy. Advanced maternal age!" She picked up her beer.

"If that's true, we'd better get cracking. I just turned thirty six." I put my hand on Chris's thigh.

His face lit up. "If that's an offer, I'm in."

"I thought we had separate bedrooms here?"

"Yeah, you do," Mary chided. "But our folks sleep like the dead. Ask Chris how many times he climbed in or out of a window—and fell."

"Are there no safe secrets?" Chris smacked his jeans. "I know it's hard to believe but I wasn't always the perfect specimen you see before you. I was a spindly dork in high school."

"They say that it's the dorks who become something in their twenties. You're living proof! Have you gone to a reunion? I bet they all want to know you now," I said, thinking about his charmed life.

Todd nodded vigorously. "Tools. They're tools just like they were in high school. It's hard to be something if you've only ever been popular, the 'apple of mommy's eye.'" Thumping his chest, he added, "It took pain and suffering to build this Temple of Cool!"

~~

Sure enough, my room was the one with the three cherubic drawings of the kids. Setting my bag on the bed, I contemplated each picture. They were drawn around the same age, if I had to guess. Beyond siblings, they almost looked like triplets. Assuming they were hung in order of age, he'd be in the middle.

I wondered how similar our child would look. The thought brought color to my cheeks. I always knew I wanted to be a mother but now, with it so close, it was spooky. I didn't run in circles with kids. Even the idea of kids was exhausting.

Finding my toothbrush, I jumped. Chris had snuck up behind me.

"Jesus Christ! You scared me!" I screamed at him.

"He scares me, too, but don't let my mom hear you."

He cowered, as I pelted him with my toothbrush. "Not cool!"

"Sorry." He took my toothbrush hand. "Did my mom leave you towels?"

"Yes, this place is like a hotel. She even left me a little soap on top of the stack."

"She is fastidious about everything she does." He turned and sat on the bed, pulling me down next to him. "I think it's okay for us to take a few minutes. I've seen you all day but I've missed you." He leaned over and kissed me on the cheek.

"Thank you for bringing me here. This feels right."

He fell back on his side, dragging me with him. He stroked my hip, a smile spreading across his face. "You're welcome. What do you think we should do tomorrow—I'm thinking dinner at an Italian place around the corner. They're family friends so I think we can have a discreet dinner."

"A 'discreet' dinner? As in—"

"Privacy. I'd hate for my celebrity to color the evening. Asking your dad to allow me to marry you—it'd be nice if I didn't have an extended audience."

"You're gonna *ask* my dad? Really?" Playfully, I added, "What if *he* says no?"

"Oh, like that's likely! Carl likes me. I can tell. He also liked my house. I'm sure he liked your Jeep. We're good. Tight, even."

"Don't go that far." If we could live the rest of our lives without being 'tight' with my parents, that'd be best for my mental health.

"Personally, I can't wait to get your pagan parents in the same room as Jonathan and Leah Sparks, Catholic Crusaders. Who'd you think'd win—faeries or the Almighty?"

I rolled my eyes. "How could faeries ever take on something called the Almighty?"

"By sheer numbers?" he asked, taking stock of his own question. "I wouldn't put it past them to have a few tricks up their sleeves."

"So, like Lilliputians, they're gonna tie Him down? And then what?" I asked, thrilled to have this time alone with my fiancé.

"Leave. Leaving is a final thing. Just leave 'em."

"And what, by faery power alone, He's just gonna stay there and waste away?"

"Or get eaten." His eyes danced. "Savages!"

"Speaking of faery power, you dazzle everyone. I watched the room light up when you came in. Your Mom, Dad—even Todd. They adore you."

"To be fair, we are talking about my parents. They brought me into this world. I should light up their lives."

"You take it for granted, but it's foreign to me. I think it's foreign to Todd, too."

"Chalk it up to 'opposites attract' then." Chris scooted closer. "After my mom tucks us in, I'll be back. Leave my side open!" He kissed me.

"Chris?" Leah called, coming up the stairs.

His eyes widened and he threw himself off the bed. The bed shook violently before it settled.

"You better be careful! One more move like that and this relic'll be done for," I said, embarrassed.

"Bah. It's fine. See you—" He met his mother outside the door.

"Hey—I was making sure that you gave Sarah towels," Chris said, putting on the charm.

"I'm your *mother*. That's not gonna work on me. Your room is across the hall." She pushed him toward his room.

"I'm sorry, Sarah. I'm old fashioned. I hope you understand." She glanced at the pictures on the wall.

"Sure. Your house, your rules. Quick question—is Chris the one in the middle?" I asked, picking up a washcloth.

She smiled fondly. "Yes. There was a short time when I took them to the store and people thought I had triplets. They were all about the same height and looked very much alike."

"They sure look like it in the sketches. How old were they?"

"Seven, maybe? Old enough to sit for a sketch."

"You've got to be kidding!"

"Yes, I am. They were done from photographs but they did have to cooperate for those!"

"Based on the pictures by the staircase, it looks like they had plenty of practice."

"There were times when they were little that Jonathan was rarely around. I felt a moral obligation to have their youth documented so when he finally surfaced, he could see what he missed."

She meant it. "You really raised them single-handedly?"

She sat down in the rocker. "It felt that way. I stayed at home. I put the kids to bed, woke up with them during the night, soothed them. I did it all. Jonathan was a great provider but he wasn't available. He was building a company. He did a great job nurturing that company, though. It's strong to this day because of his persistence."

"Is that why you stopped at three kids?" I asked, thinking that this strong woman could have raised her own army.

"That is what the Lord saw fit to give us." She paused, reflecting. "I think any more would have been more challenge than I wanted. You don't *need* birth control. You need to be in control of your body. Nothing more, nothing less."

"Sounds like advice." I felt a little uncomfortable.

She scrutinized my face. "Would you take advice were I to offer it?"

"I'll certainly *listen* to it," I said humbly.

"Be good to him, Sarah. He's a good man. He's going to make an excellent father."

Surprised, my eyebrows arched.

"It's obvious how you two feel about each other. I was prepared not to like you but you have an overwhelmingly warm energy to you. I won't even hold being a Yankees fan against you." She sighed. "I want grandkids, Sarah. Is that something you're inclined to have? He's had so many useless relationships." She shook her head. "I married my high school sweetheart. My life was set on its path so early and easily. I don't understand how you kids struggle these days to find someone. With all of the avenues for finding partners, why is it so hard to find the right partner?"

"My God! I can't tell you how many times I've asked myself that question." I cringed at my choice of words. "Sorry. Chris came into my life when I wasn't looking. I was minding my own business and he walked into my business and made me consider those questions all over again—"

"You have such a glow, Sarah. I would welcome you into this family—not that he'd ask me, but I thought you should know. I can be tough, but I can also be helpful." She stood up. "Do you need anything else?"

"Nope. I'm good."

~~

# 25

In the morning, I briefly forgot where I was until my eyes settled on the three portraits. Chris was still sleeping peacefully next to me. I studied those little faces. Could I do three kids?

I'd once had a boss who told me not to have three. 'Then you're outnumbered!' he'd said. He was serious. He'd given me all sorts of random advice that I'd held on to through the years.

Glancing at the clock, it was time to get up. I was never one to sleep in. Wishing we were home or that we had a coffee pot in the bedroom, I prepared myself. I was too old to go into Mom and Dad's kitchen and deal with them first thing in the morning.

I slid out of bed for a quick shower. Maybe Chris'd be awake by then. In the hallway, I ran into Mary.

"Morning!" she said cheerfully, about to close the bathroom door. "Do you need to use it, because I'm gonna shower."

She noticed my towel. "Do you want to shower? I can wait."

"No, that's okay."

"Chris's still sleeping?" she asked.

"Yes, I thought I'd do something productive in the meantime." I rearranged my bathing supplies.

"I can smell coffee. Why don't you go down and get some? It's just about guaranteed that Mom's already out and about. Dad's probably in the back yard. Old people get started *early*." Her eyes sparkled. "Here, I'll get you a cup. You take a butt ton of cream and sugar, right?" She popped out of the bathroom.

"You don't have to do that."

"Oh, I know," she said stopping on the stairs. "You *sure* you don't want to shower?"

"I'd rather have coffee but I'm not gonna lie—I wasn't excited about talking to parents first thing in the morning."

"I totally get it. You won't see Todd till closer to lunch. The basement has just about everything he needs. I wouldn't be surprised if they turn it into a little apartment one of these days," she said starting down the stairs.

By the time she came back up the stairs, I'd taken care of the bare necessities.

She gave me a cup. "Last chance?"

"I'm good. Thank you."

"Okay. I'll see you later," she said, closing the bathroom door.

I drank my coffee and sat in the rocker. Next to the chair was a basket of pastel yarn, knitting needles and what appeared to be a baby blanket.

I picked it up and admired her handiwork. Leah was good with needles. The blanket was probably a little less than half done but her tension and stitches were flawless. It had a Celtic knot to the pattern and was sophisticated for a baby blanket. If it weren't that, however, I wasn't sure what else it could be.

Setting it back in the basket, I realized that I was being watched.

"Good morning, Sunshine," Chris said, stretching.

"What happened to 'gorgeous?' I prefer gorgeous," I said, taking a leap at the bed. The bed lurched and fell with a thud to the floor.

"Holy shit!" I yelled, stunned.

Chris guffawed. "Nice work. Weren't you the one who told me to take it easy?"

I was bright red and flustered. "Yeah, but you're twice as big as I am!" I tried to peel myself off Chris who held me fast.

"Listen. If anyone heard that, they'd be here by now. You did us a solid." He ran his fingers through my hair.

I calmed down.

He kissed me tentatively, his hand worming its way into my pajamas.

Feeling my heat rising, I kissed him back. "You're not really gonna—we're not going to—"

With bedroom eyes, he replied, "Oh, I think we are."

~~

I spent the day lounging in the yard, learning a few new knitting moves from Leah who, having no dinner to prepare, had nothing else on her agenda but to work on the baby blanket. She enthusiastically let us know that Susan and Dan would be joining us at Giusseppe's with big news.

Chris and Todd attempted to covertly fix the bed but had no luck. It was going to require tools. When they gave up, they tossed a Frisbee around with Mary. Their dad had run into the office and said he'd be right back. No one expected to see him until dinner time.

As time ticked by, I became more and more uncomfortable. I tried to give myself a mental pep talk. When that failed, I tried to focus on their never ending game of Frisbee. The three of them were graceful and had natural athletic ability. It was a bummer to think we'd be back in New York tomorrow, living out of a less-than-homey apartment with little time for each other.

When we arrived at the restaurant, my parents were already there, hanging out with the hostess. My mother looked like she was going to jump out of her skin. She *knew* something was up, while Dad was tooling through a real estate magazine.

"*Honeeeey*!" she crooned, pulling me into a quick hug. "*Chris*!" she squealed, grabbing him with the other arm. "*Carl*!" she commanded, screeching over her shoulder.

Dutifully, Dad got up and shook Chris's hand deferentially, nodding to me.

"Thanks for coming, Lucy and Carl. The rest of my family should be here momentarily. This is my sister, Mary, and her boyfriend, Todd." Chris said warmly. "They're RISD graduates!"

"Oh! You live in Providence?" my mom asked, taking in Todd's various tattoos.

"Sure do, but not for much longer. We're going to New York," Mary said eagerly. "Love Little Rhody but can't wait for *the Big Apple*!"

My mom was staring at Todd. Smirking, Todd pulled up his sleeves to reveal more art.

"Wow, you've really got some ink, honey," Mom said analytically. "Are you in a band?"

"I tattoo for a living. If you want one, I'll cut you a family deal."

Mom put her hand protectively on her throat.

Chris and the waitress motioned us to follow them. Falling in line behind the waitress, I felt Chris's hand brush my waist as he jumped in behind me.

A back room had been set aside for us in all of its wood-paneled glory. We were going to have an Italian meal in Mama's basement complete with red gingham table cloths.

Once we were seated, Dad decided to loop back to the car for his camera. Chris trotted after him, under the guise of looking for his parents.

Mary pinched my arm. She was overwhelmed by the impending news. She was going to be the very best sister-in-law I could have hoped for.

I was relieved to see Susan and Dan. Susan was positively radiant. Setting her stuff down, she came over and introduced herself to my mother before giving her sis a hug. As we got acquainted, Chris returned with my dad as well as his own parents.

Carl looked smug. He was pleased by Chris's query and more so by knowing something that my mother didn't. Following Chris to his seat, he proudly sat between Chris and my mother. Mom reached for Dad's arm, trying to get the camera.

In typical Carl fashion, he shook her off and readied the camera for his own use.

Gina, the family friend and waitress, returned to take drink orders. Even though my stomach was turning, I was ready for something serious. I wasn't alone. Amongst the diners, the apprehension was strong and the drinks stronger.

Because Susan was at the other end of the table, Chris was trying to catch her eye. She must've sensed something was up because she did her best to avoid him. It was a bummer that she was likely to share news of her pregnancy at the same time and place that her brother would announce his engagement.

Towards the end of dinner, we were all restless. The only people who could get the show on the road were avoiding it. Mary wadded up a napkin and began throwing little bits at Chris, accompanying each with a meaningful stare. If Chris waited too long, Mary was going to announce the engagement for him. At the other end, Dan and Susan seemed to be having their own wordless conversation about who was going to make their announcement.

Jonathan stood. "First of all, what a great evening this is! It's so nice to have all of the family together. Even extended family and friends," he said, acknowledging my parents. "We are so blessed. Susan and Dan—I believe the floor is yours." Sitting down, Jonathan nodded to the wait staff to finish passing out champagne flutes.

When everyone had a glass, Dan walked behind Susan and rested his hands on her chair. "Susan and I would like to you thank you for coming out to dinner tonight. I know how challenging schedules can be." He smiled at Chris and Mary. "Until recently, I thought that the very best thing that could ever happen to me was marrying Susan. Now, I know that I've been blessed again." His eyes teared up. Setting his champagne down, he put his hands on Susan's shoulders. "Susan—" He choked on her name.

Susan slowly pushed her chair out, handed Dan his champagne and addressed us.

"Mom. Dad. I'm—I'm pregnant." Her eyes watered and she absently rubbed her belly.

The applause was deafening. Susan and Dan puffed up with pride. They were the center of attention, answering the typical pregnancy-related questions that followed.

"Susan, I could not be more excited for you and Dan," Chris said, standing. "I'd like to propose a toast to the McCleary family. May Baby McCleary join our family in good health! Congratulations!"

Smiling toothily, he waited for the well-wishes to die to a low roar. My dad had his camera affixed to Chris. I rolled my eyes. My dad would shoot anything and soon it would be focused on me.

"I, too, am thankful that we could get together tonight. It's always special to have the whole family together. Lucy, Carl—thanks for making the drive from Connecticut on such short notice. It means a lot to us." Chris looked intently at me, his eyes misting until I felt myself on the verge of tears.

"I met your daughter earlier this year and I think you'll agree with me when I say that she's a wonderful person. She has a smile for everyone. Once, I told her that she looks like she's got a secret—something amazing—and that I hoped she'd share it with me." He glanced at Leah. She was sitting on the edge of her chair, gripping the flute much too strongly. "Well, she has decided to share it with me. I asked her to marry me—and she said yes."

He looked so weak in the knees that I supportively wrapped my arm around his waist. With the hubbub that ensued, Chris turned my face and kissed me. I was vaguely aware of cameras flashing as I buried my face in his chest. It only felt like a moment passed before my mom was tugging on me, getting into the picture as well.

Everyone wanted a picture of us. It was only after the pictures that I had a chance to show off my ring and mingle with the women folk.

The Sparks women were giddy. Susan didn't begrudge me my announcement, but was appreciative that the conversation centered on her news.

She was done with her first trimester, never got sick, and was confident she was having a girl. She was due February twenty-fifth but knew her baby would humor her work schedule and come on the winter break.

I was tired and wanted to go home. I didn't realize how incredibly anxious I had been about this evening until now. I did my best to be a good future daughter/sister-in-law but my face hurt from smiling. After another hour, I was cooked.

With Chris talking to the proprietor, I made my way over to him. After accepting their congratulations, I whispered, "I want to go home."

He slid his arm around me and did a double take. "You look green. Are you feeling okay?" he asked, concerned.

"I am really tired. You know how I feel when my parents are around? This is worse. I am *tired* and yeah, I don't feel great. Probably the champagne." I gazed at him apologetically. "I know you don't get to see your family often. Maybe Mary'd take me home?"

"Of course she would but—" He glanced at his watch. "Why don't we give them another half hour and we can get outta here. Your parents should see you longer than it took to drive here."

I screwed up my face. "This is my night—not theirs."

His blue eyes scolded me. "It's a night to celebrate *family*. Let them enjoy it. Who knows when they'll see you again?"

"The wedding," I said under my breath.

He laughed. "Let me guess—we're going to have a long engagement?"

My eyes widened. "No!" I yelled. "I don't think I can handle that. I'd like to get married and keep up the momentum."

"We should figure that out, huh? But you're in the 'sooner than later' camp? Honestly, where did my Sarah go? You're officially on my schedule, aren't you?"

"It seems to me that there is no other way. If I'm not on your schedule, I'm going to miss out. So, yeah—you win."

"I wonder if your dad got that? I don't feel like I win too many!" He took both my hands. "I love you. I would like nothing better than to marry you tomorrow."

"That'd be awesome! A spur-of-the-moment wedding!" I loved the idea in part because there'd be no need to find a memorable gown, maid of honor or any of the other trappings. "Not that we have to decide this now but are you thinking traditional church wedding? Would they let a pagan such as myself in, cuz I'm not gonna lie—the idea of eloping sounds pretty good. If we could wake up and Tweet out our marriage—that'd be great."

The corner of his mouth curled into a smile. "How 'bout no church but something more than elopement? I am a traditional guy. I'd love to see you in a wedding gown." He ran his fingers through my hair. "Maybe some flowers in your hair? We could get Tilda. I'm sure she'd be thrilled. She did a great job with your dress for the gala. I like the idea of *white* and *traditional*, just this once?"

"Make *you* a deal. You get me outta here in the next half hour and I'll agree to your traditional needs." I smiled winningly at him.

~~

"Thanks again for breaking the bed, Sarah. I think you'd be better served sleeping in my room."

From the bottom of the stairs, Mary yelled, "Mom's not gonna like it!"

Waving her off, Chris flipped on the light in his room. "They're not coming home tonight—just a feeling. Your folks are staying in Boston. Mine will tag along. They've got nothing else to do." He grinned, taking my hands and backing into his room.

I did my best to smile but for once, I really wanted to lie down.

"You still look off. You feeling okay?" he asked, touching my forehead.

"I'm just tired." I put my own hand to my forehead. "I don't feel hot."

"It doesn't work like that, but I agree. You're head's not hot." He sat down. "If I promise to keep my hands to myself, will you *please* sleep with me?"

"Those words do not belong in the same sentence."

He bounced off the bed and lunged at me, pulling me down with him.

Hitting the bed, I felt a wave of nausea. I closed one eye and braced myself against his chest.

He froze. "You okay?"

I put up one finger. I just needed a moment. What I certainly didn't need was to be sick when we'd be on a plane again tomorrow. I lowered myself onto the bed and slid like an injured animal over to the pillow. "I just need a minute." I closed my eyes.

He rubbed my back. "You've never been sick since I've known you. Is there anything I can do?"

I barely shook my head. "I really need a minute. I feel nauseous. I haven't felt right all day and I was sure it was nerves, but now I'm not so sure."

The bed shook as he stood up to take off his clothes. "Do you want me to sleep somewhere else? I don't want to get what you've got."

I chuckled. "It's okay. You can stay here." I sat up and gingerly peeled off my clothes. "I'd love my bag, if you'd be so kind?"

"Will do, but you could sleep just like that. I'm telling you—they're not going to break in here. And we're getting married. What're they going to do?"

"Ha. It's their house with Mom's rules."

"Rules are *always* meant to be broken." He ducked out to get my bag.

Perched on the edge of the bed, I was irritated with myself. How dare my body betray me? I didn't have time for this!

He handed me pajamas. "Maybe you picked something up on the plane? Once, I got a call from the airline informing me that I'd been exposed to someone with whooping cough on my flight. That was a rockin' good time. Just knowing almost made me sick!" He turned on the bedside lamp.

"Could be. Another reason to hate flying." I pulled my shirt down and slid back into bed. "You look wired," I said, staring into his electric baby blues.

"I just got engaged! Hell yes, I'm awake! I want the world to know!"

~~

I felt significantly better in the morning and, after listening to the sounds in the house for a while, went downstairs to make coffee. Mary was doing a crossword puzzle.

"Hey," she said. "Do you know a word, ten letters, beginning with 'O' that means 'marked by or exhibiting a fawning attentiveness?' I think the last three letters are 'ous' but I'm not sure." She slid the puzzle towards me.

Following her finger, I read the clues for the 'ous' words. "Those're right. I don't know any of these others. Maybe after coffee?" I mosied over to the pot.

Mary parked her pen. "You're parents are fun people. Carl was showing me the announcement photos—he's such a proud papa!"

I snorted. "It's funny. I was watching everyone when Susan and Dan shared their news. Talk about *proud* papas. I totally get why women were viewed as belongings, historically-speaking. With Susan knocked up, the guys looked so proud of their own *involvement* in it. Your dad, for giving Susan life; Dan for creating a child. Even Chris looked like he wanted to claim ownership."

"They did! I half expected them to fist-bump or pull out cigars. They really do want to be acknowledged for providing the seed." Chewing on her pen cap, she added, "At least you and Susan took the heat off of me. Mom's been on my case to make some decisions about Todd. She thinks

I'm too old to be taking my time. I think she wants grandbabies from somewhere and she'll even take Todd if we move it along."

I stirred my coffee. "Do you have plans?"

"To run from marriage as long as possible," she declared.

"Why?" I asked, adding more sugar.

"Because. Life's over once your married. No offense but your ability to mix it up is severely limited."

"I thought about all that when Chris proposed. I see my life as better with him than without him. I like the idea of growing old with him."

"Good for you. I love Todd, but will I love him thirty years from now? Hard to say." She resumed her crossword. "If you don't know, that's a lot of bullshit to get divorced."

"No one can know what's up thirty years from now." I looked at the headlines on the newspaper. "D'you guys talk about the future?" My finger on the crossword, I tried to inch it my way.

"We talk about the *immediate* future but he's in no hurry. He's never once asked me any leading questions about marriage, babies or growing old. Right now, we're just trying to get to New York."

"Your family is so tight. I'm surprised you don't find it appealing—to have one of your own."

Mary slid the crossword over to me. "I like my life. I like the ability to come and go and see whomever I want. I don't see myself without Todd but at the same time—what about five years from now? Hell, what about *two* years? I'm too selfish." She leaned back in her chair. "It's not that I don't want kids ever. I just know I don't want them now."

"I never wanted babies either. I always saw myself with adult children, but babies? I glossed over that part."

"I knew I liked you. You'd have to be nuts to—well, it's the Susans of the world who were born and bred to be mothers. I am so happy for her! I can't wait to see her little peanut!"

~~

## 26

By the time we were back in New York, I wasn't feeling too good. I crawled into bed and shut my eyes.

"No chance you're gonna run lines with me, huh?" Chris asked rhetorically, standing in the doorway.

"The last thing I want to do is try to read." I cracked an eye. "Sorry."

"I'm gonna run over and see Imogen. Need anything before I go?" he asked, thumbing his script.

"Nah. Ooh, actually, give me my phone?" I said, pointing to my purse across the room.

Handing it to me, he gave me a peck on the cheek and took off.

Alone with my phone, I checked in. His tweet was big news. I wanted to hide from the world. I didn't feel up to smiling for anyone right now.

I had a million messages. Considering my news was good, I was shocked at how far and how fast it traveled. People I hadn't spoken to in at least a year were lined up, congratulating me. The cynic in me wondered how many were hoping to be invited to the wedding.

The wedding. I was completely opposed to a church wedding and was none too eager to have a big hoopla either. I wondered what an inauspicious number of guests would be. Could we get by with fifty? A hundred? God knows Chris could fill an orchestra hall with friends, and people who think they're his friends.

That inspired me to see if Jess would be my maid of honor. It was the middle of the day in L.A. but what the hell? I sent her a text.

'Jess. I'm getting married. Be my maid of honor?'

# PERFECT

As I thought about the wedding, I became more comfortable. I could totally rock a party all about me, even that white dress. When I pictured Jess dress shopping with me, she responded.

'Yes! CONGRATS!!!'

'Thanks.'

'Gotta keep this short. I'm writing. Details?'

'Only starting the planning. Feeling pretty shitty, too. Caught something on the plane.'

'Rest, darlin'. Talk to you soon.'

How many bride's maids would be sufficient? I didn't have sisters, so probably Chris's and maybe Melissa.

'Hey, Mel. Wanna be in my wedding? I could use a bride's maid.'

While I was on a roll, I also asked Mary and Susan. Mary replied uber-enthusiastically, making me laugh. She should be the one to help me with the details. She had no job, no schedule and oodles of 'can-do.'

While typing, a wave of nausea hit me that sent me reeling. I delicately set the phone down and assumed the fetal position. As I hadn't eaten in hours, I was confident there was nothing productive to be done. I just had to get through it.

By the time Chris returned, I was functional.

"How'd it go?" I asked, propping myself up.

"Great! I'm in good shape. Imogen's looking pretty ill, too. Maybe you guys swapped something. She made it through but she's looking *rough*." He appraised me. "You're looking better. Can I get you something? I think we've got cheese and beer—maybe chips."

I stuck my tongue out. "Sounds awful. I'm good. I was just thinking about the wedding."

"Oh, yeah?" he said, sitting down on the foot of the bed.

"I asked Jess to be the maid of honor and your sisters to be bride's maids—and Melissa. Have you given any thought to your wedding party?"

"Nope."

"You thinking Todd and Dan?"

"Todd's not technically family but I like him. Dan is Dan. If schedules permit, I'd like to include Ian and Tom."

"You're serious? You want them? At our wedding?"

"A—what's that saying, keep your friends close and your enemies closer? I've known them a long time. So, yeah. I'm serious. And b—I love 'em. Let's have one hell of a party."

"Okay. I guess we're on the same page. I had a very brief freak-out about the planning, but I know it's going to be all right." I inched over to him. "Mary was telling me that she used to come out to visit you. When was that?"

"As soon as I could afford to fly her out."

"We were talking about weddings and babies and she said something about not being eager to get married, that it 'limits your options.'"

"I knew she wasn't on the fast track."

"I think it's more than that. Did you introduce her to people?" From my chats with Mary, I was certain that she'd seen Ian with some frequency.

He raised an eyebrow. "She'd come and stay for a week or two at a time. Whomever was around met her."

"She met Ian and Tom?"

"Yeah, she got along famously with both of them. I wouldn't have been too surprised to find out that she was dating one or the other, but I really didn't want to know. There's something about her being my little sister." He shuddered.

"Especially with those two!"

He hit me with a pillow. "Let it go. I already told you that there are some things I just don't want to know, okay?"

I studied his face. He knew she'd had some kind of relationship with them. That was probably why he told her to stay home and get a formal education.

"So—back to the wedding." Chris tucked my hair behind my ear.

"I can't even decide on which coast. If we get married in L.A., what do we do about the family?"

"Don't worry about money. It'll take care of itself. There're all sorts of great places where we could have it."

"Any of them big enough for your legion? Between your family, friends and connections, I was thinking we might need Staples Center!"

"I thought you'd want a *small* wedding."

"I don't want anything too big, but if it's gonna be a party, let's not leave anyone out," I said, aware that this could get out of hand.

He grinned. "Nice. We should probably find a place or a date. Which do you want to work on?"

"I'd love a date but would rather have the ideal location. How about if we say within the next year and then see what's available?"

"That works." He spooned me. Kissing my hair, his stomach rumbled.

"You and that belly. Why don't you put something in it?"

"I'd rather put something in you," he said suggestively, dangerously rubbing my inner thigh.

I flipped around, mashing my body into his. I put my hand in his hair, my fingernails massaging his scalp. His body went limp.

"My god, that feels good." He lowered his head onto my cheek.

"I love you," I said, tugging at his shirt.

His eyes flashed, a devilish smile forming on his lips. With infinite speed and grace, he was off the bed. Eyeing me hungrily, he grabbed the edges of his shirt and pulled it over his head.

He slid back into position. "Continue," he said, placing my fingers on his back.

Obligingly, I dragged my nails over him slowly. It had been a long time since we'd fooled around. Baby making sex, with all its intensities, hadn't lent itself to play.

"You left your pants on?" I asked, encountering his waist band.

Desire in his eyes, he said "It's one way to slow down. We'll get there, trust me." He removed my hand, placing it on his back.

He slowly ran his stubble up and down my neck, making my body shiver with anticipation. I shoved him with my hips, knocking him off.

I imitated him. Rising from the bed, I fingered the edge of my shirt. I crossed my arms, and inch by ever-lovin' inch, eased it over my body. I dropped it on the floor.

I crawled onto the bed, savoring his chiseled face, his toned biceps.

He traced his fingers down my arm and I groaned. I wasn't sure how much teasing I could take. Pleased by my reaction, he dragged his fingers down my collar bone and around the edge of my bra.

I was more than turned on. I wanted his naked body on top of mine. As he unfastened my bra, I attempted to undo his pants. Like an animal, I tugged and yanked, my ineptitude coloring the moment.

He traded positions with me. Eyes glued to mine, he rubbed his whiskers down my chest, stopping to give my breasts more attention. I ran my hands through his hair again, wishing he were wearing sweats. Those, I could maneuver.

Making his way down to my skirt, he paused and rubbed my belly.

"You have a funky rash," he said, gently touching it.

I propped myself up on my elbows. "Huh." I touched it. It wasn't hot. It wasn't raised. It was just ugly. "Please," I whimpered, lowering myself back to the bed, "*Please* don't let it stop you."

~~

Over the next few days, life continued in much the same way. He worked. I felt poorly and spent a lot of time online. I looked at venues, dresses, and flowers while talking to Melissa, Jessica and Mary at length.

Towards the end of the week, Mary was in town and stopped by. I was curled up in bed, expecting her. When she knocked, I willed myself to rise and let her in.

"You look like hell," she said, giving me a once over. "Don't give it to me, whatever you do."

"Chris hasn't gotten it yet." I pointed at a chair across the room. "And you can sit across the room, okay?"

"How much longer are you here? Don't you miss Los Angeles?" she asked, tossing her bag on the floor.

"A little. I miss the beach but if I were there, I'd be missing your brother more."

"Good thing you're getting' hitched then!" she responded, getting comfortable. "Got a date yet?"

"Next year. I've been looking for a venue. Lots of them are booked for the next several *years*."

"At least you don't have to have it on a weekend. None of us have traditional jobs. We can do whatever works for you!"

"I hadn't thought of that. I was only looking at weekends. Now I'm gonna have to go back and look at some of the cooler ones that were booked on the weekends."

"Who's Chris having in his wedding party?" Mary asked intently.

"He's thinking of asking Dan and Todd." She was about to jump out of her skin.

"What about Ian or Tom? He's been tight with them forever."

"You really want to see Ian again, don't you? Are you still interested in him?" I asked, curiously.

The corner of her mouth curled. Her expression looked just like Chris. "Yes. Okay. Yes, I would love to see him again. He opened my eyes up to a new world. I miss it."

My mouth dropped.

"Listen, I'm telling you because I trust you and don't you ever repeat it. There are *many* reasons Chris's pretty little Ella McBride family didn't work out. It wasn't just Ian." She folded her legs up into the chair. "I got. I don't even know how to say this. My parents would disown me—I fooled around with Ella. Ian did a lot more watching than participating." She blushed. "You're the first person I've ever told. Mark my words—Ella will come out when she's much older. She likes girls."

I swallowed. "But she and Chris had quite a thing."

"I have 'quite a thing' with Todd but, I'd take Ella if she'd have me. I'd even be her dirty little secret."

"Why're you with Todd then?" I wouldn't be in a relationship with no future.

"I don't *not* like him," she said.

"There's gotta be more to it. The free tattoos?" I asked sardonically. If you knew that you liked women, why would you waste your time with a dude?

"I do like the tattoos but it's more than that. It's expected."

"What's expected?"

"That I find a guy and get married."

"But not if you don't like guys—why would you commit to that for the rest of your life?"

She picked at a scab. "I have no intention of getting married."

"Doesn't exactly fix your problem though."

"I can't *imagine* my parents finding out. They don't know, nobody knows, that I like women. I'd be disowned." She pushed herself back into her chair and relaxed.

"It's easier to do this right now. As I said, if I could be with her, I'd be her secret, no problem." She inhaled deeply. "Well, that felt good."

"Wow." I laughed, pulling her out of her reverie. "I didn't see that coming."

"I know. It's okay." She tugged on her lip. "In case you're curious, I did fool around with Ian, too. I wasn't lying when I told you that. He's masterful. And I would really like to play in his circle."

"He's with my best friend," I said coolly. "And she will be my maid of honor."

"Dammit. I didn't ask. You shouldn't've told me." Although she smiled when she said it, she looked more irritated than I'd ever seen her.

Mary jingled the keys.

"You're happy to be moving?" I asked.

"Do you want to come and see it? It's at least twenty minutes from here."

"I'll pass. I keep getting hit with waves of nausea. I'm gonna have to visit Imogen when they get home and see how she's doing. If she's over it, that means I should be soon."

"Any chance you're preggo?" Mary asked, eyes twinkling.

"I guess there's *always* a chance," I said. "I do sleep with him."

"You should take a test! It'd be hilarious if you and Susan had babies at the same time." A huge smile spreading across her face, she added, "Want me to go get one? There's a drugstore around the corner."

"God, no!" As I hadn't been off birth control for too long and hadn't had a period yet, the likelihood of me being pregnant seemed remote. From what I knew, it would likely take a year or more before everything functioned normally and at this point, I was counting on that.

"You drifted off there." She scrutinized my face, my hair. "You do have a glow about you."

I stood up so quickly that I was once again overwhelmed by the need to puke and ran to the bathroom to escape her as much as anything else.

Hovering over the toilet, I heard her, "Everything okay?"

Peachy, I thought. Gaining control, I plunked myself on the floor and freaked out. With the seed planted, I had to know or I would drive myself insane.

Minutes later, I emerged from the bathroom and Mary had the fridge open. "You've got nothing in here! Looks like I'm gonna have to go out and get something—and a pregnancy test?" She closed the fridge and ripped into a cheese stick.

~~

When Chris got home, he'd brought Chinese. Spreading it out on the coffee table, he handed me chopsticks.

"How's Imogen?" I asked, hoping she'd recovered.

"I'm beginning to think she's pregnant. I know I'm a guy, but something ain't right. And I know I can't ask her that type of question. Hey—you want to go over there after dinner? She'd tell you."

Nervously, I laughed. "Funny you should say that."

Sticking some chicken in his mouth, he waited.

"Your sis was here earlier and she thinks I'm pregnant." Cracking open the rice, the smell overwhelmed me. I corked it, setting it on the table.

"What do you think?" Chris asked, sticking the chopsticks in his container. His eyes darted over my body searching for any clues he may have overlooked.

"Honestly, no. But now that she suggested it, I'm worried."

Chris jumped out of his chair, sitting next to me. "Don't be worried. Nothing would excite me more than being a dad." He put his arm around me, comfortingly. "Do you want me to go get a test? There's a store around the corner."

"I don't know. This was not a part of my plan right now."

He chuckled. "Yeah. It is. Don't *worry*. I'm here. You will be fine. *We* will be fine." He gave me a squeeze. "You have to eat something. Rice?" he asked, opening it again.

I squeezed my eyes shut. "I can't do that smell right now." I pushed the container away. Standing up, I got myself a glass of water in the kitchen.

He guiltily resumed eating his food. "Can you smell it over there?"

I shook my head. Sipping my water, I was okay.

"Is Imogen home, d'you know?" I asked, thinking I'd let him eat in peace.

He nodded, chewing.

"I'm going over there," I said resolutely. I grabbed my purse, a bottle of water and ruffled his hair as I left.

# PERFECT

~~

Julian answered the door, eyeing me cautiously. "I hear you have the plague. We don't need that here, dear Sarah."

I crossed my arms. "I'm not leaving until I see Imogen. And hello, dear Julian."

He backed up, allowing me to enter. "Imogen—company!" he called, slinking off to the bedroom.

She was sitting on the couch, bent over a pillow, head between her knees.

"I guess that answers how you're feeling," I said, sitting in a chair across from her.

She looked up and smiled wanly. "Hey, Sarah. How're you?"

"Better than you, I guess." I nudged the barf bucket next to her on the floor. "How'd you make it through the day? Did someone carry a puke container around with you?"

She put her hair behind her ears. "Will power."

"Have you been to the doctor?" I asked quietly.

"No, but I did take a pregnancy test," she said. "It's negative. Just as well. If this is anything like morning sickness, I do *not* want to be filming and pregnant." She eased herself back onto the couch. "You? Chris said you're pukey, too."

"I've probably got what you've got. I'm nauseous off and on. When it strikes, I go *down*."

"I don't know, Sarah. Your mom forecast babies. If you're not pregnant now, you will be soon. You should buy a test just to have it on hand. Better than having to go to the doctor, in my opinion. Nothing's worse than walking out of the doctor's office finding out you're not expecting."

"You've done that?" I was surprised because I thought the baby-making part of her life had just started.

"*Long* ago. Long, long ago. I was young and dumber." She smiled ruefully. "My life would be dramatically different." Holding my gaze, she continued, "Isn't it funny how hard we run from pregnancy and then when you want to have kids, it doesn't 'just happen?' It's like perpetual body betrayal." She hugged her pillow. "You should get a test though. Even if you don't need it today, it's not like they expire."

She sat bolt upright. "Actually, I think I have a spare. I don't need it right now." She scanned the apartment, got up cautiously and wandered into the bathroom. She handed me a little pastel colored box. "It was a two-pack. I decided I didn't need a double-no."

I turned it over in my hands. I had never touched one before and it was unnerving. Reading the packaging, it could tell you within a day or two of a missed period. I hadn't had one in years so that wasn't much of a selling feature.

"You want to take it here?" she asked. "Feel free."

"Wow. These things are sensitive."

"The first time I took it, I couldn't decide if it said I was or wasn't. It had some dopey little line on it. It was so faint. It's like it left it open to interpretation. I wish I'd had two then. These though—they're obvious." She leaned delicately back into the couch.

I put it in my purse. "I was hoping you were pregnant. I'd like to know someone else who is, now that I'm ready to go through it."

The color draining from her face, she barely nodded. "There're some great books out there, too. I have one that's something like *Girlfriend's Guide* or something. I might even have it here. I think I've read it at least three times. It's as funny as it is disgusting."

"How much longer are you around?" I watched her collect herself before she answered.

"Couple of weeks? I try not to get too hung up on dates."

"Do you have other things in the queue?"

"None right away. I really want a baby to be—" She leaned over and wretched.

I stood up, taking that as a sign that I should go. "I hope you feel better. I'll see you later." I slowly inched my way to the door, waiting for an acknowledgement.

She threw one hand up and gave me a quick wave before grabbing her bucket again.

"Not pregnant," I said upon my return. "Very sick but not pregnant."

"Oh, great. Well, thank God that all of our buddy-buddy scenes are behind us. She'll have to broadcast her disease for me to get it," he responded while sitting on the couch, thumbing through a script.

"What're you up to?" I asked, checking to see if there was any Chinese left.

His smiled broadened when I threw some rice in the microwave. "What Julian's been working on. Want to read it?"

"*Twisted River*? Yes! I'd love to see it. What're you and Ian doing with it anyway? Are you going to be *in* it?" I asked, bringing my dinner back to the couch.

"Ian's expressed an interest in being in it. He asked me how I'd feel about a little directorial debut." He folded the page and set it down.

"Cool! What're you getting yourself into?" I asked, tentatively sticking a forkful in my mouth.

"I'm trying to figure that out. He's coming this weekend, so we'll see."

"Does Jess know that you two are behind this? Have him bring her, too! I'd love to see her," I added pleadingly.

"If she asked enough questions of the right people, she'd know," he said, watching me eat. "Your stomach calmed down?"

I swallowed. "Enough that I thought I'd test the waters." Poking the rice around, I said, "So far, so good."

"I don't know whether to be pleased or bummed," he said softly. "Are you going to take a test?"

I shook my head. "Not right now. With Imogen sick, I'm thinking we'll both be over it in a day or two."

"And," he said, conspiratorially, "If you're not?"

"Oh—well, I thought I would harness my Inner Imogen and just will it away. I'm fine," I said with as much certainty as I could muster.

He scoffed. "Okay then. Can we put a time limit on waiting for it to pass?"

I set my rice down. "No pressure here," I said, returning his gaze.

"Sorry. I haven't been this excited—possibly ever," he said, handing me the rice.

"And now you're going to pay close attention to what I eat? Is that how this is going to work?" I asked, amused.

He blushed. "I'm sorry. I want to be supportive and take care of you."

"How about I let you know when I need either?" I asked, taking another bite.

"You promise?"

"To what?"

"Let me. Let me take care of you."

"Sure. That means you have to be *around*. That's part of taking care of me. There will come a time when you may have to abandon your schedule and hop on mine."

"*Ours*."

"Potato-potahto. Do *you* promise?" I asked, wondering what other Chinese might be left as I scraped the bottom of the container.

Grinning foolishly, he said, "Till death do us part, I do."

~~

Ian arrived before the weekend, eager to get started. Although he had a hotel room where he dropped his bags, he became a permanent fixture. He was on our doorstep at seven a.m. with a bunch of baked goods and a messenger bag full of what looked like school work. All of his overly friendly propositions were gone. What was left was a big kid who seemed genuinely eager to work with Chris for the sake of work.

To his credit, Chris was just as enthusiastic, pouring over the details in each of his spare moments. I was pleased to get some breathing room. I still didn't feel like my old self, but seemed to get better with each passing day. While they threw out ideas, I knit a baby blanket. Ian raised an eyebrow, but other than that, he ignored me entirely.

They were planning on a low budget production and intended to maintain complete control. If things went well, they'd try to enter it in the film festival circuit. Listening to them work through everything, from the script to locations and actors, fascinated me. I knew that films required a great deal of creativity, but each time they tweaked an idea, it made the product substantively different—better.

They were thinking of shooting it in Connecticut, by the water reserve where I grew up. I spent so much time there that I knew it would provide everything they were looking for—if they could pull the proper permits. They had even asked Imogen to play Aurora Kinkade and she was considering it, in large part because it was against-type for her.

As the weekend came to a close, I was ready for him to be gone. He didn't bring Jessica with him and didn't mention her at all. I had to go to the source.

Jess'd moved. She was happy. She was writing nonstop and asked me to pinch Ian's butt for her. I wanted to delve further but she was short, 'brevity due to writing streak,' she said.

As long as we lived together, she'd never not made time for me. This was the new us. We'd support each other but we'd also give each other time and space to evolve.

I was eager to see her new digs and quite pleased that I had avoided helping her move. It felt like we just finished unboxing. I was ecstatic that she chose to have her own space instead of a dedicated dresser drawer.

That evening, I couldn't help myself. I'd spent the last several days alone in thought.

"So—" I started, getting comfortable in bed.

His head popped up from his ever-present script. "So?" he said blankly.

"Hi. It's good to see you. Can you set that thing down?" I requested, reaching for the script.

He set it down and repositioned himself, leaning on the pillows. "So," he stated.

"Is this really how life is for you?" I wasn't sure how to ask what I wanted to know.

"You've been with me for almost a year now. What are you really asking?" he said, eyeing his script eagerly.

"You haven't even finished your current film and you're not sleeping, not really eating. All you do is prepare and fixate on your next film? Is that how your life goes?" I ask, trying not to sound critical.

He continued to stare at the pile of paper on the foot of the bed. I gently grabbed his chin and rotated his face. "Hello?"

He cringed. "Sorry. I was in the middle o—I was near the end of my lines. Can I just finish it? For tonight, anyway?" He apologetically leaned in and kissed me. "I don't want to be distracted if you want to have a deep conversation but I can't do it now."

~~

## 27

I headed back to Los Angeles a couple of days later to start working on The Dress and to review places for the wedding.

It was nice to come home to freshly cut flowers and a manicured yard. Not worrying about the small stuff was a luxury.

Shortly after throwing my bags down, Tilda arrived. She only had the weekend to meet with me. She felt as I did—what that hell're we doing?

Her hair tied up in a tidy knot, she kicked off her flip flops and eyed me from all angles.

"You know, Sarah, you really are a classic beauty. You've got lots of options. Are we going traditional?" she asked, her eyes recording my body parts for reference.

"Traditional. Well, white is a yes. Chris begged for traditional. Beyond white—I don't know. I've never given this much thought before. I haven't even gone bride's maid dress shopping."

"But you've been looking online, right? You *told* me you would," she added plaintively.

She inventoried the room. "No more meeting in the pool house, huh? Your home is lovely."

"Thanks and yes, I did look. I think I need a lot of guidance. I like lace. I like glitter. I like the idea of a long dress, no trainy-thing. I don't need the big wad of fabric on my butt. I don't need sleeves but am not opposed to short sleeves. Is that helpful?" I asked, quickly running over my scattered thoughts.

"Do you have coffee? Maybe we should get comfortable and look at a few things before we really get started?" She sat down on the couch and began pulling out an assortment of magazines, a planner and her tablet.

"Sure," I said, not moving. "Are we going to look at *all* of that?" I motioned to her growing pile. "I might need to get more than coffee going."

She brought her tablet in the kitchen. "Do you know when it'll be? Are you having it here?" She scrolled wildly on her tablet.

"We hope for the next year. I'm thinking a good six months from now, like May? June? We're looking at places here, so I don't think I care a whole lot about the season." I pulled the carafe out mid-brew and poured.

"Alright. Well, I have a few traditional-non-traditional ideas to show you. Come here and bring me some of that," she commanded, not looking up.

I saw a couple of beautiful gowns. "Those are amazing but not for me. I don't think I'd ever wear something that goes all the way up my neck. That's *a lot* of lace!"

She glowered at me. "I know. What I wanted to show you about this dress is the glitzy fabric. Forget the lace and the neckline. We're looking at *parts*, Sarah, so I can get a sense of what we're building. We're not doing something 'off the rack' here."

"Is that literally glitter? They look like silver daisies embroidered in it. I'm not gonna lie, that's cool and even better if it doesn't have to have that lace."

She huffed. "This is going to be fun, I promise, but do let me show you stuff. You can tell me what you think when I ask, okay?"

My eyes widened. I'd just been reprimanded by a woman hired to build something for me. I was annoyed. I wasn't sure if it was because it felt like she was disrespectful or because I somehow felt I was better than she. I'd never been that way before. I wondered if my newfound lifestyle was somehow influencing my character in a way that I didn't see coming.

She looked up from the screen. "Sorry. I didn't mean it that way. I really like working with you, but I am used to working with people that just know how I operate." She smiled slowly and drank her coffee.

Grimacing, she said, "Holy Moses, girl! Is this diesel? That is some strong stuff!"

Over the next hour or so, we narrowed down the collective vision to something more manageable. Then, she decided to take a few measurements.

We prattled on as she worked. "Double congrats, Sarah. When are you due?" she asked, sliding the tape out from under my shirt.

I reddened. "I am that much bigger than the last time you saw me?" I asked, mortified.

"No! Not at all. You have that rash. My sister had it both times she was pregnant. I bet it itches, doesn't it? She always used oatmeal to get rid of the itch."

I felt like she could hear my heart beating. I didn't know what to say.

As she finished her measurements, she asked, "Aren't you pregnant? I'm so sorry if you're not. It's just that my sister, Becky, was pregnant last year and it looked just like this. Do you know what it's called? I forgot. It's a weird name." She scratched some numbers on her pad.

"I don't think I'm pregnant," I said. "It'd be news to me if I were."

She chewed on her pencil. "I'm sorry. You should really get that looked at. Could be shingles." She began putting her stuff away. "I will be in touch in a couple of days with fabric swatches and a couple of sketches. I think I know exactly what you want, and you're going to look ah-mazing."

Absently, I rubbed my belly. "I can't wait to see your creations. I got so many compliments at the gala."

She took another look at me, paying a little too much attention to my stomach. "I woulda sworn you're pregnant. I know I don't know you well but you look radiant. Engagement must work for you." She swung her bag up to her shoulder.

"Thanks for everything," I said, walking her to the door.

As soon as she left, I ran to the bathroom and lifted my shirt. How long had I had this stupid rash already? And was it true that the glow of pregnancy often came accompanied by an angry rash? It seemed like there was more of it now. The more attention I gave it, the itchier I became.

I picked up my phone. I hunted for information about stomach rashes and sure enough, mine sounded like textbook 'PUPP.' With my purse next to me, I willed myself to root around for the pregnancy test. I'd been home less than a day and I was staring at the little devil wondering if everyone knew more about pregnancy than I.

I crushed the box in my hand, trying to convince myself this was no big deal. The result wouldn't change anything. Resolutely, I stormed into the bathroom ready to take the biggest test of my life.

~~

# 28

I don't know how long I sat there, staring at it on the edge of the sink. Even though the little words confirmed what everyone seemed to see, I still couldn't. It was not okay to be pregnant now. I was alone now. I couldn't do this alone and I didn't know what to do with myself.

With an epic sigh, I wandered into my studio and pulled out my supplies. Over the course of the next several hours, I made two little hats, a pink and a blue one. They were really cute, considering I didn't have baby-themed supplies.

When they were done, I fiddled obsessively with an extra piece of ribbon. This was not how I envisioned Chris finding out that he was going to be a dad. We'd never Skyped before but I knew I needed to see his face. The only other option was to join him in New York. The worst part was knowing that I couldn't tell anyone but him. He had to be first.

Checking my phone, it was unlikely he was around, and for once I was at a total loss for words. I tried to remember the pregnancy books that Imogen had mentioned. When that failed, I wished that I had asked Imogen for the name of her doctor. If I couldn't tell anyone right now, at least I could be proactive and get an appointment. I considered nonchalantly texting her but knew that she wouldn't be fooled.

Instead, I settled for sending Chris a quick note asking him to check in by phone when he had a moment. I wasn't sure I'd ever asked for a phone call specifically, but I needed to hear his voice.

Cradling my phone, I went room to room trying to decide which would make the best nursery. My room had a bathtub but I really liked the front room with the view of the fountain. It felt magical to me with a view available nowhere else. The taupe walls would have to go. I envisioned a jungle scene or maybe something faery friendly to spice it up. When I was younger, I had friends in theatre who were scenic painters. If I could find one of them, it wouldn't take them but a couple of hours to put sky, atmosphere and toadstools all around.

This baby was going to have an idyllic childhood. She would be as safe as the proverbial bug in a rug, surrounded by imagination and whimsy. I'd never reprimand her for pulling out her paints and redecorating her dresser or drawing her buddies on the wall. I would encourage her to express herself and help her develop high self-worth. She was not going to work at a sandwich shop.

It didn't occur to me how little I thought of myself until that thought popped in my head. I was more than the Sandwich Shoppe and I wanted my daughter to be more than I. How much time had I wasted faithfully reporting for duty?

I wanted my daughter to be a risk-taker, a problem-solver. She wouldn't wait for the world, but would be someone who'd try anything, anywhere.

I glanced in the closet. It was a huge closet for a little person. Although my room always felt big as a child, I bet it wasn't much bigger than this closet. Hopefully, we wouldn't burden her with stuff to fill it. She'd never want for anything but at the same time, it was important to me that she learn how to be self-sufficient. She couldn't be that if we gave her the world.

I knew that having one baby meant I was committing to at least two. As an only child, I learned how to do everything by and for myself. My ability to trust that other people had worthwhile ideas took a long time to develop. It wasn't until my twenties that I became aware of the merits of being with people my age. I missed out on a lot of fun stuff as I tried to be what my parents expected me to be—a little adult robot who followed commands.

I sent Jess a text. Although I felt Chris should know first, if he wasn't available—well, she could keep my secret for the rest of eternity. While waiting for anyone to reach out and touch me, I meandered into my room and lifted my shirt. My rash was angry and I'd swear there was more of it. As a hello, it decided to itch. I didn't feel an iota different yet everything was different.

With it nearing one, I wandered down to the guest house to see what condition it was in. It looked exactly like it did when I moved in except for a couple of pictures that Jess must've left as a thank you. I opened the fridge and found a bottle of Jack with an elastic securing a note to it.

Featuring a picture of Iron Man, it said, 'Don't be a stranger.' I opened the bottle and poured myself a dainty shot. I stared at the mural. She was pretty, statuesque—static. My life had been frozen for quite a while but I was ready to embrace change. My existence was going somewhere.

My phone rang, bringing me out of my reverie.

"I found your note," I said wanly.

"What're you doing down there at this hour?" Jessica asked.

"Thanks for the picture, too. That's what I need right now: someone with iron strength." I swished the tail end of my whiskey.

"You're welcome but what're you doing down there? Aren't you way overdue for bed? How long've you been back?" she asked, perplexed.

"Came back less than twenty four hours ago. I called you and then decided to come down and see if I could see any traces of you. Beyond the bottle, you left some pictures in the living room—a gift?"

"Those're from our apartment. Chris liked them. Happy engagement!" she said merrily.

"Thanks. It's crazy, isn't it? I'm still shocked when I think about how much change has come my way this year. I'll probably never eat a sandwich again, in celebration."

"Whoa. Let's not make such sacrifices! And actually, maybe you should eat sandwiches regularly as an homage to your past. It'd keep you humble," she said.

"Yeah, that's true," I mused.

"What's up, Sarah? You sound off. You knew I was going to have to leave. I will always take your calls, even in my stardom."

I snorted. The distance between us had grown and she felt it, too. "Things are going that well for you, huh? Did you ever get the scoop on *Twisted River*?" I inquired.

"Things are going that well. I was poking around and found out who bought my book. Did *you* know that Ian and Chris are behind Doppelgänger Films?"

"That's news to me. It would explain why I found a copy of your book all dog eared and covered in pen in Chris's apartment. I asked him about it and he never did explain it."

"You really didn't know?" she asked, an edge to her voice. "I'd like to think you would've told me. You've never been much of an actress."

"What're you up to right now?" I was ready to drive to wherever she was in my pursuit of the familiar.

"I'm at home talking to you—why?" she asked cautiously.

"How'd you feel about a visitor?"

"Now?"

"Yessiree," I said with a burst of energy.

"Sure, if you want to go looking for my place. It's not hard to find but you can be directionally challenged in the dark."

I laughed. "It's not the dark. I'm just challenged."

"And it's almost two. Are you *sure?*"

"I think I am. I have your address. Can't take me too long to get there at this hour."

"Be careful, okay? You're breaking your own well-established rule."

~~

Trying to find Jessica's house was impossible. It didn't matter that my car had GPS. It didn't help that I had her on the phone. It was dark and I was out of my element. On my third pass through where her house had to be, I was pulled over. I would imagine that my slowly creeping Jeep looked like someone who was up to no good.

As the officer approached the window, I smiled shakily.

"Good evening, Officer." I kept my hands tightly on the steering wheel.

"Morning, Miss. Driver's license and registration, please," he said in a monotone.

"Did I do something wrong?" I asked, fumbling for my purse.

"Driver's license and registration," he reiterated.

Opening the glove box, he shifted and I realized he had his hand on his gun. I moved faster and dropped the pile of papers on the floor. Picking them up, I found the registration quickly and handed it over.

Taking them, he studied my face, looking for signs of impairment. I smiled sweetly in response.

"It will only take a minute," he said, returning to his car.

I watched another car pass when Chris called.

"You're awake!" he said, surprised.

"Yeppers and talking to a cop," I said, my voice quivering.

"Are you okay? What happened?" he asked unsteadily.

"I'm fine," I said, fighting back the tears.

"You don't sound fine. What's up?" he said.

"I was pulled over. I'm waiting for the cop to tell me *why* so I can get to Jessica's," I whimpered.

"Why're you headed there now? Shouldn't you be sleeping?" he asked.

I felt a tear slide down my face. "I can't be home right now, Chris. I don't want to be alone." I choked back a sob.

"You're worrying me." His words were slow, calm.

"I think you're going to have to rearrange your schedule soon," I said, wanting him to ask the right question.

"I'll be done here in days. Then I'm home. Are you okay? Seriously? Are you?" he asked warily.

"Besides being pulled over, it's been one helluva day." I sighed. "I wish you were here."

"I will be. Soon. What's made today so rough? As I remember, Tilda was coming over. You were doing some dress shopping. That didn't sound so bad. Was she unpleasant? I know that she can be abrupt."

"I did see her. She went off to sketch. I wish I had her talent," I said, drifting off into self-deprecation.

"Good. Then what's up?" He kept his voice light, lilting.

I sighed. This is not how I envisioned this announcement. Glancing out the window, I saw the officer heading my way. "Just a sec. The cop's here."

"Ma'am, please exit the vehicle," he said, grabbing the handle.

"Why? What'd I do? I have Christopher Everett Sparks on the phone. Here!" I thrust the phone at him. "This car was a birthday gift!"

He swung the door open and motioned again for me to get out. As I did, I tried to hand him my phone. "Please, he's on the phone. Talk to him!" I shoved the phone at him.

He took it, eyes never leaving mine.

"To whom am I speaking?" he asked. As Chris spoke, the officer's face softened indiscernibly. I relaxed. Chris could even charm a cop over the phone. Truly, he had super powers. The cop was nodding and took a step away from me to laugh under his breath.

The longer he had my phone, the more I wanted to scream. On the one hand, I had just been saved, but on the other, this never would have happened without Chris. I scowled at the cop now that I was off the hook.

With another muffled laugh, he returned my phone and registration. "Sorry, Ms. Riley and congratulations on your engagement. Have a good night." He turned around and left me standing, mouth agape.

I slowly returned the phone to my ear and got in the Jeep.

"Chris?" I ventured.

"Hey, there. Officer Ramirez was convinced you took my Jeep." He chuckled. "You do look like riffraff!"

"Thanks for that," I said, watching the cop car peel away.

"Are you okay now?" he asked. I could hear the amusement in his voice.

"Yep. I'm great. I'm pregnant." Even to me, my voice sounded cold and it was met with silence. I waited for what felt like an eternity before plodding onward. "Tilda congratulated me on my pregnancy. After thinking that she was telling me that I needed to go on a diet, she mentioned that my rash looked like a pregnancy thing. She was right." I paused, expecting him to say something. "I really wanted to tell you this in person." I gnashed my teeth. "You know what? Your job is getting in my way. I resent it. There. I do. I resent it." I felt relieved having said what had been bothering me for some time.

"Oh, Sarah! I am so—I don't even know what the right word is—pleased? Excited? Surprised? You took the test," he said, warmth overwhelming his words.

"I did. When everyone tells you that you're pregnant, it wears a girl down."

"I know how much you hate being the last to know," he said teasingly.

"I'm not gonna lie. It's true. And then to have to call you to tell you? I wanted to tell you before anyone else."

"But that's why you're going to Jessica's in the middle of the night, isn't it?"

I didn't reply but realized that Jess was calling. "She's calling. I gotta let her know I'm okay," I said, not wanting to let him go.

"Alright but call me back. I sure as shit can't sleep now," he said, stuffing something in his mouth.

~~

I finally got to Jessica's when she stood out on the curb to flag me down. I was less than a block from her house and had driven by it multiple times.

"Did you buy it?" I asked, setting my purse down by the couch.

"I did. When you see the back yard, you'll understand. It's like another living area with citrus trees and all sorts flowering vines. It's gorgeous and maintenance-free." She grabbed a couple of beers and sunk into the couch. "What was so important that you had to come here in the middle of the night?" She relaxed and took a drink.

I did my best to imitate her before answering. "I'm pregnant."

Jess sat up, a smile spreading across her face. "Well, m'dear. Congratulations!"

I dipped my head and gripped my bottle.

"How far along are you?" she asked, taking another drink.

"I just took the test but it was yelling at me. 'You're pregnant! You're pregnant! You're pregnant!' I couldn't believe it. I mean, I've heard denial stories before but never thought I'd question it." I set my beer down. "Do you know if I can drink these?"

She glanced at the label. "I wouldn't drink with your dad, but I'm sure one won't do any harm. Oh, Sarah! Does Chris know?"

"Yup," I said, popping the p. "When the cop pulled me over, I told him. It wasn't pretty. I cried. I don't want to be alone for this," I said quietly.

"Hon, you're *not* alone. You've got Chris. He adores you. And now, he won't be able to help himself. You will be more than his world. You're going to be his everything—if you weren't already."

"Taking that test and being alone was not cool. And now I'm looking at the first doctor's appointment. I'm sure it's not a big deal, medically-speaking, but I still don't want to do it alone."

"Listen, if you have to go before he gets back, I'll take you. We can check out Little Sparky together." She closed her eyes. "If you're freshly pregnant, your baby'll come in May-ish. Isn't that when you expected to exchange your vows?"

"Which is worse—getting married while grossly pregnant or while holding a baby?" Neither sounded picturesque to me.

"Considering it's what you both wanted, I'd say wait until you have the wee one so you can look back on the pictures and see your little person instead of the big body."

"I was just measured for my gown, too."

She guffawed. "Yeah. I think I'd wait on that."

"Why can't I do just one thing right? Why couldn't I get pregnant after a wedding? Honestly, what is his mom going to say?" I chugged my beer.

"She's going to congratulate you through tears. She's going to hug you and thank you for giving her what she's been hoping for. She's a *Catholic* mom. She's been itching for this. Your mom, too. Everyone's going to be so excited. You're going to be, too, once the shock's worn off." She leaned further back into the couch and stretched. "So, mama bear—"

"So sorry that I came by so late. I feel lame now," I said contritely.

"You can sleep here if you like. Or watch TV." She glanced at the rest of her house. "I'd give you the penny tour but you can see most of it from here, and I have a guest." She motioned towards her bedroom. "In there."

I fidgeted with my purse. "I am *so sorry*. Is it Ian?" I asked, half-hoping she'd moved on.

"It is."

"You let me come over when you had him here?" I asked, stupefied.

"Sure. You're an old friend and he's here a lot." She finished her beer and glanced again at her bedroom.

"If you want to get back in there—"

"Bah. He's fine. I'm sure he's asleep," she added knowingly.

"Because?"

"Because if he weren't, he'd be out here. He's got a bit of a Pit Bull in him." She grinned mischievously. "I think jealousy is new to him and from what I gather, it's not his favorite emotion." She closed her eyes. "Shortly after I moved in here, I had a couple friends over. He stopped by unexpectedly." Peering at me through one eye and smirking, she said, "and he let himself in. We were running through the sprinkler half-clothed. His eyes almost fell out of his head. He's mine, Sarah. If I want him, he's mine."

~~

After sleeping very poorly on the couch for a couple of hours, I awoke to Ian making coffee in his boxers. I pretended to be asleep. I wasn't overly eager to talk to him right now.

"I know you're awake. Good morning, Sarah," Ian said, taking out some coffee cups. "Are you ready for coffee?"

I jostled myself into a sitting position. "Sure. I didn't exactly sleep last night."

"Yeah, why're you here?" he asked, sweeping his hair out of his eyes. "I thought you were in New York with lover boy."

"I was, but I needed to get back here."

"Here? Then, why are you *here*?" he asked, bringing me a coffee.

"I could ask you the same thing."

"But you know the answer to that," he said evenly. "Which brings us back to you." His eyes narrowed. "Something not perfect in your world?"

"Can you please be nice to me? You are feisty this morning."

"I brought you coffee. I don't do that for just anybody." He scoured my face for clues. "Last I heard, you were engaged. Congratulations." He smirked. "You look spooked. Is that why you're here, cold feet?"

We stared at each other.

"Nothing's changed." I glanced dolefully at my black coffee.

"Not *yet*. You can still walk away."

"I can *always* walk away. I don't think a ring changes that."

"Sure." He brought a pint of half and half over.

I added some, watching the color change. "Have you decided when you're going to start filming her book?"

His eyes burned into me. "Next year. There's a lot that has to happen first. Probably start filming at about this time next year."

"Why didn't you tell Jessica that you wanted her book? Why was it a secret?"

"I wanted her to sell her book to me and I didn't think she would." He said it like it was self-evident.

"Why wouldn't she?"

"I thought she might expect to be a part of its production. That was a no-go," he responded casually.

"Why couldn't I know?" I scoured the counter for her sugar. "I didn't want anything to do with it."

"You and Jess are closer than sisters." He brought me the sugar bowl. "I suspect you'd tell each other anything. Or rather everything." He held out a teaspoon.

"And you don't share everything. Or rather anything. Except women." I tenaciously stirred my coffee.

"Your fixation with my sex life is not flattering," he said, joining me on the couch. He leaned over me. "Don't fuck with me, Sarah." His breath on my face, he was kissing distance. I willed myself to stillness, returning his hard stare.

An awkward moment later, I spilled my coffee. He touched my thigh and retreated to the kitchen.

My heart racing, I felt small and insignificant. "Why'd you get involved with Ella anyway?" I asked, reaching over him for a paper towel.

He pinned me to the counter. "Because I could." He bumped his pelvis into me.

"Unless you want to be doused in coffee, let me go." I reached for the pot. He backed up imperceptibly. "Why though? You could have anyone and you had his *sister*. Why'd you have to go for his girlfriend, too?"

Ian eyed me through his tussled hair, a tight smile forming on his lips. "Ah, you're friends with Mary. She's cute, isn't she?"

"Still—why? Why go after the women in his life when you could have anyone, anywhere?"

He leaned into my face. "Can I?" he said seductively.

"Even when you're repulsive, yes. I've gotta believe you could." I put my hand on his chest and pushed.

He covered my hand with his own. "Let's assume that you're right. Then where's the sport?"

I blushed. "You go after his girls because it's a challenge?"

"Like you said, if you can have anyone, why would you?" The warmth coming from his hand made me woozy. He rubbed his stubble on my neck.

"Stop. I am this close to stomping on your foot." I shivered. As much as I didn't want his attention, I ached for Chris.

He chuckled softly. "And that's why you're such a prize. You're a tough nut."

Putting the counter safely between us, I continued, "Why Jessica?"

His face relaxed. "I like her."

"That's it? You like her?" I asked incredulously.

"Hey, that's a big step for me. I like her. Ask anyone how many women I like."

"You're repulsive."

"And you like it. Doesn't that make you sick?" he asked cynically. "Every fiber of your being tells you that you shouldn't like me, that I'm not good for you and yet—" He reached over and tucked my hair behind my ear.

"Repugnant."

"Another time, then. You know—weddings are a great time for merriment. I'll be there, assuming we survive the bachelor party."

"Bachelor party?" How had that reality never occurred to me?

"You don't think I'd propel my boy to marital bliss without a proper send off, did you?" He grinned. "What happens in Vegas, stays in Vegas and you—you are not invited."

I sank onto the stool and held my coffee firmly with both hands.

"How much do you trust him?" His eyebrow arched. "It's going to be just as bawdy and raucous as you think it is."

"You can't stop me from coming," I said defensively.

Sardonically, he said, "You can come if you're gonna participate, and that would break his heart."

~~

## 29

When Chris finally walked in the door, I jumped into his arms.

Nuzzling my neck, he immediately put a hand on my belly. Kissing me as if I were breakable, he said, "How're you feeling?"

I raised my eyebrows. That was not the greeting I wanted. I was randy and ready for action, not a discussion that felt fueled by my pregnancy.

"I feel great," I said, less-than-enthusiastically.

He backed up. "Why're you looking at me like that? Did I do something wrong already?" he asked, a disbelievingly large smile on his face.

"I know that this is the first time you've seen Pregnant Sarah but I'm still Just Sarah, too," I said, my peevishness giving way under his gaze.

His smile broadened. "Ah! There's My Sarah!" He grabbed my chin and kissed me soundly.

My heat rising, I artfully tucked my hands in his pants. He dropped his bag on the floor. "So, that's how it is, huh?" he asked, kissing my ear.

"Oh, yes. That's how it is. From my reading, I think I'm getting randier and randier due to Baby Sparks. I want you here, now and then over there and maybe again over there," I said, pointing from the living room to the great outdoors.

"Damn, I didn't know pregnancy was going to agree with *both* of us so well!" He scooped me up and was about to dump me on the couch.

"No—let's go outside. That hammock hasn't seen any action," I said, putting an arm more securely around his neck.

Entwined in the hammock, I absently stroked his chest. "I'm glad you're here for the appointment."

He ran his fingers through my hair. "There's no place I'd rather be. I'm eager to see the little devil."

"Do you think it's a boy or a girl?" I asked, having decided it was a girl.

He put his arm behind his head. "As long as it's healthy, I don't care. We're going to have more than one, right? So, we'll get one of each."

I laughed. "Is that how it works?"

"If I'm supplying the seed, that's how it's worked for generations of Sparks. There're always a boy and a girl."

"In that order? Should we start discussing boy names?" I let my mind wander.

"No—obviously no. I have an older sister, rememb—" He paused. "Shit. Poor Suzy Q. We sorta stole her announcement and now we're going to have a baby at the same time."

"I had the same thought. Your sister has shared a lot of the spotlight with you. Gracefully, it seems." His hand had found its way to my belly again and I covered it with my own. "You're *really* into this baby, aren't you?"

"I don't see a downside. I want you. We're engaged. We're going to have a baby *and* you're horny? Yep, there's nothing wrong with my little world."

I searched his eyes. "And you're not working for the foreseeable future, right? We can have this baby together? I'm not going to be here, doing this while you phone in your support from some set, right?"

"Ouch." He brushed a lock of hair from my face. "Yes. I know what happens when I'm not available, remember?"

It was my turn to be reticent. "I'm sorry. I wasn't thinking about your last attempt at fatherhood."

He kissed my hair. "I know. There isn't a minute that goes by that I'm not thinking about you and how to support you." He jostled me. "I know how idyllic this is but there's rope cutting into my ass. Can we reposition?" He climbed out of the hammock. He had crisscross red lines pushed into his well sculpted butt. He threw his shorts on. His eyes wandered down my body.

"I'd like to offer you your clothing but you look mighty fine just the way you are," he said, picking up my clothes.

I felt very exposed now that he was partially dressed. I motioned for my clothing. I slid into my shirt, stretching it down until it covered everything. He sat next to me in the hammock, rocking it like a swing.

"What does this do to our nuptials?" he asked, stopping the hammock.

"I was thinking about that. I am not eager to be photographed right before I pop. I think I'd rather wait until we have the baby and then look like me for posterity's sake," I said, holding his hand.

He twisted the engagement ring. "It's totally up to you. I'd marry you tomorrow if I could."

"Would you really? That wouldn't leave much time for 'traditional,'" I said slyly.

"Maybe traditional isn't the end-all, be-all in this relationship." He kissed my lips. I felt myself warming up to the possibilities.

I put my hand on his chin and pushed him away from me. "Tell me more about non-traditional."

He cocked his head. "Wow, you're all over this, aren't you?"

"If I don't have to be hugely pregnant and can be married, yup. I'm all ears."

"My mom'll be disappointed. Do you want to elope?"

I hooted. "Vegas, baby!"

He rolled his eyes. "Married in Vegas? Like at a drive through chapel? That might be pushing it for me."

"I don't need a *drive through*. We can stay there long enough to have a few pictures taken and follow it up with the party." I clapped my hands like a child. "Ooh, does this mean that I can forgo the dress?" He was biting his lip. "Too much?" I asked, pouting.

"I'd really like to see you in the big, white once-in-a-lifetime gown if it's not too much to ask." He bared his teeth comically.

"Well, if we're gonna do the dress, let's figure out how to stick closer to the original plan then," I said resolutely. "If it doesn't kill me, I'll be a lot stronger."

~~

The morning of the appointment, I was thankful that we were going to be one of the first in the cue. As we sat in the waiting room, there was another young woman, rubbing her very-pregnant body while trying to keep up with her toddler. Across from us sat a couple who looked older. The woman's eyes wandered repeatedly to Chris over the top of her *People* magazine. Eventually, she nudged her partner and encouraged him to stare as well.

Chris had his arm lazily draped around the back of my chair—a proud papa. I picked up a magazine. Glancing at it, I decided to see who Chris knew.

I pointed at a picture. "D'you ever work with him?"

"Nope."

"Do you want to?"

"Nope."

"No, you don't or you just don't care?" I asked, admiring his hot body.

"Is that picture turning you on? You're flushed."

"I'm not gonna lie. I think I'm ready to screw anything that walks." I frowned clownishly at him. "Sorry. When we get outta here, I've got some needs—"

"I've never seen this side of you!" The corner of his mouth was turned up in a smile. "I've always gotten the impression that you had eyes for only me."

I closed the magazine around my finger. "Just keep your eyes where I can see 'em for the next however long and you've got nothing to worry about," I said lightly.

He tucked an errant hair behind my ear. "Strange conversation for a waiting room. You're suggesting that if the cat's away, the mouse'll play?"

Flipping again, I smirked. "Concerned that some one's gonna get a piece of this pregnant ass?"

"Hey, some people find pregnant women to be a *real* specialty item."

"Ya think?"

His mouth in a tight little line, he whispered, "I'd say Hartlass found Ella to be an exotic, forbidden fruit."

I wanted to hit myself. I'd erased her existence from my memory. "Do you spend a lot of time thinking about her? Comparing this to that?" The idea was cringe-worthy.

"I wouldn't say *a lot* of time but it has brought back some memories; thoughts about what I could have done differently."

As I debated sharing what I knew of Ella, we were called back to an examination room. The physician's assistant was nothing but professional. When she called my name and Chris got up, her jaw dropped. She recovered so quickly that I involuntarily laughed. Chris, following behind me, had fun with her.

"Mariposa, thank you so much for your help today," he said when she opened the exam room door.

She paused, flustered. "You're welcome, Mr. Sparks," she said sheepishly.

He grinned at her. "You can call me Chris."

She fiddled with her clipboard. "Chris," she said, her tanned skin reddening.

As I sat down, she entered and addressed me. "I have to take your blood pressure before the doctor comes in. Today, you're seeing Dr. Keen. She's one of our best." She took my arm and put the cuff on, giving it several hearty squeezes.

A confused look on her face, she tried it again and again. She finally looked at me and Chris. "I am so sorry. I've never had a famous client." She replaced the cuff. "Let me try one more time." This time, she focused intently on my arm and emerged victorious. "Perfect," she said as she ripped the cuff off and put it away.

"Perfect. Now *that's* what I like to hear," Chris said, sitting down in the chair next to me.

"I'm sorry. This is so unprofessional but you're one of my favorite actors, like, ever," she said, staring at him. "I—"

"You know you can't tell anybody that I was here?"

She gulped. "Oh, yes. I know that. I don't want to get fired!"

"And it's our little secret," I added. "My secret. I'm not ready to tell the world."

She nodded vigorously. "How about an autograph?" she said, patting her pockets in an attempt to find something signable.

Opening my purse, I quickly found a notepad and handed it to Chris.

"You take such good care of me," he said, taking the pen and clicking it.

After telling me to disrobe and put the charming hospital gown on, Mariposa left. I nervously swung my legs. Chris perched on the edge of the examination table, arms folded.

"I hate waiting," I said sullenly at the door.

"But think of what we're going to see. We're gonna see our little guy." He put his hand on my knee and smiled. "It's all good."

We heard a knock on the door before Dr. Keen poked her nose in, pulling the curtain away from the door.

"Hello, Ms. Riley," she said warmly. "I am Dr. Keen." She shook my hand. Recognition spread across her face. "Mr. Sparks?" she asked, extending her hand.

"Please, call me Chris," Chris said affably.

She nodded and moved to the other side of the table. "Everything looks good so far. Do you have any questions for me before we get started?"

I barely shook my head. She chuckled softly. "Well, if anything occurs to you, don't hesitate to ask—you either," she added, eyes darting to Chris. She wheeled the ultrasound machine over, rubbing slimy blue jelly all over my abdomen.

As she explained what she was going to do, she turned everything on and started pushing her little wand into my belly. She pushed, moved. She dug some more. She said something under her breath.

She paused. "It's not unusual for the little bugger to be hard to find. I'm sorry to say we're going to have to try vaginally."

I was mortified. I was going to be probed with Chris standing there? Maybe it would have been better to bang out this first appointment by myself.

Chris held my hand tightly. He looked at me so lovingly that my concern ebbed.

Moments later, she was pushing and poking again, looking at her screen and hitting buttons. After a couple of minutes, she stopped and withdrew her wand.

"Ms. Riley—I am sorry to say that I am not able to detect a heartbeat." The corners of her mouth turned down in a microscopic frown. "I am sorry. In circumstances such as these, we recommend that you give your body a chance to recover before you try again."

"Was the pregnancy test wrong?" I asked, looking for something to blame.

"That's unlikely."

"But possible?" Chris asked.

"It's very unlikely. Unfortunately, if one's pregnancy is in jeopardy, it's in the first trimester."

When she left, I wanted to cry. In such a short span of time, I'd gone from denial to excited expectation and now to grief. Chris extended his hands to help me off the table. The gesture, kind though its intention was, upset me.

"Oh, I don't need any help. I'm not pregnant," I said morosely. Easing off the table, my arms hung loosely at my side.

"Hey," he said soothingly, taking my arms and pulling me into a hug. "I'm sorry, Sarah." As he released me, he said, "On the bright side, we have time for a lot more practice."

My frown deepened. "I appreciate your attempt at humor but this isn't funny. I feel like a failure. This is the one thing you really wanted and due to my 'advanced maternal age,' I may encounter '*difficulties* with sustaining a pregnancy.' You heard her. And no nookie for twelve weeks as a precaution?" I started getting dressed. "Due to my advanced maternal age, shouldn't we be trying twice as hard before my body renegs on its promises forever?"

He leaned on the exam table and averted his eyes. "Hold on. She didn't say 'no nookie.' She said that we shouldn't get *pregnant*. That's very different."

"It's one and the same to me," I said despondently.

"You say that now, but it's not. Twelve weeks without touching you could kill me. It's been hard enough to make it *days*."

"I don't think I could go twenty four hours without sex right now." I smiled wanly. "I want you constantly. My libido is incredible."

"There's my girl!" He smiled lopsidedly. "We'll be back in the saddle before you know it."

"Not funny. I feel like a failure. I really do. When this happens to other people, you think, it wasn't meant to be. When it happens to you, it really sinks in. That's a *person* that I will never know. It hurts." I was on the verge of tears.

"I know it's not funny. I am disappointed, too, but this is just the beginning. You have to have faith that everything's going to work out. You are a very good looking, healthy woman for your 'advanced age.'"

In the car, he continued to search for the right thing to say. "You know, maybe we should get married during these three months? You look amazing. You were fitted for the dress—what d'you think?" He glanced at me, turning into our driveway.

A wedding would certainly be a distraction. Although I wouldn't call it relief, I did feel better. He parked the car and looked at me. Reading my growing smile, his face lit up.

"It looks like we're in agreement?"

"But I don't know where we're gonna find a place on such short notice," I said thinking about the couple of places we had our eyes on.

He opened the door for me. "Instead of worrying about it, let's make a few calls and get a place today."

"Man of Action, I love you," I said, weaving my arm around his waist.

~~

I never thought I'd be planning a fall wedding, but we were destined to marry in Vegas. We quickly found a place and a date and never looked back. Instead of a huge gala, we were going to have a small ceremony at Caesar's Palace and would follow it up at home with a reception.

Shortly after we made our announcement, Ian informed Chris that he'd planned an all-day, all-night bachelor party that included 'golf, gambling and girls.'

"Do you really have to have the girls?" We had this basic conversation a couple of times already. "What does that *mean*, anyway?" I wanted Chris to shoot down that part of the plan.

Pulling a raft under himself, he kicked over to my floating chair. "Are you jealous or concerned?" He latched on to my dangling leg.

"Both."

"You shouldn't be either," he said, his hand caressing my calf. "I'm getting married to you. D'you really think I'd do anything?"

"Ha! By then, it'll be almost twelve weeks with no sex. Add booze and Ian—"

"I'm not going twelve weeks without sex! And if I did, though I won't, I'm still me. Even a drunken me is no Ian."

"I know. Obviously, I know that but I don't trust him. He's said some things to me that make me wary."

"That's a good way to be with him. I'm personally glad."

"Does he have to be in charge of your party?"

"He already put it together. What's left for him to *not* do?"

"Can you come home after your 3G celebration? Like, can we rent our own room?"

"I don't want you to worry. This is my last night with the guys. Please don't lose sleep over it."

"What if I were to stay with Melissa the week between your party and our wedding?"

"I think that's a great idea!" he said, letting go of my leg and pulling himself up on the raft. He slid his sunglasses out of his hair, shielding his eyes. "You should have a bachelorette party, too. Is there one in the works?"

"I haven't had more than a minute's conversation with Jess or Melissa lately. They've been really busy."

"I hope I didn't just add to your list of pre-wedding concerns."

I stretched. "Hardly. We'll do something. The question is *what*."

~~

## 30

Days later, I finally caught up with Melissa.

"Melissa, how do you feel about some company and reconnaissance?"

"Oooh! That sounds like fun. What're we doing?"

"Ian mentioned that they're going to have a bachelor's party for Chris in Vegas and I thought—I thought it would be fun if we could *be* the entertainment."

"Entertainment?"

"Yes, I know they've got strippers coming to the room after trolling the strip."

"And you want us to be strippers?"

"I know. It's nuts but Ian told me I couldn't be around unless I was part of the package. I feel like accepting the challenge."

She hooted loudly. "Oh, my god. That's hilarious." When I said nothing, she added, "You're serious. Holy shit."

"Very." Painting my toes, I continued, "I suspect you've got all the contacts that we could ever need to do this effectively. I don't want them to know it's us. I want this to totally be under cover and a secret till death do us part. What d'you think?"

"I think you're playing with fire. Old Sarah would be up for this but—are you sure? You've got a good thing and Vegas bachelor parties can be pretty freakin' crazy."

"Hey, assuming I have an upstanding gentleman, crazy can only go so far. And if I don't—I'd like to know that, too."

"You don't trust him?" she asked, awed.

"Oh, I do. I don't trust Ian, and as Ian's behind this—I just. If they'd allowed me to come and do something else, I might be okay with it but Ian outlawed me from the city." I was peeved.

"Okay. Well, let me ask a couple of friends. I bet I can get the real deal—clothing, everything. What do you want to do about our tattoos?"

"Ask your friends. Chris gets his covered up for his movies, so the technology's out there."

"And our hair?"

"Color it. No wigs. I want to go hard core."

"You do realize that you get married the next weekend, right? You're gonna color it again?"

"Women get their hair done for weddings. I can't imagine that Chris would expect anything less."

~~

When she texted me back, she told me it was time to come out and complete the intimate research. With it being only weeks away, I felt exhilarated and ready to go. Chris was not at all surprised that I decided to go and visit Melissa. 'Have fun!' he said, dropping me off at the airport.

When Melissa picked me up, she took me straight to Cheri's. Her girlfriend, Sumi, had a robust online store. She had opened a matching parlor within the last year, out of which she operated an escort service.

Sumi was youthful, glamorous and confident. She was titillated by whatever she and Melissa had discussed.

Clasping her hands, she glided from behind the counter when she saw us walk through the door. "Melissa!" she exclaimed. "So good to see you." After giving her a quick hug, her face lit up as she introduced herself conspiratorially.

"You must be the soon-to-be-Mrs. Sparks! I'm so tickled to be a part of his bachelor party!" Her eyes danced. "Come, ladies. I've pulled some stuff together, but really—whatever you want, I've got it." She led us through a beaded curtain to a red velvet parlor.

"Whoa, this is right out of a movie," I said, taking in the volume of velvet. Running my hands down the red velvet paisley wall paper, I was impressed. It was tacky in the best of ways. "What the hell do you do back here?" I fingered some barely-there panties strewn over a chaise lounge.

"It's a show room, really. I do *this* back here. It's meant to look like a porno wet dream but it's just for show. Nothing but sales, ladies. Nothing but sales." She yanked on a rack loaded with clothing and pulled it into the center of the room.

"Were I to put on a show for the caliber of men you are expecting, I would suggest anything on this rack. If you're not quite up to these pieces, I have some more reserved stuff that'd work as well." She turned around.

When we didn't move, she said "Ladies—if you're going to wear it, you first have to touch it."

A couple of hours later, we had perfected our looks. My chosen persona was akin to a villainess. I would dye my hair red, wear green contacts and a sweet tear away bustier, garters and matching gloves—all accented in emerald green. The last real frontier was the shoes. She had about a million pairs of sky-high heels. She assured me they were essential. While I was trying on some skyscrapers, Melissa modeled her costume.

"What d'you think?" she said, pivoting in front of several full length mirrors.

Sumi nodded approvingly. "Nice. You two look like you're serving two different crowds. I like it."

Melissa was white and lacey. It gave her an innocence that was severely at odds with the design of the revealing pieces.

"You do look naughty," I said, handing her a big white feather. "I didn't think that white could be provocative, but those pieces are. What're you going to do with your hair?"

She smiled vampishly. "I'm thinking an up-do secured by a lotus flower and chop sticks." She fondled a couple of stray locks. "Do you think I need to change the color of my hair?"

"You'd be striking with jet black hair," Sumi said, finding a couple of pins and piling Melissa's hair up on her head. "Yes, black—it'll be the counterpoint to all your angelic white."

"I think she's right." I handed Sumi some hairpins. "Your skin is so fair, too. How would you feel about having blue eyes? I think you'd look Irish."

"Oooh!" Melissa giggled. "I *love* the idea! I've never played with my eye color."

"I would strongly suggest you learn to love these pieces. Work it in front of mirrors. See what you look like so that you're completely at ease when you're surrounded by the guys." She folded up my pile. "What do you intend to do?" She wrote down the code for my shoes. "I could bring a couple of my girls in if you wanted a tutorial. There're a couple who'd get a kick out of it." Her eyes darted from me to Melissa. "Do you know what service they're using?"

"Jess knows. She has access to his phone."

"How long are you in town? I don't know anyone who's had the balls to be the entertainment for their fiancé." She looked at me thoughtfully. "You're not the average housewife, are you?"

~~

Melissa and I returned to Cheri's repeatedly that week to hone our routine. The first day, we downed a bottle of Jack to get us through it. Lali and Edith were our teachers. Although they couldn't stop grinning, they took their roles seriously. They critiqued the hell out of what we were doing, but instilled confidence at the same time. It became easier and easier with each attempt.

After our last scheduled session, Lali asked "Do you know how to handle yourself when they start touching you?"

I raised an eyebrow in response while Melissa snorted.

"You should know how to get out of any situation with dignity, if you can or with haste if you must." She wasn't smiling. "Have you ever taken self-defense classes?"

Melissa nodded enthusiastically. "Mom made me when I started working for the casino. She didn't like the hours I kept and was sure that I was going to have an 'undesirable encounter' so, yeah."

Lali turned her focus to me. "Feel like learning a few moves?"

"We *know* these guys," I said, thinking that we'd never need them.

"But they won't know *you*," she said earnestly. "You'd be surprised what guys think they can get away with when they're drunk and you're being paid to prance your way out of your panties."

I furrowed my brow.

Sumi stuck her head through the beads. "She's right, Sarah. No matter how well you know them, they're not going to know you and they're going to be wasted. Better safe than sorry."

~~

With only days left, I returned to Vegas. We got our hair and nails done. We took our contacts to Cheri's and assembled our alter-egos. Emerging from our cubbies, our jaws dropped.

"If I hadn't walked in here with you, I'd never believe it's you!" Melissa said appreciatively. "There's no chance they're gonna know it's you. Beautiful!" She put her hands on her hips.

"Oh, I agree. You look like you were kicked out of angel school."

She tossed her hips around and batted her fake eye lashes. "Did you can the other girls? Are we really gonna do this?" she asked, checking herself out in the mirrors.

"I did. I took care of that yesterday. We're in it to win it now, baby."

I walked up behind her. We were the same height in heels, an imposing six-ish feet. My body had never been this toned but we'd put in so much work.

"Hey," Melissa said, turning around. "I'm sure you won't but don't forget to put on your gloves. Your tattoo'd give you away."

I looked down at my wrist. "Thanks for the reminder. That'd be it—game over."

"For real. You sure you don't want to put cosmetics on that one, too?"

"Nah, I don't think I'd fool anyone. I can't even tell I have tats on my ankles thought. That stuff is like a second skin."

I was feeling like a new person, but let Sumi have the final say. She was intrusively inquisitive, looking at me as if through a microscope.

"You're almost a different person," she said, slowly circling me for the third time.

"Almost?" I asked, curious what was left of Sarah.

"Yeah," she drawled, crossing in front of me again. "Ah!" she screamed. "I got it. Your nose. You've still got your bling. Want to change it up for a nose ring? Have you ever worn a nose ring?"

Melissa guffawed. "You woulda been undone by your twinkle!"

Sumi retrieved a sample tray. "I am all about the details." She picked through a few of them, selecting one of the smaller rings. "I think it'd be better to go with a ring than to go without. There's something about piercings that make a person so much naughtier."

~~

# 31

The night of the party, I checked in with Chris. I told him to have a good time. I felt a little hypocritical when I warned him not to do anything I wouldn't do. At the last minute, Sumi offered to tag along. Both Melissa and I thanked her profusely for the kind offer, but were eager to do it alone so that whatever happened would stay between us.

The boys had spared no expense. It was the same amazing suite they'd had when Jess visited them. Standing outside the door, we could already hear them. They were *loud* and someone was playing the piano beautifully.

With a final nod to me, Melissa knocked on the door. Repeatedly. Finally, just when our game faces were faltering, the suite went silent. The door unlatched, the piano resumed. My stomach fell to my knees when Tom answered the door wearing very little.

"Ladies!" he said, throwing his arms wide. "Welcome, welcome!"

"Great balls," Melissa flirted, acknowledging Ian's piano playing. "Can ya sing, too?" she asked, depositing her overdress in Tom's outstretched arms.

"If you make me." Ian's voice was rich and sweet—pure candy. Eyes following her hips, his fingers flew across the keys. The impromptu song was high-pitched, a challenge.

It was a smaller party that I'd anticipated. I recognized all of the faces. I glanced at Melissa, already sashaying slowly around the room, a feather under her chin. The plan was to work the room for about twenty minutes before putting on a strip tease. If things went well, we'd be out of here in two hours.

I felt more alive than I ever had. My confidence building, I locked my eyes on Chris who shared the bench with Ian. Coiling and uncoiling a golden snake bracelet from my arm, I sauntered to the piano.

Leaning across it, I breathily said, "Congratulations, bachelor!"

His eyes were glassy and he looked very, very happy. He rubbed his hands on his jeans.

"*Thank you*, brother," he said, clapping Ian on the back. "You're fucking amazing." His eyes ventured to my cleavage.

You have no idea, I thought, smiling coquettishly at him. I slowly crossed behind him, resting my bosom on his back. "How'd you like to be locked up?" I traced my fingers down his arms to his hands. In one quick movement, I had my bracelet locked around his wrists.

I couldn't see his face but Ian appreciated the move. Licking the rim of his glass, he straddled the piano bench and took a better look at the handcuffs. One of the signature pieces from Sumi's collection was a golden snake that could be worn coiled around a woman's arm or, when twisted the right way, used as handcuffs. There was no key. It took skill to get them off, more skill than most drunken men could manage.

I pulled the other one off and dragged it lazily up Ian's leg and torso. His body quaked under my touch. Leaning into his ear, I whispered, "You know your way around handcuffs, don't you handsome?"

I brushed his ear with it before going slowly for his arms.

"Oh, darlin'—you're not gonna get those on me," he said, pivoting. "I intend to make full use of my hands." He reached for my bracelet, tracing his fingers up my arm.

I batted my eyelashes and backed up slowly, coiling and uncoiling my bracelet. "Bad boys get spanked," I said, smacking my lips. "Why don't you—" I threw my hips around as I walked to the other side of the bench. "be a good boy—just this once."

He forcefully shook his head, "Not in my nature." When he leered at me, I handed him his glass. I joined Melissa who was teasing Tom and

Lucas. She took her cue to trade audiences. Tucking her feather in her hair, she folded her arms and marched over to Chris.

"Oh, honey. You've fallen into the wrong hands," she said, fingering the cuffs. The noise that came out of his mouth left no doubt that this scenario was working for him. Closing his eyes, he had a dreamy expression on his face.

"I don't think so," he said just above a whisper. "I'm right where I want to be."

I snickered from across the room, ignoring my guests. I only had eyes for my guy and I wanted to watch him. I snapped to attention when I felt Tom's hand on my garter, but I managed to keep my body languid.

"Ooh, it's a good thing—" I said, taking his hand easily off my leg and pairing it with his other. "That I have another one." I artfully wrapped the snake around his wrists, giving it a delicate yank. Tom groaned and threw his head back.

"Have your way with me, Angel of Darkness, I beg of you." He thumped the floor energetically.

A satisfied smile on my face, I cocked my head at Lucas. He looked like the frat boy who'd had way too much to drink. He was barely able to stay in his chair. He reached for my waist and pulled me into his lap.

"You're out of restraints, girlie," he said, his grip on my waist tightening.

I wiggled my butt on his legs and leaned back into him, my hair covering his face. "But I'm not out of tricks." I took his hands and set them on my chest.

He was instantly distracted. I spun out of his lap, holding on to his hand. It was a beautiful move. Ian clapped from across the room.

Ian was covetously focused on me. I had two more restraints hidden in my bustier. The ladies made sure that both Melissa and I were equipped with a few surprises that would keep hungry hands busy for a while. I plunged my hand down my cleavage and licked my lips, my eyes never leaving Ian's. He bit his lip, slowly balling his hand into a fist.

Taking that as an invitation, I danced away from Lucas. I continued to pull a black coil out of my cleavage. This time, I sat on Ian's lap and leaned into Chris. I pouted, giving the coil one last jerk as it came free. I ran it over my lips and bit it, daring him to touch me.

A lusty noise emanated from his throat. My frown deepened as I decided how to use my cuff successfully. I took a quick peek at Chris. He was inhaling my sultry perfume, another part of my disguise. Before I could turn around, Ian had my cuff sliding out of my hands and around my wrists.

"What a predicament," he growled, as I assessed my wrists. He ran his hands up my arms, and pushed the straps off my shoulders.

I whipped my head in Melissa's direction. I knew I could get out of the cuffs. That was easy, but I needed him to be distracted. Though he'd been drinking, he was a lot stronger and it would only be with his acquiescence that I'd escape.

Melissa's grin slipped. She'd just thrown on some music for our loosely choreographed performance. She tugged on Tom who nimbly stood, ready to follow her to the ends of the earth.

She turned her attention to Lucas. He fell limply out of the chair. Her eyebrows went up. No one was supposed to be dead drunk, but there he was, passed out on the floor.

She nudged him with her toe. "Looks like someone can't hold his liquor." She knocked Tom into a chair next to the piano. Hands on her hips, she bent over and licked Chris's ear. He shivered and pulled his legs out from under the piano, leaning his back on the keys.

Melissa quickly appraised the situation. She put her hands between Ian's knees and slowly spread his legs. With me sitting on them, there wasn't far for them to go. I threw my back towards her and fell to the floor. She hopped over my falling body and into his lap.

Ian laughed heartily as I slid my leg out from under Melissa's thigh. Wriggling away, I got the cuff off and silently praised her for her craftiness. She put her hands on either side of his head and yanked him into her bosom.

From my position on the floor, I admired Chris. So far, he was along for the ride but hadn't tried anything untoward. I was insanely proud of him. I didn't intend for tonight to be a test but I knew it was. I had little doubt that he was the gentleman I believed him to be.

On my knees, I crawled over to him and Tom, my breasts teasingly freed from my clothing. Getting to my knees, I drew one arm above my head and then the other, my breasts resting comfortably on the edge of the bustier. I glanced at Melissa. She was good to go.

When we were down to shoes and a thong, I didn't feel like myself at all. We sat in their laps, tickling, teasing and whispering. I felt ethereal. When we'd reached about two hours, I had a drink before retrieving my pieces.

Euphoric, I walked to a bedroom to get dressed. At the door, I was aware that I had a visitor.

"Hey, sugar," Ian said, pulling the bedroom door closed in front of my face. I felt his breath on my neck. "I didn't get your name." He eased himself onto me, an arm on either side of the wall.

"It's not sugar," I said stiffly.

He leaned into my hair, smelling it. "No. That'd be your partner. You're far too spicy." He ran his fingertips down my bare back. "I've got a couple of ideas that I'd like to share with you," he said, his finger disappearing with my thong.

I felt myself bristle, willing myself to remain loose. Too much conversation and he'd know it's me.

"Oh?" I said quietly, my mind racing.

"Mmm," he said licking my shoulders. "What would it take for you and Sugar to stay for a couple hours?" he asked, bourbon on his breath.

This was not what I had anticipated. I didn't want to turn around until I knew what I was going to do. I silently prayed that Melissa would round the corner.

When he put a knee between my legs, I dropped my clothing and braced myself on the door.

"Haven't you ever wondered about my reputation?" he asked lustily. I felt the button of his jeans pushing into my butt, his thigh lifting me lightly off the ground. "Wondered if it was well deserved?"

I shivered as he brushed my neck with his hair. His hand moved up my leg and stopped on my exposed breast, massaging it slowly. "Sugar's getting' some," he said, looking over his shoulder. "So, what's it gonna be, Spice?" he said, drawing out my appointed name.

He lowered his leg and I heard him unzipping his pants. I wanted to scream, to tell him to stop. I wanted to tell him who I was. If I said nothing and closed my eyes, it'd be over soon enough. His hand dropped to my waist and pulled me from my frozen position on the door.

"What say we invite the bachelor? He deserves to know what he's giving up." I relaxed when I realized that Melissa was banging Tom. Ian took my posture change as a yes and, with one arm around my waist, opened the door.

On the short walk to the bed, I wondered if I could work this into sex with my fiancé. I already knew that Ian liked to watch. With this as my new plan, I opened my mouth, licking my lips. "Yeah, you and Chris Sparks? That's every girl's dream." I turned around and bit his lip.

His finger nails dug into my hips and he dropped his head to my shoulder. Getting himself under control, he let go and strode into the other room.

The bedroom was exceptionally dark, designed for people who stayed up all night and slept all day. I couldn't even see my toes. I exhaled sharply, my nerves jangled.

Moments later, Ian shoved Chris into the room. He stumbled, his shoe catching on the threshold. Almost falling on me, he started laughing. His eyes were so glassy that I didn't think there was much of my fiancé there. He tried to focus on my face.

"So," he said, as I steadied him.

I moved my hands up to his biceps. "You really want to give this up, big boy?" I asked, running my hands down his arms.

He kissed my gloved fingers. "I'm not giving anything up."

I put my finger to his lips. "But you are. Till death do you part."

"Yeah, yeah," he said defiantly. He put my finger in his mouth and sucked it.

I heard Ian behind me before I saw him. He was camped out on the foot of the bed, watching.

"You're my parting present, the last piece of extra-curricular ass I will ever have." His hands perched tightly on my butt.

"Mmm." I was at a loss. As much as I wanted to fuck him, I was cheering for him to show me any sign of hesitation or guilt. I wanted him to prove to me that he would never step out on me under any circumstances.

Ian stood up and put his hands on my shoulders. I swallowed nervously as he guided me down onto the bed.

Teetering on the edge, I wrapped my gloved arm on Chris's wrist, pulling him along with me. I was on sensory overload. I leaned over and kissed Chris lightly on the lips while Ian's hands found my chest.

Chris kissed me softly, putting his hands in my hair. Pulling a little too hard, I yelped and moved closer to him.

"Sorry," he said, kissing my hair.

"Sorry," he said again, more resolutely. He pushed me away.

"I can't." He put his head in my chest. "I can't do this. You're very beautiful but you remind me too much of my girl. I can't." He pushed me into Ian's arms.

"You win," he said, getting up. Ian's arm snaked over my chest and he pinned me flatly to the mattress.

Delicately pulling the fuzzy hairs from my sweaty face, he silkily said, "I always do."

~~

What seemed like hours later, Melissa and Tom charged into the room. They fell on top of us, laughing heartily. I felt like a filthy whore. As Tom reached for me, I edged into Ian's arms. I didn't think I could handle any more debauchery. Ian draped his hand possessively across my chest.

"Hey, we thought we'd join you!" Tom said, working himself into a straddling position. "Party's not over, is it?" he asked, grasping for me.

I flinched, my skin crawling. Melissa's hair was askew, her clasp falling off the side of her head. She was obviously aroused.

Without thinking she said, "Remember what I told you—if you *ever* get the chance—" Her eyes doubled in size as she put her hand over her mouth. She giggled.

I put my hands on my face, mimicking her girlish enthusiasm. Part of me wished I'd had more to drink so I could blame my decision on it. I was also relieved that any decision I'd make, would be one that I'd remember and have to live with. I peeled Ian's fingers from my chest and sat up.

"Did you know they've named you 'Sugar'? I purred, giggling.

Tom perked up. "What does that make you—Spice and everything nice?" he asked, making another play for my body.

I rolled on to my knees and straddled Ian.

"I'm *not* nice," I said, slapping his face.

He howled and clutched his jaw. Ian laughed, massaging my thighs.

I attempted to dismount. "Where d'you think you're going?" he asked. I put my hand on his junk and gave it a polite squeeze, holding his gaze.

Tom hooted. "Definitely spicy." He exhaled sharply and massaged his chin.

"The little girls' room," I said, vaulting off of the bed.

Ian was on his elbows, mouth in a tight line. He wasn't done with me. I was going to have to move fast.

I grabbed what clothing I could see and pulled the door shut on my way out. I sighed as I stood outside the door and listened to their husky laughter. I snatched Chris's balled up shirt from behind the door. I jogged into the enormous bathroom, locked the door and showered.

Pulling on his shirt, I wandered into the living area to wait for Melissa. Chris was reclined on the couch, his phone on his bare chest.

I sat by his feet and casually touched his legs. He had such cute, well-sculpted legs with just the right amount of lightly colored hair. He opened an eye and looked at me.

"Hey," he said with familiarity.

I smiled in response.

"Please don't take it personally," he said. "You're gorgeous." He sighed and stretched. I pulled his legs across my lap.

"I didn't know until tonight just how much I love my girl." He closed his eyes. "People thought I was crazy when I started dating her. I've had some knockout girlfriends." His body relaxed. "My girl isn't an actress—not even famous." He reached for my hand. "She makes me feel good, normal."

When he opened one eye and looked at me, I blushed. I was petting his legs.

"Sorry," I said, stopping.

"Don't be sorry. *I'm* sorry." With a smile forming, he ventured, "Are you wearing my shirt?"

Turning even more scarlet, I nodded.

"It looks good on you. Keep it."

I snorted. "Keep it? Like a parting gift?" I absently stroked his leg.

He swung his legs to the floor and sat up, the fog in his eyes lifting.

Under his scrutiny, I flushed. I needed to put space between us. I felt exposed and vulnerable, like he knew who I was. In my haste to get up, I tripped on Lucas, crashing on the floor beside him. Chris jumped off the couch and lumbered over to me.

"You okay?" he asked, taking my elbow and helping me to my feet.

~~

## 32

After Melissa and I restored ourselves at her house, we went out to eat. At the breakfast table, she was glowing.

"That was something," she said.

"That *was* something," I concurred. "Something—"

"Just tell me—did you think he was amazing?" she asked. When I said nothing, she added, "No judgment here."

"I didn't *do* anything with him. He brought me in there for Chris. I've heard he likes to watch. I think he had his mind set on it." I glanced quickly at her before returning to the menu.

"You—but I thought you had sex with him?"

I lowered my menu. "Nope." The fewer words on this subject, the better.

"I thought he had sex with *everyone*." Her eyes narrowed.

"We weren't there to have sex, remember? That wasn't what we were there for."

She scoffed. "Oh, I'd say it's what we were there for. D'you know why Lucas passed out? He spiked the drinks and then accidentally picked up the wrong one."

I set my menu down. "Say what?"

"Tom told me that the intention was to get Chris a piece of ass at any cost. One of those glasses went to Chris which is why he had a hard time staying upright."

"They *drugged* their buddy?"

"I don't know if *that* was intentional."

"Do you see nothing wrong with this?" I asked, mortified.

"It is a little ugly but nothing happened. Right? Your guy is now confirmed as an upstanding, wonderful human being who thinks of you constantly."

I tucked my red hair behind my ears. "Yeah. I'm not gonna lie. When I was waiting for you, he told me about me. I wanted take him into another room and have my way with him."

Putting up her menu, she said, "Why didn't you?"

"Because I was sticking to the plan."

"Riiight." She tugged my menu down. "I'm having a hard time believing you were in there with Ian playing cards. I know I wasn't seeing straight when we fell on you, but you looked like someone who'd just had sex."

"Maybe you were seeing what you wanted to see? It was so dark in there—that's why you fell on us. I don't think you two knew where we were, really."

She coughed. "Oh, I think we knew. There's only one bed and it's only so big. Ian's a *big* dude. I just didn't care. If we're all going to screw, why not start off on the right foot?"

"The 'falling-on-top-of-your-friend' foot? That's the right foot? Dear god. What would the wrong foot be?" I asked, amused.

She let go of my menu. "If you need to live in your own world, I can respect that. I'll even try to believe you. But the funny thing is—we've all seen you naked. Who cares?"

I took a long drink of water. "I care."

~~

Back at Melissa's, I relaxed by the pool and called Chris. Although hung over, he still managed to sound like a giddy child on Christmas morning.

"Heeeey, gorgeous," he said softly. "It's so good to hear your voice."

His voice warmed my heart. "You sound like it was a late night."

"It was. Yessiree."

"Did you have fun?" I asked, waiting to see what would come out without prompting.

"I golfed well. Did I ever tell you I was on my high school golfing team?"

"That's hard to imagine," I said, adding that to my image of a gangly Chris who snuck in and out of his house.

"True story. I was good, too." The energy falling from his voice, he added, "Rusty now, for sure."

"Who came?"

"To golf? Ian, Tom, Lucas and a couple of other guys that I don't think you've met." His voice was soft, almost a whisper.

"If you'd let me, I would've liked to meet your friends," I said edgily.

"You will. Some other time." Just above a whisper, he added, "We have the rest of our lives to get to know each other."

I tried to match his energy level. "Win big at the tables?"

He chuckled. "No, but it was Ian's money. I spent a lot of it."

"That's the way to do it—on someone else's dollar." I relished the thought of Ian bleeding cash, not that he'd ever miss it, no matter how much they blew.

"Nobody won?"

"Lucas did alright. He was more interested in the girls."

"That's not surprising. That could probably be said of all your bachelor buddies."

"Where are you right now?" he asked dreamily. "I would love to rest my head on your ample bosom. I want to stay in bed and be tended. Can you arrange that?"

"'Be tended?' You want me to nurse you back to health?" I asked, amused.

"Yes," he drawled. "I want to lie here with you all day. You can be naked. You should be naked."

"You don't sound like you're really up for naked."

"How well do you know me? I am *always* up for naked. Always. That's a promise from me to you," he said earnestly.

"Then you must've enjoyed the strippers," I said, pouncing on the segue. My heart skipped a beat. And then another as he said nothing.

"Chris?" I said slowly.

"Huh?" he said.

"I thought the call dropped. Did you enjoy the strippers?" I asked again.

"This is gonna sound weird, but yes and no. One reminded me of you and it took me out of the game. She was gorgeous. Not you, but really pretty. The outfit wasn't bad either." He grew quiet.

"You left?"

He laughed sharply. "No, I didn't leave but Ian presented me with… opportunities. And I thought it could be fun. I thought about it but I left them for him."

"Left *what* for him?" I asked. "I thought they were strippers—not hookers."

"Vegas, baby," he said as if that explained everything.

"How far did *you* go?" I asked, testing what he remembered.

"I was a part of their performance. I remember getting handcuffed. That was fun. We should get some," he mused.

"Handcuffed, huh? How'd that work out for you?"

"I really don't remember when they came off. I remember Tom railing one of the girls. I remember thinking I'd like to crawl into another bedroom but I wasn't sure I'd make it."

"You had *that* much to drink?"

"I didn't think so but I must've had more than I thought. I still feel really fuzzy. Not 'hung over' fuzzy but fuzzy."

"You're a big guy. That's a lot of booze," I said scornfully.

"I don't do anything half-assed, remember?" he retorted.

"How many girls were there, what was the ratio?"

He laughed. "I can't do ratios right now. Two. The other guys went home to their women so it was just the crew."

"I'm kind of surprised two was enough."

"Now you sound like Lucas! He was expecting a harem. He passed out."

"Passed out before they arrived? That's poor form," I said, remembering how quickly he fell out of the chair.

"No, I think they were there already but like, had just come."

I gasped.

"You know what I mean, dirty girl."

"Passing out right after coming is not okay, not even with a hooker."

"You're trouble." His voice was almost inaudible. "They were something else. One looked like Poison Ivy, sort of and the other one was like a steam punk angel. She had the most remarkable green eyes."

"Sounds like you were really into the good girl. You do know you didn't have to keep up your clean image with your boys?"

"Oh, no. The angel had blue eyes. She wasn't my type. She had a sweet outfit. It's the other one that I was warm for."

"Which one reminded you of me again?" I asked.

"She. The green-eyed girl. She was smokin'."

"And you didn't bang her?"

"No, honestly. I didn't. I wanted to. I did." He paused. "Or I wanted to want to."

"That sounds goofy."

"I am goofy. I… When Ian brought me into the bedroom—do you really want to hear this or does this go in the 'I'd rather not know' file?" he asked quietly. "I will tell you anything you want to know but I don't want to hurt you and sometimes words hurt as much as deeds."

Considering my role in the whole affair, I wasn't so sure that I would ever admit to my foray into bachelor party entertainment.

"No, I'd rather know than not know everything and anything. At least then I can make my own decisions."

"Like whether or not to marry me?" He asked like it was a joke.

"You're as good as married. I'm not sure what you'd have to do or say for me to leave."

He sighed. "I adore you. I would do anything for you, do you really honestly accept that?" I said nothing. "And I—anyway—Ian had me pull my shirt off before he knocked me in there. The room was so dark that he could've been pushing me into the arms of an angry bear and I wouldn't have known till I sat on it." He stopped again. "God, thinking about it, I feel like I cheated on you. I hope you know that I didn't. I really didn't."

"Wow, you really do have the married mindset, huh? I'm sure you didn't do anything I wouldn't do," I said hypocritically.

He was silent. I wondered what he was thinking. "So, I went in there expecting to fool around. She said something about the ball and chain and you know, giving up my freedom. I told her I didn't feel like I was, like you'd never demand my freedom."

I savored his sweet sentiments. His heart was so pure that I ached in a way that I hadn't anticipated. If we'd never talked about that night, I wouldn't feel sullied—unworthy.

He continued, "She pulled me into the bed. I kissed her—this is so awkward."

It sure is, I thought, living vicariously through his eyes.

"And she reminded me of you. Or, I couldn't get you out of my head. I don't know which. I knew I wanted you and would have had sex with you right there, Ian be damned. But this girl? I couldn't do it."

"Do you expect a prize?" I asked, wanting to sound annoyed for his pseudo-indiscretions.

"No, of course not," he said, taken aback. "I am honoring your wishes for honesty. I honestly love you too much to risk—you know what? It's not even that. I didn't have any interest in screwing around. The fact is that I love you, I do. I—It felt *wrong* to touch her. I even had to apologize to her later when she was sitting around waiting for her partner."

"You apologized to a whore?" I asked, laying it on thickly.

"She didn't seem like a whore. They were calling her 'Spice.' Like, 'Sugar and Spice?' I've been around women from every walk of life who wanted a piece of me. She certainly seemed to know what she was doing but maybe I'm reading my thoughts into her behavior. My head hurts." He sighed. "Are you upset?"

~~

We had decided to spend the week apart—completing three months of limited sex with one week of no physical contact. Each day felt long and cumbersome. I texted at will to share whatever I was up to. I called at the end of the day to 'tuck him in,' as he put it.

His list of ideas for the wedding night was getting lengthy. I had a suspicion we wouldn't be leaving our suite for days.

Jess and Melissa had put together a bachelorette party for me. My favorite band for the last twenty years was playing. They'd gotten us sweet tickets and backstage passes. They were also toying with the idea of strippers, but I know I didn't sound enthusiastic.

Mary joined us Saturday morning and we went out on the town. As I had access to more money than any one of them, we gambled and drank to our hearts' content. We did alright, and took ourselves out to dinner before returning to the suite to get dressed for the concert.

While Melissa was completing the finishing touches, I received a text from Chris.

'Heading out soon?' he asked.

'Yes. So excited!'

'I got you the backstage passes,' Chris said.

'You?' I had no idea. I knew someone had connections, but I never realized that Chris used his.

Before Chris entered my life, I would have given anything to have a relationship with Diesel Nacht, the lead singer. He was the end-all, be-all of enticingly broken boys. His muscular body was covered in tattoos. He wasn't a big guy, but he gave off such an impressive energy that I wouldn't want to meet him in a dark alley. The other guys were also attractive but not as gregarious.

'I told you I could do it. Remember?' he asked.

'In the car. Yes, I remember. I thought you were full of it.'

'I am, but I did.'

'Thanks. Can't wait. Mary's here,' I added.

'She loves them, too. Have fun.'

'Yes!'

'They're staying at your hotel.'

'Oh?'

'Yes. Don't do anything I wouldn't do.'

'No problem,' I responded. I was looking forward to meeting the band and maybe hanging out, but the only man for me was not going to be in evidence tonight.

'Want to come over afterward?' he asked.

'I do, but we've come this far.'

'Rules are meant to be broken. I want you.'

'You can do it!' I said, trying to be supportive of our decision to stay celibate.

He called me.

"I want to do it," he said. "What're we accomplishing with this no-sex thing?" he whined.

"It's almost over. Just picture our wedding night," I said tauntingly.

"I think it'll still be incredible even if you come tonight," he said persuasively.

"No doubt I would if I saw you." I snickered.

"More than once. Bring your body here and you can, I will please you. I'll make it worth your time and your scruples." His sexy tone was not lost on me. It was appealing.

"It's my last night with the ladies," I said, trying on his line for size. "Try not to worry."

"Oh, I'm *not* worried. I'm horny. I like the band, too. Can I come?"

"If you come, will you leave?" I asked, sounding a bit like the principal.

"I'll come if you let me anywhere near you. We can discuss whether or not I leave," he said.

I blushed. "I think you sealed your own fate. You've gotta wait. I'm going out with the girls. Are any of the guys around?"

He cleared his throat. "Yes, Ian and Tom never left. We kept the suite. Lucas got his own room. He is pissed about missing out on my party and has had a non-stop party ever since. He's gonna be in rough shape by tomorrow, but then he's not a part of the wedding, so who cares?"

"He's hanging around for the after-party?" I asked. "Or is he going to be the only guest standing beside our parents? That's weird."

"We're not your typical couple. It'll be fine."

"Okey dokey. I'm not going to worry about it."

"That's my girl! Kicking worry to the curb. Now, about tonight—"

I hung up on him and followed it up with a brief text, 'My heart is as true as steel.' Because he had such an affinity for Shakespeare, I'd reread much of what was covered in high school. The stories were good now that it wasn't an assignment.

'But earthlier happy is the rose distilled than that which withering on the virgin thorn grows, lives, and dies in single blessedness.' I could picture him getting worked up, keeping me on the phone *and* quoting Shakespeare.

'Away with thee!' I scolded. I turned off my phone.

~~

## 33

Towards the end of the concert, I had to hit the bathroom. Because of our connection, I had access to one not far from the stage. Coming out, I ran smack into Ian. He stumbled down the hall with Mary on his back.

"Sorry!" Mary squealed after the collision.

Recognition spreading across Ian's face, he turned and smiled. "Well hello, Sarah Riley."

"Ian!" I yelped. "What're you doing here?"

"Do you know how often you ask that?" he said, bouncing Mary on his back.

"Seriously, what're you doing here?"

"I'm in town for a wedding," he teased. Mary laughed loudly, angling for a better view over his shoulder.

"And you like Dirty Charles?" I asked.

"Who doesn't?" His eyes glinted.

My eyes narrowed. "You don't seem like the type."

He shifted her weight. "Would you believe I know the drummer?"

"I didn't know that!" Mary cooed.

"You don't know much about me," he said coolly.

I couldn't tell if he was lying. He was a great actor.

"Well, whatever. Good to see you," I said, heading back to my seat.

Ian grabbed my wrist. Mary fell clumsily to her feet.

"Nice bracelet," he said, wedging a finger under my golden snake armband.

"Oh, thanks," I said, tugging at my arm.

"Where'd you get that gem?" he asked, smugly.

"Bachelorette present," I answered dismissively.

He ran his thumb along one of the coils. "Your hair's a pretty strawberry blond. You change that up for Vegas?"

I unconsciously touched my hair. Because I didn't want my hair stripped, I had to settle for a reddish hint to my otherwise blond hair.

His eyes traveled over every strand. "Cute pixie cut, too."

His eyes darted to Mary, "I'm sorry, Mare." He held his lower lip between his finger and thumb. "I've got some best man responsibilities that require Sarah's attention—"

Mary flashed us a peace sign and disappeared backstage.

"Sarah, Sarah. *Sarah*," he said, putting a hand through my hair. "You are definitely not nice."

I panicked. I pulled at my arm, losing my balance when he let go.

"*You* be nice," I said as he stepped in front of the door.

"Consider me your 'get out of jail free' card."

I hoped my expression was completely blank. My heart was pounding in my ears.

"It's not in my nature to kiss and tell but this once—I've got your back." He leaned into me. "And I'll gladly take it. Over and over."

I frowned.

"You're not very sweet either. What were you thinking?" he asked, casually crossing his arms. "I greatly appreciate your taste in accessories." He spread his legs, taking up twice as much space. "Has Jess seen those?"

I stared at the cinderblock. "You're insidious. The way you talk to me—it makes me want to vomit."

"Is that how you're spinning it? They used to say that it was your conscience talking."

"*My* conscience? You're screwing around with his sister," I spat.

He put his hands on my hips. I leaned into the wall, sinking to the floor as Mary appeared.

"What're you doing?" she asked, looking from Ian to me.

"I was telling Sarah about a dream I had. Well, I might have had. There were these two strippers who put on quite a performance."

I held my knees to my chest. He gazed down at me. "I enjoyed that dream. It's one of those dreams that I want to have again. In the daylight. Where I can appreciate it." He glanced at Mary. "And if it wasn't a dream, if it really happened—that's even better."

Mary laughed nervously. "Maybe it's the drugs, but I don't get it."

"You're a horrible person," I said in hushed tones.

"I'm sorry," he said, putting a hand to his ear. "Did you say something?"

"Yeah. You're odious."

"Am I? What have I done? I haven't hurt anyone. Can you say the same?" He offered me his hand, helping me to my feet.

In a conversational tone, he said, "Can I see that bracelet?" Without waiting for an answer, he removed it from my arm and twisted it easily into cuffs.

"This is a *nifty* toy," he said vaingloriously, restraining my wrists.

Mute, I debated my options. I could get out of them but that would give credence to what was still a bluff. "Great," I said impatiently. "Do you know how to get them off?" I waggled my hands at him. "I don't want to head backstage handcuffed."

"The show's almost over," Mary lamented. "Let's go!" she whined. "My brother'll be upset if you don't get to meet the guys."

I showed her my predicament. "Do *you* know how to get out of these?"

She zipped over and took a closer look at them, rolling my wrists around, searching for clues. "I got nuthin." She put her arm around his waist. "I bet you can get 'em off. Let her go, okay?" She pleaded. "Now's not the time."

Ian eyed us lasciviously. "Oh, I don't know. We're discussing her freedom. Which is fleeting. Unless—you say the word, Sarah." He put his arm around Mary's shoulders. "Did you hire strippers for her? Or an agreeable escort?"

"No," Mary said hesitantly. "I don't think that'd be Sarah's cup of tea—would it?"

Ian preempted my response. "There's a bathroom right there. I promise you'll more than like the tea."

I continued to fiddle with the cuffs as clumsily as I could, hoping that I could 'accidentally' unlock them.

Mary was confused. "Are you suggesting that Mrs. Sparks have a threesome?"

Ian ran his hand through his hair. "She's not Mrs. Sparks. She's just Sarah tonight."

~~

After the concert, the band came backstage. This was the first time Ian had seen Gavin in years. It was entertaining to watch all the alphas figure out the pecking order for the evening. Ian was a household name, but Dirty Charles wasn't far behind him.

Ian brought Diesel over and introduced us. He was dwarfed by Ian's hulking frame. His head shaved, he was an imposing muscle bound man of forty-some years. His tattoos were well worth reading. My inner child was awed to be standing so close to a personal hero.

The other band members, Gavin Spaulding, Quinn Sunley and Just Dirk were pure raucous eye candy.

"Are any of you actresses?" Quinn asked, inspecting each one of us closely.

Ian fake-coughed, pointing to me and Melissa.

Melissa raised an eyebrow. "I work in Vegas but I ain't no showgirl," she said demurely.

"Debatable. I'd've sworn your eyes were blue," he said beguilingly.

She laughed it off. "You've met me once. I guess I didn't make that much of an impression. My eyes have never been blue."

"In the same way that your hair's never been black?" he asked, fondling a loose lock.

She tucked it back into her pony tail. "Excuse me?" she said, batting her eyelashes.

He scrutinized her outfit for any telltale signs of her recent involvement. "How long've you been in Vegas?"

"A couple of years." She filched Quinn's open beer. She expertly avoided Ian's eyes. She put her fingers on his leather wrist band. "I can't tell you how long I've wanted to meet you!" she squealed.

Quinn's grin grew as he guided Melissa over to a couch, his hand perched on her butt.

Ian inched closely behind me and whispered into my hair, "Quid pro quo—Diesel and I are your evening's entertainment."

I took a step away from him, meeting his gaze. "Oh?" I asked, coolly.

"Yes. He's a prince. You'll love us," he added breathily.

I stiffened.

"He'll be the good cop. I'll be—trouble." He nibbled on my ear.

I pulled away.

"I knew this evening was going to be one for the record books." I pulled out my camera.

His gaze was insufferable but I refused to break the contact. Glancing over me, his eyes narrowed. He put his arm around my shoulders and drew me back to the make-out couch. Quinn and Melissa were not the only two rounding bases.

I was jubilant. If there were anything that could work against Ian, it was his aroused jealousy. His arm dropped from my shoulders. With a vice-like grip on my forearm, he said, "Diesel, it looks like you've met my girlfriend, Jessica."

Diesel kissed Jessica again before grinning foolishly at Ian. "You're a lucky guy, Ian." He leaned over her, a death grip on her boob. With one eye on Ian, he overtly stuck his tongue in her mouth.

Ian dropped down between Diesel and Quinn, carrying me with him. I screamed in surprise as I bounced in his lap. His hands flirted with my skin at the edge of my skirt.

"Ian!" Mary swatted his arm. "Sarah's white as a ghost!" She handed me a red cup. As I drank heartily, she wedged her back against Diesel, arms on Ian. She went straight for his goods. As she rubbed, his attention shifted.

He leaned over and kissed Mary, curling his hands under the hem of my shirt. It tickled and I giggled, thinking about just how bad this scene must look and wondering how ordinary it might be.

~~

Later, I woke up in a suite at the hotel with my girlfriends in different states of undress. I was in a chair that can best be described as out of the way. Whatever Mary had slipped into that cup, worked. I didn't remember a thing. Looking around through cracked eyelids, I spotted Mary's clothing balled up outside of the French doors to one of the bedrooms.

I sat up gingerly, my head pulsing. I found my camera and took a selfie before dragging myself through the suite, looking for a coffee pot. Tripping on Melissa's shoes, I kicked them closer to the couch. It was a wonder that girl had ever been married. She was a wild child, contentedly draped across Quinn's chest.

Popping in a pod, I waited for my coffee and glanced through the French doors to the master bedroom. Diesel was sprawled on the floor, face down in a pile of clothing, surrounded by bottles. Jess was nestled in Ian's arms. Even in their sleep, they were smiling.

Picking up my cup, I felt responsible for Mary and quietly looked around for her. She was in the other bedroom curled up next to a fully-clothed Gavin who was reading the newspaper. A laugh escaped me, catching his attention.

"Morning," he said.

"I found the coffee," I said. "Would you like some?"

He smiled. "Sure." He uncrossed his legs. "How'd you sleep?" he asked.

"I think I had help sleeping very soundly," I said, returning with coffee. "I don't remember a thing."

"Isn't that the best kind of bachelorette party? You can't be held responsible if you don't know what happened." Taking a drink, he winced. "And you can't feel guilty either."

I raised my eyebrows. "You look like you were above the fray. Still straight-edge?"

He smirked and set the paper down. He pointed at Mary. "This is Chris Spark's sister?" he asked rhetorically.

I nodded, leaning against the door jam.

"She's fucked up," he said. "And I know what I speak of." He smiled kindly at her, turned off the light and got up. "Congrats on your wedding," he said, motioning for me to follow him to the balcony.

It was already quite warm outside so we left the door open, air conditioning wafting over us.

"Thanks for letting us come backstage," I offered meekly. "I've loved you guys since I was a teenager."

His lips twisted. "How old are you?" He gave me a solid once over. "That'd be a compliment if you're older than you look." He took a gulp of coffee. "It was cool to get a text from Ian. I haven't heard from him in years." He leaned over the railing.

"How does he know you?"

"School," he said, holding the cup under his nose.

"Like high school?" I asked, pushing my chair closer to the door.

"I've known him a lot longer than that. He didn't really go to high school. He was home schooled—tutored—whatever he called it."

"He didn't go to high school?" I had imagined him to be the prom king, stud-of-the-football-team kind of guy.

"He caused too much trouble. That, and he was already appearing in commercials."

"Really? Which commercials?"

"The one I remember was for milk. He drank milk and became the super kid every mom's ever wanted—taking out the trash, cleaning his room, practicing the drums. He had a mop of hair. It was shoulder length and jet black."

"He still has the hair!" I said, smiling. "It's hard to picture him as an innocent kid."

"Mmm," he said, drinking. "He's never been innocent. He made trouble by any means necessary. He had a special relationship with the principal." His eyes said it all. "As a freshman, it wasn't unusual for him to be called down to the office even when he wasn't in trouble."

"He had a relationship with the principal? At the tender age of fourteen?"

"You wouldn't have known he was fourteen. He was already over six feet tall and had been wrestling for years. He was *built* and hung like a horse. We all grew up quickly thanks to him."

"Was the principal all that and a bag of chips?" I asked.

"She was older. Married—taboo. He was getting off and we're stuck in class. He had it figured out. He's always been one lucky bastard."

"Tell me something else about him that only a childhood friend would know," I said, joining him at the railing.

He raised an eyebrow.

"Gonna start a fan club?" he asked, pulling out a cigarette.

I guffawed. "Something like that."

"You girls. Did you get the ride of your life?"

I shook my hair into my face. "Um, what?"

His expression was guarded. "What do you remember of last night, pretty lady?"

"Very little."

He nodded.

"Care to enlighten me?" I asked uncomfortably.

"No." He took a drag, turning a third of his cigarette to ash. "He had a lisp. He was mercilessly made fun of. By *everyone*. I even caught the principal doing it when I was sent to the office for pissing on the wall." He stared into his empty coffee cup. "I used to be able to imitate him."

"Damn, I wonder what he did to get rid of it. You'd never know he had a speech problem. He is silky-smooth now."

He smirked. "He did a lot less talking then."

"Sounds like he had a good reason to prefer adult company."

"Oh, if you believe the stories, he was screwing better than half of his friends' moms before he was seventeen." He tossed the butt into the cup. "And I always believe his stories."

He set his cup down. "I don't know why we were friends. I wasn't the nicest guy."

"Like minds finding each other?" I asked.

He spit over the railing. "Maybe. I wanted what he had. I know that much. He had it *all* figured out."

"At *fourteen*?"

Gavin leaned his back on the railing. "I don't see that he's changed course." He scrutinized me. "Your shirt's on inside-out."

~~

The band left shortly after noon. We spent the rest of the day on the couch, watching bad movies. As my fog lifted, I started feeling anxious. No one had asked Ian to leave, and I was perturbed to be sharing my day with him. He sat in the middle of the couch in his boxers with Jess and Mary on either side, Melissa strewn loosely to Jess's left.

I took a picture.

"You should really be in the middle. Today's about you," Ian said, tapping his lap.

"Sure." I handed him the camera. "Take it for us?" I asked sweetly. He slid out from the girls and took my camera. He hooked his hair behind his ear.

I sat on Jess and Mary, arms around their necks.

"Say cheese," he said, taking several shots.

He straightened and clicked through the pictures. A satisfied smile crept onto his face. He glanced at me, Jess, Mary and back at the camera.

"There are some nice shots. Have you seen 'em?" he asked slyly.

"Ian—you gotta go," Jess said, nudging him with her foot.

"You tire of having a man-servant?" he inquired seductively. He turned off the camera and handed it to me.

"Just you. Take it personally." I threw the camera in my purse.

Melissa coughed. Mary's jaw dropped and Jessica laughed. For my efforts, he sat in my lap and put his arms around me. "I'm hard to hate," he said effortlessly, looking at each of us in turn. "But if I've overwor—"

"Trust me, you have," I said, using the tips of my fingers to pick his arms off me. "You are not all things to all people."

"What about a game of 'I never' before I go?" he asked, persuasively.

"Nope. Outta here," I said again more firmly, giving his chest a push. He eased himself into Jessica's lap.

"What if we keep it to the last week?" he asked, raising an eyebrow. His eyes darted between all of us. "Okay, the last twenty four hours?"

"Ooh, that could fill in a few blanks!" Melissa said with a giggle.

"Do *you* want me to go?" he asked Jessica, pouring on the charm. With her eyes dead, he turned to Mary. "Mary—" he intoned pleadingly.

Mary's eyes were unfocused. "I'll take you to your suite," she said, rising slowly to her feet.

I grabbed her arm. "Stay. Please." I could see how much she wanted him to herself. "He's a very big boy. He'll make it."

"I'll make it," he said, standing. "And tomorrow, you'll officially be a Sparks." He took my hand and kissed it. He closed my hand around it, curling it into a ball and fist bumped me. "Word," he said, telegraphing his message.

~~

## 34

I talked to Chris briefly in the evening, Ian's threat weighing heavily on my mind. Todd had arrived and his contingent of groomsmen was complete. When we walked down the aisle, we'd be preceded by Ian and Jessica, Tom and Melissa, and Todd and Mary, with our parents in the front row. Susan was home, bed-ridden for the rest of her tenuous pregnancy.

"How many hours is it now?" he asked, searching for any reason to keep me on the phone.

"We're at about seventeen." I was never confident about my math.

"Where're the ladies?"

"Out. They tried to take me along but I'm officially just waiting."

"Waiting?"

"Yup. To be married. I don't want to do anything else."

"Cool," he said as I heard a knock on the door.

"Just a sec. Someone's at the door." I fumbled with my phone.

Before I even had it unchained, his foot was in the door. "You can't close it," he said, a gigantic grin on his face.

I looked down at his foot and knew I didn't want to lock him out. I backed up, turning off my phone.

He walked in and swooped me into his arms, squeezing me like he'd been deprived for years.

"Hey, hey—that actually hurts!" I said, trying to get my feet back on the floor.

He loosened his grip, dragging me with him as he closed the door with his butt. Inhaling my hair, he held me to his chest. When there was enough space, I sought out his beautiful blue eyes. I'd missed him, too. He was the best kind of eye candy.

"Hello, there," I said, feeling warmth spread throughout my body.

"Hi," he said childishly, his hands tracing the lengths of my arms and holding my hands securely. "I've really missed you. Like, I didn't know I could miss you this much."

"I wasn't far."

"Maybe so but it feels like you've been hiding." He kissed my forehead.

"Isn't it bad luck for the groom to see the bride?"

"You're not technically a bride seventeen hours before a wedding, are you?" he asked. "I don't see the dress."

"And you better not! I'm not much for tradition but it'd be weird to have you here while I get ready."

"Like Cinderella then, I promise to be gone by midnight," he whispered.

I laughed. "You as Cinderella? I like the idea of you getting into my dress."

His hands wound around my waist, pinning me to the wall, "You have *no* idea how much I want to get into your dress."

I put my arms around his waist. "You're tough!"

"Who's tough? I'm ready to make sweet love to you and you've got it shut down tighter than Fort Knox. You are a tough nut."

"You can't make it seventeen hours?" I asked, mockingly.

He raised his eyebrows. "That's not the question. The question is *why* make it seventeen hours? Those are seventeen hours we will never get back."

His eyes were insistent. I kissed his chin. "Saying no to you is hard."

"Then don't." He picked me up and swept around the room. "Which one is yours?" he asked, moving towards the closest bedroom.

"You can't! You can't go in there—my stuff is spread out all over!"

"Is the dress in the pile?" he asked, walking more purposefully towards my room.

"No."

"No harm, no foul then," he said, kicking the door shut behind us.

~~

"How've we not done that before?" he asked, rubbing my bare shoulder.

"We've never not been able to do it. That's why—that and you can thank Sumi for the toys," I said happily.

"Mmm."

Time passed. Lying on his chest, it was time for me to unload. As much as the idea terrified me, I knew that he should have the opportunity to remain a bachelor.

"It's been an interesting week," I began slowly.

He put his hand in my hair. "Life with you is interesting. I wouldn't want it any other way," he said softly.

"You can say that, but I feel like there's something you should know."

He eyed me cautiously, "Why? What's in it for me?"

"I—don't you want to know everything and anything? So that you can make the best choices?" I asked, looking at his biceps.

"All of the choices I've made brought me to you, to this point." He casually stroked my back. "You are the *only* choice." He paused. "I'm happy with how things are. If you're going to shit on my parade, I don't need to know."

"What if I need to tell you?"

"What's in it for you? Are you going to feel better?" He tilted my chin up, locking eyes. "Am I?"

"I don't know that I'll feel better. It's not a 'feel good' kind of story," I said, my fingers dancing idly over his arm.

"How about this—you keep your little secret for a good five years. If, in five years, it still bothers you, you can tell me and I will be non-judgmental—how's that?"

"Weird is what that is. You can't say you won't judge. How can you not judge? Secrets are secrets because impending judgment is part of the equation."

"I always thought secrets were secrets because they were dangerous to the status quo. I'm not talking about surprise birthday parties—*real* ones are life changing. I don't need—no, I don't *want* any life changing information today. I'm right where I want to be." He pulled me more closely to his body.

"Is this secret something that is likely to happen again?" he asked.

"God, no!" I laughed.

"See—you're laughing. If you can laugh now, five years from now, it will be a footnote in our journey. No big deal."

I played with his scant chest hair. "I guess I would feel better if I could tell you."

"Hand me your phone," he said amicably.

He typed. His smile grew. What the hell was he looking at?

"Mystery," he said.

"What is?" I asked, reaching for it.

"The definition of secret," he said, showing me the screen. "Who doesn't appreciate a little mystery?" He tossed the phone on the table.

"I dunno," I said uncomfortably.

"Why do you want to tell me? So you can start with a clean slate?"

"Yes, maybe. I would like to think there are no secrets between us."

"This isn't a secret. It's a *mystery*."

"Yeah, it is."

"Listen," he said, patting my thigh. "I never asked for a flawless woman, Sarah. I was looking for the perfect girl for me. You're it. I was drawn to you on day one because of your mystery. No matter what you have to say, you're it. I want you and all of your history."

He met my eyes. "We're better together. You know it."

I teared up. To be loved unconditionally was a new promise. I had never felt so free, ready to fly.

He ran his hands through my hair, traced my jaw and tilted my chin.

"Do you love me?" he asked, his blue eyes boring into mine.

"Yes! I do. I—"

His lip curled up in a smile. "Then have faith. I do."

PERFECT

# ACKNOWLEDGMENTS

Here's to SKB for her inspiration and for introducing me to some colorful characters. Thank you, Carrie Rose for your exceptional cover art, for your spot-on help and love of commas. You are more than my sister; you are a force! And to my inner circle – thank you for wanting more and being insistent about it. Your enthusiasm was paramount and I salute you!

ALISON CLAIRE

## ABOUT THE AUTHOR

Alison Claire received a Film and Video Studies degree from the University of Michigan. As a member of the Actors' Equity Association, she has stage managed productions for theaters throughout the United States. Ms. Claire currently lives in suburban Detroit with her husband and three sons. *Perfect* is her first novel.